The King's Scepter

by

Vicki D. Thomas

The Relics Adventures

Cover Art by *Jennifer Greeff*

The Wild Rose Press, Inc.
PO Box 708
Adams Basin, NY 14410-0708
Visit us at www.thewildrosepress.com

Publishing History
First Edition, 2024
Trade Paperback ISBN 978-1-5092-5463-7
Digital ISBN 978-1-5092-5464-4

The Relics Adventures
Published in the United States of America

Dedication

This, and any future books in this series, is dedicated to my parents.
Although they have both passed on now, my mom and dad were the best examples and inspiration in my life. They instilled the value of perseverance, hard work, and the importance of following your dreams. If you have a dream, grab hold and make it happen.

Acknowledgements

First, I give my deepest gratitude to God for the impetus to write these novels. All creative thought comes from Him.

My thanks to my dear husband, Jerry. He has been patient and accepting, cheering for me, while I wrote and pounded my desk and computer keyboard in frustration.

To the gracious ladies in my writing group(s): Sunny Marie Baker, Sandra Masters, and Beth Jones, to name a few. Also, to my teachers and outside editors who went through my manuscript to eliminate an abundance of adjectives and adverbs, my many thanks. My gratitude to my editor at The Wild Rose Press, Melanie Billings, for her expert eye and gracious demeanor. She's a pleasure to work with.

My deepest thanks to the staff at The Wild Rose Press for their hard work to bring this book to print and distribution. Thank you!

I'd like to thank my readers who will read this third book in the Relics Adventures series. I hope you are as captivated with this fantasy journey as I continue to be.

Chapter 1

Tea with Coreena
Southern England, 1947

Some mornings just start out right, even joyful, and end up souring before the sun sets.

Ivan swung his long legs over the edge of the carriage and dropped to the ground. He patted Bounty's rump and dragged the flat of his hand along the horse's cheek and neck. Clutching the bridle, he glared into the animal's large brown eyes. "Stay here until I've finished with my banking. I shouldn't be too long. Do you hear me, Bounty?" His horse dipped and shook his flaxen-colored mane, suggesting he'd heard, but Ivan knew Bounty might not obey if it didn't suit him.

Wrapping the reins around a hitching post, Ivan strode toward the Graydon Village Bank, where he would withdraw money to pay his bills. He didn't worry much about money these days since his account had grown from his two trips into the West Forest. Thanks to Zephyrus and the great Kingwood Oak tree's generosity.

Breathing in the fresh morning air, his thoughts turned to Anna-Iza, the beautiful High Goddess of the forest. He recalled the scene when he approached the forest's exit only two days ago. Although affection and touching the goddesses was forbidden, the memory lingered on how she fell into his arms. Their lips came together with a soft kiss, and his heart did a little flip-flop. She'd admitted that she felt the same fondness toward him. So serious, and with Zephyrus's help, she planned to break away from her formidable Olympian Gods in a far-off eastern kingdom. Ivan hoped her request would be successful and they could be together without fear of being caught. *Will she still care for me, or will she realize our friendship was doomed from the start and turn away?*

In a few days, Ivan planned to return to the West Forest that bordered his farm in Southern England. He waited for his brother, Peter, to come home as he'd promised, but there was no sign of him. Now, Ivan worried that something terrible had happened, and Peter was unable to dodge his enemies and leave the forest unnoticed. A few days ago, Davaan sent an urgent message to Wayland and told him that Peter was in trouble and he desperately needed help. Could Ivan return to the forest in five days to rescue him? The statement was curious. Why precisely five days?

He sighed, and then someone called behind him.

"Say there, aren't you one of the Kimble boys?"

Ivan turned to face a man he'd seen before, perhaps at the Graydon Hill School Social and Fundraiser, though Ivan didn't know his name. "Yes, I'm Ivan Kimble." He bowed as he was taught by his Russian noble family, who, as cousins, had been on the far end of royalty.

"Yeah, your brother went off to war, I've heard." The man squinted as he extended his hand, and Ivan shook it. "I'm glad Peter made it back alive. I'm Jay Whittaker."

He made it back alive? Ivan pondered Jay

Whittaker's statement. Peter hadn't yet returned home from the forest, and Ivan decided not to tell him his brother had never gone to war. Instead, he disappeared into the West Forest, and there he stayed until WWII was over. It was Peter's story to tell.

"I'll be sure to mention you asked after him, Mr. Whittaker." Ivan stepped back, anxious to complete his banking and be on his way.

"Ah…and do remind him he still owes me money." Jay lifted his face and raised an eyebrow. "Think he owes the mill, too. You might tell him to make good on his promises."

Peter owes the mill? Did Jay mean the Turlow Grain and Gristmill, southeast of the village? Ivan's jaw slackened in surprise. The gristmill was his last scheduled stop for the day, where he planned to purchase cracked corn for his chickens. He gave a nod as he walked away to let the man know he'd heard, but the statements were a confusing jumble.

When Jay was out of sight, Ivan slowed his pace. His dark eyebrows came together as he thought about what the man had said. It must be some kind of a mistake, he was certain. His brother hadn't returned to the village since the war ended. Only recently, Ivan found out that Peter did attend their parents' funeral several years ago but had kept his presence a secret. *He didn't visit me. He didn't contact me. He doesn't care—does he?*

"Ivan! Wait. It's me, Coreena Filmore."

He popped out of his disturbing thoughts when he heard her sweet voice calling.

Can I be so lucky to see Dan's sister on the very day we're both in Graydon Village? She hurried toward him, her blonde hair swept along the collar of her blue wool coat, with a plaid scarf wound loosely around her neck. A package tied with twine swung from her left hand.

"Hi, Coreena." He stood frozen, wondering what to say to her.

"How nice to see you again," she said breathlessly.

In the daylight, Coreena was even prettier than he'd remembered. Her soft skin and large turquoise-blue eyes held his gaze for some moments. With a sudden jolt, Ivan realized he'd scarcely thought of her while he'd been in the forest. Perhaps he didn't much care, after all. He found that curious, as he truly enjoyed her company when he attended the Graydon Hill School Fundraising event several weeks ago. They were quite taken with each other, Ivan concluded.

He smiled at her, and she smiled back. There was a special kind of connection they seemed to share that sheltered in Ivan's thoughts only outside the West Forest—and sometimes—not even then. Ivan didn't understand it. He was certain he loved Anna-Iza, the High Goddess of the Forest. Then, how could he feel affection toward both girls at the same time? He told himself he lacked the experience to grasp such complicated things. If only Peter were home, he'd explain these bewildering thoughts and feelings.

"I'm surprised to see you in the village today." Coreena extended her gloved hand, and he bowed and kissed it. "I'm just finishing some errands," she said and drew a deep breath. A touch of pink appeared on her cheeks.

Ivan gave a polite nod.

"Would you like to step into the Crunching Crumb Tea Parlor and have a spot of tea with me?" She motioned her free arm toward the store front to the left, not far from them. "My treat, of course," she quickly added with a grin.

"That—that would be nice." He came to her side and stayed in step.

"Besides…" Coreena turned to him. "I'd like to talk to you about something, and this may be a good chance to do so."

"Sure," he answered and wondered what she wanted to talk about. Her boyfriend, who'd died in a farming accident several years ago? Their meeting at the school's fundraiser? Her future plans?

Moving to Coreena's side, he opened the door where an overhead bell tinkled a merry little tune. There were only two customers inside who appeared to be discussing a business transaction.

Coreena sat in a white wrought iron chair near the window and glanced toward the street. She brushed crumbs from the table and removed her gloves. "I love this adorable tea shop," she gushed. "The blueberry scones are delicious."

He winced, knowing he wouldn't eat anything sweet. Lowering his torso onto the chair opposite her, Ivan frowned at the hardness of the seat. He ignored the discomfort when he got a whiff of her shiny hair that smelled like lavender—and those mesmerizing turquoise-blue eyes that captivated him. After a moment, he turned warm when he caught his gaze on her, maybe a bit too long, and yet, he couldn't think of anything engaging to say.

"This is Cookie." Coreena introduced the hefty woman whose square face appeared more masculine than feminine. Her nostrils were wide, eyes deep set, and her dark chin whiskers begged to be plucked. "She's the owner and makes the most agreeable cup of tea and pastries."

Ivan gave a hasty smile. "Nice to meet you."

"Yeah, sure thing." Cookie pulled a sales pad from her apron pocket and tapped her pencil on its cover. "This your new beau you talked about earlier this week?"

Coreena bent her head to disguise her embarrassment. "Well, I…"

"We'll have a pot of tea and two blueberry scones, please," Ivan interrupted to save Coreena further awkwardness, though he did smile inwardly. He detected a strong Russian accent from the owner and was tempted to speak the language to show off, but decided against it since this was his special morning with Coreena.

Cookie gave a throaty chuckle and walked away.

"Oh, goodness," Coreena mumbled. "My face must be as red as this checkered tablecloth." She looked down at her fingers for a moment. "Those words weren't meant for publication. I guess she enjoys embarrassing people."

"It's okay. Really." Ivan finally grinned and was pleased that Coreena thought enough of him to talk about their attraction to each other.

After the tea and scones were served, Coreena added milk, and Ivan counted four teaspoons of sugar spooned into her teacup. Not a fan of sweet things, his teeth hurt just thinking about it.

"What was it you wanted to talk to me about?" Ivan wrapped his hands around the hot cup. It helped calm his jittery nerves.

"Oh, yes. You see," she said, leaning forward, "I'm quite concerned about Danny—who is not really my brother. Do you remember I told you this?"

"I do. Dan is the brother of your deceased boyfriend.

Since Dan had no one after his mother and brother died—and you lost your guardian, you live in his house in friendship and convenience."

"Yes, that's right." Coreena brought the cup to her lips and took a sip, glancing over the rim where she met Ivan's gaze. Her eyelids fluttered.

He thought highly of Dan. The boy showed responsibility and common sense when it came to taking care of Ivan's animals and farm chores when he went into the forest. Coreena had told him when Dan's older brother Phillip died, his mother died of heartbreak, and his father, having lost both of them, abandoned young Danny. It was a sad story.

"He's a good brother. Dependable and helpful." Coreena took a bite of her sugared scone and rolled her eyes. "Delicious."

"Then…what's your worry?"

"I'm concerned because he doesn't seem to have any purpose to his life. I'd like to see him go to college or a trade school of some kind. He seems to believe that his affection for Francine—you know, the banker's daughter—will be enough for him."

"W-what do you want me to do?" His eyebrows came together with genuine puzzlement.

"Danny thinks you're brave for going into the forest and coming out alive. He admires you for taking care of the farm all by yourself—that is, until your brother, Peter, comes home." She gave a quick laugh before taking another bite of her pastry. "He mentions you so often I've wondered how much of what he says is actually true."

"I'm hardly brave. In fact," he said, twisting his cup in his hands, "I don't know where he gets his opinion since I scarcely remember completing a full sentence to him. He sure talks a lot."

Coreena's serious look relaxed, and she threw back her head, releasing a burst of musical laughter. "You are so dear, Ivan. I find you quite remarkable."

Ivan didn't feel remarkable, though her opinion pleased him. He considered the foolish things he'd done in the forest—things that nearly got him killed. Fortunately, Coreena knew nothing of these incidences, and he hoped she never would.

"Aren't you going to eat your scone? I'm finished with mine." She looked at him with pleading eyes.

"Sugar hurts my teeth, and I'm not fond of blueberries." He shook his head and pushed his plate toward her.

Her face lit up with girlish excitement. "I just love sweets. I could eat them all day."

He remembered her saying this at the fundraiser when she was eating a biscuit with jelly inside. "I'll be glad to talk to Dan when I see him if you think it would help."

"Thank you. I'm sure your advice will cause Danny to seriously consider his future." She slathered the second scone with clotted cream and bit into it. Her full attention was on chewing and catching the crumbs in her left hand.

Ivan cleared his throat and hesitated a bit. "Could you ask Dan if he might come and milk my cows for a few days? I-I have some, ah…business that I have to take care of."

"Sure." A shadow passed over her eyes as she frowned. "When would you like him to come?"

"Saturday morning, if possible."

"That would be this Saturday?"

"Yes, if he can get away." Ivan was relieved when Coreena agreed to make the arrangements with Dan. That saved him the time to ride to their house, although he wouldn't have minded the trip if it meant he could see her again.

"Where are you going?" Her stare remained on him.

Surprised she'd ask, he fumbled, knowing how Coreena felt about the forest. "I have an appointment in the West Forest."

"Oh, dear." Her enthusiasm dropped. "I dislike that place."

"Why?"

"I told you, it's too dangerous to go there." Her thin shoulders slumped, and her pretty lips turned into a pout. She gazed at the half-eaten scone on her plate and moaned.

Ivan continued to stare, hoping for a sensible answer.

"Well…" She paused and glanced at Cookie moving to the businessmen's table. "Phillip went there a couple times to hunt, and it worried me. When he returned, his demeanor was nervous and even distant toward me."

Ivan cleared his throat. "I didn't think anyone was allowed to take a gun into the forest—or to hunt." He knew this because of the sign posted at the entrance and the times he'd heard the warning from the inhabitants.

Things had suddenly chilled. Coreena lowered her head with a dazed look, studying her hands resting on her lap.

He'd disappointed her and didn't know what to say to fix it. He must make a trip into the forest and help his friend, Merridyn, during her trial. The silence continued, and Ivan's discomfort grew. "I'm sorry, but I must leave." He rose from the uncomfortable wrought iron chair and, in a fake gesture, coughed into his hand, hoping to cover his uneasiness. He wanted to rub his aching rear end but knew it would be impolite in front of Coreena. Pulling money from his wallet, he laid it flat on the table.

"You may die." The girl glanced at him, her forehead lined with worry, her eyes misted.

He bowed swiftly, not knowing what more to say—or do. "I…I'd better go finish my business in town." *How can I make it clearer? I must return to the forest. My experience with girls is too limited to think of a quick, easy remark—like Peter would.*

"Come again," Cookie called with a wave, wiping her man-like hands on her soiled apron.

He stopped to glance at Coreena on his way out the door and hoped she would give him an encouraging smile. She didn't raise her head but only stared at the twisted napkin held on her lap. The little bell above the door didn't sound quite as cheery when he left.

He reprimanded himself. "I've hurt her feelings and made her sad. I should go back, apologize and comfort her, explain as best I can…but it's too late now. I would feel like a fool."

She wouldn't understand that Zephyrus, the great Kingwood Oak tree, had invited him to attend the Forest Court Trials, where Ivan would testify for his good friend, Merridyn, the gentle and thoughtful witch. She'd been accused of carelessly poisoning her little boy and husband, a most egregious crime. *What can I say to convince the jury of the High Court that it had either been an accident or someone had deliberately poisoned the potion she brewed?* He needed answers and more proof. He raked his fingers through his thick, dark hair and thought hard on the possibilities. Maybe, Pousses, the flying cat, had more details to tell about the crime. Although, he might not be forthcoming since he mistrusted and hated Ivan. For what reason, Ivan wasn't sure.

Where did their conversation take a bad turn? Until the mention of the West Forest, their discussion was lively and fun. Coreena was great company with an endearingly sweet smile. He liked her very much. Now, his stubbornness had dashed his chances with her. He felt like kicking himself for his short-sightedness. But Merridyn's life depended on his return to the forest, and he must go.

Chapter 2

Mr. Turlow's Offer

He left the Crunching Crumb, his footsteps dragging as he headed toward the bank.

It was true. The forest could be a dangerous place. On his first visit, he nearly got his head removed by Burtack, the vicious Black Knight. During his second trip, he was tied to a tree and stoned by a horde of violent trolls. He was attacked and bitten by a huge, rat-like creature whose saliva had poisoned his system. He shuddered, considering the possible outcome of his two journeys into the forest.

Coreena's assessment is quite accurate. "She's worried about me," he whispered. "That must mean she cares." The sudden realization washed over him. *He knew they liked each other…then how could he be so dense and insensitive not to know this?* Sudden warmth moved from his chest to his neck. It was obvious, and he'd missed the depth of it. He sighed with shame and remorse, knowing he may not have another chance.

After completing his banking, Ivan pulled Bounty's reins from the hitching post and hopped onto the carriage seat. He glanced around, even to the opposite side of the street, checking if Coreena was there. No sign of her. One more stop, and then he'd go home. He clicked his tongue. "Let's go, Bounty. I've done enough damage for the day." Ivan continued to stew over his rude behavior toward Coreena. *Will she forgive me?*

A vision flashed in his mind, quite uninvited and unexpected. Ivan imagined a scene where he put his arms around Coreena, his nose brushing against her silky blonde hair and pulling her close. He felt her heartbeat against his as he lifted her face with his fingers. When he brought his lips to hers, she tightened her arms around his neck. A jolt of emotion shot through him that left his hands warm and trembling.

"Good heavens!" he said aloud as Bounty swished his tail. "Where did that thought come from?" Ivan shook his head, trying to rid his mind of the charged vision. If only Peter were home, so he could explain these peculiar feelings.

His last stop was at the Turlow Grain and Gristmill, where he planned to purchase cracked corn for his chickens and to question Peter's outstanding invoices. Jay Whittaker must be mistaken about his brother visiting the mill, and how did Jay know such a thing? *If Peter came home, surely he would've stopped by the farm to see me.*

Built in 1898, the mill ground the farmers' grain harvests for nearly fifty years. The weathered stone and wood building looked its age, showing years of neglect and general maintenance.

Inside the two-story building, Ivan glanced at one of the workers and recognized the man he'd met earlier that morning—Jay Whittaker. He had his back turned, doing some chore, and Ivan slipped by, hoping to avoid him. Now it made sense how he knew about Peter's invoice charges. Ivan approached another worker wearing dirty overalls, who scrutinized him under dusty eyebrows.

"Is Mr. Turlow here?"

The man pointed upstairs to the owner's office. Ivan knew where it was, having been at the mill many times over the years, along with his father when he was alive. Taking two steps at a time, Ivan cautiously missed the spilled grease and the fifth step where it split diagonally. He heard the slow clicking of the cogwheel as the waterwheel turned and ground the grain on the bedstone below the first floor. The mill smelled with years of accumulated dust, rodent droppings, moldy corn, and wheat kernels scattered all about.

The loft opened to one large room with a slanted roof, where Mr. Turlow sat in a swivel chair with the stuffing peering out from its worn arms. He shifted papers, looking aggravated, a half-smoked cigar clenched between his teeth.

"Mr. Turlow," Ivan addressed, hoping not to interrupt the man from his frantic search through a mound of papers.

"Can't find a thing around here when Bossy doesn't show up for work," he muttered through his salt-and-pepper mustache. He glanced up with a surprised look, removed the cigar from his mouth, and tapped the ash onto the floor.

"Bossy?" Ivan brushed at a spider's web that clung to his cheek.

"That's what we call Priscilla for obvious reasons." Mr. Turlow turned in his chair and pointed behind him at the secretary's desk. "She's getting bossier by the day. But when she's gone, I can't find a thing."

"Well…" Ivan stammered and pulled his fingers through his dark, wavy hair, "I came to pay my miller's toll and pick up a bag of cracked corn." He shifted nervously on his feet, waiting for Turlow's reprimand about the unpaid bills.

"Now, that's a novelty I didn't expect. Sit down there." He wiggled his index finger toward a hard chair. "I'll find your invoice." He mumbled, "Here—no, that's not it. This is it. Kimble, Peter Kimble, right?"

"No, sir. I'm Ivan. Peter is my older brother, and he's been away since the war. I don't think he would have a bill."

"Says here he does." The man leaned forward with a grunt, his ample belly pressed against the desk's edge. He handed Ivan several invoices. Staring over his wire-rimmed spectacles that rode on the bridge of his nose, he asked, "You payin' Peter's bills, too?"

So it was true, just as Jay Whittaker had said. Ivan flipped through the pages handed to him. They were Peter's signature, no doubt. "He hasn't been back in the village since he went to war—over two years ago."

"Take it up with him—that is, when you find him."

Ivan slowly nodded. The total carried forward for almost a year—every three or four months, getting larger and larger. *Why hadn't Peter visited him when he was in the village? Why hadn't he told Ivan that he'd charged his purchases to the Kimble account?* "I'll pay all the bills in full," Ivan blurted, his heart heavy with disappointment.

"Not your responsibility, but..." The man removed his cigar and placed it on the edge of his desk. He coughed into his hand and wiped his mouth. "I sure appreciate your honesty."

"I'll ask Peter when I see him." Ivan pulled his wallet from his trouser pocket and counted out the total amount. "I'm sure there's a misunderstanding." The frown stayed while he considered the situation. This meant that Peter had come home several times and driven away with a wagon full of wheat flour, or corn meal—or both.

"Your dad's, that is, your farm is about an hour from the West Forest's border, eh?"

"That's right." Ivan wondered why the man would ask about it.

"Good man, your dad." His brow rippled with sympathy. "Sorry to hear about the train wreck that took your parent's life." Mr. Turlow stamped the bill *paid* and handed him the receipt. "I liked doing business with him. That's the only reason I've been lenient with your brother's debt."

"T-thank you."

Ashamed that Peter had been negligent—even dishonest, Ivan's eyebrows pulled together in a disagreeable frown. Had his brother charged his orders and then didn't attempt to pay them? What did Peter do with the grain orders? He felt hurt and deceived. His gaze darted around the room. The upper floor was covered with boxes carelessly stacked, layers of grain dust, old used furniture, and broken machinery parts.

"I'm wondering…" The big man rested his arms on his desk, folding his hands together. "Would you be interested in working here at the mill on Saturdays and vacation days? When you're not in school, I suspect it's pretty slow on the farm during winter. It'd mean extra money for you—and a big help to me."

Thinking about it, Ivan knew he'd be good working at the mill. There were times when he came with his father and imagined how the ancient machinery functioned. The sluice that carried the water that rotated the waterwheel, the simplicity of the cogwheel as it turned the top stone over the bedstone and ground the wheat into flour or corn into corn meal.

"Yes." Ivan paused briefly and then added, "Yes, that would be fine. When do you want me to start?"

A grin spread across Mr. Turlow's face. "That's the way we Russians like our decisions, eh? Quick and confident."

His dark eyebrows shot up. Ivan knew from years of doing business, and the man's accent, that he was Russian, but he'd never mentioned it before unless it was to his father when Ivan wasn't present. *I've certainly met my share of fellow countrymen today.*

"Your father and I discussed our country and how we managed to leave just when the Bolsheviks overthrew the provisional government, taking power from the Romanovs."

Mr. Turlow stared at Ivan and lifted an eyebrow, like he was waiting for a response or a confession.

Ivan swallowed and pressed his lips together. He'd never mentioned his almost-royal Russian heritage for the fear that he and his family would be found out. Ivan learned that his teacher, Mrs. Hambuckle, knew of their royal heritage from Peter, but she'd promised to never tell. Their parents made a point that silence was the only way to protect them from being discovered. Discovered from what? *After all this time, are our lives still in danger?*

"How about in a week?"

"What? I..." Ivan stumbled. "Best make it two weeks. I have things—arrangements..."

"Sure. Of course." Mr. Turlow coughed again, a sound that rattled deep into his lungs. "I'm getting too old to be here in this drafty, decrepit old building, breathing grain particles all day." He pushed up from his chair, stood with effort, and shook Ivan's hand in agreement. "See Bossy—I mean Priscilla when you come. She'll explain what you need to know."

Ivan left the Turlow Grain and Gristmill and plopped the bag of cracked corn into the buggy. Glancing over his shoulder, he scanned the littered yard of useless, rusty junk along with a few clucking chickens pecking at the ground. He scratched his head and scowled, wondering about the bills that Peter left unpaid. Did he take bags of milled grain, never intending to make good on them? Or had it been someone else pretending to be Peter? With a sinking heart, Ivan admitted that the signatures belonged to his brother.

Anxious to be home before it started raining, he gave Bounty's reins a quick shake. He turned in his seat, glanced at the mill, and pursed his lips. The strange happenings left him bewildered and a bit out of sorts. *How did this day turn so dismal?*

Chapter 3

Zephyrus

A dark-haired lad will come seeking and find maturity, wisdom, and friendship.

He will risk his life for the Forest's survival. The oath of the Forest is to keep him alive

The Black Book of Pearls. Chapter 77, Verse 7

Sir Zephyrus Westwind Barkay, the great Kingwood Oak, stood in a wide clearing in the West Forest, surrounded by a thick grove of brother oaks. His bright green eyes appeared through his rough bark, and he blinked. Above a tangle of twigs, serving as a mustache, his wide nose pushed out with a squeaking sound. At last, his thick lips appeared right where they belonged. He yawned, and his eyes gently closed. The closer winter came, bringing the threat of freezing temperatures and strong winds, the more naps he took, as did the other Forest trees and creatures.

His branches had dropped their crimson and golden leaves as the days grew shorter and colder. He was aware that his age of over a thousand years was taking its toll. Some days he felt the chill even more strongly in his roots. The time would come when he'd again have the legs of a man, as he did long ago when he was king of the now-abandoned kingdom of Helvaka.

This prophecy, told in the Black Book of Pearls, had

yet to be fulfilled. As each century passed, he strengthened his resolve to be patient until he'd be released from his duty. His long sigh fluttered the cluster of leaves that still clung to his powerful branches.

Zephyrus's greatest hope remained with the young boy, Ivan Kimble, who had all the necessary qualities for survival in the Forest. Even Zello, the castle dragon, recognized this. When Zello came forward to share his findings, Zephyrus lifted his twig and moss eyebrows in agreement. "He's a very special boy. But I thought the same of Peter, and I fear he has betrayed us."

Disgust registered on Zello's face, and he grunted. "If I ever see Peter again, I'm going to fry him with my breath and eat him in one gulp."

"That's probably not a solid idea, Zello," the Great Oak cautioned. "We all make mistakes and can't see past our own selfishness."

Zephyrus returned to the present with a jolt. "What's that noise?" Zephyrus's heavy-lidded eyes shot open and darted to and fro.

There came a steady rumble. The earth shook, and branches trembled. A roaring wind that seemed to come from all directions sent dried leaves, twigs, and dust whirling.

A grayish-brown plume of smoke rose between the forks of an old tree stump not far from Zephyrus.

"I wish to enter," the loud voice demanded.

Tereus, the Demon of the Dark Underworld, forced his ghostly image through the stump's unprotected opening. The wind suddenly died.

"Why should I allow you to show your disgraceful self?" Zephyrus bellowed. "It's forbidden for you to appear above ground. The rules are clearly written in the

Black Book of Pearls, our Forest's Bible."

"This is only my phantom image, you know that. I can do you no harm," Tereus said in his smooth, condescending voice. "Now, I wish to have counsel with you. I need to warn you of impending danger that I sense beneath the earth."

"The only danger in the deep caverns is you." Zephyrus raised his twig-tangled eyebrow and grimaced. "We can protect ourselves. Now, go away."

"My dear brother, Zephyrus. Please allow me to materialize, if only for a few moments—to see the sky, to smell the fresh autumn air, and to feel solid ground beneath my feet."

"You are not my brother! I've told you, I don't claim you."

A thick puff of smoke, obscuring Tereus from below his knees, billowed through the opening and swirled skyward. He was yet a man—a beast of a man. His naked chest, shiny with sweat, festered with burn marks and scars. His large hands gripped the hilt of a broadsword housed in a leather scabbard that rested on his hip. A set of lethal-looking white horns curved back on his bald head. In front, two pairs of smaller ebony horns protruded from his forehead. Everything about him radiated evil.

"You would be wise to listen to me." Tereus snorted as he leaned forward. A scowl lined his scarred face.

"What could you possibly tell me that my sources don't already know?" The Great Oak knew Tereus was crafty and deceptive. It'd been this way for a thousand years, even when they were young boys. *If I allow Tereus to show himself fully*, Zephyrus worried, *it could give him new powers, and he may rebel against his imprisonment in the underground caverns.*

"My advice is for the advancement of your kingdom." Tereus swept his huge arm through the air. "Perhaps one day we will rule the Forest together. You and me. Can you imagine how strong and rich it could become with us working together for the betterment of the West Forest?"

Zephyrus knew that Tereus believed he deserved to be king since he was the eldest male in the Barkay family. But the townspeople and tradesmen of Helvaka had seen him as greedy, a liar, and a tyrant. The High Intervener, the Forest's God, *intervened* and forced Tereus to live in the fiery underworld as punishment for his wickedness. Having a void above ground, Zephyrus's spirit was imbued into the Great Kingwood oak. There he ruled for centuries and centuries with his fair-mindedness and kind heart.

Though Zephyrus wanted to learn the information Tereus allegedly held, he was profoundly aware his brother was never to be trusted.

"Then it is agreed." The demon's voice was only a bit contrite.

"You are not allowed to come forth in the flesh but only as an apparition. You may appear for a short stay. Is that clear?"

Tereus's yellow-tinged eyes, like that of a reptile, gave evidence of his anger.

The longer Tereus remains, Zephyrus agonized, the more powerful and dangerous he could become.

Fire suddenly exploded from the aperture, with smoke trailing as sparks flashed upward, though they did not appear to burn Tereus. "I came here to make a deal." He glowered. "Ask me two questions, and you answer one in exchange. Then, I will return from where I came."

Zephyrus thought on the proposal, watching the sparks fizzle and extinguish themselves mid-air. Pausing for some moments, he wondered if he were playing a fool to trust his deceiving brother. He asked his first question, "Do the five Ancient Relics yet remain in the West Forest?" He wasn't certain Tereus knew the Golden Lantern had been found and returned by the young lad, Ivan Kimble. It now hung safely in the Sanctuary of Truth, a cathedral-like cavity in Zephyrus's trunk.

"What makes you think I know the answer?" Tereus's jaw tensed, and his nostrils flared.

"You follow numerous paths through your underground corridors and hear many confessions. It's in your best interest."

To Zephyrus's surprise, Tereus answered, "I'm sure most of the relics are somewhere in the West Forest. As you know, they are not of much use on the outside, where they lose their magical properties and power."

"And the Black Book of Pearls?" Zephyrus eyed him with suspicion. "You didn't know where it was during our last—let's say, disagreeable encounter."

"Is that your second question?"

"No. Merely a confirming one."

"I don't know where it is, and that was my question to you." Tereus wiped dripping sweat from his brow with his big hand. "If I knew of its whereabouts, you can be sure the words would be changed to better suit me and my ambitions."

"I'm sure they would."

The Great Oak considered his second question. "The man in the hooded gray cloak—the traitor who nearly ended my life by striking me with the poison-edged Silver Axe, was it my beloved and trusted friend who stayed protected at the castle?"

"Why Zephyrus," Tereus shouted for all the Forest to hear. "I'm surprised you haven't yet figured it out. Is it because your pride won't allow you to admit that Peter, your golden-haired chosen one, has betrayed you?"

"I have suspected it."

"Yes. Your attacker was the very same young man that you've loved for so long. Peter came willingly to the side of darkness. I only hinted promises of power and riches, and he was snared by his own greed—as most men are." Tereus laughed while he gloated.

"He's only a boy!" Zephyrus teeth audibly ground together.

"I've tried to warn you of man's lower nature to adopt and follow evil, but believing only the best in people, you are deaf to such things."

"Perhaps," he said with a long sigh. "Then again, perhaps not."

"You will see." The demon spread his muscled arms wide. "There is little difference in men's selfishness. I know because I share their tendencies."

Zephyrus was silent while the dark truth ripped through him, cutting him to his very core. He wouldn't allow Tereus to see his vulnerability. His beloved Peter had betrayed him, and tried to kill him, and then planned to join Tereus to take over the Forest. *Is it possible that Ivan has the same deceiving nature?*

And then, it was as though Tereus read his thoughts. The demon lifted his head and stared with a cynical grin on his lips. "You foolish, old, naïve tree! Do you really believe that simple-minded farmer will be of any future use to you? The younger Kimble boy will disappoint you, just as all the others have."

Zephyrus released a low moan. Tereus now knew that Ivan was Peter's younger brother. *What must I do to protect the lad?*

"For my one question…" Tereus's eyes grew narrow while his forehead bunched with impatience. "Do you agree to partner with me and rule the Forest in an iron-clad grip?"

"You will be no partner of mine. Not ever."

Tereus roared and pumped his fists into the air. "You will regret your hasty decision and die a slow, torturous death because of your short-sightedness. Mark my words and write them in the Black Book of Pearls. You *will* regret this."

"Be gone with you!"

With that powerful command, Tereus screamed, and red hot sparks pinged from the fire that shot from the tree stump's opening until he faded and was sucked into the dark hole he'd materialized from.

"Good riddance," Zephyrus said as he spit in that direction.

Chapter 4

Return to the Forest

"It's about time!" Wayland the Wolflord pulled on his horse's reins. The animal whinnied and spun around. Ivan had only just entered the West Forest when Wayland met him. There, he reached forward and grasped Ivan's forearm, squeezing twice in a warm greeting. It was the sign of friendship they and the Elftens used for loyal friends. Next to him, Gan-let, the Wolflord whose horse danced with nervous feet, reached for Ivan's arm and made the same gesture.

Alfred and Canute, Ivan's beagles, barked, jumped, and ran in circles. They must've remembered the smell of the Wolflords. Though they were once werewolves, they had suffered through the *transition* and were now fully men.

"They'll get used to us in a short time." Wayland grinned at the frantic dogs.

"Sorry I'm late," Ivan called. "I had to finish my chores and take care of a sick heifer. Everything is in order now."

"That's good." Wayland leaned from his horse and stroked Bounty's forehead, but the animal raised his head and shook it offensively. "The trial will start soon, and everyone's asking for you."

"Me?"

"That's right. I understand you'll be speaking on Merridyn's behalf. Convince the jury she's innocent of the crime. You promised Zephyrus, remember?"

"I said I'd attend, b-but I didn't know I was to speak. I can't talk in front of people. They scare me." His mouth went dry.

"You only need to ask a few questions while the jury makes the final decision." Wayland frowned, appearing unsure of his statement.

"Yeah, easy," Gan-let said, using multiple hand gestures, his familiar way of communicating,

Ivan tried another excuse to let him off the hook. "I haven't heard all the facts yet." He glanced up, searching for Pousses on a limb of an old alder tree at the Forest's entrance. "I wonder if the cat is here."

"Why do you want that mangy ol' sourpuss?" Wayland scrunched up his face. Gan-let rolled his eyes.

"He seems to have a lot of helpful information about Merridyn's crime—the person who is suspected of poisoning her little boy and husband." Ivan searched the branches above, hoping Pousses was listening from his favorite perch. Sadly, he wasn't there to give Ivan further advice.

"The cat does have his opinions, no doubt." Wayland rubbed his hairy wolf ears. "Since he has the ability to fly, he has the privilege to go when and where he wants. You may've noticed Pousses is not real fond of Wolflords."

Ivan knew the persnickety cat didn't like him much, either. Reviewing aloud what he'd learned on his last trip to the Forest, he listed the points Pousses had made. "He told me it was one of those shrunken wizards."

"Shrunken?" Wayland's dark eyebrows lifted.

"Cecil, the troll, who is too short to reach Merridyn's cottage window and drop the poison into the potion she was brewing."

"I could believe Cecil was involved." Gan-let twisted his mouth in disgust. "He and some of his followers are nothing but a nuisance in this Forest. But what could Cecil's motive be to do such a thing?"

"Well, I-I…" Ivan's gaze swept in the distance as if the answer might be there, but he couldn't think of one. "This means it had to be someone taller who either lifted Cecil to the window or they dropped in the lethal dosage."

"Good deduction, Ivan, but why would this *someone* lift that stout sack of flesh to the window when they could've done it themselves?" Wayland's voice peaked. "Who might that be, and why?"

A frown cut deeply into Ivan's forehead. "Oh! It just came to me. Pousses suggested there was a ladder hidden behind some ivy next to the cottage wall."

"That could be your answer, then," Gan-let said.

"Pousses also asked me to get the blacksmith's boy to speak—suggesting he knows what happened."

"Little Benny, the mute?" The Wolflords said in unison.

"Yes. I think whoever did such a thing threatened Benny to keep quiet, and now he's too terrified to talk."

Wayland raked his fingers through his thick, black beard, scratching as he went. He turned to stare at Gan-let. "This is more complicated than I'd thought."

"It always is." Gan-let shrugged.

"That's what I think, too." Ivan shifted in his saddle while he considered dismounting to stretch his legs and sore backside. "Now, add the likely suspect into this twisted tale."

"Who would that be?" Wayland squinted, giving him a skeptical look.

"Lyla. Merridyn's older sister." Ivan watched their faces to see if they were in agreement.

"It doesn't really surprise me, though I don't know much about her." Wayland let out a sigh. "I've heard she's a jealous, scheming witch. It was her that sent Merridyn to Troll Transformation Prison. You remember?"

"So I've heard." Ivan nodded. "Though it doesn't mean she slipped the poison into the potion, does it?"

"Let's hope the truth will come to light." Wayland lifted the reins of his horse. "We need to be at the Forest Court Trials in a few minutes." He waved his arm forward.

Following Wayland's lead, Ivan tried to steady his cold hands. "What if I don't make a convincing case for Merridyn's innocence? Will they hang her?"

"Don't worry." Gan-let jerked his hands in several directions. "Zephyrus and Lord Graydon, the Lord of the South Castle, will see that justice is done. Their wisdom and fairness will prevail."

The comment calmed Ivan only a little. *What does Zephyrus or Lord Graydon know? How can they help me be convincing?*

The Wolflord rested his hand on Ivan's forearm. "Only one more piece of unexpected news."

"What now?" Ivan's back straightened.

"After the trial, we'll go find Peter, as planned. That will probably be tomorrow, mid-morning. But...the location has changed."

"Wh-where are we going?"

"The Mountain of Smoke and Fire," Gan-let said and lowered his eyes.

"Oh, no." Ivan choked. "The most awful place in the entire Forest, I've heard." He tried to recall what Joseph, the spirit imbued in the Golden Lantern, had told him during his first visit to the Forest. "It's where the relics were kept after being stolen from the sanctuary. A—a monster lives there, called the Women of Flame. And, and—a blood-thirsty goblin named Hoxx and his horde of followers. They are savages."

"They are ghouls, a name that certainly fits." A muscle jerked in Wayland's jaw.

Ivan's teeth chattered. *What are ghouls? Humans? Animals? Ghosts?*

They slowed their mounts to hear each other.

"I've heard the King's Scepter may still be there in the mountain after it was stolen nearly ten years ago." Gan-let shivered. "I don't know if it's true, but it may convince Zephyrus to let us search for your brother. So far, we haven't explored that horrible hellhole."

Wayland gazed off into the distance and pursed his lips. "We'll worry about the King's Scepter later. Right now, we need to make our entrance and take our seats before the trial begins. The barrister is a real stickler for punctuality."

Ivan suddenly had new worries. He'd hoped he'd never need to enter the awful Mountain of Smoke and Fire. The stories he'd heard were too terrifying. But then, so was Helvaka, the ancient kingdom where they'd first planned to go.

"Why did our destination change?" Ivan drew to the side of Wayland's horse. "I mean, it was all arranged to meet in the ruins of Helvaka, and then—who made the decision?"

"My brother, Davaan." Wayland bunched his wide shoulders. "He formed a friendship with Peter who asked—no—begged that we meet and rescue him in five days."

"What's the mystery about five days?" Ivan peered at Wayland under the shadow of his eyebrows, waiting impatiently for an answer.

"I understand that Tereus summoned Peter to meet and have counsel with him there. Apparently, the demon has a new plan. Don't know what it is, though."

Ivan recalled Davaan had volunteered as a messenger, but it made no sense. *How dangerous is their mission?* He bit his lower lip. What must they rescue Peter from?

As frightening as the stories were, he'd go to the dreadful mountain to save his beloved brother. *I'll have to worry about that later. Now, Merridyn's life is at stake.*

Wayland indicated for them to quickly follow.

Ivan was both awed and intimidated by the vast setting as he, Wayland, and Gan-let rode into the circular clearing where Zephyrus, the Great Oak stood. Though he'd seen it many times, it still inspired him. People stood and cheered, welcoming them with wide grins as the newcomers entered. Some clapped their hands, while others hooted with joy and pumped their fists into the air and whistled. Canute and Alfred abruptly stopped. Their hind legs quivered, reacting to the sudden noisy crowd. They scampered for cover and hid under a cloth-draped table placed in front of Zephyrus.

"The applause is for you," Wayland said, glancing at Ivan. "Accept it with a smile and look confident."

"Why…why me?"

"You're expected to speak on Merridyn's behalf and bring out the truth," Gan-let confirmed with a nod of his head.

Zephyrus's twig eyebrows rose with relief, and his bark lips spread into a wide grin. "Ivan, Wayland, and Gan-let, welcome. We are happy you could join us."

Ivan felt a flush climb his neck and turn his face hot. He sputtered, trying to explain his tardiness, but Zephyrus politely cut him off.

"Delays are expected, my lad, but I'm pleased you made it here for this important occasion."

Closing his mouth, Ivan had no idea the Forest Court Trials event would be so elaborate. There were rows and rows of rough-hewn wooden pews, separated into three sections in a wide semi-circle, all positioned in front of Zephyrus. They lined up precisely from the front to the far distance. People were milling about and talking. Some were already seated and whispering with vibrancy. He glanced about, looking for Sebastian. *Where is he?*

The new arrivals slipped off their horses. "I didn't know there would be so many folks." Ivan's bottom lip trembled.

"They were all invited." Wayland nodded. "They have the right to know what goes on in their Forest home. Some couldn't come, of course, having responsibilities."

Every person and creature Ivan had ever met in the vast woodland seemed to be there. He stretched his neck to spot Anna-Iza in the crowd with her sister goddesses. But he didn't see her. Maybe they wouldn't come, having duties that kept them away. The free trolls, in the very back of the pews, were arguing and pushing at each other. Cecil and Maloof, also amongst them, were guarded by several armed soldiers. Kaleido-birds paced to and fro. Fetters, their male leader, strode and strutted with his flock of females. He fanned his colorful tail which vibrated with changing citrus colors, indicating the bird was either nervous or felt threatened.

Apparently, this was *the* yearly event that no one missed. Many farmers, craftsmen, and shopkeepers turned their heads and stared at Ivan. He pulled up his shoulder to hide his face. *What did I do to garner such attention?* The first row was filled with Elftens, wearing white tunics, black leggings, and boots, with their long legs stretched out. Several Wolflords from Wayland's pack also occupied the front row until someone with an air of authority gave a sweeping motion with his hand, suggesting that Wolflords and Elftens should move to the fourth and fifth rows. They didn't appear happy about the change of position, though most complied. Wayland, the leader of the Wolflords, and Sytha, the leader of the Elftens, stubbornly remained.

Sytha jumped forward and grasped Bounty by the reins, and Ivan slid off. Tapping a Forest servant's shoulder, the Elften ordered, "Take these horses to the stable and care for them." He grasped Ivan's forearm and squeezed.

"What kept you? We're about to start." Sytha frowned.

"Sorry." Ivan repeated what he'd told Wayland and Gan-let about the sick heifer, and Sytha nodded. Dusty from his journey to the Forest, Ivan brushed his jacket and trousers with the side of his hand.

"Where's Merridyn?" Wayland skimmed the crowd, standing on his tiptoes to get a thorough look.

"We're watching for her and Lord Graydon's safe

arrival." Zephyrus scanned the visitors in the pews and quickly counted heads.

Ivan moved closer to the Great Oak and said in a low tone, "Who are you looking for?"

Zephyrus whispered in return, "I'm searching for Lyla, Merridyn's sister. She needs to be here to answer some important questions. No doubt she will make a theatrical entrance."

"Oh," Ivan said, though he wasn't sure what Zephyrus meant by *theatrical*.

A lady and a young boy rose from their seats and made their way forward. She wore a big grin. Wayland opened his arms wide and embraced the lady. "This is my wife, Willa, and this—this shy little fellow is my son, Cactus." He scooped up the boy. "He's four years old now. Such a big boy, too."

"I didn't know you had a family." Ivan's brow lifted, pleasantly surprised. He smiled widely and bowed to Wayland's wife. "I'm most happy to meet you."

Her dark brown hair, tied back into a ponytail, accentuated her soft, pointed wolf ears. She wore a long peasant-style dress with a thick navy shawl resting over her shoulders. The open tote she carried bulged with small toys and what may have been a half-eaten chunk of bread, along with a boy's knit sweater.

Cactus turned away and buried his face into his daddy's shoulder. He had all the characteristics of a young wolf. Dark eyes and small wolf-shaped ears peeked through his straight black hair.

"Hello, Cactus," Ivan greeted.

"They wanted to meet you." Wayland looked proudly at his family and rested his arm over Willa's shoulder.

"We'd better be seated." Willa took Cactus from his father's arms and hustled back to their places.

Tanner, an Elften, strode toward Ivan. "After the horror of your last visit, I was afraid you might not return."

Ivan thought about the attack of Kagutt, the Vaguer-beast. It nearly sucked out Ivan's Essence from his brain, leaving him as a walking corpse until the end of his days. Even now, the memory caused him to tremble. If it hadn't been for Peter, who shot a golden-tipped arrow into the Vaguer, everything precious about Ivan would be gone. After such a nightmarish experience, he didn't wish to return. But then, here he is, keeping his promise to Zephyrus and Merridyn.

The accused witch had pleaded with Ivan to return and save her from a life sentence in Troll Transformation Prison, a place not fit for any living being. Thinking on it, Ivan could hardly refuse both of them. Merridyn was his friend, and she depended on him to bring out the truth. *But what do I know, and what can I say to defend her?*

"Here they come!" someone called in a strong voice as Lord Richard Louis Graydon's carriage, drawn by four magnificent horses, raced toward them. A large, decorative South Castle crest painted on the door showed two proud gryphons with a fiery background. Ivan wondered if the two half-lion, half-vulture creatures would be as revered after the public learned of their bird-napping. They were accused of snatching the kaleido-birds and delivering them to the Dark Army for food.

About twenty of Commander Simon's uniformed men followed the royal carriage, riding proudly on various shades of chestnut horses. The lead soldiers carried colorful castle banners while their helmet plumes swayed in the wind.

When the carriage came to a stop, a footman jumped down from his seat and opened the door. Though the lord's expression was grim as he stepped out, he looked splendid in his royal-blue velvet coat with matching long pants and a gold-buttoned vest. He bowed to the crowd and then reached for Merridyn's gloved hand. She kept her gaze down and carefully lowered the hood of her crimson-colored traveling cloak, but she did not smile. Her honey-blonde hair was swept up in a mass of curls and pinned with sparkling diamonds.

Her rich woolen dress, simply cut, was slimming to her small chest and waist. The high neck, edged with ecru lace, framed her delicate chin. A small purse with a beaded cord hung over her shoulder.

Ivan couldn't take his eyes off her. She was elegant. So different from the weeping, smudge-faced girl wearing a torn, soiled dress when they'd first met her near the troll prison.

"Welcome," Zephyrus's voice boomed over the crowd. "I'm so pleased to see you."

Merridyn raised her head for a moment and swept the audience, and then she stepped from the carriage to follow Lord Graydon's lead.

"The witch is guilty beyond a doubt," a mean, raspy voice shouted for all to hear.

Ivan's jaw clenched, and his eyes narrowed. He swung around to see who had made such an ugly remark. If he spotted him, he might put his fist into the man's mouth, but he couldn't determine where the comment came from.

Sytha nudged him. "Don't let remarks like that

bother you. Some people enjoy agitating the situation."

Two Forest servants led the carriage horses to the stables, located northeast, behind Zephyrus and a solid stand of trees. Simon and his specially selected garrison turned their mounts and followed, brushing away the dust from their uniforms.

Commander Simon called to Canute and Alfred, his hands cupped around his mouth. They shot out from under the table where they'd been hiding and raced toward him. Their ears flopped, and their tails wagged swiftly. Ivan knew the commander loved beagles, having had one of his own until a Swamp Dragon ate him. Even now, the memory of Simon's loss brought tears to his eyes.

"I'll keep them by my side and out of mischief until the trial is over," Simon yelled, and Ivan waved in agreement. It took a load off his mind, and he sighed with relief.

"Ivan, my lad." Lord Graydon gave him a genuine smile though his face was lined with worry. "You are to sit in front, next to Merridyn." He took her hand, and she followed him toward their seats while motioning to Sytha and Tanner to sit near them. Others took their places as summoned, while many seemed to understand they belonged in the second and third rows.

"Why are the trolls wandering free in the back?" Ivan tipped his head in their direction. The trolls included Maloof and Cecil, who'd captured Ivan and threw stones at him. *I should wish them ill with a long prison sentence, but I don't, and I won't.* It was difficult to determine, as all the trolls pretty much looked alike, but he'd never forget Maloof and Cecil. They grunted and snorted, making half-human sounds, pushing at each other clumsily.

"Many are free trolls," Wayland said, "guarded because they can be so unruly."

Ivan knew all about that.

"Maloof and Cecil will be chained and brought forward by Sergeant Pezzuline when the time comes." Wayland jabbed his thumb behind him, indicating where they were held captive.

"Will you bring charges against them?" Merridyn inhaled a deep breath.

"I—I don't care to." Ivan rubbed the side of his forehead where a rock had hit him hard enough to knock him unconscious from his horse. He glanced at Sytha and Wayland and then into Zephyrus's troubled eyes. "Maybe that can be overlooked." Ivan hoped.

"You must tell your story." Sytha, who hadn't yet taken his seat, placed a hand on Ivan's shoulder. "It will be up to the seven members of the jury to judge them."

"Probably send them back to Troll Transformation Prison," Tanner casually added.

"Where are the goddesses—Anna-Iza?" Ivan stared west on Sir Barkay Road, hoping to see them riding their magnificent Andalusian horses. *Did my friends notice how nervous I am, asking about Anna-Iza?* He stuffed his cold hands into his jacket pockets and bent his head.

"I don't know." Sytha raised his shoulders. "I'm sure they'll be here since Merridyn is their good friend. Perhaps they will be along later."

Just as Sytha finished his comment, walking slowly to the right of Zephyrus, were Anna-Iza and Diana holding hands. The other eleven sister goddesses followed, each wearing various colored cloaks with hoods covering their heads. They continued to the third row since Simon and some of his soldiers occupied the entire second row.

Anna-Iza turned and made her way to where Ivan stood.

He gulped air, and his throat caught. With his focus on her welcoming smile and blue-green eyes, he returned his most confident grin, remembering the kisses they'd shared on his previous visit. She must've remembered, too. A slight blush touched her soft cheeks.

"Anna-Iza." Ivan bowed. "It's a pleasure to see you again."

She curtsied and said, "The pleasure is mine."

She's here! More beautiful than ever. Her auburn hair with touches of gold curled under the edges of her hood. He was so happy he nearly laughed out loud but then held his outburst in check. No one must know of their deep affection for one another. Ivan cautioned himself to remain emotionless, but it was nearly impossible. It was forbidden to touch a goddess, especially by a mortal person from the outside. They both knew this.

Merridyn rose from her seat and walked toward them. "I'm glad you're here. I'm worried," she whispered.

"It will be okay." Ivan faked assurance. But he wasn't sure and wished he had a chance to talk with Pousses when he'd first entered the Forest. *Where is that fussy cat when you need him?*

"Have you gathered anymore information that will help Merridyn?" Anna-Iza gazed into his eyes.

"No. I arrived too late and didn't have time to question Pousses further. Perhaps Zephyrus has learned something."

Vicki D. Thomas

"Oh. Please excuse me, Ivan." Anna-Iza gave him one last pleading look. "I must have a private word with my friend, Merridyn. I hope to see you later when we take a lunch break."

"I would like that very much." Though he stepped back and made space for the girl, he didn't want to.

The goddess tucked her arm through Merridyn's when she approached, leaned forward

and spoke softly into her ear.

What did she say? Ivan pressed his lips together and wondered.

As he watched them leave, his hands trembled, and his mouth went as dry as the scattered leaves on the Forest floor. *What if I humiliate myself during the trial? Or make accusations against someone—like Cecil or Lyla, and it proves to be false.*

Turning to Sytha, his tone low, he said, "I can't do this. If I make a mistake or say something wrong, Merridyn may be condemned to prison. That would be a terrible burden for me to live with."

"Don't worry. With your keen sense of truth and justice, you'll do just fine." Sytha gave him a reassuring nod. "If you get a chance to ask questions, I'm sure they'll be meaningful ones. Remember, it's up to the jury to deliver a fair verdict."

Ivan wished he was as confident as his Elften friend. The positive thing about this day was that his dear Anna-Iza was here, and he relied on her presence to give him strength. *Did she think about me after we parted from the Forest? Does she still care for me and want to be in my arms, kissing me?* Ivan gave a cold shudder and considered the worst.

Soon, Lord Graydon and Merridyn took their seats

in the center front, as instructed by the court announcer. Ivan sat next to Merridyn, with Sytha and Tanner located to Lord Graydon's left. Wayland and Gan-let squirmed, and it became clear that eight to a pew was two people too many, especially with the broad-shouldered Wolflords. Besides, they must leave space for Sebastian. They rose grumbling and moved to the second pew on their left and sat in the front seats.

Ivan suspected that Tanner, who had a crush on Merridyn, would've preferred to be near her to comfort her, but that wouldn't be the case during this trial. He kept peeking in her direction.

Merridyn wore a stoic face and stared ahead. Once, she glanced up and gave a hasty look at Zephyrus, who winked at her. Anna-Iza and her goddesses, seated in the third pews with their hands folded and resting on their laps, were quiet and somber.

Ivan leaned toward Merridyn and Lord Graydon and whispered, "I suppose you both know about the workings of this important autumn event."

"Ah, yes." Lord Graydon stroked his goatee. "They can be quite entertaining and lively."

Ivan wondered why the lord answered in such a flippant manner. *Does he take the proceedings seriously?*

"I've attended many," Merridyn's chin quivered when she spoke, "but never in the seat of the accused."

"Are—are you confident about the trial?" Ivan crinkled his brow.

"I'm sure of my innocence." She squinted at him. "You don't always know which way the truth will blow during a Forest Court trial."

"You'll be fine, my dear." Lord Graydon patted her

41

slender hand. "Once they hear the phony testimony from your accusers, the seven jury members will proclaim you're innocent. You'll be free to live your life." She gave a polite nod, but didn't appear convinced.

"By the way," Lord Graydon said, his eyes narrowed, "where is the Long Dark Cloak—Sebastian?"

"I've asked the same thing." Ivan stared at the huge door in Zephyrus's trunk. "I haven't seen him since I arrived." He stuffed his hands into his jacket pockets, feeling lost without the garment over his shoulders.

"We're right behind you if you need anything." Simon cupped his hands around his mouth, directing his remark toward Merridyn. The men in his garrison confirmed their commander's statement while squeezing into seats, jostling for their places.

The trumpet blew loud and clear. The trial was about to begin.

Chapter 5

Rules of the Court

"Please take your seats," the court announcer called in a deep voice, looking quite official in his long, black robe with sleeves flapping. He stepped behind the podium and paused as the people moved to find a last-minute seat.

It grew quiet until Wayland's son, Cactus, cried out from several pews back, "I want to go home, Daddy. I'm scared." Wayland gave a little chuckle and turned around to wave.

"Hear Ye. Hear Ye," the announcer called. "The court will now come to order on this day of November 15, 1947. The honorable Sir Zephyrus Barkay presides over the Forest Court Trials and will be the final judge, deciding a man's—or a woman's—innocence or guilt. The revered Lord Richard Louis Graydon, owner of the South Castle and our West Forest, will also determine innocence or guilt if there is any doubt or dispute."

The man making the announcement shifted his thin frame and called, "Clerks, will you please settle at the table near Zephyrus and record the awards, announcements, and each testimony to the best of your ability?"

Bowing in the announcer's direction, sober faced as pieces of wood bark, the clerks took their seats.

The great door in Zephyrus's trunk opened with rumbling and creaking, all familiar sounds to Ivan. To his surprise, Pousses, the persnickety flying cat, dashed out, raised his feathery wings and lifted into the sky. Circling, he landed on one of Zephyrus's low branches, tucked in his tail, and settled there. Sebastian stepped out slowly, wearing the same beige tunic and baggy leggings that he always wore, with the Long Dark Cloak draped over his arm. He gave a high wave with his free hand to Ivan and walked toward the front pew.

They embraced and patted each other on their backs. "I was worried about you," Ivan said.

"It was a bit chilly this morning, so I stayed inside, but I brought the cloak for you." Sebastian placed it around Ivan's shoulders, making a fuss by adjusting the fabric over Ivan's jacket. He leaned close and said in a quiet voice, "I've had private words with Pousses, and you are right. He has helpful information regarding the *possible* culprits. Unfortunately, being a cat, he's not allowed to give testimony."

"I know this—but why?" Ivan groaned.

"A court rule." Sebastian shrugged. "Animals are not allowed to testify. In Pousses' case, he's uncooperative, temperamental, and not very well-liked."

"But…he has evidence." Ivan felt frustration rise in his chest. "Isn't that what's important?"

"I don't make the rules here, and, what's more, I don't happen to agree with this one."

Ivan scooted toward Merridyn, making space for Sebastian. As they shifted, Ivan was anxious to hear what Sebastian had learned while in the tree's sanctuary with Pousses.

Taking his seat, Sebastian nodded to the others in

the front pew. He gazed at Merridyn. "Good luck, my dear lady."

Merridyn bowed her head and reached for Ivan's hand. "I'm scared." She shivered.

"Don't worry. Everything will be fine." Ivan wished he believed his own words.

Bartholomew, or Bart as people called him, the blacksmith at the Witches' Village, carried little Benny in his arms, with his wife at his side. He fretted over the boy. "Don't worry, Benny, no one will hurt you." They took their seats in the pew when several forest people made space for the family.

Curious about Bart's remark, Ivan wondered if someone had threatened Benny not to talk about the allegedly guilty person. *And who would that be?*

The court announcer turned to the podium, where he encouraged a smooth and fair trial. Finally, he extended his open hand toward the illustrious Golden Lantern, with the spirit of Joseph imbued inside, and thanked him for his light and warmth on this cool morning.

"It's my pleasure to be here and to serve my master, along with all you dear folks," said Joseph in a gravelly voice. For emphasis, the lantern shot out a streak of fuchsia-pink and violet light that raced to the south and passed over the crowns of forest oaks. The audience oohed and aahed.

Cactus shouted from his seat, "Look, Daddy! The light is running away."

Wayland cracked with laughter. He rotated, glancing over his shoulder. "That's my boy!"

"I believe we are all in place." Zephyrus chuckled. "You may proceed."

The announcer unrolled a scroll, flattened it with his

palms, and cleared his throat. "The rules of the Forest Court Trials are as follows:

1. No weapons allowed in the court or in the Forest. The exception to this rule is Commander Simon and his men.

2. Disruptions during testimony will not be tolerated. Booing, cheering, or throwing foreign objects, coaxing, verbal taunts, or threats during interrogation are strictly forbidden.

3. If you must leave the premises, please do so quickly and quietly, so as not to disturb the line of questioning or to influence the outcome in any way.

4. Once the accused party has been deemed guilty by the jury, Sir Zephyrus Westwind Barkay may confer with the victim or victims and in private, hear their last defense. Zephyrus will have the final say before the sentence is approved."

Rolling the scroll, the announcer tucked it into the wide sleeve of his robe, and stepped back from the podium. "I now present Sir Zephyrus Barkay, our most-esteemed and much beloved Master and Peacekeeper of the Forest. First on his agenda is the Declaration of Gratitude."

Someone hissed from Ivan's right and several rows behind. "I came for a hanging, not all this useless babbling."

Zephyrus opened his eyes wider, and his thick bark lips tightened. It was clear he wasn't pleased with the mean-spirited comment, but this time he ignored it. "Good Morning," he called. "Welcome once again to our Forest Court Trials. I see many old and new faces. I hope this shows our Forest community is growing. We have a number of testimonies to present. I encourage you to stay the full day, share lunch with us, and be witness to all. If the trial goes longer than planned, we will serve dinner, and the barracks will be made ready for your evening use."

The people clapped and cheered their appreciation.

Zephyrus introduced the three clerks by name, who sat with stacks of parchment, quills, and bottles of ink in front of them. They did not look up but were already writing feverishly, recording Zephyrus's every word.

"My most important announcement," Zephyrus's said, his gaze coming to rest upon Ivan, and Ivan immediately shrank in his seat. "Is my profound gratitude to a young lad who entered our Forest only a few months ago and has enriched our lives more than I can say—or repay."

Warmth crept from Ivan's chest, moving to his neck and face. He wished he could pull the cloak's hood over his head and disappear, but that would be impolite.

"Will you please stand, Ivan Kimble?"

Mortified, Ivan never expected to be singled out in front of all his friends and strangers. Lord Graydon was the first to stand and clap, followed by Simon, Merridyn, Anna-Iza, and the other twelve Forest's goddesses. Sebastian stood, pulled Ivan to his feet, and patted his back. All were clapping with vigor. Someone gave a shrill whistle. Ivan was sure it was Commander Simon.

"I have a gift for you." Zephyrus winked at the boy. "Sebastian, would you do me the honors?"

Sebastian stood and fumbled under his own well-used traveling cloak, looking muddled while he searched for something.

The crowd rose to its feet and threw arms into the air, shouting wildly.

"Now settle down, my friends," Zephyrus said and chortled lightly, "or we'll never get through the trial." He continued, "For returning the Golden Lantern, which is now hanging safely above me—it is the first of the five missing Ancient Relics, stolen ten years ago, and has now found safety in the Sanctuary of Truth—we are truly grateful."

Ivan diverted his eyes to the lantern, where he tried to find an escape from all the attention. He wiped his forehead with the palm of his hand, hoping he could sit quietly and the trial would officially begin. Rotating toward Lord Graydon, he saw a twinkle in his eyes and a smile forming under his white mustache.

Sebastian lifted the amulet, encompassing a ruby-red stone, hanging on a sturdy gold chain from inside his cloak's pocket, and draped it around Ivan's neck. "Congratulations," he said and stood on his tiptoes to kiss both Ivan's cheeks. He stepped back for all to see the glimmering, heavy piece of jewelry.

"We award you the Golden Medallion of the Forest, given for valor and bravery." Zephyrus's bark face took on a proud look. "It signifies our appreciation and everlasting friendship. This necklace gives you unhindered entrance into the Forest, as well as a few other meaningful perks, anytime you choose—except, of course, when the trees are dormant for the winter. The reason being, I fear you'd find it quite dull here when the trees give into the Big Sleep." He chuckled.

Commander Simon and his soldiers murmured in agreement.

Ivan forced a smile and tipped his head as Sebastian hung the amulet around his neck. Pride suddenly swept through him. He'd won the trust and love of the Forest.

He couldn't have guessed this celebrity moment had been planned for him. In awe, he studied the design and center jewel. The Forest certainly awards a lot of medals, he thought. Not that long ago, when Ivan visited the castle, he'd been given a silver necklace from Lord Graydon that protected him from Vaguer attacks. *Is it because of the many risks I've taken to survive the dangers in the Forest?* He gulped past the lump in his throat.

Ivan bowed to the audience for their goodwill, and his eyes met Anna-Iza's. The hood of her riding cloak, now resting against her back, showed her face aglow. She waved and clapped with enthusiasm. Her eyes shone bright with tears. To avoid staring at her, Ivan turned to the front and focused above Zephyrus's thinning crown of leaves. *Who would think attention would be so painful?*

"I-I-well, I…" Ivan's cheeks felt hot. He lowered his head, fingering the amulet, pretending to study it until he cooled off.

"For all these examples of good citizenship and your concern for others, Ivan Kimble, we award you with this Golden Medallion, sometimes referred to the Forest's Medallion of Bravery, to wear with pride." Zephyrus clicked his wooden tongue.

"Th-thank you very…very much. I-I…" Not knowing what to say, he nodded and took his seat. After some time, the applause died down, and Ivan drew a deep breath. He hoped it would be the last that Zephyrus pointed him out to the crowd.

"I'm proud of you," Merridyn whispered. Studying the jewelry for a moment, her face lifted with admiration. "You deserve this medal and appreciation for all you've done." She took Ivan's arm and squeezed affectionately.

"Congratulations, sir." The announcer stepped back and gave a practiced bow.

Chapter 6

The Forest Court Trials

The court announcer stood and gestured behind him. "I present the seven jury members." They entered the area, following each other in a rigid line. Standing before the richly carved and polished pew in front of the spectators, they waited for a prompt to sit. Their brilliant white robes, made from plush velvet, were tied loosely with double golden cords at their waists. Ample hoods covered their heads, shadowing their eyes.

Ivan wondered if they hoped to stay anonymous for their own safety or had other reasons. They bowed in unison to the audience, sat, and smoothed their luxurious garments with their palms.

With scarcely a lapse in breath or wasted moment, the announcer called Lord Graydon to the front. He bowed low and moved to a small table behind the podium.

Lord Graydon pulled on his fancy coat sleeves and stood erect behind the wooden stand. He coughed lightly into his palm and then stroked his goatee. "As you know, we try to include as many cases as are needed in the Autumn Forest Court Trials. There seem to be a number of unresolved circumstances that require our attention. I ask your indulgence."

"Regarding Zello, our renowned dragon..." The

lord paused, and glanced at the audience. "He has been exonerated—that is—forgiven for burning down the dragons' stable. He deeply regrets the accident."

"Then, where is he? Zello should be here to make his own case, don't you think?" A man far back in the pews shouted. It sounded like the same spiteful voice that had earlier called for a hanging.

Ivan gritted his teeth, tempted to turn and look again. *Who is the man making these nasty remarks?*

Sebastian leaned into Ivan and whispered, "That rude person is Raleigh Malicotte, the castle's Animal and Game Keeper."

"Shut up, Raleigh," someone barked.

Ivan hoped he'd see Zello and hear his testimony about the stable fire and for illegally taking the Golden Lantern. Lord Graydon had arranged a private inquiry where the revered dragon wouldn't suffer public humiliation, thanks to Sebastian and Ivan's encouragement. After some consideration, Zephyrus also agreed to the arrangement. Maybe, the audience would've been more sympathetic had they heard Zello speak in his own defense. *Well, they would never know.*

The lord raised his head. "You will recall the fire was an accident. When Zello tried to relight the wick of the Golden Lantern, he didn't realize a spark jumped from his fiery breath and smoldered in the stable's straw. I believe many of you have already read this in the South Castle's Weekly Crier. I preferred the information not be printed until after the verdict was declared." His scowl showed his deep disapproval. The audience looked sheepish, and none uttered a peep.

"However…" Sebastian stood and raised his hand. "Zello has agreed to help rebuild the stable, and workmen are now constructing the framework for it. We're hoping some of you fine men will volunteer to assist with this important project."

Simon nodded, murmuring his compliance. His soldiers groaned. They must've realized they would be called upon, once again, to help with the repair work. A few lifted their heads and looked sympathetic. When Sebastian sat, Ivan faced him, and they exchanged winks and a quick grin.

"What about the dragon having the Golden Lantern in his possession?" The voice sounded like Raleigh's, once again. "It's illegal, isn't it? Punishable by death?"

"He's getting more and more belligerent," Sebastian informed Ivan behind his cupped palm.

Though Ivan had never met Raleigh nor heard his name before, he was certain he wouldn't like him much.

The disgruntled gamekeeper grumbled about the lack of fairness and justice. Next to him someone hissed and said, "Keep quiet and listen. Lord Graydon and Zephyrus are the law here."

"Would you continue, my lord?" the announcer acknowledged with a slant of his head.

Lord Graydon clutched both sides of the podium and leaned into it. "Thank you for understanding." He faced the audience and grimaced. "The next consideration on the agenda, I'm sad to say, concerns our gryphons, Huntington and Piccadilly. They are now permanent stone pillars and will hold up the pediment at the entrance of the castle—forever." He wiped moisture from his eyes. "Since the time they were gifted to the castle, the creatures have been free to leave their marble posts at midnight. Their duty was to patrol the Forest and keep it safe, but they betrayed us by snatching the kaleido-birds to feed the Dark Army." The lord sniffed. "They'll never be free to fly into the sky again."

Standing in the back of the pews, the kaleido-birds squawked and flapped their wings. Justice finally prevailed. Ivan noticed Fetters dancing in a circle, fanning his colorful tail of vibrating pin feathers.

Several people in the audience were visibly shaken and choked after the announcement.

"Nothing more can be done." Lord Graydon lifted his shoulders. "They violated our Forest Laws. Zephyrus and I agreed to condemn them for their criminal behavior." He bowed to the crowd, blew his nose into his handkerchief, and returned to his seat. Merridyn took the lord's hand in hers and stroked it affectionately.

The court announcer stepped back. Mortimer Tink, the heavy-set Forest Court Barrister, moved laboriously to the podium and unrolled a thick scroll. His white-curled wig had seen better days. "I believe we can cover the next case on the agenda before lunch." He lifted a gold watch from his vest pocket under his black robe and studied it for a brief moment. "Ah, yes." He returned the watch to his pocket. "The Case of Cecil and Maloof." Clearing his throat, he said, "As you know, at one time, Maloof was a most-honored wizard, and Cecil was his Wizard Advisor. They were both respected and held in high regard. Nearly a decade ago, the two were found guilty of their crimes against the Forest and sent to Troll Transformation Prison."

The barrister continued, "After a time, the two traitors were *transformed* into shrunken trolls. Once again, they are before the council for their dreadful deeds." The barrister turned a tad to his right, exercising caution that his wig didn't pull away. He called loudly,

"Sergeant Pezzuline would you please bring the troll prisoners forward?"

The sergeant led them to the front, yanking on the chains that were attached to handcuffs. Ivan watched them stumble forward, jerking and resisting their captivity. Their time in prison had reduced them to a size no taller than about four feet. Maloof was devoid of hair, with lichen-like growths clustered over his head. Sebastian had once told Ivan the trolls were not in favor of cleanliness. Cecil snarled while Maloof made pitiful cries like an injured animal. Ivan felt sorry for the little runt.

"No. No hiding behind the pedestal." Barrister Tink extended his hand in a halting motion and gave them a noticeable push. His lips curled under his gray mustache. "Here to the side, where the audience can see and relish your guilt."

Maloof's head swung from side to side, scanning the crowd. His frightened eyes settled on Ivan, and deep ripples creased his thick brow.

Coaxing his spectacles down his nose, the barrister silently read the words on the scroll. "Grievous indeed," he muttered. "Maloof and Cecil, we have proof you left the parameter of the Forest about five or six years ago and did, at that time, visit the Kimble farm. For those of you that don't know where it's located, it's about an hour or so from our border." He wagged his finger in a northeasterly direction. "Be aware that our creatures are prohibited from leaving the limits of the Forest. There is some evidence that you both made a second trip some years later, but we have no real proof of this." He gave a swift glance at Pousses, who was stretched out on one of Zephyrus's lower branches. The barrister ran his fingers down the flattened scroll on the podium, mumbling through the script.

Ivan pitched his head back. He wasn't sure the trolls made a second trip, and he wondered if Peter shared the information with Zephyrus. Judging by the barrister's glance, perhaps it was Pousses who snitched. Privately, Ivan had told Sebastian and Lord Graydon about the trolls' first visit, but he didn't expect it to be used against them. *After all, what damage had they done?*

When Maloof bobbed his head up and down, Cecil jabbed him with his elbow.

Did Maloof understand what he'd just admitted?

"Is that a 'yes' for the both of you?" the barrister asked, bending toward them with a condemning scowl.

Cecil glared at the crowd, baring his teeth. "None of you have a right to judge me." He hissed, raised his fist, and shook it. "I am a great wizard and advisor to this— this idiot next to me. I've done astonishing wizardry in my life until you pompous arses condemned me to that disgusting prison." He jerked at his chain and growled like a mad dog.

"That's your opinion, Cecil." Barrister Tink sneered. "At the time, the Council of Seven found you guilty and sentenced you to prison for a full year. It seems it wasn't nearly long enough." He read further. "Oh, and it would seem, Maloof earned himself a ten-year stretch. It doesn't appear he has learned much discipline from it."

Lord Graydon shook his head, pressing his lips together with distress, his eyes closed.

Did he blame this dilemma on his own carelessness of the trolls' betrayal and bad behavior?

"The second infraction…" Barrister Tink ran his

index finger down the parchment once again. "Cecil, you are accused of possessing and throwing fireballs. I see we have a witness who is, at this time, resting on one of Zephyrus's lower limbs. What say you, Pousses?" The barrister lifted his double chins and addressed the cat with a raised voice.

Indeed, there Pousses stood, his back arched, his tail held straight. He meowed a high-pitched sound, "Guilty! These patches on my fur are proof of where the fireball singed me. It came whizzing at me from Cecil's wicked troll hands, but I couldn't jump out of its way fast enough."

Lord Graydon's face scrunched with anger. The flying feline was one of his favorite pets.

Scratching his sideburns, Ivan blinked. *Didn't Sebastian just tell him that cats couldn't testify in a trial?* No one spoke to dispute the statement, so Ivan stayed silent.

"These weapons are illegal in our Forest, Cecil. Where did you get the fireballs?" The barrister leaned toward them with an accusatory snarl.

Cecil growled and glared at the crowd.

Barrister Tink released a loud puff of air. "Well," he said and grunted with disgust, "we'll learn about their origins, and the responsible culprit will surely suffer the death penalty."

A few in the crowd gasped, shifting in their seats. Others snickered and seemed to agree with the suggested threat.

"The third infraction against Cecil and Maloof..." He stretched his hand toward Ivan and splayed his fingers. "We know you captured and stoned this poor young man, our honored guest from the outside. We also know you treated Sebastian badly by striking and poking him with your swords."

Ivan shrank into his seat, wishing the stoning incident hadn't been reported. It was all too embarrassing. He had been saved by the Elftens' timely arrival, and his bruises healed by the Long Dark Cloak. *Why mention it?*

Sitting next to him, Sebastian wrinkled his face and frowned. "I didn't tell anyone except Zephyrus, and I'm sure Lord Graydon didn't snitch, either."

"Then, who did?" Ivan raised his brow.

"I suspect Tereus arranged the attack and influenced the mindless trolls," Sebastian said. "Once the demon beneath the earth gathered the information, he would find ways to broadcast it."

"Do you have anything to say—Maloof? Cecil?" The barrister glowered at the prisoners.

Maloof looked up at the barrister. Tears rimmed his eyes. He wiped them away with his stumpy fist. "L-lan-ern." His speech stumbled. "Lan-ern mine." Turning, he pointed to the Golden Lantern that hung on one of Zephyrus's branches, spreading its light and warmth. The troll swung his finger at Ivan. "Him takes lan-ern, and no gives ta Maloof." A pitiful cry left the troll's lips. He wrapped his short arms around his chest, swaying from side to side. "Mine, mine, mine," he cried.

Ivan shifted forward on his hard seat, feeling sorry for the poor creature. "I-I-the lantern wasn't mine to give, Maloof. Do you remember I told you it was broken? Now it's fixed, and it belongs here—with Zephyrus."

Maloof turned his squat body and stared up at the Great Kingwood Oak. "Your lan-ern?"

"Yes, little fellow."

Overwhelmed with pity, Ivan ignored the court's protocol for speaking out of turn. "I have a lantern on my farm, and I'll give it to you as a gift." After he said this, Ivan worried whether it would be safe to give the clumsy troll a lantern with which he might burn the entire Forest down. He wished he'd stayed quiet.

A crooked-tooth grin spread wide. "Mine? Warm and bright," he blubbered.

"Those details can be worked out later." The barrister waved his hand impatiently. "Do you, Ivan Kimble and Sebastian, wish to press charges against the trolls for stoning you?"

"No, I-I…" Ivan shook his head.

Sebastian studied the two prisoners for some time. He must've been thinking about the treatment he'd suffered. In a soft voice, he answered, "No…no charges."

There were mumblings and whispers of discontent amongst the crowd. It seemed they had hoped all the trolls—especially these troublemakers, would again be sentenced to prison or hung.

For the first time that morning, Barrister Tink whacked his gavel on the pedestal for order. "Let it be recorded that Maloof and Cecil will not be charged for throwing stones at our honored guest, or Sebastian, but—they will be charged with leaving the Forest years ago and for the possession and use of illegal fireballs. And lastly, for having stolen the Golden Lantern. All of these crimes are very serious." A scowl gathered on his forehead. "I sense that Maloof is not malicious, perhaps dimwitted, and led astray by Cecil and his evil doings. However…it's not for me to say."

59

Maloof looked at the ground, kicking his ragged sandals into the dirt. He hacked a wad of phlegm from his throat and gave it a careless long spit, nearly hitting the barrister's polished boots.

Barrister Tink jerked his foot away, glowered, and turned red with anger. "Your sentence will be determined by the seven jury members behind me." He gave a swift glance in their direction.

"You, Cecil, will also be sentenced later by these same men, and, I must say, it doesn't look very favorable. I will enter my opinion to hang you."

Cecil's eyes rounded, and his mouth dropped open.

Ivan gasped, as did many in the audience.

Throwing back his head, Cecil screamed, "No! I'm a great wizard with strong powers. If you punish me, I'll exact vengeance on you." He spun around and tried to run, but Sergeant Pezzuline held the chain in a tight grip. The troll plummeted to the ground, screaming revenge.

"I'm afraid you sealed your own fate, Cecil, by involving Maloof in your twisted plans and corrupting the Forest." The barrister snarled. "Remove the trolls from court and hold them."

As the sergeant and a few soldiers dragged them away, Cecil jerked on the chain and continued to threaten and scream at his accusers. "You'll be sorry for this, I promise. Tereus will make you pay."

Maloof followed, looking a bit befuddled. He clapped his hands and sputtered, "Dat good, dat good."

Ivan couldn't help but smile. Sometimes, Maloof behaved like a nitwit. Other times, he seemed to understand a dire situation. You couldn't be sure about rocks or trolls.

Shortly, the people must've gotten a whiff of

something cooking. They shifted in their seats and smacked their lips. "That smells delicious," a soldier behind them remarked.

"It must be time for lunch," Ivan said happily.

Lord Graydon ran his fingers through his wavy white hair. Worry lines crossed his brow, though he seemed a bit relieved. "Excellent. I believe justice will finally be served on those two."

Remaining quiet, Ivan nodded. Now they knew that Cecil was aligned with Tereus, just as Pousses had said. He'd also said that Peter was in allegiance with the same master. *Is it true? Did Peter obey Tereus and all his malicious schemes?* A cold shiver shot up Ivan's spine.

"I'm not sure I like how this is going." Merridyn took a deep breath. Her dainty chin trembled.

"Don't you believe Cecil is guilty and deserves just punishment?" Ivan asked. He couldn't say the word "hanging." It reminded him of his own grotesque dream where Merridyn was made up like a clown, her wrists tied, and the rope around her neck was slung over a limb of the big red oak.

"I do, but…" She lowered her eyes.

"But what?"

"I'm wondering if Cecil is also involved in my case. I've heard he has a friendship with my sister, but I can't prove anything."

"Do you think Cecil put the poison in your potion?" Ivan eyed Merridyn closely. *Did Pousses tell her about the connection between Lyla and Cecil?*

"Sssh." Lord Graydon pressed his index finger to his lips. "It's not good to talk about it right now. Too many ears."

Zephyrus announced lunch was being served, and

all were welcome to partake in a lovely meal and hot tea provided by the generosity of Lord Graydon and his staff. The people clapped and cheered, leaving their seats at once.

Ivan jumped up, rubbing his aching rear end as privately as possible. His stomach growled shamefully. Hearing the rumble, Lord Graydon chuckled.

Chapter 7

Lunch Break

The morning turned warm. Ivan removed his jacket, folding it neatly on the pew seat. He pulled the Long Dark Cloak back over his shoulders and reached for Merridyn's hand. Instead, she hooked her arm through his. "I need to steady myself," she said, her voice shaky and apologetic. "My trial is next, and I'm not sure I can bear it."

Sebastian and Lord Graydon followed them to the trestle tables laid out in the open meadow to Zephyrus's right. In that way, the Great Oak could watch and listen to his subjects and enjoy their gaiety. The Elftens, Wolflords, and Simon's soldiers all moved swiftly to find bench seats that were closest to the kitchen and they would be served first. At least, that's what Ivan figured.

As the crowd grew, searching for their special place to sit, Simon's men rushed from the storage sheds to carry more benches and position them beside the established tables. Damask tablecloths were quickly spread and smoothed by the many servants' helpful hands. Fine silver cutlery was placed alongside fancy linen napkins. Ivan remembered Zephyrus had insisted the tables be presented like royalty for the people of the Forest. This event was no different.

"Bring hot tea," one of the servants shouted to

another.

Maynard, a familiar Forest face, gave Ivan a nod when they made eye contact. Standing at the opposite side of the table, the servant held a domed silver platter where hot steam escaped around the edges and delicious smells wafted in the air. Ivan's knees went weak with hunger.

Looking a bit dazed, Merridyn said, "I believe I'll go sit with my friend, Anna-Iza and the goddesses, if you don't mind."

"Sure." Ivan stopped while Merridyn pulled her arm from his. "Please tell Anna-Iza—well, tell her that—that I'm glad she's here, and I hope to see her later." Merridyn gave what Ivan thought was a knowing smile and walked away.

"Here! Come sit over here with us." Commander Simon waved vigorous arms. Ivan and Sebastian moved in his direction. "We have a lot to talk about." Simon scooted down the bench, making space for them. Alfred and Canute woofed and turned in circles, happy to be close to their master again. Or to be fed—which was more likely the case.

"They were good dogs, Ivan. You have them well trained." Simon reached down to scratch their ears, murmuring affectionately. "It wasn't until they heard the word *lunch* that they sat up and started barking."

Rolling his eyes, Ivan grunted. "Well trained, huh?"

Wayland waved as he passed. Holding Cactus in his arms, he found seats for his family near the end of where Sebastian and Ivan sat.

The Elftens walked toward a lone table. Ivan knew they ate differently than all the rest, preferring slightly cooked or raw vegetables, fruits, and nuts. Sytha sat first and waved to Ivan.

After the Wolflords found a suitable bench, Wayland doubled back to where Ivan had just managed to tuck in his long legs. Bent at his waist, the Wolflord whispered into Ivan's ear. "My brother, Davaan, confirmed early this morning. We're all set for our journey to the Mountain of Smoke and Fire. My wife and Cactus don't know anything about this, so don't mention it—or they'll worry. Okay? I'll send them home with Lord Graydon in his fancy carriage. Cactus will love that."

Ivan agreed with a tip of his head. "Of course, but Zephyrus must be told where we're going."

"That's exactly right." Sebastian's bushy eyebrows came together, causing his spectacles to slip to the end of his pointed nose. "There's no negotiation on this matter."

Wayland didn't seem too happy about it, but he agreed. "Sure. Zephyrus must be told."

"I'm anxious to see Peter and find out what kind of help he needs." Ivan pressed his lips together until they turned white. "Wayland," he said, "I'm very troubled."

"It'll be okay. After a good night's sleep and the trial is over, we'll leave early tomorrow."

Trays of food came sweeping in, carried by the many servants of the Forest. Maynard, with his rust-red hair, familiar in his black waistcoat and starched white shirt, seemed to make an effort to reach Ivan, his friends, and Lord Graydon. He bowed and showed the array of food on the silver tray. The rush of good smells made them shiver with anticipation.

"What's this?" Simon leaned over his plate and poked at what looked like a medium-sized pie with something fluffy, baked to a golden brown that covered it.

"Why, it's Cottage Venison Pie topped with whipped potatoes, sir. Surely you must've eaten it at the castle many times." Maynard closed his eyes, looking both offended and defensive.

The commander finally grunted, and after tasting a reluctant forkful, he seemed to agree that it was delicious.

Ivan took a bite of the Cottage Pie. "It's wonderful." He nearly moaned with pleasure but knew it was impolite, even in the relaxed atmosphere of their meadow luncheon.

Shortly, another servant placed a large platter of smoked root vegetables on their table. "Eat up. There's plenty more of these." He bowed and moved away.

"Merridyn is terribly anxious." Ivan sliced a cooked rutabaga and turnip into small bites and asked Lord Graydon in a quiet voice, "Do you believe she has a chance?"

"Oh, yes," the lord said. "Although, I'm concerned her sister, Lyla, hasn't yet shown."

Ivan poured hot tea into their cups. "I'd like to ask little Benny a few questions. I was led to believe…" He glanced at Lord Graydon. "Pousses suggested that the boy might've seen something—a troll near Merridyn's cottage, but Benny doesn't talk."

The lord nearly choked on his tea, and a dribble caught on his white goatee. The cup shook in his hand. "Why didn't Pousses tell me this? It makes all the difference, then." He began to tremble all over. "I must go see that spoiled cat and get the information firsthand. This changes everything." Lord Graydon pulled his bony legs from the crowded bench and wiped his mouth on a napkin. "Excuse me," he said as his voice trailed. Lines deepened on his brow as he briskly walked away.

"Was that the right thing to say?" Ivan turned worriedly toward Sebastian.

"Probably the best thing you could've said. Otherwise, if Lyla does show up with all her venom, I don't believe the verdict would go well in Merridyn's favor."

****

The trumpet blew twice, a sign for all to return to their seats. The seven white-robed jury members filed in and sat quietly, pulling their hoods forward, ensuring their faces were not visible. They neither looked at the audience nor spoke a word.

All those returning from lunch approached with a buzz of conversation. There were several bursts of laughter and jostling to take their seats.

Barrister Tink reached for his wire-rimmed spectacles from his shirt pocket beneath his robe. He rested them on his nose and began reading directly from the scroll flattened on the podium.

"Merridyn Hempstead versus the Council of the Witches' Village. Case Number 7. Hmmm...not many cases against them in all these hundreds of years. That's commendable."

Zephyrus interrupted and spoke, "Excuse me, Barrister Tink. Could I request that four strong soldiers come forth and take the witness chair from the Sanctuary of Truth?"

The soldiers dashed ahead, as though previously informed, and waited until the huge door in Zephyrus's trunk opened, squeaking and rumbling. They disappeared inside for a moment and grunted as they pulled out a heavy, ornate chair and positioned it near the podium. Barrister Tink turned his head and stared at it. He seemed puzzled, like he'd never seen it before.

Merridyn jerked when her name was called.

"Would the accused please come forward and take the witness chair?" Mortimer Tink motioned with a tip of his hand.

It was the most elaborate chair Ivan had ever seen, with royal crimson upholstery and a matching tufted seat and back. Its thick arms and legs were intricately engraved with what appeared to be a mix of dragons and gryphons in flight, along with twisting vines, acorns, and oak leaves. The most jarring feature was the face of a hideous gargoyle carved into the back of the tall chair, glaring with sinister black glass eyes. Though considered a protector, this gargoyle was the ugliest Ivan had ever seen. It resembled a goat with a thick brow, giving it a cynical and angry appearance. On the top of its head was a single horn with two large ears on either side. The audience gasped and whispered to each other. *Did they never see such a thing from past trials?*

Ivan shivered at the thought of getting close to the carving.

When Merridyn stood, Ivan leaped up and reached for her forearm, sensing her legs were unstable. He led her to the imposing chair, where he helped lower her onto the plush seat. The gargoyle's foreboding eyes stared above and beyond her head toward the audience, threatening and watchful. After she sat, his menacing mouth relaxed and closed.

Merridyn removed her gloves and twisted them on her lap.

"In the spring of this year, April 23, 1947, it was reported that you, a witch of high standing in your village, renowned for your potions and remedies, concocted a cure for a cold for your four-year-old little boy and your husband of five years." The barrister raised his eyes, peering over the rims of his glasses. "Is this correct?"

"Y-yes, sir," her small voice said.

Glancing at her pale face, Ivan saw tears welling in her eyes. She was remembering that horrible day—the day she lost them both.

"We understand the mixture went awry, reportedly through carelessness on your part and, as a result…" Barrister Tink turned to her and said in a gruff voice, "Your family died an agonizing death. Is this true?"

"I-I—yes, it's true, they did die an agonizing…but I didn't, no, I wasn't careless…" She choked on her tears, now flooding her cheeks.

"I object," Lord Graydon said and rose to his feet. "Barrister Mortimer Tink, your opening statement is most uncalled for. You've already condemned this dear young lady, and it will influence the jury as well as the audience. I must insist, no more alleged comments on Merridyn Hempstead's actions."

The barrister curled his lips. He frowned and grudgingly tilted his head.

Ivan gave the lord an admiring look for his boldness and an encouraging smile to the distraught lady. It seemed to help…somewhat.

Merridyn pitched back her shoulders and then swung her head toward a sudden movement to her right. A look of horror covered her face. Her mouth parted.

All attention turned in that direction.

"Ahhh, Lyla." The barrister's eyebrows rose with pleasure. "We are just about to start questioning the suspect."

Lyla gave her sister a disdainful look, not saying a word, and squeezed into the front pew next to little Benny and took his hand in hers. While the mother didn't protest, Bartholomew, Benny's dad, scowled and looked irritated.

It was difficult for Ivan to see clearly, but he did notice Lyla leaning over and saying something to Benny and his mother. The witch's blood-red lips stretched victoriously.

"She does look the part of a witch," Ivan said in a low voice to Lord Graydon. Her glossy black hair hung long, nearly to her waist, with two beaded braids hanging down on the right side of her head. Her eyes were traced with black pencil and accented with dark lashes. The black lace dress she wore hugged her slender body while dark hose covered her legs. The only thing missing, Ivan mused, was a peaked witch's hat and a deadly wand—or maybe a broomstick. He'd seen pictures of them in children's books when he was young, and Lyla certainly fit the image.

When the audience quieted down, the barrister continued his questioning.

"Miss Hempstead, could you please tell us what was in the potion you made on that fateful day?"

"I-I…nothing unusual, nothing harmful. Herbs and grated roots, onion and garlic broth, a small quantity of diced red mushrooms to help my husband and little boy sleep peacefully."

"Could too many mushrooms be poisonous?"

Ivan knew about them. His two beagles had sniffed

the mushroom powder on his first visit to the Forest, and shortly thereafter, they crawled under some holly bushes and went to sleep. Several hours later, they returned with no harm done. He'd also talked with Merridyn's neighbor about a possible overdose. Again, it was stated that they would not kill a person—though too many might give them a severe bellyache.

"N-no sir," she raised her face and forcefully spoke. "Many people from my village already know that I excel in potion preparation. They know this because I have arrested their pain, stopped the spread of diseases, and I've cured many of their illnesses in the past. Do you really believe I would be so careless with my own beloved family?" She inclined forward. Her eyebrows drew together in a sharp point. "It comes from years and years of study with the elder healers in our community, much reading, note taking, and hours of devoted practice."

Lyla crossed her arms. "Humph," she said and purposely distorted her lips.

"Go on, please, Miss Hempstead." The barrister cleared his throat and shifted his weight.

"On the day in question..." Merridyn ignored Lyla's response and continued, not giving her a moment to sabotage her testimony. "My little boy caught the cold that my husband was suffering from. I mixed the ingredients into a pot on the stove, next to an open window."

"And did you, Miss Hempstead, leave the house at any time while the potion was on the stove?"

"Why...yes," she answered, looking into the distance as she'd just now recalled the fact. "Come to think of it, I did."

"Well, isn't that a convenient detail you've just remembered?" Lyla mocked.

Heads turned toward the sarcastic remark. Wayland's wife loudly shushed her.

The barrister didn't reprimand Lyla, though he should have. Ivan wondered if the two of them were part of a plan to destroy Merridyn, but he couldn't imagine the reason.

"And where did you go when your young son and husband were sick in the next room?"

"I went to the root cellar where I grow my own small crop of red mushrooms. They must be kept moist and in the dark for at least three days before using."

"Did you see or hear anything out of the ordinary when you went to the cellar?" The barrister made a quick note on the parchment.

"No. I was intent on picking the best and freshest." She scanned the crowd, judging their reaction—or was she searching for an ally?

"She's such a liar!" Lyla jumped from her seat. "My arrogant, self-absorbed sister screwed up the potion and now tries to find someone to blame. I've never heard of such madness. You"—the witch screamed, shaking a long manicured finger—"you deserve to hang, and I'm going to see that it happens. You are not fit to live in our village."

The audience choked on the girl's spiteful words. Merridyn let out a painful cry of disbelief. Tears streamed down her flushed cheeks.

"Stop!" Without realizing it, Ivan was so angry at the bitter remark that he shot from his seat and turned on Lyla. "Y-your opinions are not allowed in this court." He fisted his hands. "Barrister Tink is doing the questioning—the j-jury will make the decision. And—and Zephyrus will see that justice is done." He was shaking so hard he could scarcely get the words out. Only because of his affection and belief in Merridyn did he find the courage to shout the irate statement in front of the audience and his friends.

The crowd clapped and cheered for Ivan's outburst. Apparently, they valued the drama, and he was sure they were pleased he'd spoken up. *It's clear they love and believe in Merridyn.*

When Ivan glanced over at Zephyrus, he saw a huge grin on his bark lips. The Great Oak gave him a wink.

Merridyn dabbed her eyes, and she mouthed to Ivan, "Thank you."

Chapter 8

Merridyn's Trial

"Eh-hem." The barrister's lifted his head with a show of superiority. His nostrils flared. "Young man, as *you* have stated, I'm here to do the questioning. Allow me to do my job." He glared at Ivan, and then with a quick nod at Lyla, he motioned for them to both sit. "Let's continue and hear the remainder of Merridyn's testimony." Moving his finger down the scroll, the barrister appeared to search and find his place. "So…you put the red mushrooms into the stewpot?"

"Yes," she said, her voice trembling. "I diced and added them slowly. When three minutes had passed, I strained the mixture into two delicate porcelain cups, adding several teaspoons of sugar to mask the unpleasant taste. As I've stated, my husband and boy were in the same bed so I could check on them. They drank their potion and curled up into each other's arms. I left the room when it seemed they had fallen into a peaceful slumber."

"But they did not." The barrister stared at her and lifted an eyebrow. "They did not have a peaceful slumber."

Merridyn bent her head, clasping her hands together as though in prayer, silent for some moments.

"Miss Hempstead?"

"I heard them groaning, calling for me, and then—a scream—like they were being…"

"Being?" The barrister leaned in her direction.

She shook her head. Her shoulders slumped.

Ivan wished he could go to her. Hold her, and ease the pain of that horrible day.

Sitting to his right, Sebastian patted Ivan's knee. "She must relive this for the court jury," he said softly.

"Is it possible, Miss Hempstead," the barrister said and emphasized, "that someone dropped something lethal into the potion while you went to the cellar?"

"Well," she hesitated, taking a deep breath and sniffed. "I suppose someone could've done such a thing, but I can't imagine anyone so cruel, so hateful."

Lyla shot to her feet, her voice high-pitched. "There was no mystery person outside your window!" She stomped her foot and shook her fist at her sister, who sat rigid in the witness chair. It was most comical when Lyla discovered her childish foot stomping had caused her high-heeled shoe to wedge solidly into the ground. She struggled to pull it out, getting angrier and angrier at the chuckling audience. Even Ivan covered his mouth, trying to stifle a laugh.

"Do you need help?" the barrister said and made a move toward her.

"No!" she shouted and, with some effort, jerked her shoe from bondage.

Sebastian leaned toward Ivan, his hand against his mouth, hiccupping with laughter. "Zephyrus wrapped a root around Lyla's shoe, ensnaring it into the earth." He whispered, "Good trick, Zeph' ol' boy!"

"I wondered how such a thing could've happened." Ivan snickered.

Zephyrus slowly closed his eyes and tightened his wooden lips to hide a grin.

Lyla jabbed a finger at Merridyn and continued her tirade. "She was careless, thinking she's so perfect and righteous. My sister is a danger to the village and that's why she was confined to Troll Prison. We witches voted for this after she murdered her family, and as far as I'm concerned, the sentence still applies."

Bartholomew said in a loud voice, "We witches don't remember voting on such a thing. It was all your doing, Lyla."

The barrister heard the comment and made a note of it.

Lyla's face turned bright red, her slender arms crossed in front of her chest.

"Calm down, Lyla." Lord Graydon slowly lowered his hands. "We want justice here, not hysterics."

Lyla bunched her lips with narrowed eyes fuming. She gave Lord Graydon a baleful look.

"Yes," the barrister said, leaning an arm on the podium. "We want justice, certainly."

Arms crossed over her chest and her lips in a pout, Lyla raised her nose into the air.

Sweeping his big head right and left, the barrister said, "Who amongst you was there in the Witches' Village that awful day at Merridyn's cottage, number 13?"

"Benny. Benny," Ivan said, directing his low voice in the boy's direction. "Now is your time to speak."

The boy buried his face into his mommy's shoulder, shaking his head.

"No one! See, no one was there." Lyla shot from her seat and raised her voice. "Doesn't that tell all? Only her—only Merridyn herself is to blame."

"Let's please be…" the barrister began.

The angry witch leaned forward, her dark eyebrows jammed together. She shouted, "Stop wasting precious time and condemn her with a life sentence in Troll Transformation Prison! She'll be in good company with Maloof and all those dreadful, worthless trolls."

One of the seven jury members grumbled. "Will you please keep that woman quiet? She has no right to speak out of turn and give her biased opinion during the trial procedure."

"There's a first." Lord Graydon turned to Ivan and whispered, "We've never heard one of the jury members talk during questioning." His eyes twinkled. "Though I am rather amused."

"Things are getting out of hand," Zephyrus moaned and rolled his eyes toward heaven.

"Will you please sit?" Bartholomew demanded. He jumped up, gripped Lyla's arm, and dragged her to a seat in the front row where he sat. Tanner frowned but squeezed tighter in the pew, allowing the witch her space. "Now be quiet!" Bart grouched.

The audience mumbled. Many clapped in agreement. "Way to go, Bart!"

Pousses stood on one of Zephyrus's low branches and arched his charcoal-gray body, lifting his wings as if to send a message. The cat stared at Ivan and meowed.

Is it a sign that I'm supposed to understand? Fingers spread wide, Ivan shrugged. He still had no proof against Lyla, as disagreeable as she was.

"Why don't we all take a short break and cool off a bit?" Barrister Tink cleared his throat and marked a spot on the parchment. "I'm told there are scrumptious desserts and hot tea being served."

Heads bobbed in agreement. The clerks lowered their quills to the table with an audible sigh of relief.

The barrister called to Ivan in a gruff voice.

"Yes, sir."

"You will remember when the announcer read the rules of the Forest Court Trials. These outbursts are not allowed, and I may have to excuse you from…"

"Of course, y-you are right. I apologize." Ivan bowed, swiveled abruptly, and marched toward Zephyrus. He grinned as he moved away, knowing he had avoided a scolding from the barrister.

"Wait for me." Sebastian pushed up from the pew and followed on cramped legs.

"What is it, Ivan?" Zephyrus beheld the lad with kindness. "You look frantic."

"I need to talk to—where is Pousses? I have some questions to ask him—it's important."

"He's up there somewhere." Zephyrus looked upward. "I feel him scratching against one of my limbs."

"Pousses, please come down." Ivan backed away, scanning the branches for the feline. "I must speak to you." His jaw clenched. This was his last chance to hear the truth.

The cat took wing and flew to a lower branch, not far from the Golden Lantern, who had extinguished his light since the day had turned sunny and warm. "What do you want—you woke me from my catnap?"

"It's not looking positive for Merridyn. Her wicked sister is tormenting her, trying to influence the barrister and the jury."

"I was wondering when you'd ask me." The cat yawned like it all bored him.

"If it was Cecil who put the poison in the potion, how did he reach the stewpot?"

"I flew to Merridyn's cottage a couple days ago," the cat said, "to confirm that the short ladder hidden behind the ivy was still there. But that probably doesn't mean much since I can't testify," Pousses said with a twitch of his whiskers. It was clear the cat was insulted.

"It means everything!" Ivan felt a weight lift from his chest. "Cecil used the ladder to reach the window and dump in the poison."

"I told you before, get Benny to talk," Pousses emphasized. "He was there that day to play with Merridyn's little boy, but he was sick. It's quite possible Benny saw what happened. You need an eyewitness."

Ivan leaned against Zephyrus's trunk, arms folded, wondering how a mere cat became so smart. "Why is life so complicated in the Forest?" He sighed.

Zephyrus gave a little laugh. "Life is complicated everywhere. We must be wise and seek the *truth*. Sometimes it's harder to find when the truth is obscured by human deception."

"I don't believe Benny will say a thing against Lyla." Ivan watched the people rush to the tables where pots of tea and tasty sweets were being served. He wished he could join them. A cup of tea would be just the ticket for his dry mouth. "She has him scared to death—and maybe threatened his life."

"Ivan, my dear lad." Zephyrus grinned. "I'm surprised you haven't guessed it yet. All you need do is to ask Lyla to take the Truth Chair, and, having no control over her words, she will admit everything."

"Oh, yeah." Pousses bobbed his furry head. "I'd forgotten all about the magic in that ancient chair."

"What?" Ivan's eyes widened as he stared at Zephyrus. "Do you mean the witness chair is really a *Truth Chair,* and if anyone sits in it, they must be honest?"

"That's exactly what I mean. It takes control of your subconscious and forces the truth to be told. We've secretly named it the Truth Chair, though few know this." Zephyrus wiggled his twig-eyebrows. "The High Intervener helped put magic into the old frame, but the head of a gargoyle was my idea. You must admit, it's very clever."

Ivan wasn't sure if it was or not. He had yet to test it.

"Please don't tell anyone about it, however," Zephyrus said.

"No. No, of course not. Then, the barrister will call Lyla to sit in the chair."

"Yes, and here's the catch. It must be *you* that interrogates her."

"M-me? Why me? Surely there are better qualified people—the barrister, he—"

"As you may suspect, Barrister Tink is dazzled by Lyla. He is not the right choice to question her."

"Then," Ivan pleaded, "how about Lord Graydon, or you, or Sebastian—maybe Sytha, the Elften. They should be the ones to question the witch. I don't even know her."

"You wear the Forest's Golden Medallion." Zephyrus glanced at the heavy disc around Ivan's neck. "It is more special than you realize. It gives you the power to influence and make a difference where honesty is desired. That said, you must appreciate the gift you've been awarded. In the wrong hands, it could be a disaster."

"Yes. But…how will the chair reveal dishonesty?"

"You'll see when it happens."

Ivan lifted the metal disc that rested against the Long Dark Cloak and traced his finger over the ancient rune, gaining new appreciation for the medallion. When he flipped it over, he recognized the image of Zello and Zephyrus etched on the back. "Does the barrister know—I mean, about the Truth Chair?"

"No."

"The clerks?"

"No."

"The jury?"

"Yes, all seven of them. It makes their job so easy. I don't know why I pay them for their services." Zephyrus chortled.

"B-but what would I ask her?"

Pousses rolled his yellow eyes, like Ivan didn't have a functioning brain. "You could start with, where were you on the day of April the 23rd of this year?"

Ivan thought it was a logical suggestion.

"Soon after the break, I'll request that Barrister Tink allow you to call a witness." Zephyrus closed his eyes and considered his own suggestion. Then he opened them. "The barrister will not challenge me. You will escort Lyla to the Truth Chair and ask her a few questions. I'm sure you'll find your path from there. Now off you go—we are about to resume the trial."

Chapter 9

The Truth Chair

The pews filled up quickly, and the people seemed in a better, almost cheerful frame of mind after their hot tea and a wide selection of desserts. Sytha and Wayland asked Ivan why he'd missed such a fine array of treats. Shaking his head, Ivan mumbled that he had spoken to Zephyrus. The Elften and Wolflord glanced at each other, a look of curiosity on their faces.

Barrister Tink was about to make his opening remarks when at the last minute, several people walked hurriedly toward their seats.

"So sorry," Willa, Wayland's wife said, waving her hand. "I got a bit delayed waiting for our time in the privy with little Cactus, here."

Ivan smiled while the barrister frowned at their tardiness.

Lord Graydon also strolled toward the pews with Merridyn's arm tucked through his. Her face was pale, her legs wobbly. "I hope you all enjoyed your lovely sweets and tea," he called, gesturing his hand toward the audience. "My thanks once again to the gracious castle staff for their preparations."

The people clapped and mouthed their approval. Seated several rows back and to Ivan's right, a lady was still stuffing scones and biscuits into her mouth, trying to catch the crumbs in her open hand. He watched her for a moment and licked his lips.

"Excellent." Lord Graydon took his seat next to Merridyn, giving her an encouraging smile. She didn't seem to share his optimism, for her expression remained grave.

Turning around, the barrister appeared to check that all seven jury members had returned and were comfortably seated. His opening remark caused Ivan's chest to turn hot and his head to buzz.

"Merridyn, I'm afraid your innocence doesn't look very promising. Unless you can tag the perpetrator who put poison in your—ah, concoction—you may very well return to prison, or even worse."

A pitiful, low scream escaped from Merridyn's throat and grew louder. "No. Oh, no. It can't be. I'm innocent. I've already lost so much, please…" Now the tears came, rushing down her flushed cheeks, and her body shook violently. Lord Graydon put his arms around her shoulders and held her tightly, whispering into her ear.

Ivan wondered what the lord said to her after she'd been threatened and may be sent back to the most degrading prison in all of England.

Zephyrus interrupted the gasps and murmurings from the people. "Excuse me, Barrister Tink," he said, "but I request that you call upon Ivan Kimble, the bearer of the Forest's Golden Medallion, to ask a few questions of Lyla."

Taking a step back, the barrister's face bunched with what looked like insult and resentment. He paused for some time, working his mouth up and down before answering. "Well, yes, of course, sir. You are perfectly in your right to call upon whom you deem adequate for—interrogating the lady."

"Yes, I certainly am." Zephyrus's twig mustache twitched in the most delightful way.

Ivan slowly stood, his hands shaking, uncertain of what he would ask. "Lyla, will you please s-sit here in this f-fancy chair?" He grasped the cool metal of the Golden Medallion, hoping it would suddenly give him the confidence he needed to ask the right questions. *Isn't that what Zephyrus told me, that the medallion would give me the power of influence*? He didn't know what that meant, but if it would grant self-assurance to speak and not make a fool of himself, then it would more than serve its purpose.

"Why call on me?" Lyla's body stiffened. "I didn't poison my family." She sneered at her sister. "I didn't murder two people through my own carelessness."

"We are only trying to find the truth. W-would you…?" Ivan stepped toward the heavy chair and rested his cold hand over the gargoyle's wooden head carved on top of the frame. He jerked it away. The ugly monster with dark glass eyes was too frightening to touch.

The girl reluctantly moved toward the chair and pressed her hand against the crimson velvet cushion testing for softness. It must've met her approval, for she sat and then lifted her nose into the air, tightening her bright red lips.

Ivan turned sideways to the audience so they could view him and Lyla at the same time. He took a deep breath.

"D-do you have family, Lyla—that is, besides your sister?" He didn't know why he started with such a personal question when Pousses had already told him what to ask.

Her face seemed to relax a bit, and her shoulders lost their stiff, defensive look. "No family." Lyla's upper lip curled when she pointed at Merridyn. "Just her. Our parents were killed by a couple of stinkin' trolls that snuck into our village. They did away with Mum and Dad. It was the last time they attacked—you can count on that!"

Ivan thought it was interesting, if not ironic. A sign outside the Witches' Village forbid trolls to enter, yet Lyla held a friendship with Cecil. The once great wizard who had been reduced to a troll for his crimes against the Forest.

"I have no parents, either." Ivan bit his lower lip and looked into the distance. "Only one brother, you probably know that." He studied her face to see if she would acknowledge his remark—that she knew Peter. "I know it's lonely not having parents."

"Well, yes, it is." Lyla's eyes eased their wary look. *She must believe, since I'm an outsider, that I'm too timid to challenge her with tough questions.* "My parents were killed in a train crash just outside of London. I miss them every day."

"I'm sorry," she said, sounding almost genuine.

"Tell me, where were you on the day of April the 23rd when Merridyn's husband and child died?"

"M-me?" She sputtered, and put her fingers over her mouth. A startled look appeared on her otherwise relaxed face. "I-I was at my cottage, picking lavender and rosemary from my small garden."

"—And, and then what?"

"W-well, I took a walk."

"Anywhere near Merridyn's cottage?"

"Actually, it was. I went there to meet someone."

"Who would that be?" Ivan turned to glance at Zephyrus, whose bark face showed extreme pleasure. *Is the medallion working, yet?*

"It was, um, let me think…" The gargoyle's eyes suddenly lit up and shone bright red. "I was to meet…a…C-Cecil, the once great wizard of the Forest." Her voice became louder, and she shook her finger at the people. "You all seemed to have forgotten how magnificent he was, all the things he did for you—for the betterment of the Forest. And he still could be great if you'd give him half a chance to change back into a man-wizard."

"Not possible," Sebastian said dryly, and he crossed his arms over his chest.

Lyla scowled at him. "I promised Cecil that if he helped me with this one little favor, I'd put in an encouraging word to the council to forgive him. But I see you have unforgiving and hardened hearts."

"I thought trolls were not allowed in the Witches' Village." Ivan cocked an eyebrow at her. "It's written on the wooden structure at the front entrance." After his pointed remark, Ivan didn't know what to do with his hands. They seemed to hang tense at his sides with no purpose, and so he shoved them into the pockets of The Long Dark Cloak.

Her eyes opened wide, showing astonishment that Ivan would know about the sign. "That's true, but Cecil came at my request. He wore a little girl's dress and a bonnet. Therefore, he wasn't really a troll."

The gargoyle's eyes blinked red.

"Why was Cecil dressed like a little girl?"

"So no one would recognize him, of course."

Hesitating, Ivan allowed the comment to sink in, not just for his understanding but also for the jury.

"Why didn't you want him recognized?"

"It should be obvious." She scowled, and her tone was impatient. "He's a troll, and trolls aren't allowed in our village. You just said so yourself."

Ivan inhaled deeply. Was she confusing him and the audience on purpose? "Why did you want Cecil to meet you?"

"I asked him to slip a strong sleeping potion into my sister's stewpot on the stove."

With surprise and disgust, the audience gasped and whispered to each other. Merridyn bent her head and wept softly into her handkerchief.

"Couldn't you have done this yourself? You're taller than Cecil."

"Oh, no. Someone might see me. I stayed well out of the way, hiding behind a neighbor's cottage."

"Did you know the potion on the stove was meant for her husband and son for their bad colds?"

"No. And it didn't matter. She was always brewing up some smelly remedy to heal people. Merridyn is so impressed with herself and her abilities that no one is her equal, you see?"

"Then, you were jealous of your sister's talents?" Now, Ivan's mouth felt like dry tree bark, and it was difficult to form his words. He had moved into touchy territory.

The imposing chair struck again. The gargoyle's red eyes brightened, forcing truth.

"Yes, I'm very jealous of her, and you would be, too." She gripped the sturdy chair arms. Her teeth clenched until the grinding sound was heard in the front row. "It's always been that way, you see? Ever since we were little girls, and now, my envy has turned into bitter hate."

There was a rush of moans from the audience. Several scratched their heads in dismay. Sytha and Tanner turned to elbow each other, apparently enjoying the spectacle.

For a moment, the witch in the chair frowned, looking puzzled.

Ivan shot a glance at Zephyrus. *Should I go on?* The tree's expression was blank. *What more can I ask her?* He thought about Merridyn and how she'd suffered those awful months in Troll Transformation Prison. He took a deep gulp of air and decided he must bring the truth fully to light or make a complete fool of himself.

"Is that why you had Cecil put the poison in Merridyn's potion? Because you hated your sister and wished her dead?"

She looked up at Ivan and hesitated for a long time. Then she let out a terrible scream, her eyes narrowed with fury. "I didn't know it was poison. I didn't know! Cecil brought that fishy-smelling stuff and poured it into the potion. He said it would put her into a light stupor."

Ivan paused and waited for her to regain some composure.

She tipped her head back, her mouth opened wide. "I think Cecil lied to me."

"Cecil is kind of short to reach the window by Merridyn's stove." Ivan had observed this during his first visit to the Witches' Village. Watching her closely, he wondered how much longer he needed to go on.

Rigid with anger, Lyla said, "The ladder, you idiot. There's a short ladder hidden behind the ivy that climbs up the wall of my sister's cottage."

"Oh, I see." Ivan waited after the outburst. A lump crawled up his throat. He wished she wouldn't yell at him and call him an idiot. He was already nervous about asking penetrating questions.

Unexpectedly, Lyla's hands covered her face. Her forehead lowered until it touched her lap. She released loud sobs. "Oh, High Intervener, what have I done? I only wanted her to sleep deeply." She looked up, scanning the audience. Thick makeup dissolved around her eyes, sliding down her cheeks, and spittle dripped from her mouth. "Cecil promised me she would sleep for several hours—that it wouldn't harm her. I didn't want her family to die."

Ivan hesitated for a moment, his thoughts scrambled. "Why did you want her to sleep?"

"So…" Her sobs trailed to a whimper. "So I could search for the deed to her cottage. You know?" Wiping the tears from her eyes, she stared at the black makeup smudges on her hankie. The dark spots baffled her.

"It was meant to be mine," she continued with complete confidence. "Cottage number 13 on the Sacred Hill. It has special properties where our ancestors were buried. I'm the eldest, but *she* took it from me because she married first. Th-then I would be admired and respected in our village—a trusted potion-maker, a great spell-caster, a witch well loved in the community. Do you see? I just wanted acceptance and to be loved."

The jury members leaned forward, looking shocked at such words. Several pushed their hoods back as though they couldn't believe what they'd just heard. Apparently, they'd never witnessed anything as disturbing as this.

"I thought her husband and boy were off fishing at

the east end of Emerald Lake, where the Swamp Dragons once lived. You know the place?" She seemed to plead with her eyes for understanding.

Ivan met her stare and nodded.

"I didn't know they were home, sick with colds." Wailing in her own defense, she stuttered a cry of helplessness. "I didn't know. I didn't know."

"Did you believe Merridyn was preparing potion for herself?" Ivan looked just above Lyla's head to see if the gargoyle was as shocked. His gleaming red eyes showed that he was.

"Well, sure. Sometimes she tested her own brew to see if the ingredients were just right."

It suddenly occurred to Ivan with a jolt. *The fishy smell, the agonizing death. Was it the poison from the Swamp Dragon's venomous tail? Was it the same as on the Silver Axe that struck Zephyrus's side—nearly taking his life?* Ivan forced his teeth together, not mentioning it, as it had no bearing on the trial.

"Lyla," the barrister interrupted, his eyebrows lowered with remorse. "Do you understand what your foolishness, your jealousy, your self-centeredness has done? Though unintentionally, you poisoned Merridyn's family. And to cover your mistake, you blamed your sister and sent her to Troll Prison? Do I have it right?"

The gargoyle's eyes open wider, flashing red.

It may have grinned. Ivan couldn't be sure.

"Yes," she said, dropping her chin. "I've been very bad."

"Why—why did you cause Merridyn to suffer even more by condemning her to that ghastly prison?" Ivan glared at her.

"Well…because…it would turn away any suspicion

from me. My sister would be kept in prison, and no one would suspect what I'd done, nor would they trust her testimony."

Breath seemed to leave Ivan's lungs. He suspected his response was identical to most of the audience. Bartholomew's wife wiped her eyes while little Benny tried to comfort her with his arms around her neck, patting her back. Merridyn shook her head, shoulders bent, sobbing even harder. She couldn't believe her own sister's cruelty.

Ivan finally took in air, hoping to find the strength to complete his questioning. He unclenched his fists. His palms were sore where his fingernails had dug in. "Why did Cecil help you?"

She looked over her shoulder at Zephyrus, her eyes begging. "Don't you see? I didn't mean to harm her husband and boy. I only wanted to put my sister to sleep and take the cottage that was rightfully mine."

"My question is, why did Cecil help you?" Ivan forced a stoic face, as revolting as Lyla's testimony was. He felt it was imperative that she repeat why Cecil would do such a wicked favor for her.

"Cecil is a good friend and was a mighty wizard at one time…and he was willing. That's what good friends do for each other."

The gargoyle's eyes spun in their sockets.

"Oh, Lyla, dear sister," Merridyn mourned, moved beyond grief. "Why didn't you tell me this? We-we could've made some kind of arrangement. Built onto my cottage…something. It wasn't worth the years of jealousy you've endured. It wasn't worth my family's life."

"It doesn't matter." Lyla snuffled and waved the

comment away. "I'm so accustomed to hating you that I don't know what I'd do without that emotion. It's what helps me endure every day. Do you understand?"

"No. Not at all." Merridyn sat up, and she slowly shook her head. "I don't understand."

Ivan's eyebrows rose. He'd never heard such a thing in all his life. Hating someone so deeply—your own sister—that you depended on that emotion to help you make it through each day. Dark. Terrifyingly dark.

Sensing the audience was tense with anxiety, stunned, and overwhelmed, Ivan said, "One last question, Lyla, if you please."

Lyla lifted her eyes and looked at Ivan with tears wetting her cheeks and her bottom lip quivering.

"Did my brother, Peter Kimble, have anything to do with this scheme of yours?" Ivan took a step back and hardened his arms. *Why did I ask such a question in front of all these people? What if her answer is yes?*

"P-peter?" She appeared confused why Ivan would ask such a question. "I did ask him to help me—he's tall, like you. No need for a ladder, and he's a familiar face in the Witches' Village, often helping in Arnie's bakery. Peter wouldn't have looked out of place, don't you see?"

Nodding, Ivan's chest tightened, waiting for her answer.

"No. He didn't want any part of my plan. Just walked away, shaking his head. He's kind of a snob. Did you know that about your brother?"

Ivan stared at the ground, the pressure released from his lungs and filled with fresh air. *My brother had nothing to do with the awful poisoning. Peter is innocent.* With that, Ivan bowed low, thanked Lyla in a quiet voice, and quaking all the way, returned his seat.

The jury looked as shaken as everyone else.

"Thank you, Ivan Kimble, for your expert questioning." The barrister coughed into his hand. "Now I know why Zephyrus called on you."

Though he was relieved that Peter hadn't been involved, Ivan's heart was heavy with sorrow. He'd heard the most pitiful testimony from a beautiful witch who'd allowed her jealousy and hatred to kindle and grow.

Merridyn rested her head on Ivan's shoulder and wept softly. "You are incredible. How did you know how to make Lyla tell the truth? My own sister—so scheming, so manipulative, so vengeful. What a waste of the human spirit." After a moment, she rose and stood before her sister, who cowered in the Truth Chair. "Lyla, though it will take a long time, I'll try to forgive you."

"No. I deserve to go to prison and regret the things I've done for the rest of my life. I'm a murderer," she said and sighed. "Perhaps I'll hang from the big red oak. That would be a fair penalty, don't you agree?"

It was then that Ivan realized the woman in his dream that'd been hung from the red oak was not Merridyn at all. It had been Lyla. He held his head in his hands and groaned. It was just as Merridyn had said—such a terrible waste.

There came a long, loud meow from one of Zephyrus's branches. "Good job, Kimble," Pousses said from his perch. Then he pushed off and spread his wings. "Just in time for my dinner at the castle."

Ivan watched Pousses rise to the sky, his charcoal-gray wings flapping. He circled and headed southwest. Drained of emotion and energy, Ivan wished he could disappear into the barracks, collapse on a bed, and sleep until morning.

Standing, Lord Graydon turned and rested his hands on Ivan's shoulders. "Your questioning and delivery were exemplary. I'm most proud of you, young Ivan." He kissed him on both cheeks and smiled broadly.

Allowing for a moment of joy, Ivan gave a nod of gratefulness.

Then, the lord reached for Merridyn's hand. "Congratulations. The truth is at last known. I'm sure the jury will find you not guilty and consent to your complete freedom. However, I'm afraid there will be a heavy penalty for Lyla."

"Prison?" Merridyn asked in a small voice.

"Probably," the lord answered, though he didn't sound real positive. He arched his back. "I'd better make one last announcement. Excuse me." He moved to the front, held up his hands to the stunned crowd, and thanked everyone for attending. "Stay around, and dinner will be served shortly. I promise you, it will be a grand feast. For those of you who have traveled far for the trial, I repeat, the soldier's barracks have been made ready for your stay tonight. This may be an excellent idea." The lord glanced skyward. "It will be dark soon, and it looks like rain in a few hours." He bowed, and the people clapped for his generosity.

"Lord Graydon, is there nothing we—I can do to change her sentence?" Merridyn's lips quivered. She dabbed her eyes and stared at him. "I don't want her to go to that dreadful place."

He studied her for a few moments.

Ivan hoped the lord would come up with a kindly solution. Perhaps imprison Lyla at the castle where the treatment would be more humane—or ban her from the

Forest forever.

"As you know, it's up to the seven jurors, Merridyn. It's not for me to interfere in this decision. I'm sorry."

She tipped her head and gave a slow nod. "I know." Putting his arm around her shoulders, Lord Graydon led her to the open meadow where the meal was being served.

Ivan and Sebastian followed, feeling both happy and glum.

Chapter 10

Meeting the Goddess

"You should've had a slice of apple pie," Wayland said to Ivan as they left the dinner table and walked toward the gravel path that led to the barracks. "It was very good."

"The mince pie was better," someone yelled after them, and the man laughed.

"I…ah…you know I don't eat anything sweet." Ivan grinned.

"Hurts his pearly-white teeth." Sytha teased, showing his own perfect mouth and making a face like a ferocious dragon.

"That was one intense trial." Ivan shook his head and puffed out a breath.

"Yes." Sebastian nodded. "I believe justice was done, and now Merridyn is free."

"What do you think the jury will do about Lyla?" Ivan and Sytha asked at the same time.

Sebastian shrugged and didn't answer.

"Oh, Ivan, my lad," Zephyrus called. "Have a moment for me?"

Ivan, Sytha, Wayland, and Sebastian turned to their right and stopped in front of the Great Oak.

"He did a good job, didn't he?" Sytha patted Ivan's back and ruffled his dark hair. "I was surprised you asked

Lyla all the right questions to relax her, and then you pulled the truth from her."

"Yeah, that was pretty amazing. How did you do that?" Wayland narrowed his eyes and gave Ivan a long, hard stare.

"Darned impressive, I'd say." Sytha winked at Ivan, causing him to believe that Sytha probably knew about the magic Truth Chair. It wouldn't surprise him since the Elftens seemed to have a privileged place and thorough knowledge of the Forest Kingdom.

"I won't keep you long. I know how weary you must be." Zephyrus eyed Ivan and Sebastian, his thick bark lips pressed together with concern.

"It's been a long, tense day, that's for sure." Sebastian threw Ivan a sympathetic look.

The Forest servants were busily cleaning the tables, removing plates and platters, congratulating each other for the fine meal they'd prepared and served efficiently.

Canute rubbed his tired head against Ivan's trousers and whimpered. Alfred sniffed Wayland's black boots and suddenly leaped back, where the smell of werewolf lingered.

"We'll leave and take Alfred and Canute to the barracks with us," Wayland said. "I think Zephyrus would appreciate some privacy with you."

With that announcement, Wayland, Sytha, and the brother beagles made a motion to leave.

"By the way," Sytha called behind his back, "Maynard has prepared room five for us. Just knock, and we'll let you in."

Ivan tipped his head with understanding and wagged his finger at the beagles when they hesitated. "Go with them. They'll take good care of you. Oh, and could you please give them a bowl of water?"

"Sure thing," they answered.

****

"You did exceedingly well, Ivan," Zephyrus said as his twiggy eyebrows rose. "I'm very proud of you,"

"I was thinking the same thing." Sebastian's gray eyes caught the glint of the lowering sun and sparkled.

Ivan's hand circled the medallion around his neck. "I was trembling so hard, I scarcely knew what I was saying. It was because of this gift that gave me the courage to be in front of people and ask those questions, wasn't it?"

"Not necessarily." Zephyrus relinquished a short laugh. "The medallion was helpful, that's true—it gave you some confidence, but the poignant questions and your thoughtful delivery came from your own heart, as I knew it would."

Ivan shot him a curious and skeptical look.

"Yes, *you,*" the tree insisted.

Zephyrus's comment sunk in for a moment or two. Then Ivan took a couple steps closer and asked, "Did you hear that Peter had nothing to do with the poisoning?"

"I never thought he did." Zephyrus raised an eyebrow.

"And did Commander Simon tell you that Peter saved me—my life—from Kagutt, the horrible Vaguer? I would be dead now and without my eyes in their sockets if Peter hadn't come to my aid and killed the ghastly creature."

"Simon did tell me of your brother's brave act."

Coming beside the lad, Sebastian admitted, "I also told Zephyrus. I reminded him that my powers of healing and protection had faded because of the rain, and I could do nothing to help you."

"Peter is to be commended, and he will be rewarded for his bravery." Zephyrus looked about. A pained look flashed in the tree's eyes. "Where is he? I thought he'd attend the trials, as he often did in the past."

Ivan wondered how much Zephyrus had learned about Peter's questionable behavior. Hearing the doubt in the tree's voice, Ivan shrugged one shoulder and turned his eyes to the ground. Though he suspected where Peter was, based on Davaan's message, Ivan decided not to bring the subject up.

"We'll talk to you about that tomorrow," Sebastian interrupted. "As well as our travel plans. Now, I believe our hero needs to get some sleep."

"Sure," Zephyrus said. "Oh, by the way, some great news. Merridyn spoke with me just after the trial. She requested that their Witches' Village be accepted into our Forest Kingdom with all its rules and laws. She thought they'd be safer as a unit instead of having their own separate colony. I agreed with her and told her I was very happy with their decision."

Both Sebastian and Ivan were pleased about the announcement. "I knew it had to happen sooner or later." Sebastian grinned, and his eyes glowed bright with pleasure. "Their village will be stronger. And we can help them with any future turmoil."

Zephyrus agreed, matching Sebastian's joy. "Goodnight, then. I'll see you tomorrow after the morning meal."

They returned to the narrow pathway. Ivan took Sebastian's arm to steady him over the rough gravel and led him toward the barracks.

Once out of earshot, Ivan said, "We'll ask Zephyrus

about going to the Mountain of Smoke and Fire tomorrow, but he may not allow it."

"I've been thinking about that very thing. You'll have to plead your case."

"My case?" He jerked back, and his eyes grew large.

"Like…how you want to find Peter and convince him to come home with you. That you need him to help you on the farm."

"Oh," Ivan replied. "That's true."

In the distance, a nightingale sang, and then, another joined her. It was a sweet sound that carried not a worry in the world. If only life were so simple, Ivan mused. He wondered if it was going to start raining soon as it had turned colder, and a breeze sent a chill down the back of his neck. *A warning?*

As they turned to their left, where the barracks lined up like a continuous stone-and-wood-roofed city, Anna-Iza leaped from a bench where she'd been sitting. She gave a little wave and called Ivan's name.

"Anna-Iza! I thought you and your sister goddesses left on your flying steeds by now."

She smiled and curtsied to Sebastian. "No. Diana and I decided to stay the night and rest after the long and trying day. We are pleased our dear friend, Merridyn, was found innocent of the terrible poisoning she was accused of. I'm grateful for your questioning skills and fair-mindedness."

"That's generous of you, Anna-Iza." Ivan averted his gaze. "But I wasn't that confident. It could've been a disaster."

"Well…" Sebastian pulled his arm from Ivan's hold. "Perhaps I'll go on to the barracks—it's room five, you know?"

"I do know, yes." He stared at Anna-Iza and studied her face. An auburn curl rested on her forehead, giving her a sweet and innocent look.

"Goodnight, then, goddess." Sebastian's brows wrinkled. The old man turned and slowly moved away.

"Can you stay and talk for a few moments?" Anna-Iza motioned toward the bench as she shyly gazed into Ivan's eyes.

"Sure." Joy rose in his chest, and his heart beat faster. Now he didn't feel tired at all.

She returned to the bench, snugging her riding cloak around her chest to ward off the chill. Ivan sat next to her, willing himself not to grin and seem too eager. He remembered with jubilation how they'd kissed and held each other before he'd left the Forest several weeks ago. Was it so short a time? It seemed like months had passed since she allowed him to take her into his arms. At that time, she confessed she'd spoken with Zephyrus about being released from her allegiance to her strict gods in the east. *Does she have an answer for me? No, likely not. It's probably too soon.*

An uninvited question entered Ivan's thoughts with a jolt. *What about my affection toward Coreena? My heart sored when I held and kissed her. The same bewildering feelings overcame me with Anna-Iza. It doesn't make sense. Can I care deeply about two lovely ladies at the same time?*

Anna-Iza traced Ivan's slanted eyebrow with a delicate finger. "Why so suddenly glum? Did I say something to offend you?"

"No—I—that is, a disturbing thought flashed through my mind."

"Can you share it with me?"

He forced a smile. "Perhaps some other time. For now, we are together and that's what's important."

"You must be worried whether my Olympian gods in the east will release me from my goddess position so we can be together—forever." She stroked his cheek.

Ivan gave a nod, feeling guilty for the deception.

"Zephyrus hasn't gotten an answer, yet," she said, "but I'm hoping it will be soon."

"I'm hoping the same." Ivan glanced over the treetops and into the night sky and tried to find the words to change the conversation. "I must say, I've never heard anyone speak the way Lyla did. So full of hate and vengeance against her own sister."

Anna-Iza's pretty, full lips pressed together before she spoke. "I've known Merridyn a long time, and we are solid friends. She often spoke of how spiteful Lyla was toward her, and she wondered if her being married and having a darling child had caused Lyla's jealousy. Any attempt to repair the rift between them was met with scorn. Today, at last, we found the deep-rooted reason."

"Who would believe it started over a small plot of land and a tall house?" Ivan shook his head.

"Jealousy is a wicked partner, Ivan. It will steal all your peace of mind and any love that's in your heart."

Ivan gave her a slow and thoughtful look. He believed her words were wise and quite profound. "Have you had experience with such a feeling?"

When she shook her head, the hood slipped to her shoulders. "No. Not me, nor my goddess sisters, but between Zephyrus and Tereus. Their hate was so strong that it divided their kingdom for at least a thousand years. Zephyrus became king of the above world, and Tereus, fierce with jealousy, was confined to the underground caverns."

"Yes, I know these things. Like the demon Tereus is, he gathers followers wherever he goes, demanding they do the dirty work for him." Ivan scowled when he thought about Peter's involvement with Tereus and his harsh commands. Just how deeply Peter was bound to the demon, Ivan wasn't sure, but he hoped to find out and change Peter's loyalties.

"Then you know about the once great Kingdom of Helvaka?"

"Yes, I do. At least parts of it."

Several passing soldiers' footsteps crunched against the gravel pathway. Their heads turned and spotting Ivan and Anna-Iza, they waved and smiled. "Well done there, Kimble," one man said. "Happy to have you as part of our Forest."

"Thank you," Ivan called in return. He smiled broadly and was happy they'd made the remarks in front of Anna-Iza. He sat straighter, and his chest expanded with pride as the men walked on.

To his regret, another man strode by. Sebastian had said that he was Raleigh Malicotte, the Animal and Gamekeeper at the castle. He threw Ivan a hostile look and spat. *What's his problem?* Ivan wondered and was glad when Raleigh didn't stop to harass them.

"You did an exceptional job questioning Lyla." Anna-Iza gazed at him. "Were you coached by Zephyrus?"

Ivan couldn't tell her about the Truth Chair. Zephyrus had asked him to keep its powers a secret, and so, he felt like a fraud accepting compliments for what he'd done. "Pousses was a big help. He may be persnickety and mean-spirited sometimes, but he was generous with his information about Merridyn. He suggested I question little Benny about that day, but Benny refused to speak, even to the very end."

"He was frightened that Cecil would harm his mum and daddy."

"How do you know?"

"Well," she said timidly, "Pousses talks to me, too. He said that Benny was warned by Lyla that if he told what he'd seen that day at Merridyn's cottage, Cecil and Peter would…would kill his parents. Isn't it dreadful to scare a small child?"

"Yes, terrible." Ivan took a sharp intake of breath. "Somehow, Lyla had managed to bring Peter into this sham of a tale with an outright lie."

"I believe she was trying to degrade Peter and your reputation so Zephyrus would banish you from the Forest in disgrace. She's a devious witch, not at all like the rest of their village."

"Maybe that's why Benny was so scared of me. He knows Peter and I are brothers, and he believed we would harm his parents if he snitched." Ivan shook his head, feeling sorry for the poor little mute. "He may find his voice now that Lyla and Cecil have been taken away."

"I hope so. His silence is agony to his parents."

Ivan reached for her small hand and held it in his own. "You are very wise, Anna-Iza."

She blinked. "Thank you."

He hoped to keep her talking as long as possible, to hear her sweet voice, to look into her lovely blue-green eyes. "Your hand is cold. Are you cold, too?"

"Yes, a bit. But we have so little time to meet and talk."

Sytha called from a distance, "Hey Ivan, we want to turn the lantern out. Are you coming to bed?"

"I'd better go." He sighed. "It's been a very long day for all of us." He turned to her and shyly lowered his head. "May I kiss you goodnight?"

Anna-Iza smiled sweetly and leaned toward him. "I would like that very much."

His arms went around her, and he drew her close. His heart beat fast as their lips met. Their kiss seemed to last only a short time, deep and caring—even loving. When they parted, he inhaled deeply and then slowly exhaled. "Anna-Iza, I…I…"

She touched his lips with her finger. "No need to say it. We both know how we feel, and it brings such joy to my heart."

"Yes, me too, but I'm wondering…"

Wayland yelled, "Ivan—sometime tonight if you don't mind! We have to talk."

He slowly released his hold on the goddess and rose from the bench they shared. Helping her to her feet, Ivan asked in a quiet voice, "Will I see you at breakfast?"

"I regret we must leave early tomorrow morning. There's much to do with the lavender we have harvested and dried in our sheds. We make soaps, perfumes, and shampoos." She pulled her leather gloves from her cloak pocket.

Ivan's brow lifted. "So that's where the lavender fragrance comes from. It's everywhere, and every lady in the Forest wears it." He smiled at his own discovery.

"I wouldn't expect a man to be aware of such a thing." She touched his nose with the tip of her index finger. A playful grin curved her lips.

Before she turned to leave, he leaned forward for

one last kiss. Then he hurried away, wishing he could stay by her side.

Chapter 11

The Barracks

Wayland leaned against the door frame of their room, his arms folded, tapping his foot. "Where have you been?" He scowled. "I thought you'd just say goodnight to Anna-Iza and then be on your way."

"I—that's what I'd intended, b-but—"

"Oh, never mind. Come in and get ready for bed."

Canute and Alfred dashed over to greet their master. Ivan dropped to his knees, stroked their heads and down their backs. They jumped at his chest, licking his face and hands. Canute's tail whipped crazily. "I'm sorry I left you alone most of the day," he said to them, "but it couldn't be helped."

Coming from the bathroom, Sytha wore a long nightdress and was towel drying his silvery hair. "It's all yours." He motioned. "Your saddlebags are draped over the headboard."

Ivan hadn't given his meager possessions a thought until Sytha had mentioned it. In the corner, Sebastian sat on a tattered wicker chair with a book on his lap. He cocked his head and pulled on his beard. Ivan supposed it was because he'd arrived late.

The room had three narrow beds. Sytha stood by the one nearest the door, wiggling his toes on the cold, bare boards. Alfred watched the toes move with interest, giving his opinion with a sniff and a sharp woof. When Ivan looked down, he was surprised to see the Elften had six toes on each foot. He wondered if it was a characteristic belonging only to Sytha, or was it a trait common to all those in the Elften Colony?

Following Ivan's stare, Sytha answered the curious look. "It's a sign of royalty, inherited from the very first king of the Elften Kingdom." He grinned, nodding his head. "Good thing it wasn't six noses. What would I do with all *those* on my face?"

Sebastian and Wayland exploded with laughter. Ivan laughed, too, when he realized Sytha was joking.

Ivan was pleased that Sebastian's frown disappeared as his laughter turned into hiccups. He rose from his chair, and in a hushed tone, his scowl returned, and he said to Ivan, "We should probably have a talk." He pressed his hand against his bent back, moaning. "Can't they make a more comfortable chair in this darn Forest?"

Coughing into his hand, Ivan looked away, hoping an interruption of any kind would distract Sebastian's lecture. *Was it something about my questioning Lyla?*

"We need to discuss our presentation to Zephyrus tomorrow." Wayland tried to stifle his laughter after Sytha's nose comment.

"Right." Ivan removed the Long Dark Cloak from his shoulders, draping it over Sebastian's uncomfortable chair. "Will it be difficult to convince Zephyrus we are going to the Mountain of Smoke and Fire tomorrow?" He stared at each of them. "Is there no other place to meet Peter?"

"I'm only telling you what my brother, Davaan, told me." Wayland's cheek muscles jerked. "We're to meet him tomorrow, sometime in the early afternoon, near the second cave."

"Will that be enough time to eat breakfast and ride to the top of the mountain?" Ivan raked his teeth over his lips.

"If we skip breakfast and start out early, we'll be okay." Sytha yawned. "In that way, if we are delayed for any reason, we will meet Davaan on time."

"That sounds logical," Ivan said, though he and his beagles would hate to miss a morning meal. Since Sebastian was a spirit and didn't eat, it wouldn't matter to him.

"I think we should have breakfast." Ivan thought about his beagles. "Who knows when we'll have our next meal?"

"Let's sleep on it." Sytha lifted the covers from his bed and slipped his long, thin frame between the sheets. He hummed with pleasure. "I like the fresh smell...lavender, I think it is."

With a smile, Ivan recalled Anna-Iza telling him about the products from harvesting their lavender fields. He cupped his hands over his mouth, directing his remark to Sytha and Wayland. "I'll bathe, and then we can talk more."

"Don't depend on any hot water." Wayland gave a chuckle. "We tried to tell you not to linger, or you'd be left out."

Ivan pursed his lips and frowned. They were correct. The water was cold and caused Ivan to shiver until he completed his shower and pulled on his nightshirt to his knees.

By the time he finished, which wasn't very long, Wayland was snoring, and Sytha lay on his side with the coverlet pulled over his delicate, elongated ears.

"I know you never sleep." Ivan moved toward Sebastian and sat on the edge of the only empty bed nearest where Sebastian sat fidgeting.

"I'm worried about your affection for Anna-Iza." He eyed him with a hard stare.

Ivan now realized why the spirit was none too happy with him. Before Sebastian could scold him further, he quickly changed the subject. "Will Zephyrus let us search for Peter in that dangerous mountain?"

"It's hard to say. He wants you all safe, of course—and the mountain is not a safe place. On the other hand…" Sebastian looked over the wire rims of his spectacles. "Zephyrus would certainly respect your wish to find Peter. Just why that rebel brother of yours can't come to us, I sure don't know."

"It's a mystery to me, too. I'm wondering if Peter is being held prisoner and can't escape from the ghouls. Or…"

Sebastian's bushy eyebrows rose. "Or what?"

"Davaan may be luring us into a trap where we'll be skinned alive by those horrible creatures."

"I don't think that's the case." Sebastian hesitated. "I'm almost positive."

"Maybe…" Ivan placed his palm over his mouth to stifle another yawn. "There's a good chance we could find the King's Scepter in the mountain if the rumor is true."

"Possibly, but I wouldn't put much trust in that tale. True, it was there years ago, but we don't know if it still is." Sebastian reached for the Long Dark Cloak draped over his chair and handed it to Ivan. "Better wear this tonight for extra warmth. It will be chilly when the fire in the grate dies down."

Ivan did as Sebastian suggested and threw the cloak around his shoulders. He allowed his head to droop, his eyelids to flutter, and maybe…Sebastian would forget about questioning him about Anna-Iza. He didn't wish to explain his deep feelings for the goddess. After his long, tense day, he realized he *was* exhausted.

"I think it's time for bed," Sebastian said quietly. "Goodnight, Ivan."

Crawling under the covers, Ivan turned onto his side with his damp head nestled into the pillow. Canute gave a woof and curled up beside the bedpost while Alfred trotted toward the fireplace and lay down near the stone hearth. Then all was quiet.

Ivan drifted off.

Shortly, he heard the thunderous rain beat against the shingled rooftop. The room turned chilly, just as Sebastian said it would. He pulled the cloak to his chin. A dream came quickly where he walked into a huge, cold cave, dark as midnight. He heard whimpers of pain and smelled evil—metallic-like, mixed with sewage, or could it be rotting skin pulled from a living man? In his dream, he trembled at the very thought of it. Paralyzed with the fear of danger, he took cautious steps forward with his back pressed to the rough cave wall, his hands feeling their way as he inched toward the sound of painful cries. Where are Sytha and Wayland? Aren't they following me? He wanted to call out to them but was afraid it might alert the bloodthirsty ghouls if they were waiting for him inside.

Turning onto his back, Ivan shivered in the cold of the room, willing his frightening dream to end. But it continued.

A familiar and welcomed voice called into the black

abyss, and Ivan could hear footsteps dragging in his direction. "Little brother of mine. Where have you been? I've waited days for you."

When the owner of the voice stepped near, and a sudden light illuminated the naked body, Ivan threw back his head and screamed, "Oh, God. My High Intervener!" It was Peter. He had no skin. None on his face—only bloody blonde hair and no covering on his feet or hands. His tall, nude figure was red-raw, weeping blood and yellowish pus that dripped from his torso.

"Those filthy buggers split my skull and took my brain, too," the skinless man said angrily. "They could've left me with something."

Feeling himself teetering with nausea and terror, Ivan groaned and doubled over, holding his stomach, praying he wouldn't vomit. "Peter!"

"Wake up, Ivan." Sebastian's image released from the cloak in a swirl of fuchsia and gray smoke, and he shook Ivan by the shoulders. "A most grotesque dream at that," Sebastian said and gasped,

"Oh, Sebastian, it was just horrid. Peter—it was Peter and…"

"Sssh. I know by the way you moaned and tossed it was dreadful. Be still now, and let Sytha and Wayland get the sleep they need." Sebastian soothed Ivan's sweaty forehead with his bony hand. "Yes, my young friend. It was a most terrifying dream. May the power of the High Intervener not allow this dream to come true."

Canute whined, a familiar sound that told Ivan his beagle needed to go out.

Awake from his fitful sleep after his loathsome nightmare, Ivan sat up and swung his legs over the edge of the bed. He shivered when his feet touched the cold floor, and then he stretched, trying not to revisit his awful dream. "Come on, boys," he called.

The morning light was easing over the horizon when Ivan opened and held the door. Alfred and Canute raced from the room, turning in circles, woofing at each other.

Ivan grinned at their antics. The beagles found pleasure in everything around them. A soft trilling of some sort of bird broke the quiet of morning as if coaxing the sun to rise higher. The earthy smell of the Forest mingled with Ivan's excitement to find Peter. Today he would see him. He thought about the dream he'd had as he sat on a damp wooden bench in front of their room at the barracks, waiting for his beagles to join him. "I'm glad to have my skin and hair," he whispered, and ran his palm across his face. What if those horrible ghouls attack me or my dogs?

Sebastian joined him on the bench. "Are you worried?"

"Yes. I didn't sleep well."

"I know. You woke up flailing your arms and groaning. Not loud enough to wake Sytha and Wayland, I don't believe, but troubling to me."

"I'm sorry. This may be a wild goose chase—or Peter could be in grave danger if he's anywhere near that frightful mountain."

"That's true." Sebastian lowered his head, studying his fingers. "I'm against this journey, you know that. I almost hope Zephyrus denies you making this trip. A ghoul is a vile and barbaric creature—they—"

Ivan raised a halting hand. "Last night, I dreamed about what they do to intruders."

"Better you know in advance and not be shocked—or skinned. If Peter had any consideration for you and your friends, he'd meet you at the bottom of that mountain, and he'd follow you home from there."

"He wouldn't lead us into danger. He's my brother and only wants what's best for me and his friends. You remember he saved me from Kagutt. What's worse, a Vaguer or a ghoul?"

"They're both freaks of nature and misfits. I've often told Zephyrus they don't belong in our Forest."

"What does Zephyrus say about that?"

"He says it will all come to be in due time, and only the High Intervener knows that time."

Ivan bent to stroke Canute's head and allowed him to lick his hand while thinking about Sebastian's comment. Alfred demanded his share of attention from his master and thrust his wet nose under Ivan's forearm.

"By the way…" Sebastian's bristly white eyebrows lifted. "Zephyrus and I are mighty proud of you the way you conducted the trial. It was a lot to ask of you, one so young, but you were the best person to do the job."

"Why is that?"

"Your honesty and integrity. Your unselfish nature—all dependable and solid qualities."

"Well, I don't know about that, but the outcome amazed me, too. I was so nervous speaking in front of those people—my friends—my tongue stuck to the roof of my mouth."

Sebastian gave a snort of laughter.

"Besides, I just let the words take their own course." He hesitated and considered how the trial played out. "The Truth Chair impressed me most. It's an amazing piece of furniture." Talking about the trial made him uneasy, and he squirmed on the hard bench. He helped to condemn Lyla to Troll Prison—or worse, but it didn't make him feel any better.

"The Truth Chair couldn't have forced the truth from Lyla if Mortimer Tink had interrogated her. He doesn't have the same humble and honest character as you."

"You know all about the chair, then?"

"Of course, I'm a spirit, but others are not to learn of it." Sebastian turned a serious face to him.

"Zephyrus already warned me not to tell. Where did it come from?"

Sebastian pressed his lips together. "A thousand years ago, it was formed by the High Intervener from the wood inside Zephyrus's trunk. Now known as the Sanctuary of Truth. It has come in mighty handy on several occasions."

"Does Peter know about the chair?"

"No, he was never told." Sebastian paused like he might do more explaining, but he changed the subject. "Say, it looks like your beagles are hungry, sniffing around the bushes. You'd better get dressed, and we'll have breakfast."

Lifting his head, Ivan said, "I believe I smell fried sausages and mushrooms." He rose at once and went inside to put on his clothes and wake his friends. This morning they would learn if Zephyrus would agree to their journey to the most dangerous mountain in the world.

Chapter 12

Breakfast Brawl

Shortly, Ivan, Sytha, and Wayland, with Sebastian dragging behind, approached Zephyrus. Canute and Alfred chased each other in the circular clearing that surrounded the Great Oak until they spotted a mole and took off after him, barking madly.

"Don't go too far," Ivan yelled.

"Aha, good morning, my dear Forest friends." Zephyrus beamed. "I had all night to think on the trial and was pleased that justice was done. I knew you'd do well, Ivan Kimble, and get to the truth of the matter."

"Th-thank you, sir. I had my doubts. But it seemed to turn out just right. Merridyn is free, and Lyla...well, I'm afraid her plight will not be so good."

"I'm glad it's over, too." Sytha scowled and pulled on his delicate Elften-ear protruding through his silvery-fine hair. "We've all known Merridyn for years and have loved her greatly, but to hear the venom that came from Lyla's red-serpent lips was particularly painful." He glanced over his shoulder at the breakfast tables and shifted on his feet. It was obvious he was anxious to leave, stop the idle chatter, and skip breakfast.

"I agree about Lyla," Ivan said. "After witnessing two sisters who should love each other, but one hated the other. Well, it was heart-wrenching."

"Things are not always the way we'd like in families," Zephyrus said, raising his eyes to the overcast sky. "Just look at the dissension between Tereus and me. He chose the path of cruelty, wickedness, and dishonor to our kingdom. Whereas I found that love, kindness, and justice are a better fit for man and life." His sigh went deep.

"You will excuse us, sir." Sebastian bowed to Zephyrus. "But we should have a quick breakfast and feed Alfred and Canute. Then we'll come back to have a word with you."

"Certainly. I was just about to suggest that." The Great Oak closed and opened his eyes as if giving his full approval for them to take leave. "One of the Forest's servants wanted a private word with me, and I see him coming this way. We won't be long."

Maynard hurried toward Zephyrus, a dark look on his face. *What is his problem?* Ivan wondered. The foursome nodded at the servant as they passed him in a hurry.

They strode toward the open meadow where the trestle tables were once again covered with fine linen tablecloths and napkins. Ivan breathed in the delicious smells of breakfast as he tugged the Long Dark Cloak around his neck to warm himself. The aroma of freshly baked bread wafted through the air and mixed with fried wild boar bangers. They selected a table where Sytha sat on the end with Ivan next to him while Sebastian struggled to swing his legs under the table on the opposite side. They were amused watching the beagles jump at Ivan's legs, begging for their share of breakfast.

Wayland took his place across the table from Ivan, Sytha, and Sebastian, clearly disappointed they were not yet traveling to their destination. "We should be on our way," he quietly grumbled. "If there's any kind of delay, we may not meet Davaan and Peter when and where we'd agreed."

"I feel the same." Sytha tucked the edges of his napkin in the neckline of his white tunic.

"I say we just go." Wayland threw his arm forward in the direction of the mountain. "Why wait around here and waste time? We have a long, steep road to travel."

"I don't like it any more than you do." Ivan frowned. "I'm worried about Peter's safely."

Sebastian turned his thin lips into a grimace. "Zephyrus wanted us to have our nourishment and then talk to him."

"The longer we wait, the harder it will be for Davaan to make a connection. He may not be waiting for us at the second cave, and that would be a bad sign." The Wolflord muttered other worrisome words, but Ivan couldn't hear them since his beagles were barking to be fed.

Maynard moved hurriedly toward them and laid out the cutlery beside each fancy plate and a tea cup. "Good morning, Ivan!" He waved and bowed to them. "I've been told to serve you at once. That you have urgent business."

"Why did you have audience with Zephyrus a few moments ago?" Ivan's curiosity pushed to the forefront.

Looking to the end of the table next to them, Maynard tightened his jaw. "An unwelcomed guest who makes trouble wherever he goes."

"Oh, I see." Sebastian nodded. "Rude-Raleigh."

Ivan stretched his neck and spotted the man that had passed him and Anna-Iza while they were sitting on the bench the night before. Raleigh had spat upon the ground showing his disdain. He'd also made nasty remarks during the trial that no one appreciated.

The tables filled up with Forest people, Elftens, Wolflords, and a number of soldiers who would help clean the area after the guests had left.

"Where are Commander Simon and most of his men?" Ivan looked around, searching.

"They left early this morning to escort Lord Graydon and Merridyn in his carriage to the Witch's Village," Maynard said.

"I hope Willa and my son will enjoy their ride with them." Wayland's frown nearly covered his dark eyes. "If Cactus throws a tantrum, I'll have to take them home on borrowed horses. Willa wouldn't be too happy about that."

"Oh, yes, sir," a passing servant stopped and assured. "Cactus was not pleased about being awakened at the early hour, and he let everyone know it! I sent them away with a light breakfast basket. They did, indeed, ride in the fancy carriage, and it seemed to thrill the young lad."

"That's my boy!" Wayland slapped the top of his thigh and laughed.

"If you would be so good," Sytha said and held up his hand for Maynard's attention, "to fill a couple rucksacks with food for our journey."

"Yes, sir. I'm already working on it, and I'll pack food for your beagles, too." Maynard stooped to whisper into Ivan's ear, "Anna-Iza asked me to tell you that she and her goddesses left at dawn. She was sorry not to say goodbye this morning."

Ivan thanked him, and held back a shy smile. Anna-

Iza had thought to bid him goodbye, and happiness rushed through his heart. Glancing at Sebastian next to him, Ivan saw the same scowl he'd seen while in the barracks. It was clear the spirit was not in favor of Ivan's affection toward the goddess. But their feelings for each other were theirs alone, and Sebastian had no right to interfere. *Did he?*

Forest folks and staff crowded the tables to join in the enticing breakfast. Plates and cutlery clinked against each other. Teacups were filled while serving platters of food moved from one person to another in quick succession. Faces looked tired, their voices low after the previous long day of the Forest Court Trials.

A couple of men near the end of the second table laughed, and one said, "I'd like to see both witches hang from the big red oak. Hear their breath choked out of them, dangling there."

Ivan and Sebastian gasped.

"Who said that?" Ivan half stood from his seat, looking for the ill-mannered person. He spotted a man wearing a pale green uniform with his head tipped back, chuckling with amusement. Ivan knew who he was.

"That's a terrible thing to say." Sebastian growled.

"No!" the same man shouted at Maynard. "I told you I wanted my eggs cooked with no runny yolks. You think I'm uncivilized?" He shoved his plate away. The irate man turned his angry face and glared at Ivan, though Ivan couldn't imagine why the runny eggs were his fault.

Sebastian leaned and whispered to Ivan, "That's Raleigh Malicotte. He's Lord Graydon's Animal and Gamekeeper at the castle."

"Yes, I know." Ivan brought his teacup to his lips, sipped the hot liquid, and tried to calm his rising anger.

Wayland called loudly, waving his hand, "Maynard, we're in a big hurry here. Could we please be served?"

"Yes, sir! At once," Maynard said. Within moments, the servants carried full breakfast plates for the three of them.

Raleigh shot to his feet, and his lips curled into a sneer. Apparently, he didn't appreciate being ignored or the preferential treatment toward Ivan and his friends. "I don't like you," he yelled, jabbing his finger in Ivan's direction. "Not you, not your brother. You are frauds and cheats. You may've bamboozled most of the people in the Forest, but you haven't fooled me. Not even with that phony medallion you wear."

Ivan jerked back, his shoulders stiffened. *Why do so many people in the Forest pass judgement on me, and my brother, when they don't even know us?*

Wayland and Sytha struggled to stand, their nostrils widening with rage, but Ivan placed his hand across the table on the Wolflord's forearm to stop him. "Let it go. It's not worth a fight."

"You're a coward, right, Kimble? Think you can come into our Forest and get everything you want. Be the big hero. Even fool Zephyrus."

"You don't know anything." Ivan's jaw clenched while finding his restraint waning. The hard tone in his own voice surprised him.

Raleigh leaned forward with both hands flat on the table. "I do know that Zephyrus's *special boy* believes he can push his way into our Forest and win popularity, corrupt the females, and get away with it."

Now he'd gone too far. Heat rose from Ivan's chest, shooting to his neck and face. If Raleigh referred to Merridyn or Anna-Iza, Ivan wasn't about to let the crude remark go. He struggled from the bench, his fists ready to defend the ladies' honor. Surely anyone in the Forest would do the same.

Raleigh ran around to the end of the table, where Wayland and Sytha rose from their seats, prepared to intervene.

"Stop this, Raleigh." Sytha's light-colored eyebrows jerked inward. "You have no right to accuse our friend." He turned and held out his hand as a warning to Ivan. "Don't. This only complicates our delay, and Raleigh's got bigger problems of his own."

Ivan's anger came to a fast and full boil. "Let go of my arm, Wayland," he said, wrenching away. "He has no right to insult me or the ladies this way." When Ivan jerked loose, he upset his plate of eggs, bangers, and beans that Maynard had just brought. The entire plate and cutlery flew off the table, dumping the contents on the damp ground. *This isn't me*, Ivan thought. *My parents taught me to control my anger, and here I am, begging for a fight with the gamekeeper.*

"It will pass." Sebastian grabbed Ivan's shoulders and struggled to hold him. "Just cool off."

The breakfast guests all turned to see what the commotion was. Some stood and cheered Ivan, challenging him to fight the troublemaker. Seemingly, Raleigh wasn't a favorite in the Forest. It was past the point of stopping a confrontation. Fiery revenge etched Ivan's face. Recalling the crude remarks Raleigh had made during the trial, Ivan dashed toward his irate opponent.

He heard Sebastian's words of caution, but Ivan ignored them.

Raleigh landed the first blow, striking Ivan hard

with his fist.

Ivan's cheek instantly burned and throbbed with pain. Stumbling back, he whipped his arms for balance and just caught himself. He inhaled a deep breath, and his eyes froze into a furious glare. Turning swiftly, he dived forward and struck the angry man's jaw. The beagles barked ferociously at their master's attacker.

Shaking his head, Raleigh staggered a few feet and wiped the blood dripping from his mouth. He cussed under his breath and came at Ivan a second time with arms bent and hands balled. "You dirty traitor. Get out of our Forest." He swung just as Ivan ducked.

Ivan grabbed him from behind and tightened his arms around Raleigh's chest.

"Stop this fighting," someone yelled.

"Let me go, Kimble, or I'll knock your head off." Raleigh struggled for air under his opponent's restricting hold.

Ivan released Raleigh and gave him a shove, nearly toppling him to the ground. In a flash, the gamekeeper turned and rushed toward Ivan madder than ever, his teeth champed, his brow wrinkled with fury. He jerked his arm back and prepared to let it go.

"Get him, Ivan. Knock the bugger down," Wayland yelled.

"Teach him some manners," Maynard shouted, punching at the air.

Thinking only of his survival, Ivan raised his arm and landed a powerful blow to the man's chin. He quickly jumped back, gasping, and flexed his knuckles. "That stung," he whined.

Shaking his head, Raleigh bent from his waist, looking like he was about to ram into Ivan with full strength. He stopped and teetered. His eyes rolled up into their sockets, and his mouth dropped open, battered and bleeding. Wayland rushed forward and grabbed Raleigh around his waist as he spun and allowed him to slowly collapse onto the ground. "He's out!" the Wolflord announced, raising his arms high. "Fight's over!"

Staring wide-eyed at Raleigh, still quaking with fear and rage, Ivan felt the sudden flush of shame. *What would my mother and father say if they saw me brawling like a drunken street bum?* He lowered his head, holding his bruised hand against his chest. He noticed blood dripping from his nose and mouth onto the Long Dark Cloak. He reached for his handkerchief and pressed it against his face and patted the blood away. It pounded with pain, but he didn't think anything was broken.

"Take him to the barracks," a stout man from the second bench said. "Clean him up and sympathize. We all know it's been difficult for him."

"Seems Raleigh is a rabble-rouser no matter where he goes," one of the two men said, who'd been directed to help. The older man of the two stepped forward, lifted Raleigh under his arms, and forced him to stand. "Come on, mate. We'll lead you to your bed."

"What's been difficult for him?" Ivan manipulated his jaw with his uninjured hand to see if it had been broken or dislocated. "I-I-didn't mean for that to happen," he said in a regretful tone.

"Yeah," the stout man explained. "Raleigh's wife left him about three months ago. Has a little girl to care for. He's been real irritated these days. When he's feeling better," the same man said to the other, "tell him he may as well return to the castle. There's nothing here for him."

"I'm so ashamed," Ivan whispered, staring at the mess he'd caused. They took their seats once more. His hands trembled, his knuckles pulsated with pain, and his legs felt boneless. "What caused me to be so reckless?"

"You're getting to be quite a hot-head," Sytha said, poking Ivan in the ribs. He chuckled, trying to ease Ivan's shame.

Ivan frowned, not thinking it funny. He stared at the scuffed earth where they'd just fought. "I should've had more control," Ivan said. "My parents taught me…"

"Passivity," Sytha finished in a quiet voice.

"What does that word mean?" Wayland moved his food around on his plate, seemingly discouraged because his eggs and bangers were now cold.

"It means he doesn't care, or—or he's indifferent," Sytha explained.

"I care," Ivan defended. "If I didn't, I wouldn't be here looking for Peter."

"Sometimes you have to fight to save yourself, your honor, and those you love," Sebastian said and swirled into the Long Dark Cloak, giving a customary push as he entered. Ivan wrapped his tender knuckles around the fabric, and they instantly healed.

"You've shown a great deal of courage," Sebastian said. "We've all watched it happen—or heard about it later. Fighting for the Forest's benefit."

Ivan's dark eyes squinted until his curiosity sought the meaning of Sebastian's comment. "What do you mean?"

"I'm saying, when you first came into the Forest, you were, ah—submissive and quite unemotional. I suspect it had much to do with your upbringing. I'm beginning to see that your parents disapproved of any show of anger or violence."

"That's the way of royalty." Sytha lifted his eyebrows, his voice edged with cool resentment.

"You are royalty?" Wayland stopped chewing his toast long enough to stare wide-eyed at Ivan. "No one ever told me that."

"You don't have to know everything." Sytha took a long gulp of tea, pushing his vegetable plate away.

Wayland scowled and then stuck out his lower lip. "Well, how did you know, Sytha? Did Ivan tell you?"

"No. Peter told me soon after we'd first met, and he asked me not to say anything. At first, I didn't believe him. Thought he was trying to impress me, equalize us because I'm next in line to rule the Elften kingdom. But it's true. Isn't it, Ivan?"

Ivan lifted one shoulder and peered up slowly. "It doesn't matter to me. It was a long time ago, and I've never cared for royalty like Peter does."

Wayland kept staring at him, his heavy dark eyebrows raised and then lowered. "Imagine that," he finally said and put his fork down. "I'm surrounded by royalty and didn't even know it."

People went back to eating. Maynard moved swiftly, bringing another full plate of hot food for Ivan and Wayland along with a fresh pot of tea. "So sorry, Ivan, sir. Raleigh can be unpredictable at times. During my earlier meeting with Zephyrus, I asked if he'd encourage the gamekeeper to leave and go home."

"Sure," Ivan said. It was difficult to chew with his swollen jaw and chin. He touched the bruise with his cold fingers, not wanting Sebastian to heal him. He deserved to feel this pain for his lack of self-control. The only good thing to come from the brawl was that Alfred and Canute woofed down Ivan's breakfast that had scattered on the ground. Ivan turned cautiously in his seat and glanced at Zephyrus, who probably saw the entire disruption. He couldn't determine how Zephyrus felt about it, but Ivan was certain he'd be reprimanded.

"You'll excuse me," Sebastian said after he'd pulled himself from the cloak. He rose from the wooden bench and stepped out carefully. "I'll check if Zephyrus is ready to see us. I'm getting as impatient as you are." He made his way toward the Great Oak, shaking his head as he went.

"Well, since you stirred my curiosity," Wayland said, "what kind of royalty are you? Like a king or something?"

A silence ensued between them. It seemed Ivan wasn't going to admit anything. He took a bite from a wedge of toast, chewing with some difficulty. While *slow* was his usual method of eating, it seemed he took even longer to swallow with his sore jaw. Nor could he make enough spit to soften the toast.

"His family is related to the Romanovs, the once, long-time ruling family of Russia." Sytha's crinkled brow showed his hesitation, but Ivan didn't stop him, or respond. "Your father was a cousin or some distant relative to the czar, wasn't he? Then your parents secretly left their country when things became...well, violent. Seems the ruling class was losing support and loyalty from their countrymen. Changed your name to Kimble, right?"

"Something like that," Ivan answered in a soft voice. He continued to move his food around on his plate, avoiding either Sytha or Wayland's probing stares. He hoped no one was eavesdropping.

In a short time, Sebastian returned and said, "I'm not here to give my opinion about royalty. Only to hurry this interrogation along. Shall we go now?"

"You and Peter were born here? In England?" Wayland ignored Sebastian's prompting.

Ivan gave a brief nod and dragged his fingers through his thick, dark hair until the strain in his shoulder reminded him of that injury.

"I believe Peter's lifelong passion is to sit upon a throne—any throne." Sytha glanced at Ivan and continued. "He felt that your father should've inherited the kingship and the position handed down to him. That same driving force has gotten him into a lot of trouble. I mean…"

"You probably know more about it than I do," Ivan said, forcing a stoic face. "But I'd appreciate your silence on this subject."

"Sure." Wayland nodded. "I'm no tattletale."

"We three were famously close when Peter lived at the castle." Sytha tipped his head toward Wayland. "We did everything together, enjoying our adventures—and sometimes a little bit of mischief." He chuckled. "Then, maybe earlier this year, Peter changed, and he changed quickly. Didn't he, Wayland?"

"Seemed to." Wayland eyed Ivan even more closely. "Most times, I was in my village taking care of my family and wolf-brothers, so I couldn't always join their wild pursuits." He rested his elbows on the table, laced his fingers, and sighed.

Sytha came near the truth when he described Peter's motivation. Ivan worried what Tereus might do to Peter if he severed his allegiance from the demon—that monster of a man who roamed the dark caverns beneath the earth.

"Why did you never tell me the brothers were royalty, Sytha? I thought we were good friends." The Wolflord moped, unable to hide his hurt feelings. In those moments, he looked a lot like his young son, Cactus, Ivan observed.

"I assure you, we are the best of friends, including Ivan here. Please understand it wasn't my story to tell. It's Peter's and Ivan's."

"But, you just told it." Ivan looked up under his eyebrows.

"Yeah. I guess you're right. Sorry."

Wayland blinked and turned his face away.

Maynard hurried toward them and announced that Zephyrus was now ready to see them.

Chapter 13

Convincing Zephyrus

"Well…" Wayland paused. He faced Zephyrus with a puckered brow. "Ivan has a request of you."

Hoping for more support, Ivan swung his head around at Wayland.

"Only fair," Wayland emphasized. "It's your mission and your quest."

Is Wayland resentful toward me because I didn't divulge my royal heritage to him? Sometimes, even good friends must find forgiveness in their hearts for lack of disclosure.

Sytha folded his arms over his long, thin chest and took two steps aside for Ivan.

"Make your case." Sebastian flapped his hands, trying to hurry the discussion along.

"What can I do for you, Ivan?"

"I-I have heard…" Ivan shoved his cold, shaky hands into the cloak's pockets. "That is, I'd like your approval to go to the Windemere Mountains and search for Peter."

"He actually means the Mountain of Smoke and Fire, located in the Windemere Mountains," Sytha corrected in a dry tone.

Ivan gave Sytha a nervous stare. *I'd hoped to avoid the mountain's terrible name. It sounds so—deadly.*

"What! I can't have it." Zephyrus's tangled-twig mustache quivered as he spoke. "It's a dangerous place—why, there are ghouls there. Do you know what they do to trespassers?"

Ivan jumped at the outburst. A petrified look covered his face.

"They'd rather eat you than allow your presence." The entire tree shook, as he said those shattering words. "Haven't you told Ivan how degenerate they are?"

"You see," Wayland stammered in his own defense, "my brother Davaan, who you know is still a werewolf and probably feared by the ghouls...well, he delivered a message about a week ago that Peter is at the mountain and needs Ivan's help."

"You must convince them, Zephyrus, of the risk they're taking," Sebastian said.

Ivan's breath stopped in his throat, wondering whose side Sebastian was on. "But why would Peter call on me—us, to a place if it's so dangerous? Does he want us torn apart?"

"He must be in a lot of trouble, possibly held a prisoner." Sytha thrust his opened palms toward Zephyrus. "We just don't know."

"Peter can't be their prisoner." Wayland turned and confronted Sytha. "He met Davaan a couple of times in the early morning, asking for help. Just why he didn't escape at that time and find refuge somewhere, I don't know, and Davaan didn't know either."

"Tereus must have a strong hold over him." Sebastian scratched his head, looking more perplexed than ever.

Reaching for the medallion that hung around his neck, Ivan cupped his hand over it. "I came to the Forest to find Peter—that's all I've ever wanted." He stared up at Zephyrus, feeling his eyes mist with tears. "I didn't want to kill Burtack or his brother; I didn't want to fight your Forest war or to fly on Fluorescence's back, risking my life to catch the Golden Lantern. I only wanted to find my brother and bring him home with me. Now, he needs my help, and I must go to him, even if I have to make the trip myself." He pulled a hankie from his pocket and wiped his eyes. Sebastian put his arm around Ivan's waist.

"Ivan, it's just that…the ghouls, the Woman of Flame, they…" Zephyrus's bark lips pulled downward, seemingly at a loss for a convincing answer. "You are so young, Ivan. Your life just beginning." Ivan's tears momentarily halted the tree's dire warning.

"I don't care about those creatures. Maybe they're a myth," Ivan said fervently though he knew they were not. "I want to start our journey. Right now, before it gets too late in the day." He swept his arm toward his companions. "They're willing to go with me. We have our protection." He rubbed his hands against the Long Dark Cloak and glanced at Sebastian thinking of his healing abilities.

"We'll take The Challenger with us," Sebastian said quietly. "That is, with your permission, sir."

"I have my wand." Sytha patted the leather quiver held by a strap crossed over his chest. "Who knows?" He shrugged. "Could be that Peter will meet us at the foothill of the mountain. Plenty of places to hide there."

"And," Wayland jumped in. "I'm good with a sword and knife, as well as being strong on a horse. Having been a werewolf, I can smell and see trouble miles away. Together we'll protect each other." A look of enthusiasm lit Wayland's face that Ivan hadn't seen before.

Zephyrus's frown seemed frozen.

"We've heard…" Ivan ventured his last attempt to convince. "The King's Scepter is somewhere in the mountain."

"I don't like it." Zephyrus's gaze shifted from one person to another. "Your lives and your skins are worth more to me than any Ancient Relic. How about contacting Commanders Simon and Gifford—between them they have four hundred men? There is protection in numbers," he logically stated.

Shaking his head, Wayland pulled on his dark beard. "Davaan was sure about who could be part of this hunt and rescue mission. Although Sytha wasn't included, he insisted on coming, and I agreed at once."

Are we losing the argument with too much explaining? Ivan wondered.

"We must make a decision, sir," Sebastian said, his face scrunched with a painful look. "With your approval, we can be on our way at once and arrive before midafternoon. Those hills are treacherous any later than that."

It was clear Zephyrus was not persuaded. His reluctance told the whole story. "You have no alternative plan to escape the ghouls if you're captured in their cave home."

Sytha jumped in and said, "My father told me you've talked about eliminating that wicked collection of flesh-eaters for over a hundred years. It only gets worse as their numbers multiply, unchecked."

"I'm aware of this, Sytha. It is a timing issue that must be considered," Zephyrus said in a strong tone. Their eyes met and locked. The Elften nodded slightly as though he suddenly understood Zephyrus's words. "As you say." He stepped back and gave a polite bow.

Ivan noticed the exchange and wondered what it meant.

They fidgeted under Zephyrus's challenging stare. He was right. They didn't have a backup plan for their own safety. Since no one dared to visit the area, they had no idea if there was another way out or other hazards they weren't aware of.

"Mind you," Zephyrus said after a moment, "I'm not agreeing to this plan of yours, but if I did, what route would you take?"

"The foothill route." Sebastian pointed to the north and slowly moved his finger to the left. "We'd follow it west and climb the rocky path until we come to the second cave opening. Davaan will meet us, and we'll leave our horses there."

"It's possible you'll see several druids on your way. They usually use the Foothill Road, but have no encounters with the ghouls. Perhaps they know of a more favorable route, one that's safe. Of course, with their unique method of transportation, it's understandable how they avoid the creatures." Zephyrus's wooden lips pulled up in one corner, leaving Ivan to wonder at the statement, *their unique method of transportation. What does it mean?*

They were getting more impatient while Zephyrus seemed to solemnly think on the matter. His lips were moving, but no words came out. Tangled eyebrows moved up and then down, ending into a deep scowl. Zephyrus stared over their heads in a southerly direction, looking like he suffered greatly.

Ivan kicked at some wet leaves on the ground,

figuring the Great Oak was trying to find reasons to deny their perilous journey. He could understand Zephyrus's reluctance to let them go. It could be a dangerous mission.

Finally, Zephyrus mumbled, "I will make some contacts this morning, that is if the Underground-Root system is working properly, and I think it is."

"Then, that means—" Sytha was quick to respond. "We should get our horses and prepare to leave?"

"Who are you going to contact?" Wayland asked.

"I'll have Zello meet you at the foothill path of the mountain."

Each looked at one another. Doubt and fear flashed across their faces. It was bad enough the four of them planned to make the journey on horseback, but to invite Zello, the Forest dragon? You can't hide a dragon. His appearance would alert every ghoul that lived there.

The door in Zephyrus's trunk creaked open. "Step inside, Ivan, and take The Challenger. May the High Intervener be with all of you."

He did just that, and shortly, they gathered their supplies from Maynard, mounted their horses, and waved to Zephyrus as they trotted north.

****

Sytha, who usually seemed so confident and sure, was now scraping his teeth together. He glanced from side to side. He rode his pale blue horse, not saying a word.

Blue horses—still an oddity to Ivan that he couldn't get used to.

Part of him was elated to be on his way to find his brother, while the other part of him dreaded their frightful journey of the unknown. He stared at the hazy mountain ahead, thinking about what he'd agreed to. *I've talked my good friends into going to the most dangerous and gruesome place in all the Forest, and we may not leave alive.* For a moment, he wanted to call it off, go home and feed his chickens and clean the barn. He thought of Peter's plea for help. *No. I won't abandon my brother, and I hope he escapes this terrible predicament.*

They left the graveled path that many horse hooves had beaten down, beyond the wooden barracks, and the bench where Ivan sat next to Anna-Iza the evening before. A flash of her sweet countenance rushed through him. If only she were here in her crimson riding cloak waiting for him. His chest warmed, and he ached to hold her in his arms.

Alfred and Canute followed happily along with their master on the oak-edged trail. Stopping from time to time, they barked at small rodents or a flock of sheep with a shepherd guarding them as they passed in the distance.

They trotted beyond a grove of brother oaks, the ground carpeted with dead leaves. Squirrels chattered and ran up the tree trunks, where they hesitated and watched the strangers ride by. *Everything seems quite ordinary.*

"Don't get too dreamy." Sebastian coaxed his old gray horse next to Bounty. "We must stay alert, even now where it is presumed safe. Get used to looking behind you and over your shoulder. It may save our lives."

He understood and nodded while shifting The Challenger to a comfortable position at his side.

"It's great to be with you again, Ivan Kimble," the sword said.

Ivan knew the sonorous voice along with the strong bond of friendship they'd formed when they'd traveled together, and The Challenger's quickness that saved his life several times during two prior trips into the Forest. "Yes, I'm grateful to have you with me."

Bounty was not so happy carrying the extra rucksack of food, Ivan's saddlebags, and a rolled blanket that Maynard had supplied for each of them. His fussy horse didn't like anything unusual or burdensome bouncing on his rump. He stretched his long neck to take a nip out of Wayland's stallion, but fortunately, the animal jerked forward before any damage was done.

"Stop that, Bounty." Ivan pulled his horse's head toward him and cuffed him on his cheek. "You're mad because I left you at the barrack's stable for one night. It couldn't be helped. Didn't they feed you well? Clean water? Hay and a handful of oats?"

"I don't think we'll make it in time to meet Daavan," Wayland grumbled. "We shouldn't have stayed for breakfast or waited for Zephyrus to make up his mind. The older he gets the longer everything seems to take."

"For good reason." Sytha stared ahead. "First, he's over a thousand years old. All the oaks know the winter's frost is near, and the tree's sap is returning deep into its roots. You've seen Zephyrus's branches dropping their leaves the colder these days become. Second, he's got good reasons to worry about us."

"I know that." Wayland snorted, though it seemed to do nothing to rid his anxiety.

Hoping to ease the tension, Ivan said, "I've noticed that Zephyrus has no acorns."

"He's far past middle age," Sebastian explained, riding next to Ivan. "There will be no more acorns from him to feed the squirrels or pigs."

A sweeping lawn of purple heather in bloom appeared in the distance, blanketing the gentle foothills with color. It was calm and peaceful, and Ivan wished he could share the sweet smell of earth and its vegetation with his brother.

"Know what that is, Ivan?" Sebastian pointed off to their left.

He shook his head and said, "It's an impressive oak tree standing alone in a clearing—much like Zephyrus's domain, only not nearly as large."

"Remember when Joseph and I discussed the Circle of Enchantment?" Sebastian turned to Ivan. "A Dwelling Place for Enlightenment?"

Sytha snapped his head to the right, giving them a stare that Ivan couldn't figure. Maybe Sebastian shouldn't have mentioned it, although Ivan had learned of the tree on his first trip into the Forest.

"It has something to do with Maloof's fall from grace," Ivan said. "He lost his High Wizard standing, and then he went to troll prison for ten years."

"That's right." Sebastian patted his animal's neck. "Well, now that you've seen it, stay away."

"It's beautiful." Ivan gasped and continued to stare. A straight, proud trunk, its branches were thick with gold, red, and purple leaves.

The tree seemed to sing to them, calling for attention with a soft, haunting voice.

"It looks harmless enough," Ivan said.

"Well, it's not," Sytha barked. "Its power to draw in people and corrupt them is immense. Don't tempt it."

"I don't plan to." Ivan raised his shoulders and glanced away.

As they traveled, Ivan thought about Sytha's harsh warning. He remembered the story about the enchanted tree. What actually happened to cause Maloof's decline under the oak tree's spreading branches? He suddenly wondered if Peter had chanced a visit to the Circle of Enchantment.

"If it's so dangerous," Ivan asked innocently, "why doesn't Zephyrus have it destroyed?"

Wayland said after a long silence, "I wondered the same thing."

"My guess?" Sytha twisted in his saddle and spoke clearly, "It's because Zephyrus doesn't choose to. He feels that this tree, which was first meant for good to ease the grief of losing a loved one, is still a brother oak and should not be taken down. Maybe one day, its original purpose will return and soothe those who need comfort with its gentle songs."

Pulling on his frazzled white beard, Sebastian glanced up. "It was Tereus who poisoned the tree by injecting his evil into its roots. I'm sure of it. Maloof was a victim who met a lovely demigoddess there for consolation, and then, well…it was too late. The evil enveloped him, and he couldn't escape its hold." Sebastian heaved a sigh. "That's enough about the tree. Let's watch for any danger ahead."

Well, now I know. Ivan wondered why the information was so difficult to share with him.

"It's a matter of timing," Sebastian simply explained, answering the question on Ivan's mind.

Wayland led the way where they connected with Foothill Road, giving the Tree of Enlightenment a wide berth. The rains from the evening before made the road muddy with deep puddles to maneuver. Bounty whinnied with irritation. He pulled to the right side and munched on wet grass until Ivan gave him an encouraging nudge to his ribs. The animal shook his light-colored mane and moved on. The other horses did the same.

"I didn't know this road was in such bad shape," Wayland griped, turning toward Ivan as if apologizing.

Ivan pursed his lips but wasn't really concerned. A little mud didn't deter him. He had other worries—like finding Peter—alive. The same for his beagles, who were wise enough to leave the sloppy road and trot on the grassy area. It surprised Ivan that Wayland still seemed a bit out of sorts. He'd never heard him quite so cross in the past and figured he must be troubled about their journey to the dangerous mountain while trying to meet Davaan as scheduled.

The morning is gloomy and gray, just like Wayland's mood, Ivan thought. No birds sang their charming songs in the massive oaks and ash trees as they passed. A wild boar stuck his nose out from behind a cluster of gorse bushes and grunted at Alfred and Canute. The beagles jumped and let out a yip, backing away to avoid a confrontation. *Maybe they are finally learning not to chase bigger animals than they are.*

"Ignore the big brute," Ivan called to his dogs. "He's looking for acorns and beach masts that have fallen from the trees." Swallowing hard, Ivan tried to get the feel of something scratchy past his own dry throat. They hadn't yet started to climb the foothills, and already he was plagued with doubt. *Is Peter still alive? Did Davaan decide to leave his hideout and abandon the mountain?*

The gnarly old oaks thinned after a half-hour ride up the first hill. They rode single file on the thin path that looked to be carved out by deer hooves and other four-footed animals.

"Let's stop here and water the horses," Sebastian said as they approached a clear, slow-moving stream. "We'll save our canteens for later when we need a drink, and who knows when the next river will show itself?"

Ivan looked up and down the river to be sure there were no Ratlings prepared to jump from the cattails and reeds and pounce on them. They were frightful creatures, rat-like and as big as ponies. He shivered just thinking about them and their poisonous teeth that had bitten into his side, nearly ending his life.

No one argued with Sebastian's suggestion to stop, especially Ivan, whose rear end felt the irritation of his saddle.

Sytha swung off his pale blue horse with the energy and skill of a practiced acrobat. His animal drank thirstily. Ivan and Wayland dismounted and bent to their knees, cupping cold water into their hands. All except Sebastian, who was a spirit and had no need to quench his thirst.

"Look!" Ivan pointed excitedly. "A blue-back turtle—in the creek."

Sebastian leaned over to see it. His voice rose with excitement, "Imagine that. I didn't think they inhabited this area."

The amphibian stared up at them.

"I haven't seen one of these since your first trip into the Forest. Remember, Ivan? You told me a turtle talked to you when you snuck into the Forest as a little boy."

"Yes, I remember."

"What did it say?" Sytha's gem-blue eyes grew large. "They are very rare."

"I think it said, 'My spirit will go into you.' Something like that. I don't know what it meant, and then it died."

The Elften gave Sebastian a long, curious look, blinking several times. "How did it die?"

After a few moments of uneasy silence, Ivan lowered his eyes and admitted, "Peter threw a big rock and killed it."

"Why did he do that?" Sytha's mouth dropped open.

Ivan pulled up his shoulders. He didn't want to admit, "Just to see it die. But Peter isn't that foolish boy anymore."

Sebastian turned away, shaking his head slowly. "A terrible thing," he muttered.

"We'd better go." Wayland stood and brushed wet leaves and mud from his knees after kneeling at the stream's edge.

As they rode up the first of many hills, the oaks thinned even more and were joined by pines and tall firs. A hawk left the spindly branch of a tree, chasing a few blackbirds. It was comical to watch—if any of them were in the mood to laugh, which they were not.

"You haven't said much." Sebastian moved his gray mare next to Wayland, who stared at the rocky mountains ahead. Ivan encouraged Bounty to move closer, wanting to hear Wayland's response.

"The climb will be hard on our horses." Wayland's thick eyebrows pulled into a deep frown.

"We'll never make Davaan's meeting in the midafternoon."

"D-do you think your brother will wait for us?" Ivan sympathized with Wayland's worries.

Glancing at each of them, Wayland shook his wolf-like head. "I just don't know. My thinking is different than Davaan's, now. He's more impulsive and, if I might say, self-centered. That's understandable, I suppose. Their pack is accustomed to thinking of their own safety and their bellies first, and most everything else is secondary."

Ivan knew from past remarks that Wayland's greatest wish was that his brother, and the other werewolves in the wild, would make the transition into a man as Wayland had done, and they'd live in the safety of the Wolflord's village.

"It's important to show Davaan that it's better to leave his werewolf life behind." He pulled at his dark mustache, scowling. "I try to set an example of good behavior, loyalty, and dependability. If we are late, I'm afraid he'll think I don't keep my word. Do you understand my thinking?"

"We'll do the best we can," Sebastian answered. "That's all that can be expected from us."

They heard a grunting commotion coming from the border of brush and small trees.

"Rutting season of the deer?" Sytha raised his slender torso from the saddle and scanned the area.

Dashing from a clump of brambles and yellow gorse, a wild boar appeared. When his squinty gaze met the travelers', he swung in an arc and ran back to his hiding place like he was being chased. Shortly, seven roe deer, small and delicate, each about the size of a dog, ventured from the thickets. Even from a distance, Ivan saw their slender legs quivering, their eyes large and frightened.

"Something's wrong…" Ivan's stomach knotted, bringing on a flash of pain.

"The deer are easily frightened." Wayland indicated with a dismissive wave of his hand. "I don't believe there's danger here."

Then, they saw it.

Chapter 14

Strange Visitors

Above their heads, a flat, rectangular object slowly lowered toward them. Bounty snorted and pounded his hooves. The beagles jumped and barked at the large shape coming from the sky.

"Aah," Sebastian called. "The druids have found us."

"D-druids?" Ivan watched as the thick carpet neared the ground. Sitting cross-legged were three men in brown-hooded robes with gold braided ties around their waists. The heavy-set man in front appeared to be most uncomfortable while trying to uncross his thick legs. He removed his hands from the wide sleeves of his garment to steady himself and tried to stand.

Wayland leaped from his horse, moving quickly to help the teetering, bald-headed druid step from the carpet. The other two druids sitting behind him leaned over the carpet's edge where it hoovered inches from the damp earth. They seemed concerned about what they might be landing on.

"What is it?" the heavy-set druid asked the thinner man.

"I thought I saw a beetle."

"Oh! That will never do to harm one of God's creatures." His partner agreed with a brief nod.

Alfred and Canute whimpered and then barked ferociously at the newcomers. Ivan shushed them. He knew it was an odd sight, and he was trying to absorb it with some amount of common sense, but it was slow in coming. People don't fly on carpets, although he'd read fables like this when he was a youngster.

"Welcome, welcome," Sebastian called as he slipped off his horse, his arms thrown open. "I didn't think we'd have the pleasure to see you again so soon. It's only been a couple of months."

Ivan joked silently to himself. *Of course. A mystical forest wouldn't be complete without a flying carpet of druids, would it now?* Didn't Zephyrus mention they used an unusual mode of transportation? This must be what he was referring to. The beagles stopped barking when the other two druids stepped to the ground. Studying the carpet's thick woven pattern, Ivan could made out a scene of deer in a forest, twisting vines, forest birds, and friendly druid figures all living peacefully together.

Moving toward the visitors, Sytha bowed with respect to the Master Druid, apparently having some familiarity with their customs. Wayland and Ivan also bowed but remained in their places, gaping.

They spoke a language that Ivan surmised must be Elften, though Ivan had never heard Sytha speak in his own tongue before. When the heavy-set druid responded with a tip of his head, Sytha motioned to Ivan. "He wants to speak with you."

Ivan's eyebrows rose, astonished to be singled out. He hoped Wayland followed behind, but he held back.

"This is Rounds, Master Druid of the Wise," Sebastian said, "and these are his brother druids, Indez and Zupine." Rounds and Indez lowered their brown hoods and returned Ivan's polite bow.

"We're pleased to meet you, Ivan Kimble," Rounds said, his voice higher than Ivan would've expected. "Our greetings to you, Wayland the Wolflord." Now, Wayland moved closer and joined the others.

"It's good to see you again." Wayland grinned. "It's been a long time."

"Yes," Master Rounds replied. "When we first met, you were on all fours and howling. I was very pleased you went through the transition. Zephyrus tells me glowing things about you and your pack—that is, your colony."

Plucking at his wolf-like ears, Wayland smiled widely. "Yeah, that was a long time ago. Not only have I transitioned, but many of the werewolves that terrorized this region also turned and became men."

Indez nodded several times, seemingly pleased. He was brown skinned and smiled with white teeth at the four travelers. They must've known all about the transition, Ivan surmised.

Rounds appeared as his name suggested, round faced, with a thick middle. Even his feet were wide, pushing through his leather sandals. "I'd like to say," he addressed Ivan, "we've heard a great deal about your courage, and we admire one so young who has generously helped the Forest."

"He has," Sebastian confirmed with a prideful grin.

"We recognize the Forest's Golden Medallion that you wear around your neck," the druid named Indez said. He was taller than Rounds with a hooked nose. "These medals are not presented to men carelessly. They are earned for exceptional bravery and merit."

"And yet," Zupine said, keeping his ample hood over his head, shadowing his face and eyes, "you look young to have received such a treasure. How old are you?"

"I-I turned fifteen—several months ago." Ivan wondered how Zupine could *see* anything. He noticed the tall, thin druid had no pupils. His eyes were white, and his complexion pale without the benefit of the sun. His long face was passive, with a heavy lower lip that did not smile. In fact, they scarcely moved when he spoke. The look of him frightened Ivan, not knowing what those empty eyes could see.

The blank-eyed man's voice was thin and cracked from what seemed a lack of use or a tortured larynx. "You are much admired, Mr. Kimble. Your visit to our Forest is blessed with charges of enchantment."

Ivan frowned briefly, wondering what the "*charges of enchantment*" meant. *These druids say some strange things.*

"Now," Rounds said, "what is it you seek from the Brotherhood of Druids?"

Though the Master Druid had asked the question, Ivan suspected he'd already been informed of the nature of their journey.

Rotating to Ivan, Sebastian gave a nod. Ivan supposed it was his turn to speak.

"I—we are traveling to the Mountain of Smoke and Fire where I've heard my brother, Peter, is hiding. He's in some kind of trouble and needs our help."

Staring up at the lad with compassion in his small eyes, Round's brow furrowed. "You'll forgive me, but when I received Zephyrus's message this morning, I questioned his sanity. He asked us to meet you here and try to dissuade you from this foolish endeavor. Brother or no brother, it's not worth your lives."

"We've already been through this argument with Zephyrus, and we believe it's worth the risk to help our friend." Sytha pressed his lips together and adjusted his bow and quiver that hung over his shoulder.

Relieved to hear Sytha's remark, Ivan released a lung full of air. "Do you know of an escape route, or another passage to the second cave, where we believe Peter may be hiding—maybe a backway?"

Bounty tossed his head, and the reins jingled his impatience. He whinnied loudly to be sure his master had understood. Wayland must have felt the same way as he shifted from one foot to another, stroking his thick, dark beard.

"No druid has ever gotten close to the ghouls' territory—or have we ever wanted to—with one exception." Pulling his hands from the sleeves of his robe, Rounds pointed at Zupine. Flexing his fingers, he gave a mysterious tip of his head. "He knows about the damage a ghoul can do to your body—and eyes."

Without hesitation, Zupine lowered his hood, untied his belt, and slowly pulled opened his robe. He wore a linen loincloth, sandals, and nothing more under his robe.

They gasped and sputtered. Sytha twisted away, dry-heaved, and his chest quivered. Sebastian lowered his head.

Zupine's body was a patchwork of red scars and brownish flesh stitched together—a ragged pattern that climbed from his belly to his neck. It looked like healing had been slow, painful, and was still in progress.

"It wasn't put back together well," Zupine explained

with a tormented tone. "The damage was almost beyond our doctor's ability, and the Long Dark Cloak couldn't be called upon with such short notice to heal me."

Sebastian raised his head briefly and looked away. *Was it shame that caused him to hide his face?*

"It took him months to recover," Indez said. "The constant infection was the worst because the ghouls are filthy and diseased."

Zupine's resigned face neither smiled nor grimaced, but he closed his brown robe and tied the belt with practiced hands without the aid of his sight.

"Why…" Ivan paused. "Why didn't you call on Sebastian and the cloak at once to heal you?"

"An understandable question, Ivan Kimble." Zupine turned in Ivan's direction, staring, unseeing to some distant place. "Druids have, what may seem to you, uncommon codes and rules. We don't depend upon outside help. Like the Witches' Village, we aren't an official part of the West Forest, and therefore, we don't burden our friends with our troubles."

"Friends and neighbors are here to support one another, to help them whenever possible," Ivan said, hoping he didn't sound too pompous or pushy.

"It is for us to give and not to take," Indez said.

Something about their code didn't seem quite logical. Ivan was tempted to inform Zupine that the witches did, indeed, just join the Forest, accepting their rules and regulations. But then, he decided it wasn't for him to reveal it at this time.

Rounds cleared his throat. "Maybe it doesn't make sense to you, young man, but we druids are a proud and isolated people and don't wish to trouble or obligate anyone."

When Sebastian shook his head, Ivan let the subject go. Still, he was curious about their peculiar behavior.

"There is a back entrance to the cave, but you'd have to travel from the west side of the mountain and enter from there. I don't advise it because, having little coverage, you can easily be spotted by the horde." Zupine turned toward the group, his blank eyes glaring in the direction of the mountain. "The horses should stay in the second cave. It's small, but there's space for your animals, and you won't need to walk so far if you must travel to the ghoul's main cave. It should be safe if you are not gone too long. I believe there is a stream nearby." He paused and looked down at the dogs. "That includes room for your beagles."

How did he know Alfred and Canute are beagles?

"As you near the highest mountain," Zupine continued, "the trail is treacherous, and you'll have to travel on foot. Leave your supplies behind. If there is any smell of food or blood, they will be drawn to it."

Ivan wanted to ask Rounds if he knew Peter, but he stopped, not comfortable delaying their journey any longer. Right now, he couldn't bear to hear a bad report about his brother if that would be the case.

"We really must go," Wayland mumbled just loud enough for them to hear. He moved toward his horse and took the bridle in his hands. "There's someone waiting for us, and his guidance is important." He groaned impatiently.

The Master Druid shook his round head with barely enough neck to be convincing. "I wish you'd change your minds. Perhaps your brother will meet you somewhere near the base of the foothills."

"If only that were true," Ivan said softly.

"It's rumored the King's Scepter is in that terrible mountain." Sytha seemed to recover from the shock of seeing Zupine's ravaged body, but he wisely avoided more than a glance at him.

"We know for certain the mountain dwellers *do* have the King's Scepter, and we realize how important it is to the Forest's well being." Rounds swept his pudgy hand toward the blind druid. "He traveled there and tried to take it from them so he could present it to Zephyrus as a gesture of our goodwill. This is the result of Zupine's generous heart. Just what use it is to the ghouls, I'll never know."

"The huge ruby embedded on the top of the scepter transmits no power, nor does it emit light or magical properties while in enemy hands," Indez said for their complete understanding.

"How did you know about the scepter, and why did you go it alone?" Sytha asked.

"I looked into our Pond of Visions." Zupine blinked his vacant eyes. "There, I saw the scepter in the hands of Hoxx, who rules the large horde of that degenerate, savage community. I felt the need not to involve any of my brother druids, trusting my ability to find my way, to move and hide quickly." His attempt to smile froze on his distorted lips. "As I have said, by returning the scepter, I'd hoped to please Zephyrus and help make the Forest safer for all."

"Noble gesture," Sebastian said in a dull voice.

Rubbing his own eyes, Ivan was grateful to have full vision.

Wayland fell against his horse, his arms draped across the saddle. His patience waned further.

"You would be wise to leave this awful place now

and avoid the ghouls, Ivan Kimble," Rounds said pointing east where they should return. "While they are poor fighters, having only crude weaponry, they make up for it in large numbers with sharp teeth and claws that can—well, you see what they can do."

"Their culinary choices are repugnant, and they will cannibalize everything and anyone living." Zupine's thick bottom lip trembled. He looked worriedly at each traveler.

"Yes," Ivan replied. "We've heard." He thought back to his dream about Peter having no skin to cover his body—and no eyes. Ivan's chest tightened, and his breath came in a jerky motion.

"Then you've also heard of the Woman of Flame, who resides deeper in the mountain? She protects the ghouls from invaders." Round's voice was stronger and more forceful. "She lives in the river that flows through their cave home, and she never leaves it."

"Since she can't feed herself," Indez continued, "the ghouls must take care of that task."

"A perfect symbiotic relationship," Sebastian said.

"Yes." Indez glanced at him.

"What does that word mean?" Wayland asked Ivan.

"Um. It means they depend upon each other for their survival. She protects the ghouls, and the ghouls, in turn, feed her." Ivan frowned, and thought on it. He was pretty sure his meaning was correct.

"Do you still insist on making this journey to the mountain?" Zupine's head turned toward Sytha, Wayland, and then with raised, non-existent eyebrows, he seemed to search Ivan's soul.

What is he seeing?

"We...are," Ivan said shakily.

"Then we can only send you on your way with blessings from the Brotherhood of Druids." The Master Druid bowed and pulled the hood over his shiny head. "Incidentally," he said to Ivan, "I'd do the same as you to save any of my druid brothers. It is our Code of Love and Fellowship."

"Just as we would harm no living creature, be it beetle, or deer, or man," Indez added and gave a hint of a smile.

The comment caused Ivan to breathe a bit easier.

With the help of his two comrades, they lowered Rounds onto the colorful carpet. There, he sat, cross-legged, pursing his lips. Zupine and Indez stepped behind him, and with somewhat greater ease, they sat, shoving their hands into the sleeves of their robes.

"Thank you for your advice," Ivan called as the carpet rose slowly from the ground. It struggled to rise higher like the load was almost too much to bear for a mere piece of woven fabric.

Rounds leaned toward the edge and said, "Hold fast the ones you love. They are your lifeblood. It is for them you risk your life." He straightened and adjusted his hood. "Come visit us sometime. You are always welcome to our west mountain home."

"We would like that," Sytha called back. They waved at the departing visitors.

"That's sensible advice," Ivan shouted after them and softly repeated, "Hold fast the ones you love. They are your lifeblood." *Yes, that's why I need to find Peter and take him home.*

Chapter 15

Mountain journey

Sytha and Wayland rode on either side of Ivan, more for his protection than for conversation.

Ivan's faithful dogs followed behind Sebastian, who squirmed on the back of Old Bones, watching for invaders.

"See the beautiful foothills—bluish with stands of fir trees and pines," Wayland said, sweeping his arm in an arc. "I'd forgotten how lovely this area is." He seemed in happier spirits now that they were moving again and making good distance.

They encouraged their horses up a rocky path that zig-zagged. It switched directions going up one mountain, leading to another. After some time, they came to a flat area in a small valley where pines grew thickly and lush grass covered the ground.

"Let's stop here." Wayland came to a halt near several ancient, downed trees, which gave them privacy and a perfect place to sit. He scanned their surroundings and must've decided it was safe to have a picnic. "We need to hurry, but we'll have our lunch and rest our animals."

"Hallelujah!" Sebastian sang. "I'd like to stretch these weary legs."

Each pulled rucksacks from their horses along with

their canteens of water. Bounty turned his head toward Ivan and snorted his disapproval. "It isn't that heavy, you big baby," he scolded and made an ugly face. Straightening The Challenger at his side, he thought about removing it, but after seeing Sebastian's scowl, he readjusted the weapon and sat on the log.

The sandwiches were thick and meaty, slathered with some kind of sauce that Ivan couldn't name, but he liked the flavor very much. The beagles jumped at his knees, begging to be fed. "Just hold on," he said and laughed. "There's plenty here for both of you."

"These vegetables are fresh." Sytha ate a raw carrot and, with his knife in hand, he quartered a rutabaga. While crunching on a celery stick, he rolled a radish between his fingers. "A nice variety, and just right for me." He grinned.

Wayland sat on the log and reached out to stroke Canute's head. "I keep thinking of Zupine and those terrible scars. I wonder how he escaped such a nightmare attack."

"I don't want to think about it," Ivan mumbled, slowly chewing his sandwich and apple.

"Maybe someday Zupine will tell us." Sytha turned an inquisitive eye toward Sebastian. "Do you know?"

The spirit leaned over with his elbows resting on his knee, his hands clasped together. The look on his face was one of pity. "It was as Zupine told you. He took it upon himself, foolishly, I might add, to sneak into the ghouls' mountain home in an attempt to snatch the King's Scepter with his wish to present it to Zephyrus. How he got away, I don't know."

Between bites, Ivan said, "High price to pay."

"Yes, indeed." Sebastian nodded. "He was aware of

the danger but thought he could accomplish the task single-handedly because of his gifts of stealth and quickness."

"Could you've healed him?" Sytha lifted a light eyebrow at Sebastian.

"Yes. Had they contacted me or Zephyrus, I would've mended his flesh. You heard Rounds say they don't call on others to solve their problems but only depend upon themselves."

Ivan understood why Sebastian felt guilty. Given a chance, he could've mended Zupine and saved him all the pain and agony he'd suffered.

Sebastian's voice quivered with remorse. "I say, in this case, their code of conduct is not wise, but how do you change centuries of rules?"

No one asked any more questions. It seemed the subject was too painful to revisit. They fell silent, seriously considering what lay ahead. Ivan picked up their lunch leftovers and stuffed the waste in Wayland's empty rucksack.

A sudden feeling of both thankfulness and fear rushed over Ivan. "Why are you doing this?" He turned and addressed his companions. "Knowing how dangerous our mission is?"

"It's our job," Wayland answered first. "This is what we do as inhabitants of the Forest. It's to our benefit to protect our homes as well as others—to keep it safe for our own *'Women of Flame.'* " He gave a little chuckle at the statement.

"…And, for the children," Sytha said and waved his hand. "They will one day inherit the responsibilities, duties, and joys of our Forest."

"And, for you, Ivan." Sebastian met the boy's

worried eyes. "It's for you…because we care."

Warmth rushed up Ivan's face, causing a blush, he was sure. "I…thank you…for your courage and kindness."

Mounting, Wayland announced, "Now the real climbing begins. The mountains ahead have dangerous switchbacks, and the air is thinner. I'm sorry to say, I don't know about the caves that Zupine mentioned, but they should be easy enough to find."

"If there's a cave one and cave two, I assume," Sebastian said sensibly, "the third must be the home of the ghouls and found at the very top." The others nodded, recalling that Zupine had told them this. Ivan supposed, silently, that Sebastian was reviewing their plight with some nervousness.

Several hours passed as they rode on and searched for the first cave. Canute and Alfred panted and lagged behind. Their horses were also feeling fatigued and stumbled over ruts and rocks on the unpredictable path. Sebastian's dusty gray horse kept his head lowered to the ground, plugging along wearily.

"It's late in the afternoon," Wayland mumbled. "I'm worried that Davaan won't be waiting for us, and we may be on our own."

Sytha and Ivan gulped.

A light cloud of ash floated down on them, making it obvious how the area got its name. They could smell the plumes of smoke before they could see the flames that shot from the mountaintop. The breeze carried it down, acrid and putrid, as it fell on them and their surroundings. Stepping back and rearing, the horses seemed to sense the danger ahead. Wayland, a descendant of the wolf family, was particularly sensitive to the odor.

Ivan held his nose and asked, "Do they know we're here? Is the smoke a warning that intruders are entering their territory?"

Sebastian shrugged his shoulders. No one had an answer.

"Where's the trail?" Wayland turned to his riding companions after they'd rode to the crest of a big hill. "It seems to have disappeared."

"We haven't seen or heard any wildlife after climbing the first foothill," Sebastian said. "I suspect the native animals know where they'd end up if they ventured here."

"Look!" Ivan pointed to a spot where two steep hills came together, forming a small dip in the landscape. "There's a cave hidden behind some bushes and pines."

"You have good sight." Sytha gave Ivan a wink. He pulled his blue horse to the right, riding slowly down the incline toward the cave that Ivan had spotted. The others followed. Canute and Alfred stared at each other. They let out a whimper and then trotted behind.

The sun lowered while a chill replaced the warmth of the day. Ivan knew his beagles were tired and needed rest. He hoped Davaan and Peter had changed their minds and would be hidden in the first cave waiting for them, and then they could all go home.

"Be careful at the entrance," Sebastian warned and dropped his unsteady legs to the ground. "Anything could be in wait, ready to pounce on you."

Ivan pushed off Bounty and ran to support the old man around his waist and held him upright.

"Do you see anything?" Sytha stepped behind Wayland, peering past him into the darkness.

"No, but I smell decaying bones and rotten flesh. This is either a dumping ground for the ghoul's waste or another dining room." Wayland walked slowly into the cave, kicking a few femur and rib bones to the side. A human skull wedged between a couple rocks seemed to stare up at them with a dire warning.

Ivan bit his bottom lip and turned away. It reminded him of his frightening dream where Peter came toward him with flesh clawed from his body.

"I don't smell anything." Sebastian stepped into the opening and squinted. "But…"

"But?" Wayland repeated.

"I hear moaning."

"Yes, I hear it too." Wayland cupped the palm of his hand around his wolf ears. "It sounds like someone's hurt. Maybe it's Davaan." He started to rush into the dark cave.

"Or maybe it's Peter." Ivan's breath quickened.

"Wait!" Sytha grabbed Ivan's arm. "Let me go in first." He pulled the bow from his shoulder and notched a golden-tipped arrow.

"We need a torch more than we need a bow and arrow," Ivan said sensibly. "The Golden Lantern would suit me just right about now."

Sytha returned the items to where they belonged and pulled his wand from a thin leather quiver. When he gave it a tap with his index finger, a bright light instantly appeared and illuminated the cave.

"That's better," Ivan said, and when he turned, he noticed Sebastian wasn't behind him. Spinning around, he walked out into the late afternoon. "Aren't you going with us?"

"No. I'll stay here and watch the animals—be sure

the horses get some grass to eat and drink from the little stream over there." He indicated with a sweep of his hand. "Alfred and Canute are weary, and I'd like to rest until you find out what's moaning inside. It's possible Zello may show up and wonder where we are."

"Ah, I'd forgotten about Zello meeting us." Ivan scratched his head.

Hearing their names mentioned, the beagle's whined, wanting attention and to follow behind their master into the cave. "No. You stay here." Ivan bent to his knees and stroked their foreheads and dark noses. "It may be dangerous in there."

Though he didn't like leaving Sebastian alone, he could see the old man needed rest. Ivan asked, "Is this the second cave where we are to leave our horses and climb on foot?"

Sebastian lifted his shoulders. "I don't think so. It's too far from the main mountain. There must be another cave ahead."

"Ivan. Ivan. Come here." He faintly heard Sytha call his name from inside the cave.

"Go." Sebastian gave him a gentle push. "We'll be safe."

"Alfred and Canute stay and protect Sebastian." Ivan rushed into the dark hole of the unknown.

"The moaning seems to be coming from over this way." Wayland stopped and listened for the sounds, stepping gingerly past a pile of bones. He pointed. "A couple of sheep heads gnawed clean."

After Ivan entered the opening, he didn't watch where he was going and tripped over a rib cage that looked like it belonged to a small deer. He tried to jump clear of the entanglement but couldn't catch himself fast enough. Down he went onto his hands and knees. "Ooowah!" he cried.

"Are you all right?" Sytha and Wayland rushed to their friend's side. Together they lifted him under his arms to his feet from the dirt floor.

"I punctured my hand when I fell on a bone." He shook it, and then put it into his mouth, where he sucked the bleeding wound. "It stings terrible."

"Sebastian, will you—where is he?" Wayland turned and searched. "I thought he was behind us, picking his way carefully."

"He volunteered to watch the horses and my beagles at the entrance," Ivan said, cradling his injured hand next to his chest, now throbbing with hot pain.

Wayland took a handkerchief from his pocket and wrapped Ivan's wound. Patting him on his back, he said, "It looks pretty deep. Sebastian must heal it at once. You don't want to get an infection. Heaven knows what kinds of germs infest these scattered bones."

"I—I'll wait until we find out who's doing the moaning. Maybe it's Peter."

The groan became a scream coming from the darker recess of the cave. Ivan pulled back. "Is it a trick?" His teeth suddenly chattered. "Could it be ghouls who are luring us in further so they can attack us?"

Moving closer, Wayland drew a deep breath and asked with a shout, "Davaan, is that you? Where are you? It's Wayland."

"Oh, Wayland, m-my brother. I-I'm here, behind some large boulders."

"This way." Wayland stepped over the loose rocks and dips in the cave floor. "I can hear his fast breathing—and terrible fear."

Sytha and Ivan tried to follow the surefooted Wolflord, but their instincts were not as keen, and their movement not as sure.

Waving his wand in front of him, Sytha placed his hands on the boulders and peered over them. "Hold on—we're here."

"Dear Davaan." Wayland dashed around the pile of rocks and went to his knees, cradling his brother's head in his lap. "What happened to you?" Frantic, he lightly touched Davaan's bare chest with his fingers. Blood oozed from his wounds, and his shirt was shredded.

"Where were you? I waited and waited at the second cave as we agreed. When you didn't come, I ventured down to the first cave, thinking you might be here." He groaned. "One of those flesh-eaters found me just as I reached the entrance, and he attacked. He pounced on me so fast, ripping at my flesh, that I scarcely had time to *turn*. I was in so much pain." He whimpered and tried to move.

"Please, remain still." The stutter of shame filled Wayland's voice.

Sytha and Ivan caught up and kneeled next to Davaan. Ivan smelled the blood, a lot of it, as it seeped down the werewolf's side and puddled around him on the cave floor.

"Another ghoul showed up, grabbed at me, and started clawing. He sunk his teeth into my chest and arms, ripping some skin away, and—he ate it. I fled and ran far enough until I finally *turned* into a werewolf. I stopped and leaped on him, chewing at his throat. I tore the other ghoul to pieces, too."

"Where are the bodies?" Sytha's forehead wrinkled. "I didn't see them outside."

163

"There." Davaan pointed weakly to a darker part of the cave. "I managed to drag them over and hide them in case others showed up. That's why I bled so much—the effort it took." His chest rose and fell quickly, as the terror must've revisited him. "Ooh, it burns and throbs. Wayland, please help me."

"Were there others following you?" Sytha quickly asked.

Davaan groaned and arched his back. "I-I don't know. All I could th-think about was turning as fast as I could, or I would die. Help me."

"We will, at once." Wayland looked up with enlarged eyes. His dark beard trembled. "Ivan, can you make your way out of the cave and ask Sebastian to throw his spirit into the healing cloak?"

"Y-yes. I'll go."

"Take the wand. It will light your way to the outside. If it goes pale, tap it with your finger, and light will reappear. Like this." The Elften tapped the smooth crystal wand, where golden bands circled it, and light flashed from its tip. He squatted to Davaan's side, inspecting his raked arm. "Just hold on. We'll get help."

"Bring a canteen of water," Wayland yelled in Ivan's direction after he'd spun to leave.

Darkness behind him replaced his lighted path.

Ivan clumsily tried to retrace his steps following the wand's illumination. He stumbled a few times. His injured hand was now aching, the pain almost unbearable. He crunched his teeth, thinking of Davaan's agonizing condition and his desperate cry for help.

At last, he focused on the dim light of early evening at the cave's mouth. "Sebastian, Sebastian," he called. "We need you."

"You sure do! What happened to your hand?"

Ivan glanced at the bloody handkerchief, nearly saturated. "Not for me," he said. "It's Davaan. He was attacked by a couple of ghouls and needs your healing."

Turning to look at the horses grazing peacefully, Sebastian was satisfied they would be safe. Alfred and Canute scampered from behind rocks near the entrance and darted toward their master, barking eagerly. For only a moment, Ivan bent and scratched their heads. His painful hand wouldn't allow him further delay.

Sebastian dissolved into a smoky-gray wisp and threw himself into the Long Dark Cloak that Ivan wore. The phenomenon still astonished him, though he'd experienced it many, many times before. His agony was so great that Ivan tripped again before straightening upright. He quickly wrapped his hand around the garment's front hem. Instantly, the excruciating pain disappeared. The punctured skin came together and healed under the protection of Wayland's soiled handkerchief. "That feels just right." He sighed with relief. "Thank you, Sebastian."

"Always ready to help when I can."

Ivan grabbed Wayland's canteen, shaking it to determine how much water it held. About half full, he judged. "Stay," he said to his beagles, "and protect the horses." Holding up the palm of his now healed hand, he raced into the cave with Sebastian, who shot questions from the cloak about Davaan.

"He's in a bad way—in danger of going into shock," Ivan said a bit breathless. "The ghouls raked his chest and arms to pieces before he could *turn* into a werewolf—and when he finally changed, he chewed them apart." Ivan stepped through the bones and rocks, clutching the wand in front of him.

They heard Davaan's wail of suffering. "This way." Ivan stepped hurriedly where he knew the injured man lay behind the large boulders.

"He's not doing so good." The wand's light caught Wayland's tears that streamed down his face. He continued to hold his brother's head in his lap, soothing his brow with his fingertips.

Ivan pulled the cloak from his shoulders and draped it over the now shivering Davaan. His teeth chattered, and his bloody arms jerked.

Chapter 16

Davaan

"Y-you are none too early." Wayland's voice trembled. "He doesn't have much longer."

An agonizing gurgle rolled from Davaan's throat and then, "Aah," he exhaled deeply. "Wh-what magic did you just use on me?"

"Never mind now, brother. As long as you are healed and feeling better."

"I don't know about being healed, but the fire is gone from my chest and arms. Thank you all."

"Here, take a drink." Wayland took the canteen from Ivan and lifted Davaan's head. He gulped the water and didn't stop until it was empty.

"I couldn't get close enough to the stream without tearing more flesh from my body." His statement sounded like an apology. "I was craving water."

They were quiet, not speaking for some moments, waiting to see if Davaan would fully recover.

Sebastian materialized from the cloak in a swirl of blueish-gray smoke, tugging on the garment as he left it. He studied the red scars on Davaan's chest with care. "It must've been terribly painful. I'm so sorry."

"Where are the bodies?" Sebastian's forehead wrinkled. "I didn't see them outside."

"There." Davaan repeated the explanation and

pointed weakly to a darker part of the cave. "I managed to drag them over and hide them in case others showed up." His chest rose and fell quickly, as the terror must've revisited him.

Now that Davaan was no longer in danger, Ivan was about to speak of Peter's whereabouts, but Wayland spoke first.

"I'm so sorry we were delayed," Wayland said. "We got a late start because Zephyrus couldn't make up his mind."

"Not really his fault," Sytha defended. "Zephyrus didn't want us to make this trip. He was dreadfully worried we wouldn't survive."

"That's right." Sebastian stood to his feet from where he had crouched nearby.

When Ivan made his way toward the stream, he washed the blood from the handkerchief and his hands. He splashed water on his face and took a long drink. When he returned, he said, "I think we should go back to Zephyrus. Coming here was a dangerous mistake. We must take Davaan to the castle's infirmary to rest and be sure he's completely healed." He handed the wet handkerchief to Wayland.

"You may be right," Sytha said. "If we only knew where Peter was, we could collect him and be gone from this blood-thirsty mountain."

Ivan saw a chance to ask a burning question. "Where is Peter, and why did he choose this awful place to meet?"

Davaan appeared to study Ivan for a moment. "I can tell you're brothers. Both tall, same angular faces, and straight noses." He hesitated. "Fifteen, aren't you?"

Ivan nodded, wondering what it had to do with

finding Peter.

"Your brother talked about you all the time. He's very proud of you. Says he can't live up to you or your father's expectations of him."

"What did he mean by that?" Ivan's dark eyebrows puckered.

Davaan stretched his legs out and moaned. "Don't know. You'll have to ask him."

"Is Peter safe?"

"As far as I know, he is. He's in the Mountain of Smoke and Fire because that's where Tereus ordered him. Wanted to negotiate something, Peter told me. When you didn't show up in the second cave—like I said, I rode down here looking for you."

"But why did he choose this—this terrible place to meet when it's so dangerous?"

Davaan blinked a few times, and scratched his wolf ears. "Peter does what Tereus tells him."

Ivan shivered hearing the comment. *There must be more to the story.*

"Now, I think we should leave this cave." Davaan rolled to his side and groaned.

"Where's your horse?" Wayland glanced around.

"He took off when I was attacked and is probably ghoul-meat by now." Davaan twisted his lips and made an angry face. "That's probably why no other ghouls came after me. They were enjoying a feast."

"Do you feel well enough to sit up?" Wayland asked.

"I'm stiff and sore, but with your help, I can manage." His brother put his arm around Davaan's back and tugged him into a sitting position. Davaan stroked the garment that lay over his body. "What's this cloak thing over me?"

"It's the Long Dark Cloak." Ivan was surprised Davaan didn't know about it. But then, why would he? He'd lived his life in the wilderness as a werewolf.

"What does it do?"

"It heals a person when imbued with the spirit of Sebastian." Ivan thought how fantastic it must sound to a werewolf who only knew survival and chasing wild animals to eat.

Davaan seemed to think on this a moment and then asked, "How can I get me one of these?"

"Sorry." Sytha gave a short laugh. "It's one-of-a-kind, and it belongs in the Sanctuary of Truth."

"And where's that?" Davaan handed the cloak to Ivan, who draped it over his arm, inside out, to avoid the blood and pieces of skin where it clung.

"In Zephyrus's trunk, where all the Ancient Relics are supposed to reside," Sytha said.

"Isn't that a big tree of some kind?" Davaan's interest seemed to peak.

"A huge oak tree." Sebastian stretched his arms wide.

"Thank you for healing me, Sebastian. If you and that black cloak ever need a new home, you can come live with us werewolves."

Sebastian snorted with good humor.

"Enough questions for now," Wayland said impatiently. "Let's wash ourselves in the stream that flows outside the cave and prepare our dinner."

Ivan reached under Davaan's arm to help him stand with Wayland on the opposite side.

"Here, take my jacket." Wayland slid it from his shoulders and placed it on his brother to cover the red scars on his chest. "You might as well throw away that bloody shirt you are wearing." He motioned toward the shredded garment.

"No! It's a reminder of what those vile creatures did to me. They will pay for this vicious act of savagery. There will be no leaving until we purge these mountains of them."

"Suit yourself." Wayland's heavy dark eyebrows lifted. "I'm here with you unto the end."

Davaan nodded his appreciation with a determined look on his face.

Just how he planned to do this, Ivan couldn't figure. He counted: Wayland, Davaan, Sytha, Sebastian a spirit, and me. Not much of an army. Not much of a fight. Not much of a chance. They would be annihilated. Ivan's jaw muscles tightened.

Leaving the cave, they towed Davaan until he garnered enough strength to stand on his own.

Ivan washed the cloak in the stream and gave it several swift shakes to remove the excess water. "I hope it'll dry quickly, or you won't have any healing power."

"Spread it over these rocks, and maybe the sun will do its job." Sebastian patted the rocks nearby.

Wayland and Davaan removed their clothes and with no shyness, took each other's hands and waded into the cold, clear stream. They squealed and threw their arms around their chests, shivering to their knees. "Wolf dung, that's cold!"

Sytha and Ivan chuckled.

The two brothers dried themselves on a sleeping blanket and redressed in their dirty clothes.

Just outside the cave's entrance, they sat on the ground to ration their food. Sytha and Ivan brought three canteens of water from their horses. For a while, they ate in silence as they no doubt thought about the possible battle on the mountain summit.

Ivan could no longer hold back his questions. "I don't understand. Why did Peter insist we meet him here? He's free to come and go as he pleases, isn't he?"

The werewolf's eyes appeared dazed as he stared at the sandwich he'd been served. "I could go catch a doe for our dinner if you'd like," he muttered.

Wayland gave a short huff of laughter. "Maybe some other time, huh?"

"Well…" Davaan slowly began, "Peter is a person of his own ambitions."

"What does that mean?" Ivan gave Canute a slice of mutton from his sandwich.

"How much do you know about Peter's…let's say, adventures?"

Shaking his head, Ivan shrugged. He wanted to know everything, so he pretended he knew little, which fact, he didn't know much.

"Some time ago…" Davaan paused and took a long gulp of water. "Peter gave his allegiance to that devil, Tereus, who lives in the underground caverns. Tereus promised Peter he'd make him king, and he'd sit upon the Forest's throne. Your brother believed such a position was owed to him, because his—your parents came from a kind of royalty, he told me."

It seems, Ivan pondered, *that everyone knows about our royal heritage in spite of trying to keep it secret.* "I tried to warn him that Tereus wasn't to be trusted when I met Peter at the edge of the Forest on my first visit. He promised to come home but didn't." A frightening thought came to him. *Is it Peter's plan to have me—us—*

ripped apart by the violent ghouls? Is his loyalty sacrificed to that terrible creature below ground?

"He's a hard-head, that's for sure. Foolish and shortsighted." Davaan took a big bite of his sandwich. "Not too bad." He licked his fingers.

"Then..." Ivan's voice quivered as he verbalized his concerns. "My brother is bound to Tereus, who has control over the ghouls, and that's why Peter moves freely among them?"

An uncanny silence followed. "Something like that." Davaan's nostrils widened. "I'm sorry I had to tell you. Peter told me that in the beginning, he'd hoped to gather information from the Dark Army and report it to Lord Graydon. I don't know if that was true or not, but he got himself in too deep, and now he doesn't know how to get out, though he insists he wants to leave Tereus's stifling hold. Since you've earned some amount of clout in the Forest, he thought you could help him be free of Tereus. The big question is, how do we plan his escape without all of us getting skinned alive?"

"That's enough for tonight's discussion." Wayland stood, sounding weary. "It's too late to travel. Let's clean up and try to get some sleep. We'll tackle the problem early tomorrow. Come, Davaan, you can share my blanket with me."

Sebastian shook his head and glanced at Ivan. "I don't like what Davaan just said about Peter. Is it too late to free him from Tereus' tight hold?"

Ivan closed his eyes, lowered his head, and pressed his lips together. Tomorrow they'd have to solve big problems on how to find Peter and help him escape the dangerous mountain.

Shortly, Ivan stretched out his bedroll to the right of

the cave opening and called his beagles to him. "Stay by me, but bark your heads off if you see or hear anything dangerous."

When a tawny owl hooted in the night, Canute barked. "Not him, Canute. The owl is harmless." He laid back and fell into a disturbed sleep where gloom and fear threatened to smother him.

****

The sun rose over the horizon, though its warmth wouldn't follow for a couple more hours. Wayland and Davaan were sitting up and talking in low tones. *Is Wayland discussing his wish for Davaan to transform into a man?*

Turning onto his side, watching the two brothers, Ivan thought about Peter. *Does he want fame so badly that he'd risk my life and his friends in order to sit upon a throne?* When he found Peter during his first visit to the Forest, he learned that Peter was obsessed with becoming a king. Royalty meant nothing to Ivan, and he told his brother this.

Seeing the warm colors of morning change, Ivan's thoughts glided to Coreena. *That pretty blonde-haired girl with turquoise-blue eyes misted with sadness, who worried about my safety. She was right, the Forest could be a dangerous place, and I'm squeezed in the middle of danger and death. I miss her and wish I could relive our last meeting at the Crunching Crumb, where they'd shared tea and scones. If only I hadn't hurt her feelings and walked out on her. What an insensitive thing to do. I should've flirted a bit, although I'm not sure I know how to do that. Will there be a next time?*

****

"Good morning," Sebastian said to Ivan. "Sleep

174

well?"

"Don't be so cheery," Davaan said, jerking the meager blanket he'd shared with his brother and draping it over his shoulders.

"As well as can be expected on this hard, cold ground," Ivan said. "I'm worried what the day will bring." Alarmed, he sat up. "Where's Sytha?"

"Not to worry." Sebastian waggled his finger toward a bushy area. "He's doing his business."

After a quick breakfast, with only a few morsels and fruit to share from their rucksacks, the group mounted. Canute and Alfred sniffed around for more to eat, but there was nothing to give them. Though Ivan apologized, it didn't fill their empty bellies.

Davaan climbed behind Wayland on his horse. "We'll look for the second cave and check if Peter returned there and is waiting for us." His tone was hopeful.

The morning warmed—almost too warm—unusual for this time of year. Ivan wedged his fingers between his throat and the cloak's ties, trying to cool himself. Most likely, it was fear and uncertainty. If only it were over, and Ivan and Peter were traveling back to their farm.

A rabbit screamed and raced across their path. Sytha's horse reared and skittered. Bounty jumped and backed into Old Bones. "Whoa, boy," Ivan soothed. "It's only a small rabbit."

"It could be our lunch." Davaan licked his teeth, and his eyes went wide with hunger.

"We can't risk the delay or the commotion," Sytha said, dropping his hand from his bow and arrows. "You wouldn't think there'd be anything living in this area that the ghouls haven't already consumed. More importantly, the smell of a bloody carcass might attract attention to us."

Ivan pulled in a shallow breath. Was the rabbit's scream a warning?

Pine and fir trees thinned the higher they climbed. Ivan looked up, wondering where the second cave was located. They negotiated a couple switchbacks, causing a dizzy feeling from weaving back and forth. *How much longer did they need to travel?*

"There it is!" Ivan stood in Bounty's stirrups, throwing his arm toward a dark opening that could've been mistaken for a shadow since the sun hadn't yet reached it. A few scraggly pines and bushes growing from the rocky ground nearly obscured the opening, but it was easier to spot as they drew closer. They heard a snort, followed by a soft neighing. *Peter or Davaan's horse?* Ivan's mouth dropped open, wanting to yell with happiness. He must have hidden in the second cave just as Davaan had suggested.

Swinging off Bounty, Ivan gave his mount a quick pat on his neck and ordered, "Stay here."

"Wait up!" Sytha hollered. He ran after Ivan, his wand shooting a stream of light from the tip into the dark tunnel.

Ivan rushed inside, pausing after only a few yards. "Peter? Peter, are you here? It's Ivan." He waited for a few moments listening for a response. Sytha came beside him, slowly waving his wand in front of them. The cavity lit up, showing a predictable dirt floor and slick rock sides.

"What's that—over there?" Ivan pointed to the back, toward the west wall of the second cave.

When a horse nickered, they stopped and listened. Drawing closer, Ivan exclaimed, "It's Darkly. Peter's horse! Where are you, Peter?" he called desperately. "I'm with Sytha."

"We should've had Davaan follow us." Sytha moved over the rocks with a careful and lithe step. "He made the arrangements with your brother."

Only the dripping of water off the cave's wall broke the gloomy silence until a flock of bats left the ceiling and wall crevices, darting madly toward the exit. They both ducked and covered their heads with their arms.

"Whew." Ivan exhaled. "That was scary. I almost fainted from shock."

Sytha put his hand on Ivan's shoulder. "Since when are you afraid of a few little ol' bats?"

Carefully, Ivan approached the horse and patted its cheek. "Darkly, I won't hurt you. Look, he still has his bridle and saddle, and that means Peter can't be far away. Where's your master?" he asked the horse, feeling sad and disappointed.

"Blasted!" Sytha said. "He's not here. That means we have to walk up to the big mountain and find a back or side entrance. It's getting riskier, and I don't like it. But..." He halted and pointed into the gloom. "I see something protruding over there."

Behind a pile of rocks, the end of a large sack stuck out. "Peter brought us something, I'm sure of it." Sytha rushed toward his finding and dragged the bag from its hiding place. He removed the string and stared inside. "Just look at that! Anything you'd want for a delicious lunch—and more."

Ivan grinned. His stomach already rumbled with hunger.

"Let's show it to Wayland and Davaan. The beagles will be especially happy." Sytha handed his wand to Ivan to light their way while he hefted the bag over his shoulder.

"Come on, Darkly." Ivan reached for the horse's reins and he followed.

"What's this?" Wayland scurried in their direction when they emerged from the cave. He helped settle the sack onto the ground. "A bag of rocks?"

"Peter thought to leave some food." Ivan's tone dropped. "But he's not here—only his horse."

Alfred woofed and then whimpered. Clearly, he was not happy being left behind. The beagles backed away when the black horse lifted a foot and pawed the ground.

Sebastian approached Darkly and stroked its forehead and neck. "You are a striking stallion," he mumbled. "Now, where is Peter?"

Chapter 17

The Attack of the Ghouls

"We'll leave our horses here in the second cave," Wayland said, "and travel on foot. It'll be easier to dodge any lurking ghouls if we have bushes and rocks to hide behind."

Ivan clutched his hand over the hilt of The Challenger, grateful to have it by his side.

"I noticed a stream and a couple of pools of water in the cave, so the animals will have something to drink." Sytha brushed off his white tunic and dark leggings, which by now had become soiled with mud and dirt. "Do you suppose the stream runs from the top of the mountain all the way to the last cave where we found Davaan? If so, maybe that's how Zupine escaped the ghouls." When no one answered or showed much interest, he shrugged and dropped the subject.

It was a bit early, but since they'd not eaten much breakfast and were concerned for their next meal, Wayland pulled various items from the bag. "The bread feels almost fresh," he said, squeezing it to prove his point. "And look, a few cans of cooked venison. Vegetables—blah, not for me." He handed them to Sytha. "Some apples and green beans. Here's a jar of jam—good on bread." He licked his bottom lip.

They'd hurriedly finished their early lunch and filled

their canteens at the stream. Remembering Zupine's warning, they stashed the food bag and their rucksacks behind an alcove in the second cave.

Ivan stooped and ruffled Canute and Alfred's ears. "You'll have to stay and protect the horses until we return. Do you understand?" They looked up at him with sad eyes and whimpered at their master's departure. "Stay," he repeated.

They set out on foot, where they traversed a trail that appeared to wind up to the final mountain. Ivan took a deep breath. *What awaits us? Is Peter sitting on a ghoul throne, next to Hoxx, holding the King's Scepter? I don't think so. It would be a stain on our family name—not that anyone would ever know—except me.*

An hour passed as they trudged up the rough terrain, shifting the canteen straps over their shoulders, alert for anything suspicious. Their surroundings were quiet, not a sound. Though he missed his beagles by his side, Ivan was satisfied they were safer at the second cave guarding the horses. Sebastian did not stay behind to watch the animals—his services would be needed if they collided with the ghouls.

The warm sun disappeared. The sky grew stone-gray as rain clouds formed. They all seemed to notice the change in the weather at the same time, and worried looks etched their faces. At one point, they stopped to rest their weary legs and took refreshing drinks from their canteens.

Wayland looked past a few spindly trees and stared. "The mountain is smoking again, but I don't see any fire."

"I keep wondering if it's a warning to uninvited visitors like us," Sebastian said. His eyebrows lurched.

"The mountain and ghouls won't give you any notice." Davaan rubbed the flat of his hand over the scars on his chest. "They'll stampede us in a moment and peel our skins for their dinner." He turned to spit. "Savage beasts!"

"I thought Zephyrus wanted to rid the Forest of those horrible creatures." Wayland met Sebastian's gaze, challenging him for an answer.

"Zephyrus wants a lot of things for the betterment of the Forest, but it takes scheduling and the cooperation of our garrisons." He raised his shoulders. "Time eventually solves all things."

Wayland blinked and pulled his head back, like he didn't understand the comment or didn't believe it would ever happen.

Ivan held out his palm. "I felt a few sprinkles."

"It's clouding fast. We'd better hurry." Davaan stared at the sky, and he twitched his nose.

They agreed and plodded on.

Stepping next to Sebastian, Ivan took the old man's arm to help him navigate the loose stones that dislodged and tumbled down the mountainside.

"The trail on the right seems to go back on itself." Wayland turned and gave a nod toward the same direction they'd just come. "It could lead to a back way. We should follow it."

"I think we should continue in this direction." Davaan pointed to the left path. "It seems to climb to the top and will take us to the main entrance."

"How do you know? You've never been here before." Wayland's dark eyebrows jerked in, and his nostrils widened.

"I still have a werewolf's instinct, you know?"

Davaan shot back, his voice terse.

"Is that to say that I don't, just because I've transitioned into a man?"

Davaan's shoulders rose. "Could be. Otherwise, you'd have smelled my blood and those dead ghouls back in the first cave."

"Well, I didn't smell anything except wet earth. I was too worried about what was groaning in the darkness. I was worried about you." Now Wayland moved closer to his brother, his breathing fast, and his fists tightened at his side.

"If you were so worried about me, why weren't you on time? I wouldn't have been attacked and nearly clawed to death."

They glared at each other, their bodies quivering with anger.

Ivan intercepted. "I'd give anything to have my brother with me so we could argue. I miss him so much."

The wolf brothers relaxed and lowered their heads in shame. They stood for a few moments, staring at the ground. Wayland lifted his eyes, gave a glance at Davaan, and after some hesitation, they threw their arms around each other. "You're right," Wayland said. "We're lucky to have each other. "Now, let's follow the trail that Davaan suggested." He picked up his canteen that had dropped to the ground and patted his brother's back.

Sebastian bobbed his head, obviously pleased about the end of the heated argument.

Without further discussion, they continued on the upward path to what they thought was the main entrance to the cave—and where they'd hoped to find Peter.

A cold wind rushed toward them, and the sprinkles became stronger. Smoke that spewed from the mountaintop blew away and disappeared.

"What are we to do?" Ivan asked, pulling the hood of the Long Dark Cloak over his head.

"Keep going and watch your footing," Sytha replied, making a sweeping hand toward the mountain ahead. He checked his bow and arrows and then stroked the leather quiver with his wand that Ivan had returned. Exhaling, he seemed satisfied.

It occurred to Ivan with a nasty jolt that Sebastian's powers of healing could fade if the rain drenched the Long Dark Cloak that Ivan wore over his shoulders. They would need its healing ability more than ever during their journey into the deadly mountain.

"Sebastian," Ivan called and halted. "Please disappear into the cloak. This rain is doing you no good."

"A capital suggestion! I'm slowing you down with these old legs of mine." His spirit turned into warm brown and lavender smoke, swirled into a circle, and vanished into the cloak's fabric. The spirit gave a little push against Ivan's back when he entered. "Aah, much better." Sebastian sighed.

"That's amazing." Davaan stared wide-eyed at the phenomenon. "The cloak has many mysteries. What does Sebastian do in there all day?"

Stifling a laugh, Ivan shoved his cold hands into the cloak's pockets. "I've never asked. Someday he'll have to tell us." He heard Sebastian's low chuckle.

Ivan removed and folded the cloak. He shoved it under his jacket and buttoned it to his neck.

"I look like I've just had a huge meal." Ivan laughed and patted his bulging belly.

"I think it'll work," Sebastian's voice was muffled. "Keep a watch for Zello. He may yet meet us somewhere on the mountain."

"But he hasn't." Wayland snorted. "You can never depend on that spoiled dragon."

"We have to keep going." Sytha wiped the rain from his eyes. His long, silvery hair and face were soaked, as was everyone's. "The trail is already slick." His next step proved this when he slipped on some wet, dark stones.

Usually so graceful and quick on his feet, Sytha tried to right himself. Davaan rushed and grabbed him with strong arms, preventing an injurious fall.

"Thanks," Sytha said, throwing Davaan a grateful glance.

Off to their right was a cluster of mountain bushes woven with sharp thorns. Ivan saw a mouse peek out his head and then dash for cover. *Wouldn't my beagles enjoy chasing a rodent?* He greatly missed their company, but he was glad they were safe in the second cave along with the horses.

"Someone's coming!" Wayland stopped abruptly and held up his right hand.

"I smell them, too." Davaan's gaze darted all around. "Ghouls are coming down the path toward us, grunting and snorting like rabid dogs. Let's hide—there, behind those thorny bushes. It's our only chance."

"Have your weapons ready," Wayland said as he pulled his knife from a sheath attached to his belt. He dropped behind the shrubbery.

They all squatted on their hands and knees in the mud, hiding while the rain continued to saturate their heads and clothing. For a moment, Ivan felt the urge to sneeze, but he held his muddy hand over his nose and mouth and managed to smother it.

"You are right. Ghouls! " Ivan hunkered a little

lower. Since he and Sytha were the tallest, the scraggly scrubs barely hid them.

The ghouls' big feet slapped against the wet path. Their clothes were tattered and filthy. They wore shapeless tunics or ragged knee-length breeches with sleeveless tops made from skins of some kind of animal, tied with strips of hide for closure. But it was their faces that caused the group to gasp, except for Davaan, who'd already had battle with them.

"Their heads are too big for their squat bodies," Sytha whispered, with the palm of his hand held against his mouth. "The ugliest creatures I've ever seen."

Ivan had to agree. It was like as their long, grayish faces had melted. Tiny eyes, a wide extended nose that met and overlapped their bottom lip, with two teardrop-shaped nostril holes on top. Their flesh appeared soft, folded over itself under the eyes and cheekbones with drooping skin around their necks, arms, and bare legs. Light or deep-brown tuffs of hair peeked in all directions.

"You should see this collection of misfits," Ivan said quietly to Sebastian.

"How many?" Sebastian spoke from the cloak where it was tightly stuffed under Ivan's jacket.

"Three, I think." Ivan wondered if more trailed behind.

"Take a look at those lethal claws." Davaan shook his head, frowning. "That's what ripped my chest and arms apart." He snarled, and his shoulder muscles tightened. "I'm going to get them all."

"Hold on, brother," Wayland said. "Give them a chance to get closer."

"What if they go to the second cave where they'll find the horses and my beagles?" Ivan scowled. "We must do something."

"I plan to." Suddenly before their eyes, Davaan stood from behind the bushes, his head began to shape-shift into the werewolf that he was. His nose and mouth elongated into a pointed maw, his body distorted, growing long forearms and strong hind legs. Brownish-gray hair sprouted, growing thick and protective on his torso and limbs. Buttons popped off the jacket that Wayland had lent him, and his trousers ripped both inner-leg seams.

Wayland shot up and moved next to his brother. "No, Davaan, don't. We'll help you destroy them."

"You can't stop me now." Claws extended on his large paws. Davaan's jaw opened wide, showing sharp teeth, ready to tear his enemies apart.

The ghouls stopped and stared. Their small eyes opened wider, and their mouths formed a distinctive circle as they watched a man turn into a dangerous beast.

Ivan saw the transformation, just as astonished as the ghouls. He jerked The Challenger from its scabbard, his hand shaking so hard he could scarcely hold it.

Standing slowly, Sytha pulled his wand, rolling it between his thumb and two fingers as though biding his time, evaluating the situation. A smirk of superiority played on the Elften's lips.

Fully changed, the werewolf leaped at the first ghoul, who held a short-handled axe in his hand. He knocked the ugly creature onto his back. Next to him, the second ghoul fell because of the impact, kicking his thick legs into the air, trying to scramble to his feet. He bellowed in some garbled language that was not understandable—and no one cared.

"Here's a lesson to you!" Davaan pinned the first

ghoul, and with unrestrained anger, he chewed through its throat, spitting away the muscle and sinew. He stood on all fours panting, his eyes burning with hatred. He sunk his claw into the ghoul's chest and raked it all the way down to its groin, shredding the dirty tunic as he went. "There, you savage beast. How do you like your flesh being ripped to pieces?"

"Go, Ivan!" The Challenger yelled. "Kill the third ghoul before it attacks."

Wayland was in a dance of stealth and skill, wielding his knife against the second ghoul, who'd clumsily stumbled to his feet. *Wayland was playing with him.*

Ivan rushed forward. The Challenger rose. He gripped and followed the command of metal, ready to strike and remove the ghoul's big head. The creature snarled, baring teeth, and gave what sounded like a chuckle, muffled through his odd-placed nostrils. For some reason, it unnerved Ivan, and he froze.

"Strike, now," The Challenger shouted, "or he'll get away and snitch."

Raising the sword once more, Ivan's lungs throbbed with heat and fear. When the ghoul backed away, ready to run, Ivan swung his weapon with all his strength, aiming for the neck. Meeting his mark, the head went flying and landed with a splat in the mud. The squinty eyes closed. Ivan couldn't dwell on having killed another—man? He turned to see Wayland crack the second ghoul in his mouth with a swift kick of his boot, breaking its front teeth and jaw. Grabbing the axe, Wayland tightened his hands around the wooden handle and brought it down swiftly. The sharp edge thumped against the creature's skull, cracking it open.

"Bravo." Sytha clapped. "You all did an exemplary job." Leaning back, he crossed his arms and showed a contented smile.

Ivan gave the Elften a *look*, while wanting to collapse with fatigue onto the ground and recover his breath. He wished he had four legs like Davaan for support. After a moment, he wiped the blood from The Challenger's blade on a small patch of wet grass and shoved it into the scabbard buckled at his waist.

"I commend you," The Challenger said to Ivan in a sonorous voice. "You haven't forgotten the moves you've learned. In fact, you've improved your speed and accuracy."

It was no consolation to Ivan. "I promised myself I'd never kill another man, but look…"

"I understand better than anyone, Ivan," The Challenger sympathized. "I've killed more men than I care to revisit. Remember when I told you this? You must protect the ones you love no matter the cost."

"Yes." He lowered his chin and closed his eyes. "I remember."

"Let's drag the bodies behind the bushes." Wayland grabbed the ghoul's bloody and severed head and gave it a toss in that direction.

Davaan was turning back into a human…his cranium changed first. The thick hair dropped away, and his expanded jaw receded. Eyes moved to the front of his face, and his dark, full beard returned. Shoulders widened to accommodate his arms, and his wolfish hind legs straightened to human thighs and calves. Feet appeared, with five toes on each foot. His chest heaved for oxygen—his rage still boiling. In a swift move, he pulled his now ripped, seamless trousers over his hairy legs.

"Your zipper's open." Sytha pointed with his wand in a casual manner.

Glancing down, the werewolf turned pink with embarrassment, and then he snickered. His anger subsided.

"It's a small thing compared to the ragged rips in your trousers," Ivan said with innocence.

Sytha, grasping the unintended irony, tipped back his head and laughed along with Wayland. Ivan didn't understand what was so funny, and that made the comment that much more hilarious.

"Are you mocking me?" Davaan zipped up while his laughter faded into hiccups.

"You'll excuse my lack of involvement," Sytha said with an air of arrogance. "There were only three of them, and you handled the job like experts."

Wayland snorted. "You can take the next three ghouls that come along, then."

"There'll be plenty where we're going." Davaan smoothed his straight, dark hair and lifted his eyebrows at them as a dire warning. "Now, where are my shoes?" He looked around until he found them half buried in the mud. "Dang it!"

When he examined a long scratch on his arm, Wayland winced at his bloody and torn shirt. Thankfully, it wasn't too serious and the only injury they'd suffered.

"I think it's time I came out to be helpful," Sebastian said.

Ivan unbuttoned his jacket and removed the cloak, giving it a shake.

Wayland wrapped the hem of the Long Dark Cloak around his arm. "You know what to do, Sebastian."

After a few moments had passed, Wayland let out a relieved puff of breath. "Many thanks."

"My pleasure to be of service." Sebastian worked his magic and sealed the cut.

Sebastian materialized quickly with a swirl of ochre-colored smoke and changed into a man. He adjusted his rumpled, tan-colored tunic and pulled the sleeves to his wrists. His hair was disheveled, and his face grave with concern.

They congratulated each other on how well they worked together, and after only a brief hesitation, they dragged the three corpses toward the bushes and rolled them into the thorniest parts.

"That's one fancy sword you have, Ivan." Davaan stared at the weapon covetously. He reached out, and Ivan handed it to him to examine.

Ivan pointed at the ornately carved hilt, embedded with a golden cross and images of oak leaves, acorns, and vines that twisted around it. "It feels just right in the curve of my hands." He ran his fingers down the flat of the silver blade that read in English Gothic script, *The Challenger*. "We've fought many enemies together," he said with pride. "Without this weapon by my side, I'd be dead and forgotten by now."

"Ah, you are a good student, Ivan," The Challenger said, "and I'm proud to fight with you for the betterment of the Forest."

"Ooh!" Davaan leaped back, his mouth opened. "It talks. A piece of metal actually talks. What do you think of that, Wayland?"

Wayland let out a squawk of laughter. "So does the cloak when Sebastian is inside, you may have noticed— as does the Golden Lantern when Joseph's spirit resides there."

Davaan licked his tongue over his teeth. "How can I get me one of these things?"

"Sorry." Ivan took the sword and shoved it back into the scabbard.

"It's another one of those Ancient Relics you talked about?" Davaan stared at it, and his eyes opened wider.

"No," The Challenger said. "I did not choose to become an Ancient Relic. In my thousand years, I've killed many men and don't wish to kill more. Though it seems, I must. I'm a servant and a defender of Zephyrus and our magnificent Forest."

"So many things I didn't know about." Davaan scratched his forehead and glanced at his brother.

"There are more mysteries to learn in our mystical Forest." Sytha tapped the quiver that held his wand. "You'll learn them as you go."

"We'd better leave now." Wayland gave his brother a nod.

They cautiously followed Davaan up the trail.

Chapter 18

The Mountain of Smoke and Fire

The mountain rumbled and belched a long puff of smoke along with spurts of fire, affecting the sky overhead to turn hazy and gray. Wayland slowed his pace and stopped. Turning to Davaan, he said, "They know we're here."

Davaan shook his head. "Maybe not. Anything could set the mountain off at any time. Only the Woman of Flame has control of it. I think that's the rumor, but I can't be sure."

The remark calmed Ivan—somewhat. His belly was already tight, and he felt more uncertain as they continued to climb. Glancing around, he saw no place to hide or take cover, only a few large boulders and wind-whipped shrubs here and there. At least the rain had stopped, and they were drying out. Still, their damp clothes were uncomfortable, clinging to them. Fortunately, The Long Dark Cloak had been protected.

When they rounded the next bend of the mountain climb, they knew they were finally approaching the top. Sytha lifted his head and pointed. "There, behind that huge outcropping of dark rocks and ragged pines."

"What?" Wayland stared.

"I believe it's the ghoul's cave home."

"I don't see it." Ivan squinted in the distance.

"That's because the entrance has a large gray stone covering it." Sytha faced them. A deep scowl wrinkled his pale forehead.

"Now, why would they do something stupid like that?" Ivan asked.

"Yeah, how do they get in and out?" Wayland took a step forward, cocking his head. "They must use a back or side entrance like Zupine said. Or, maybe they know we're coming and closed the hole."

"That's a frightening thought." Davaan drew to his brother's side, and they walked together.

Continuing on, they stumbled up the slippery path. Just as they reached the outcropping of rocks, they heard countless pounding feet.

"Oh, no," they groaned as quietly as they could.

"It's horse hooves." Ivan ducked behind the rocks, as did the others. "Do ghouls ride horses?" He pulled The Challenger from its hold and squatted lower. He had trouble keeping the thumping of his heart quiet, certain it would alert the unknown threat that approached.

Hundreds of mounted men thundered in their view and halted near the cave's entrance.

Ivan sighed with relief when he spotted their uniforms and flag colors that he recognized from his first visit during the terrifying Forest War.

Commander Simon's soldiers appeared with blue plumes atop their helmets, carrying Forest-colored flags, breastplates, and shields that were slick with rain. The green plumes of Commander Greendyn's soldiers, who patrolled the northern region of the Forest, rode behind Simon's regiment in an orderly fashion. The men gripped swords, bows and arrows, spears, and mace, looking determined and impatient. Rounding the rocks,

Sytha waved vigorously to several of his own Elften brothers, who were positioned in front of the Wolflords, all armed for battle.

Davaan approached Commander Simon with dread in his voice. "What are you doing here? You weren't supposed to be part of this rescue. I promised only a few of us for Peter's safety." He turned and motioned for Wayland, Sytha, Ivan, and Sebastian to join him.

Simon tugged at his large bay horse's reins and removed his silver helmet. "More importantly, what in the world happened to you and Wayland? Did you already slay half the ghoul population?"

"Three ghouls met us on the lower part of this mountain and attacked us." Davaan tried to pull his shredded shirt together.

"I hope you won the battle, but I'm not too sure," Simon said and shifted his weight. "To answer your question, we received emergency orders from Zephyrus to wipe out the ghouls. I was worried we might be too late to save you five vagabonds from their dinner plate." His deep frown showed his fatigue and worry.

"So, Zephyrus finally decided it was time to rid the Forest of this menace?" Davaan cupped his hands around his mouth for his words to be heard over the noise and confusion of the horses.

"Zephyrus recalled what they did to Zupine and what they could do to you," Simon yelled back, looking directly at Ivan. "Those vile flesh-eating creatures don't belong in our Forest—or anyplace in the world, for that matter. Their eating habits are a real embarrassment."

Pivoting his head, Simon asked, "Where are your horses and the beagles? Did you leave them behind in one of the caves?"

Wayland answered, "We thought it would be safer for them, and they wouldn't get hurt."

"Good decision." Simon saluted and wiped the dampness from his brow.

"How did you come without us seeing you?" Ivan asked.

One of the soldiers pulled off his helmet and answered, "There's a west side path, though longer, but not so steep. It allowed our wagons to make the assent more easily and for the men to stop and take a break from time to time. You know, eat and pee in the bushes." He grinned.

"Though longer, it was the best route for us," Simon said. "Besides, since you trudged up the east side, this gave us an advantage of covering any escape route for the ghouls."

"Dismount, men," Commanders Simon and Greendyn shouted, and the soldiers threw themselves off their horses, stretched their legs, and examined their surroundings.

Approaching the giant round stone with a large hole in the middle, Ivan rubbed his hand over the rough surface, and Wayland touched it with his fingertips. "It looks like a huge millstone, doesn't it?" Ivan said and patted it several times, testing its solidity.

"How will we remove it?" Wayland's brow crinkled.

"I'll take care of that little detail." Sytha withdrew his wand. "Let me know when you and your men are ready." He turned on his heel and addressed Commander Simon.

"Hold on a minute." Simon slipped off his horse and stepped closer to Ivan. He reached out and fingered the medallion around Ivan's neck and gave a quick but genuine smile. "Congratulations. You'll be fighting the Woman of Flame because of this medal."

"Me? Why?" He panicked. "How did I suddenly move into the most dangerous position of battle? I'm not experienced to kill the monster that lives inside—whatever she is."

Simon's eyebrow rose with a look of sympathy. "You wear the Forest's Medallion for Bravery, and you have The Challenger at your side. I watched at the trial as Zephyrus awarded you this honor. These should protect you, and it qualifies you for the job."

"B-but, Simon. I don't want the job. What if she-she blows fire at me? I'll be fried like an egg in an instant."

"Only two members of the Forest are honored to have this medallion. You and Zello. Our Forest dragon was summoned to meet us here, so we'll have to be patient until he arrives. In the meantime—" Simon turned and shouted at his soldiers. "—A few of you, give your horses and protective gear to our brave warriors here."

Wayland and Davaan climbed on the backs of dark chestnut horses, but they declined the helmets and shields offered to them. Sytha selected a light-colored animal with a blonde mane and tail. It neighed at the Elften, lifting his beautiful head with approval. "I guess that endorses my selection," he said, stroking his mount's glossy neck and combing his fingers through her silky mane.

"And you, Ivan, wait until Zello arrives." Simon finished, "—for your ride."

Fear shot across Ivan's chest and arms. "M-my ride—on Zello?"

Simon waved Ivan's comment away.

"How many men do you have?" Sytha interrupted Ivan's sputter of fear.

"About two hundred total—a hundred are mine and about the same for Greendyn's soldiers, something like that." Simon turned to point. "In the rear are five wagons, several carrying food and medical supplies. The Elftens and Wolflords will be lending their special expertise to the final battle. I believe we will claim victory for the mountain. Peace will finally return to this northern part of the Forest."

"But at what cost?" Sytha clutched the quiver's leather strap that held his magical wand.

Simon's response was a raised shoulder and a shake of his head. "Whatever it is, the price must be paid." His gaze met with Ivan's stark face.

Ivan's attention swept over the troops, watching them act bravely, anxious to fight the blood-thirsty creatures inside the cave. He was thrilled the commanders and soldiers had showed up to fight the battle with them. Though pleased that Zello was expected, he couldn't figure how the dragon fit into this plan of attack.

"There's never a guarantee in combat," Simon said. His men remounted, checking their weapons.

"Simon?"

"Yes, Ivan."

"How-how do I fight this Woman of flame? I can't kill a woman, n-no matter how ferocious she is."

"Don't think about that." Simon slapped his gauntlets against the palm of his hand, his eyebrows drew together. "I've heard a distant rumor that she's in disguise and will morph into a strange kind of dragon after she sheds her outer female skin."

"Simon?"

"Yes, Ivan."

"I'm terrified." He swallowed hard and wiped sweat from his brow.

"You have every right to be," the commander replied. "And—where is that darn dragon, anyway? He was supposed to be here by now and help us." Simon's impatience increased. "Well, we can't wait for our privileged dragon to join us." He growled and spat on the ground.

The armies moved into position near the entrance. Ivan, Sytha, Wayland, and Davaan sat on their borrowed horses behind the first twenty hand-selected soldiers who would enter the cave first.

"I think it's best you disappear into the cloak where it's safe," Ivan said to Sebastian, who now stood on the ground next his mounted friends.

"My very intentions." With that statement, Sebastian swirled into a bluish and violet smoke and entered the garment. "Be careful, Ivan, and don't do anything foolish."

"That's what I'm hoping." His voice squeaked.

"Roll away the stone," Simon shouted.

Withdrawing his wand, Sytha tapped it with his index finger. Light exploded from the tip as he waved it into the air. An arc of illumination shot charges of lightning that circled the stone as though electrifying it. Within moments it began to move at Sytha's bidding, rolling back slowly as it crunched gravel beneath its path. He coaxed it to move back farther and farther until the mouth of the cave showed its menacing blackness inside.

Two of the front soldiers raised Forest flags with an

image of Zello blowing fire from his fierce snout. The other eighteen hand-selected men rode into the cave. Their horses' hooves split solid layers of dirt where hundreds of ghouls had trampled the earth. Brittle bones littered their pathway, stripped clean, and tossed carelessly next to the damp walls. Commander Simon bellowed an order to the remaining soldiers, "Some of you stay outside and guard the entrance. Others must leave their horses and come in on foot. If there is an onslaught of ghouls, you'll want full use of your weapons."

"It's mighty dark in here," Lieutenant Pezzuline turned to say. "You may not need your helmets either. They will only impair your vision." With that, most of the men removed their head coverings and dropped them near the opening of the cave. A couple soldiers, accustomed to following up, retrieved them for safekeeping.

Ivan entered the bleak hole, covering his nose with the sleeve of the Long Dark Cloak. His eyes watered from the overpowering stench. Men behind him coughed and gagged while Ivan's borrowed horse whinnied and balked. Sytha, now next to him, leaned over his horse and heaved. His delicate stomach churning, the Elften threw up a second time. The wand's light flickered as it bounced over the cave's interior until he could wipe his teary eyes and right himself in the saddle.

"This is a miserable place." Wayland coughed as he made the comment.

After some moments, Ivan's eyes adjusted. He looked for any signs of Peter or someone human, but there were none. *Where is the horde of ghouls we expected to find when we entered the gloomy hole? Are they hiding—waiting for the best time to attack?* All was quiet except the rushing river that flowed in the back of the cave, giving off sudden bursts of flames on the surface. *What caused the leaps of fire?*

He was glad Alfred and Canute were not with them to get into trouble. They'd likely bark and jump at the ghouls until they rebelled, cornered and angry.

The cave was humongous, wide with a high ceiling, and dripping water down the black walls. To their left, a steep, crudely chiseled stone stairway climbed to the second floor. Ivan remembered the Ancient Relics were once held captive in an upper cave after they'd been stolen from the Sanctuary of Truth. Joseph, the spirit imbued in the Golden Lantern, had told them he hung on a ceiling hook and was held as a prisoner. Joseph further explained that Cecil, the troll, had eventually taken the lantern away.

Along both sides of the cave walls were a series of dark, roughly arched doorways—hiding whom or what? Ivan sucked in his breath, imagining a swarm of flesh-eaters stampeding the soldiers and horses, attacking them, chewing their skin and muscles, and spitting out their bones.

"Charming accommodations," Sytha said sarcastically, tilting toward Ivan.

Wayland laughed nervously. "Take a look at that." He pointed to the right of the staircase.

They turned to see a long, stone dais with rough columns on both sides. It had two stone chairs with a faded British Crown print fabric covering them. Above the thrones, carved into the wall, were portraits of Hoxx and what must have been his queen. "What a handsome couple," Wayland snickered.

"It's devilishly hot in here," a soldier fanned his face. "Do you suppose the water in the river is fit to drink?"

"I wouldn't." Davaan shook his head.

Ivan wondered about the water, too. Sweat collected on his chest and under his arms. His hairline, saturated with wetness, threatened to drip into his eyes. He wanted to loosen the Long Dark Cloak and remove his woolen jacket. But he didn't dare.

They moved toward the flowing river, back into the cave, where it was much cooler. There were no signs of the inhabitants, only the sounds of horses whinnying or soldiers mumbling and giving orders. Suddenly, a series of wall torches lit the inky blackness. Ivan jerked back in his saddle, startled by the brightness. "Who lit all the torches?"

A series of snaps sounded, along with a click. Then a loud bubbling noise—like that made by a giant sea creature rising from the ocean. Up, up, out of the water came the shape of a huge woman who let out a long earsplitting scream. As her tall figure rose higher and higher, orange and red flames were drawn from the water, encompassing the lower part of her nude torso.

Davaan's horse reared, and Ivan's animal pulled back, its eyes bulging. Reaching over, Wayland grabbed the bridle of Davaan's steed, trying to soothe him with a calming voice. "It's okay, boy. It's okay."

The woman's long dark hair swept back from her high forehead and cascaded down her front, where it covered her nakedness. She was about the biggest and ugliest creature—woman—Ivan had ever seen. Flames reached to her navel but did not burn or consume her. And yet, he felt the intense heat on his face and hands.

With terror in his voice, Wayland said, "She's one mean-looking Amazon!"

Noticeably masculine in build with a square jaw, huge eyes, and flaring nostrils, the Woman of Flame glared at the soldiers that crowded in and gawked at her.

"There she is!" Sytha pointed and pressed his lips together. "The very thing Zephyrus tried to warn us about."

"I-I never imagined she would be s-so large and—terrifying." Ivan's teeth chattered in his own ears.

"Stay focused on her alone." Sytha raised his wand to illuminate her full body. "Once your attention is averted, she may fry you with her hot breath."

"Why would she do such a thing?" Ivan's chin trembled.

The woman crossed her muscular arms over her chest. Her penetrating gaze moved from Ivan and scanned the crowded cave chamber. Lifting her head, she blew flames from her mouth as if punctuating her first question. "Who are you that enter here uninvited?"

When no one answered, she said, "Foolish men who wander into my cave home and offer themselves for dinner. Who will be first?" Her mocking smile revealed long, yellowed teeth while a wisp of gray smoke seeped from her nose.

"Speak!" Her strong voice vibrated off the cave's ceiling. "Why have you come?"

Forcing himself to answer, Ivan said, "I-I'm here to find m-my…" His fear betrayed the words that stuck in his throat.

"I know you." Her wing-shaped eyebrows lifted high as she leaned frighteningly close.

Ivan shrunk back, her foul breath nearly causing him

to faint.

"You are that boy from the outside that I've been hearing about, a hero of sorts. What do you want?"

He stared into her eyes, not daring to look away. "My b-brother. I'm looking for my brother, P-Peter. I've heard he is here, and I've come to take him...away."

She blinked. "Your—ah, yes. I do see the likeness. Both tall, your faces are the same shape, but your hair is dark as this cave, and his is light as the sun."

"Yes! Yes, that's him. Is he here? I know he wants to go home."

"Does he, now?" She sneered.

Chapter 19

Riding Zello

One of the soldiers coughed into his hand. *Or was it a warning from Commander Simon?* Ivan tried to swallow saliva that never materialized. *Did I say something wrong? Should I have said nothing but only challenged the Woman of Flame to battle?* He tried to steady his horse. It had the good sense of not wanting to be in the presence of this menacing woman—whatever she was.

"I'm sure Peter wants to go home." Ivan tried to keep his voice steady. "He asked for my help."

"Oh, did he now?"

He gave a nod and closed his mouth, no longer trusting his own words.

"Keep still, Ivan," Sebastian whispered from the cloak. "She's playing with you."

"Well, Peter is here," she said. "He is our prisoner, chained to a wall in an upstairs chamber."

Ivan gasped. "Peter is here—chained?"

"You better not hurt him," Wayland yelled, raising his fist and shaking it.

"Hurt? Hmmm…" She allowed another wisp of smoke to curl from her nostrils. "He did mention this morning he didn't feel so well. The ghouls have tortured him only a little bit—but for good reasons, I assure you."

"Why?" Ivan was stunned. He thought his brother was on friendly terms with the ghouls, who were controlled by Tereus, the demon of the deep caverns. *Is Peter no longer in allegiance with Tereus?*

"Peter had pledged himself to us. But now we are sure he has betrayed us by inviting you and your army to destroy the ghouls. That is not a nice thing to do." She let out a loud roar and sent a long column of fire that shot over the heads of the soldiers. Their horses jumped, knocked into each other, bucked, and screamed in terror.

No wonder Davaan cautioned them about inviting others. Did Peter turn away from these blood-thirsty heathens, endangering his own life?

"No! It's not Peter's fault." Davaan rushed his horse forward at the woman, waving his arms to get her attention. "I told them not to bring other warriors—that it wasn't safe. I made that very clear. But Zephyrus sent the soldiers on his own accord for this boy's protection."

"Hmmm. Is that so? Well, it doesn't much matter. The damage is done." The fire-women lifted her head, indicating the subject was closed, and she yawned in their faces.

Ivan gulped, wondering if they'd soon be cooked alive.

"What's that around your neck?" Her focus suddenly changed as she bent forward and stared at the circle of metal around Ivan's neck. Her eyes opened wide.

He touched the Forest's Medallion for Bravery, wondering why a piece of jewelry would interest the fire-and-smoke-spewing Woman of Flame.

"It-it was awarded to me just yesterday—for reasons—" He couldn't think fast enough to give her a good answer, afraid anything he said would sound like a challenge to fight.

The woman pulled back, making a choking sound. Her brow rippled with what might've been shock. "I know of only one other living creature who was awarded such an honor, and that was Zello, the Forest's dragon."

Ivan's eyebrows shot high. *How did she know Zello?*

She hummed and pursed her thick lips.

When a shadow passed over the entrance, blocking light from the outside, a commotion broke from the soldiers and commanders. Something had drastically changed. Simon and his trusted men in front turned around and gawked. Simon's eyebrows lifted, and then a grin spread over his face.

"Well, speak of the rascal himself!" The Woman of Flame's upper lip pulled into a suspicious grimace. "What in blazes are you doing here?"

"Zello!" Simon pulled his horse aside to make way for the dragon to enter. His men did the same, realizing the dragon's bulk needed a wide berth.

"Our loyal castle dragon," Wayland yelled, pumping his fist into the air.

"Hello, cousin!" Zello's deep voice rang out and bounced off the cave walls. "Step aside, men, let me through."

"Cousin?" several people echoed, and they turned to stare at each other.

Ivan compared the two. "The Fire Woman is related to Zello? How can that be?"

The dragon lowered his shiny-webbed wings next to his large, dark body while the soldiers and Wolflords jerked their mounts away for their honored guest.

"We were hoping you'd come," Commander Simon

said and saluted.

"I was ordered here by Zephyrus." The dragon swiveled his long neck, studying the layout of the enormous cave and the army that surrounded him. His feet crunched noisily on a thick layer of bones under his immense weight. "Ah, I see you've all met my cousin, Manila, also known as the Woman of Flame."

Simon's jaw tightened.

"We were once close friends." Zello's glare softened a bit. "But she chose a more dangerous path."

"And why are you here?" she asked with a cold scowl, leaning back, her arms once again crossing over her immense chest.

"Now, why do you think?" Zello lumbered near the river, drawing in closer to his cousin. "I'm here to tidy up, do some light dusting, sweep these filthy floors a bit." He hunched his massive shoulders, chuckling at his own joke.

Some of the men laughed, probably from a feeling of relief.

"I didn't know Zello had a sense of humor," one of the Wolflords said.

"Whew. You sure keep it hot for a cave." Zello gazed around, like he was searching for an outlet of cool air.

It occurred to Ivan that Zello might not be too fond of him, since he'd snatched the Golden Lantern from his claws when Ivan was flying on the back of Fluorescence. At the moment, there didn't seem to be any animosity in the dragon's eyes—maybe he didn't remember the incident. Ivan hoped.

"Do you plan to do battle with me, cousin Zello? Not a wise idea. If so, you will lose your life."

"You knew this day would come, Manila, when all the conditions were just right."

"What conditions?"

"Me being here, for one." Zello snorted. "My good friends are in danger of your hot breath and your horde of ghouls." He eyed the many arched doorways lining the cave walls. "Where are your little flesh-eaters? I expected them to greet us—maybe throw a party. Have a bit of dinner and cake together. You know, nice and friendly like."

"They are here, never doubt it, and we will enjoy a fine banquet tonight."

Ivan shivered all the way to his knees, wondering how Zello could be so frivolous with his conversation. For a moment, Ivan imagined what it'd feel like to have his chest raked into patches of skin. *Is it too late for us to escape?*

Raising his head, Zello roared, blowing out a stream of fire and smoke that could rival the mountains eruption on any day. Horses screamed and struck the air with their front hooves, knocking into each other. Soldiers struggled to stay seated and pulled back on their bridles. "Whoa, boy, whoa," they called, fighting to bring calm.

"Very impressive, Zello. You always were a showoff." the woman mocked while flames from the river suddenly exploded, sending flashes of fire into the cave's interior. The men in front jerked their horses back so as not to be ignited. Ivan and Wayland ducked, covering their heads with their arms to avoid the dangerous sparks.

Laughing, Zello taunted his cousin, "When we were youngsters, my fire used to scare you." He hunched down and tucked his long tail around his body with purpose.

"Not anymore. I've grown up and have an army of my own. They have sworn their allegiance to me, and I protect them from intruders like you. You'd better get out now before I give the command to my little flesh-eaters—as you so fondly call them, to attack with a vengeance."

Turning to face Ivan, Zello said, "Step here on my shoulder and grab one of those fleshy spines on my back and pull yourself up."

"Wait—me?" He hesitated. "You want me to—?"

"There isn't much time," Sytha warned. "She'll soon release the ghouls, and we'll be forced to do battle with them. The idea is to kill her before she has a chance to sound the alarm." The Elften stroked his borrowed mount to bring her under some control.

"But, Sytha, why me? Isn't it enough I killed Porcupine, the Swamp Dragon? I killed two men in Tereus's army, and—and—?"

"Very simple decision." Zello's eyes became larger as he gawked at Ivan. "You wear the Forest's Medallion for Bravery. I have the same medal, and it hangs around my neck. See here." He motioned with his chin. "That means we are a good fit and are meant to fight together. Now, get off your horse and climb on."

His heart pounded rapidly, his mouth dust-dry, but Ivan slipped off his steed and approached the great dragon. It was the closest he'd ever been to him. He glanced at the glistening brown-shingled scales that covered the dragon's body. He remembered the musty smell, a mix of mildew and dust.

"Zello. Please. This is not for me. I've come to find my brother, not to be fried by the Woman of Flame. How about Commander Simon—he's—"

"Stop stalling." Zello flattened his bulk even more to the cave floor to accommodate his rider. Indeed, a duplicate medallion hung from the dragon's neck, swaying, catching flickers of light from the wall torches.

Reluctantly, Ivan stepped onto Zello's muscled forearm, clawing his way up, his hands so cold, he could scarcely grab hold. He was hoping someone would suddenly call out and announce it had been a mistake and that Sytha or Wayland would do the job. Ivan slipped when his boot went out from under him. Just as he was about to tumble down to the floor, he felt Zello's nose catch his backside and give him the upward thrust he needed.

"That's it." Zello raised his head. "Pull yourself up and straddle the open space where the triangular spines have been removed for a rider."

Ivan faltered. His boots kept slipping on Zello's taught muscles. At last, he reached the top and eased his leg over the opening. He settled down and clung to the dragon's fleshy spine in front of him.

"Now hold on tight," Zello instructed and huffed.

His breath coming in gulps, Ivan followed Zello's advice. He repositioned The Challenger at his side when it twisted under his leg.

The soldiers, Elftens, and Wolflords cheered and clapped. "Well done," Sebastian said from the cloak. "Now, do try to stay seated—and stay alive!"

Once on, Ivan shifted but couldn't find a comfortable position. The musty odor of the dragon that he remembered from his first encounter with the flying beast was stronger now, and it reminded him of a damp, mildewed water closet.

Manila let out a loud roar that circled the cave and vibrated off the ceiling. "If you fight me, cousin, my ghouls will tear you and all these men apart."

"I will fight you, and I will win." Zello lifted his snout into the air in a show of defiance.

"So be it." The woman's large eyes glazed over with a white film. Her skin began to split from the top of her skull and then rolled over itself slowly to her feet that were planted in the river. It looked like a thin rubber suit as it folded and slipped down into the water with a splash.

How will she manage to get her skin suit back up over her huge body? Ivan wondered.

A strange-looking beast struggled from the human skin, appearing to look only a bit like Zello. Her head was large like her gigantic winged body. A wide, rough snout resembling a crocodile opened to reveal rows of sharp, yellowed teeth. There were two pairs of horns that swept behind her ears and followed the curve of her backbone. When she stretched herself straight, spines lined the entire length of her, ending at a powerful tail that lashed out like an angry whip. Her muscled arms and legs twitched from either being released from her outer skin or anticipation for the battle to come.

"This handsome creature is Manila," Zello introduced. "Now, there's no need for me to lower my voice. She's mute and can only hear and smell when she's disguised as the Woman of Flame."

Behind him came gasps and shocked conversations from the men. They were as stunned as Ivan after witnessing the strange transformation. The mutant dragon appeared every bit as ferocious as Zephyrus had warned. She bellowed out a heavy stream of red flames.

Her long, dark tongue flickered rapidly, guiding the fiery discharge over the heads of the soldiers.

"Two things you should know." Zello rotated his head to address Ivan. "Even though she has wings, she can't fly—they are only for balance. She can't get her own food to feed herself. That's why she needs the ghouls. They are her food finders. In turn, she protects them from intruders—like us."

"That's a c-comfort to know," Ivan stammered, though he already knew about the symbiotic relationship between the Woman of Flame and the ghouls.

"Do you see those two small knobs on the top of her head, just in front of the pair of long horns? Those are *sensors*—cut them, and it's like a death knell. She won't be able to see anything, and her balance will be compromised—but she can still blow fire, so we must be careful."

Manila raised her wings, stretched, and flapped them in a threatening manner, but Zello had said she could not leave the ground. Ivan hoped this was true.

"Y-you want me to remove those little knobs on her head? How will I get close enough to do that? S-s-she'll gouge me with her horns or fry me with her hot breath." Ivan shifted on Zello's back and wiped his sweaty hands on the Long Dark Cloak. He wished he were riding Bounty and on his way home with his beagles trotting behind. This assignment was beyond his ability and his darkest imagining.

"I'll try to get close enough without endangering your life." Zello turned his head and stared.

"Your thighs are quivering. Are you scared?"

"Out-of-my-mind-terrified."

Chapter 20

Battle with Manila

"Now, hold on!" Zello opened his ribbed wings, took a few lumbering steps, and kicked off from the bone-strewn floor. He rose slowly with pounding effort, far above Manila's head. The huge cave allowed space for him to gain altitude and fly unhindered in any direction. His plan, the dragon told Ivan, was to come in from a high position and catch his cousin off guard, where Ivan would swing The Challenger and slice the sensors from her head. It sounded so simple.

A rise of noise and commotion below momentarily distracted Ivan. He glanced down, seeing men pump their fists into the air, yelling their good wishes.

"This species," Zello said, "cannot release fire when their throat is extended vertically. Any other position is a fire zone."

Ivan's teeth knocked together. He didn't care to test Zello's statement.

Just then, Manila released a gravelly rumble deep in her throat. Zello said she couldn't talk as a dragon, but she could certainly roar! He knew at once the sound was a dire warning, and then…

The thunder of hundreds of screaming voices poured from the arched doorways from both sides of the cave. Ghouls raced out with blood-thirsty cries of battle, waving their clubs, swords, and spears, above their heads. Some had bags of stones over their shoulders and were throwing them at the soldiers and their mounts. Below, Ivan spotted a frightened horse that reared and pawed at the dank air. Neighing in terror, it stumbled and fell onto its side. The rider screamed and tried to push the horse from his legs. Davaan rushed to the soldier's aid seconds before the ghouls reached him. He jerked the limp man onto his own stallion, where he draped him over the saddle. When their enemy grabbed at them, Davaan gave several swift boot kicks, knocking the attackers to the ground. Jerking his horse into the thick of battle, Wayland joined his brother to fight off the horde.

Commander Simon shouted an order, "Kill them! Kill them all."

The soldiers reacted immediately. Hundreds of the creatures collapsed, thrust by the sword or trampled by horses. They were an odd sight. Their faces looked like their skin had drooped in layers of ashen rubber. When they spoke, their words were mumbled beneath their bulbous noses that overlapped their lips. Maybe they said no words at all but screamed cries of death at their attackers.

A sweep of Sytha's magic wand tore the weapons from many of the ghouls' hands, and after that, they were easy targets. Two finger taps on the wand sent a thin stream of lethal light, and their animal skin clothing burst into flames. They yelled and rolled on the moist cave floor trying to extinguish the fire, but there were too many, and they were too close together. Shortly, they were charred crisps. More ghouls raced in, ignoring their burning comrades, and were trampled in the dirt by the soldiers' frenzied horses.

Clusters of female ghouls stood near the arched doorways wearing deer or goat skins that were haphazardly stitched together as tunics. Some held bundled babies in their arms, others with children clutching their mother's hand or garments, their small eyes wild with terror.

It saddened Ivan to see so many ghouls crumble under the soldiers' blades, moaning their last breath. He knew it was the wrong emotion, but he pitied them just the same.

"Pay attention, Ivan!" Zello turned his head and yelled. "Our first attack is only to test her range—her fire, her claws, and teeth. Do you understand?"

"Yes." His voice trembled. There was so much noise and commotion he wondered if Zello heard his response.

Lifting and lowering his great wings, Zello curved and dove directly at the mutant dragon. Her head swung from side to side as though trying to pick up the danger signals. Ivan swallowed and clutched harder at Zello's fleshy spine with one hand and gripped The Challenger with the other. He extended the sword in a threatening manner, knowing he would not strike—not this time. At the last moment, Zello banked to his left and twisted to avoid his cousin's flames. The maneuver would've worked perfectly had Zello remembered Manila's mouth of dangerous teeth. Her head darted toward him, and her mouth snapped shut.

Zello screeched, "Aaargh! You vicious reptile, you chomped off my toe." He continued to rise, shaking his hind leg, trying to rid himself of the throbbing pain. Blood spurted out, falling below, consumed in the river's flames.

Manila ate the toe in one gulp with a sneer of satisfaction on her lips. And then, the ultimate insult— she gave a loud burp.

After several flights around the mutant's head, Ivan was getting a feel for balance on the dragon's back. *How does Zello plan to bring me close enough to slash Manila's sensors?*

"I'm going in for another strike," Zello said, shaking his foot to ease his aching toe. "If you can't remove her sensors, then cut her throat."

Extending the Challenger's blade as far as he could, Ivan swung with full might, but he missed the target. When Zello jerked back, Manila let out a blast of fire that Ivan felt on his right leg, and he was pretty sure Zello felt the heat, too.

"Owww," Zello screamed. "That was hot under my tail, you stupid lizard! Let's try this from a different angle, Ivan." Pumping his wings, rising above, he was in a temporary safe zone—high enough to avoid a blast of fire if Manila decided to release it.

Though she had no real use of her wings, her instincts worked well for her. She seemed to anticipate Zello's pattern of flight and Ivan's strikes. Trying to bluff her had met its purpose—now was the time for The Challenger's ultimate blow.

Zello dove toward his cousin. Again, Ivan leaned into his target, swung the great sword, and connected with—nothing. He groaned with disappointment.

"Sorry," The Challenger said. "You must get closer so I can catch her sensors that are not very big."

"New plan." Zello twisted his head to face his rider.

"W-what's your plan?" Ivan's voice croaked like an injured frog.

"I call on your faith in me," he said. "I have a Forest Medallion for Bravery, just as you do."

"Couldn't we wear her down to exhaustion," Ivan whined.

"Not likely. We're doing all the work."

"I guess you're right. Tell me, then."

"I want you to fall, just as you did when you rode Fluorescence, the flying horse, and you caught the Golden Lantern. Remember? Scream to make it seem real, and that will confuse—and delight her. Grab Manila's head and hold on, then cut her sensors. When that's done, I'll swing by to catch you in my forearms."

Ivan didn't have a chance to ask further questions or to review the plan. He hoped he understood the instructions well enough to save his own life. Now his heart thumped against his chest in earnest. He glanced down into the flaming river where he would end up if he fell. It was too dangerous to imagine a positive outcome.

Circling, circling, Zello hovered over Manila's head. She looked up and followed his pattern, though doubtful she could see anything. The position strained her neck, just as Zello had said. Unable to blow fire at such an angle, she lowered her maw and roared with savage anger.

"Watch out." Zello propelled his huge wings backward to avoid the flame. He struggled to maneuver his wings and stay airborne for some minutes. Zello let out a gruff sigh. They were fortunate this time to only feel the searing heat.

"Can we do this?" Ivan asked The Challenger as he gripped the sword's golden hilt.

"We've been through tougher battles, Ivan," The Challenger answered. "Allow me the freedom to help you."

Abruptly, Zello flipped around and sped toward his cousin. "Now, Ivan!" He gave his head and large body an unexpected shudder, and Ivan was thrown off into the empty abyss. As he tumbled, he screamed midair—there was no faking this!

Frantic to catch hold of something, he dove toward Manila. As long as he didn't waver and she didn't jerk her head aside, he might find a welcomed neck to cling to. A terrifying plunge, even though it had been loosely planned.

Ivan let out a terrified scream. Now, she can impale me on her horns or fry me with her hot breath. If Manila drops me into the River of Flames, she'll trap me with her foot and laugh while I drown. Ivan quaked at the multiple ways to die.

When he landed with a thump against Manila's neck, he wrapped his legs and a free arm around her, his breath coming in short gasps. The Challenger shook in Ivan's hand as he pulled it back and swung the blade with full force over her head. He cut one of her horns that went sailing into the darkness. She shook violently. The burning pain of losing a horn must've sobered her and made her angrier. Ivan held on tighter. Lifting The Challenger with a strained arm, the sword slipped in his hand. He immediately grabbed hold and repositioned it. At last, with great effort, he sliced one sensor on top of her head and then the other. Blood gushed out in hot spurts, splashing Ivan's hair and face.

"Aaaarrghh!" Manila shrieked and howled. She must've realized she'd been tricked by her cousin, along with an inept kid. Her neck swayed, and her body trembled. Gurgling sounds rose from her throat. Her wings beat wildly, trying to keep upright, and rid herself of the excruciating pain.

"Zello!" Ivan screamed. "She's going down—catch me."

He lost his grip on her wobbly neck and was thrown backward, tumbling through the air. *When will Zello rescue me? Will he let me fall and die in the river now that he's done his part? Is this his plan to get even with me for taking the lantern?*

Long claws grabbed him around his chest, piercing his flesh. Ivan screeched, twisting his body in anguish.

"Sorry," Zello said. "I miscalculated your fall just a bit." He drew Ivan close and pressed him to his chest, where Ivan could hear the dragon's thrumming heartbeat.

Manila wavered for one final moment, and then a long exhale gurgled from her throat. She collapsed into the river, splashing water and flames onto the dirt floor.

Ivan wailed from Zello's piercing, sharp claws.

"Hold still," Zello warned. "Or I may drop you."

Looking down to distract his fear and pain, Ivan watched while hundreds of ghoul bodies were being stacked by the soldiers, Elftens, and Wolflords, against the walls of the cave. Davaan was working feverishly, jerking the ghouls from their fallen positions, dragging them away. He slung a dead body against a wall with great force, and its skull exploded. The werewolf's nostrils opened wide, and his face scrunched with vengeance.

The soldiers continued to fight, but they managed to pause long enough to cheer for Ivan's success. "Our new dragon rider," Lieutenant Pezzuline chanted from atop his horse. "Way to go, lad!"

Zello carried Ivan out into the open and laid him on the ground, hovering over him like a worried cat over her kittens. The fresh air filled Ivan's lungs, but when he breathed in deeply, his chest shot with agony.

"Pull the Long Dark Cloak over your chest," Sebastian said, "and I'll heal those claw wounds, along with a couple of cracked ribs." Groaning, Ivan grabbed the front hem of the garment and wrapped it around snuggly. He was lucky to have the cloak with its healing powers.

"Sorry about those ribs." Zello lowered his head in shame. "I should learn to be gentler with the fragile bodies of humans."

Wayland and Sytha hurried out of the cave toward Ivan and fussed over him when he tried to rise to a sitting position. "You're bleeding a great deal," Sytha said, touching the wetness on the side of the cloak.

"It's okay," Ivan said and exhaled. "Sebastian has just healed me."

Giving the lad an admiring grin, Zello blinked his heavy-lidded eyes. "We did it! Didn't I say we'd work well together?"

"Just great," Ivan said with sarcasm edging his voice. He collapsed back onto the patch of dried grass to rest his tense legs, surprised he was still alive.

"You're shaking all over." Wayland went to his knees and soothed Ivan's brow with his palm.

Zello lowered his head and asked Sebastian, "How about healing my toe? It throbs terribly."

"Wrap his foot with the hem," Sebastian said.

Ivan sat and offered the hem of the garment to Sytha.

"I can heal it, but I can't grow another for you," Sebastian mumbled.

"Bring your foot closer to Ivan." Sytha pulled the hem of the cloak over Zello's toe.

Zello hummed with joy. "Thank you, Sebastian." And to Ivan, he said with pride, "You are a brave warrior. I see why you were awarded the Forest's Medallion for Bravery."

Ivan grinned to receive such a fine compliment. He nodded and rose from the green patch of lawn. "I feel the same about you, Zello." He reached up and stroked the rough scales on the dragon's head.

Zello moved to reenter the cave. He was actually strutting like he'd done the entire thing himself, mumbling words of praise about his clever plan to save Ivan and destroy Manila.

"Arrogant dragon," Sytha chuckled.

"Let's go find Peter." Ivan rose to his feet, and for a moment, he wobbled. "I guess I should be careful after such a dizzying ride." Sytha and Wayland grabbed and steadied him.

"Here." Wayland offered him his canteen. "You need to drink after what you've been through."

Ivan gulped the water down, surprised at how parched he'd been. "Can we go find Peter, now?"

His friends tucked their arms through Ivan's and led him back inside the suffocating stench. To their joy, the cave had cooled off now that the stone had been rolled away, and the river's fire was extinguished.

The soldiers and Wolflords continued to kill the dwindling ghouls, dragging them to the wall as quickly as they fell. *Are there more to annihilate in the upper chambers of the cave?*

Manila had collapsed with a large part of her body still submerged in the river while her neck and head lay on the bank. She wheezed, and her eyelids fluttered.

"I'm sorry it came to this," Zello said as he hunched close and placed his chin on top of her bleeding head. "You chose this pitiful life. I tried to tell you almost a hundred years ago not to get tangled with Tereus, but you argued that it was power and the coddled life you wanted. It looks like you got what you wished for. Now that your ghouls have been slaughtered, you have no subjects to serve you."

She blew out a long breath, her eyes rolled up into her head, and there by the River of Flames, Manila died…the last of her kind.

After a few moments, Zello sniffed and said, "She was a freak, you know. Born that way. Never fit in with the other dragons who tormented her about her odd shape and ugliness. So Tereus gave her another body to disguise her bad looks. I tried to help her, be her friend, but she chose her own path to follow."

Though Ivan sympathized, he needed to find his brother. Nothing else mattered.

Chapter 21

Hoxx

Zello's eyes turned glassy. Moving with a slow, lumbering walk, he said over his shoulder, "I'm going outside to grieve."

"Sure," Ivan said, watching him go. "I-I'm sorry for the loss of your cousin."

Quick movement caught Ivan's attention on the chiseled stone staircase that led to the second floor. He was sure it was Hoxx, the blood-thirsty leader of the ghouls that Ivan had heard about. He wore a tattered purple robe with ermine trim around the neck and down the center front. Its hem dragged on the dusty steps. A gold crown rested on his big head. Hoxx sneered and dashed to the top of the landing. Once there, he stopped and turned, challenging Ivan with a frown to bring on a chase.

"Look! He has the King's Scepter." Ivan waved his hand to get someone's attention, but there was so much racket and chaos he thought no one heard him.

Wayland slid off his horse, his chest heaving. He removed his gloves and shoved his knife back into its scabbard. "I've killed my share of those foul creatures. It's a good thing they're poor fighters—no stamina, no common sense. Simon's men can drag them off into piles, and later we'll burn them."

"Listen, Wayland." Ivan gripped the Wolflord's forearm and pleaded. "I saw Hoxx going up the stairs with the King's Scepter in his hand. Let's go after him, or he might blame Peter for this entire massacre and kill him." They gingerly picked their way through the cave, avoiding frightened horses and sickened by all the blood and ghoul dismemberment. It was a cruel mountain. Ivan would be happy when they left, and he'd never return.

Wayland spun around and gestured to Sytha and Davaan to follow. "We're going to find Peter. Ivan believes he saw Hoxx going up the stairs holding the King's Scepter." He grabbed Ivan's hand and pulled him toward the steps. "Let's hurry before he gets away."

"Now things are getting interesting," Davaan said while he and Sytha propelled off their horses, handing the reins to a nearby soldier. "Take them outside and give them water." He indicated with a jerk of his thumb. The soldier grabbed the bridles, not questioning a command from a wolfish-looking person.

Ivan took the stairs two at a time, and the other three dashed behind him. At the top landing, they hesitated, not knowing into which of the three chambers Hoxx had disappeared. Davaan cocked his head and grimaced. "We'll try this smaller one to the right in case it's a trap."

"Your werewolf instincts must be working with full power," Wayland said to his brother with a wink.

Ivan pulled The Challenger with blood pounding in his heart. *What if we enter the cave and hordes of ghouls race at us? What if Peter is there, his skin raked off his body from head to foot? Isn't that what I dreamed a few nights ago? Am I ready to grieve the death of my brother because we are too late to save him from the dreadful flesh-eaters?*

"Be careful, Ivan," Davaan hollered and backed away from the entrance of the lesser cave, listening.

The air stunk of wet fur and putrid meat.

Yelling like a pack of frenzied wolves, more ghouls suddenly rushed out, pushing at each other, their weapons drawn. Ivan swung The Challenger, removing the heads of the first three in succession. Avoiding the beheaded bodies, Wayland knocked several of them onto their backs and thrust his knife into their chests. Coming behind with a serious look on his face, Sytha pulled his wand from its quiver and waved its light across the ghoul's bellies, splitting them in half. Their gruesome insides spilled out onto the stone floor, making it slippery and dangerous. Ivan had the sudden urge to turn his face and gag if there wasn't the fear that more might attack.

"Nice work, Sytha ol' boy," Davaan said, and he jabbed his lethal knife into the bellies of several more attackers. "You're lucky to have that magic stick of yours to slaughter these creatures at a distance." But Sytha had gone even paler than his usual coloring as he turned to dry heave onto the dismembered bodies.

Poor thing. Ivan's dark eyebrows came together. He placed his hand on Sytha's shoulder and gave it a friendly squeeze. "Are you okay?"

"I'm-not-sure. Give me a minute to get past all this slaughter. It doesn't come easily to Elftens."

"It doesn't come easily to an outsider like me, either," Ivan said. "I hate it."

"And…I must be careful how much I use my wand. My father monitors its use, and I'm sure he's fuming right now."

"Drag the bodies away, or we'll trip over them," Wayland shouted, and his brow wrinkled with disgust.

He grabbed a dead ghoul with his free hand and slung it to the side. "You deserve it for what you did to my brother, you uncivilized vermin."

They paused at the entrance, wondering if more of their enemy would surprise them and rush out, shouting their gibberish. Peeking around the opening, Ivan waved his hand in front of his face. "It's dark in here. Sytha, give me some light." The Elften didn't hesitate, in spite of what he'd just confessed about his father's disapproval. Sytha reached for his wand, tapped the surface with his index finger, and at once, light shot forth. It looked like a small meeting room, sparsely furnished with a long rough table and chairs. Weapons crudely carved were hung on the walls, as well as several slingshots, axes, and bows and arrows. *The air smells stale and rotten, like the cave floor below. Carelessly tossed skeletons and skulls appeared to be mostly sheep, deer, and some fowl. A wild hare or two.* Ivan guessed.

"Could be used for storage," Ivan said. "Wood pieces, carving tools, and workbenches." He backed away, his eyebrows slanted. "Let's try the next cave to the left. Maybe Peter's in there," he said and started to walk in that direction.

"Don't be so bold," Sytha scolded, grabbing the cloak's sleeve to slow Ivan down. "We'll all go together and be better prepared."

His Elften friend was right, of course, but believing they were close, Ivan was even more anxious to find his brother. He cupped his hands around his mouth and yelled into the entrance of the cave hole, "Peter. Where are you? It's Ivan—we're looking for you."

They heard a pitiful groan and froze there on the stone landing. *Was it a trap?*

Sytha was the first to enter the large cave, his wand extending forward, shooting light into the interior. "Well," he said sarcastically, "our flesh-eating king awaits us on his royal throne." For a moment, the Elften cautiously held the others back. He stepped in, looked around, and then motioned for them to follow.

"Where? Where is the ghoul king?" Davaan asked, lowering his voice. Sytha didn't answer but only scanned the room and fixed his light on the far end cave wall.

The huge space was shadowed behind crudely built stone partitions in dreary darkness. Ivan thought it must be the bedroom. He saw several lumpy mattresses that lay on the floor with crumbled blankets on top. The middle of the room held a crooked table and several hand-hewn chairs, with a beat-up wardrobe closet having no doors, pushed against the side wall of the cave.

When they heard strange whimpering sounds from the back of the inky gloom, Sytha sent light in that direction. In the corner sat a mother, probably Hoxx's queen, for she wore a thin golden crown. Her hairy legs were drawn up to her chest, where she held onto five or six young ghouls of various ages huddled against her, their eyes wide with terror.

There, to the right of his queen, sat Hoxx on a chiseled stone throne in his purple robe, gripping the fluted handle of the King's Scepter. A sword lay at his side. His grin was cold and scornful. The teardrop nostrils on top of his rounded nose expanded rapidly— in and out. His beady eyes dared Ivan to take the scepter from him.

"Be careful," Wayland bellowed, holding out his arm to stop his friends. He indicated another smaller cave opening to his left. "Could be a hoard of them hiding there."

Did Hoxx set a trap for them?

Ivan felt pity for what must have been Hoxx's queen and his family. They had inherited this degrading way of life with no means to escape.

Just as Sytha, Wayland, Davaan, and Ivan moved toward Hoxx, Commander Simon and several of his men flooded the doorway. "What do we have here?" Simon mocked, his sword gripped hard in his hand.

"Hoxx holds the King's Scepter," Ivan shouted excitedly to Simon.

The Commander's shrewd gaze traveled to the small cave off to their left. His shoulders straightened, and his head lifted. He motioned with a nod to his men, and they moved closer to the opening and listened.

Following the soldiers, some strong instinct stirred in Ivan and pushed him forward past Simon and his men into the small cavity.

"Peter! Oh, Peter," Ivan shouted. "What have they done to you? More light, Sytha."

"Oh, no." Sytha gave a cry of horror. "They've tortured him."

Ivan went to his brother, whose arms were stretched up and cuffed, chained to the cave wall. Slumped over and shirtless, his chin rested on his chest. Peter's bloody ankles were bound and shackled where the metal cuff had cut into his flesh, causing them to bruise and bleed.

Is he still alive? When Ivan's arms circled his brother's torso, Peter screamed, "Ooh. Oh, no!"

Ivan pulled away and discovered his hands were wet with blood. "What did these hideous creatures do to you?" He examined Peter's back and saw ugly crisscrossed stripes, some infected, weeping pus. They had whipped him and torn his flesh. Tears fell down Ivan's cheeks as he murmured his brother's name repeatedly, clutching him at his waist.

Wayland returned to the large main cave and howled at Hoxx, "Take these shackles off him right now!" The leader of the ghouls sat there in a stupor like he didn't understand.

"We're going to get you out of here." Ivan couldn't breathe—his chest tightened. "Hang on, Peter."

"L-listen, please, Ivan." Peter gasped, his eyes rolling in their sockets. "I was s-so wrong. Tereus is evil. He wouldn't let me go—threatened I'd be eaten alive—would kill you, too. You must get away."

"Don't worry about that. First, we have to get you out of this terrible place."

"You m-must understand…" His brother raised his head, sputtering past the blood dripping from his mouth, "I thought you—and Davaan could help me escape, un-unseen, but the ghouls spotted me, and I was captured." He groaned in a fit of pain, and his head dropped forward.

The female ghoul, cowering in the dark corner, untangled herself from her children and lifted a set of keys from the wardrobe with no doors. Cautiously she took them to Ivan, and he grabbed them from her hand. Then, remembering his manners, he thanked her. *Did she understand my gratefulness?*

Hoxx stood quickly and huffed at his queen, but she ignored him. His scowl deepened.

Davaan and Wayland held Peter under his arms while Ivan worked the locks. His hands turned cold and trembled so hard that he couldn't get the key in the keyhole. Wayland lifted Peter's chin, and they looked with horror at his face. His right eye was badly bruised and swollen, his mouth bleeding, and there were cuts on his cheeks and forehead. A nasty red rash showed around his neck that was probably from rope burns.

"Do you want me to work the key?" Wayland asked.

"No!" Ivan snapped. The key finally released the rusty lock, and Peter fell forward. Chains jingled and clanked when Wayland and Davaan caught him, guiding him gently to the stone floor. Peter cried out in agony.

To Ivan's surprise, the ghoul queen rushed over with a ragged blanket that smelled of urine and vomit. She tossed it toward Ivan, not getting too close, her eyes strained wide with fear. It seemed she had intended to place it under Peter as he was lowered to the floor, but she wasn't fast enough. Ivan thanked her once more and quickly bowed. It occurred to him she may never have experienced kindness or gratefulness in her whole miserable existence. She tipped her head and blinked, then scurried away toward her frightened family.

Dropping to his knees next to his brother, Ivan stroked Peter's forehead. "What have they done to you?"

Peter groaned.

"I've missed you so much—and—and I love you," Ivan said and allowed the tears to flow down his cheeks.

Peter raised his head. "Ivan. Where…have you…been? I was waiting…"

"I'm here now, and Sebastian will heal you." Ivan jerked the Long Dark Cloak from his shoulders, though he felt vulnerable doing so, and laid it over Peter's battered body. "You can heal him, can't you, Sebastian?"

Before Sebastian could answer, Hoxx shot up from his throne, a furious look distorting his ugly face even more. He let out an odd muffled scream where his big, overlapping nose prevented clarity. It seemed Hoxx didn't want Peter healed but to suffer the punishment due him.

"I will heal you, Peter," Sebastian said softly from the cloak. "It's been a long time since I've helped you. Now, relax and feel my curative power circulate throughout your body."

Anxious moments passed.

Peter whimpered a sigh and fell into a deep sleep. "Let him be for a while," Sebastian said. "His body needs to neutralize the pain and horror that he's suffered through—for who knows how long?"

Hoxx screamed an undiscernible sound while pumping the King's Scepter above his head.

"Attention," Simon shouted from where he stood at the arched stone doorway. "We've got more visitors." Ghouls crowed into the cave opening, having responded to their leader's muffled cry for help. They pushed at each other to enter, waving their weapons aggressively. The soldiers jerked their swords, and the slaughter began again. Ivan saw the ghoul queen covering her eyes and crying out a mournful wail. The children, not understanding the intruders' violence, sobbed along with her.

Davaan dragged the slain creatures from the floor and into the large main room, where he stacked them near the wooden wardrobe. His hard face and clenched jaw told of his fierce anger.

Ivan stared at the King's Scepter, gripped in Hoxx's stumpy hand. The long handle was forged of gold with a large faceted ruby on top and encircled with delicate filigree that laced its hold.

The scepter didn't belong to Hoxx and his horde. It

belonged in the Sanctuary of Truth, inside Zephyrus's trunk.

Crunching his teeth, something feverish overcame Ivan that he couldn't understand, driving him to covet the rare and valuable relic. He would proudly return it to Zephyrus, and the Forest would be that much safer and closer to being complete. His act of gallantry would repay Zephyrus for his kindness. It occurred to him in a flash. These thoughts were exactly Zupine's motivation for retrieving the scepter.

"Watch over Peter," Ivan said to a couple of Simon's soldiers, and don't let anyone near him or the cloak. They nodded, not questioning the young boy who'd barked orders at them.

"Where are you going?" Sebastian called from the cloak now draped over Peter, warming him. "Ivan, did you hear me? Stay here and let the commanders and soldiers do their job."

Ignoring the advice, Ivan moved stealthily in Hoxx's direction, hardly conscious of the clamor from the fighting that surrounded him. Approaching the leader, Ivan reached out his hand and demanded, "Give me the scepter. It's a sacred relic and unlawful in your hands." He wondered if the leader understood his words.

Hoxx twisted his lips and made a snorting sound like he was laughing through his heavy nose. He held out the treasure to Ivan, tempting him, and then pulled it back, crossing it over his chest.

The Challenger rose from Ivan's hand, taking over with its own power to protect Ivan from Hoxx's sword that suddenly appeared in the ghoul's grip. The two weapons came together with a resounding clank, then another. Ivan was no longer a novice when it came to sword fighting. He knew his strengths from battles that he'd fought in the past. Hoxx must have realized this, too, for he stood and raised the scepter high over his head in his other hand. The light from the ruby blinked red and flashed at the ceiling. *Is it a warning?* Ivan moved closer, and his left hand reached toward the scepter. Hoxx pulled back, and his hard breathing sputtered. Believing this was his only chance, Ivan lunged toward the fluted handle, opening his palm to grab the prize, abandoning all caution.

"Ivan—no," the voice from The Challenger screamed.

The ghoul gripped his sword and leaped forward, plunging it deep into Ivan's belly.

Ivan screamed with pain, knowing at once he'd made a terrible mistake. The sharp blade burned like the hottest fire. He wheezed and struggled to catch his breath and footing.

Harsh, threatening words vibrated from somewhere in the cave: "You are meant to die, Ivan Kimble. You fell into my trap. Your time has now come."

So, the ghoul king could talk? No—the voice belonged to—Tereus. Ivan's true nemesis. *Is he here, hiding in the cave?*

Heads turned. Soldiers' mouths trembled, eyes stared, horrified. Sytha shot to his feet from where he squatted near Peter.

In spite of the burning pain, Ivan lunged and grabbed the King's Scepter from Hoxx's tight fist.

The ruby-carved stone projected its bright light, scattering a red and golden glow that cast its beam on the ceiling and the dark cave walls. Furious he'd been stabbed through his own carelessness, Ivan jerked the scepter from Hoxx's hands. In a flash, he swung it with such ferocity the ghoul's head exploded like a club smashing against a pumpkin. Pieces of skull and brain went flying.

Coreena's angry face blazed before him in a vision. "I told you! I told you the Forest is a dangerous place."

Chapter 22

Sytha's Decision

Ivan stumbled back, wrenching in agony, his forearms pressed against his stomach while trying to regain his balance. He held The Challenger in one hand and the scepter in the other as his legs weakened. Sytha and Wayland rushed forward, catching Ivan at his waist and easing him onto the cold, gray floor. He groaned and released The Challenger but held the scepter in his grip. A soldier retrieved the sword and held it. Even with Ivan's arms wrapped around his wound, the hot blood saturated his shirt and jacket. He tried to turn to his side, but the pain was too great. Darkness shrouded him, and the frenzied commotion around him spun in a frantic circle. His mind whirled off into another world. A place that Tereus inhabited and ruled—from hell, where he'd earlier heard the terrible threat.

"It's your meddling that's caused Peter's betrayal. Now you'll both die," the voice boomed, followed by maniacal laughter.

At that moment, Davaan and Lieutenant Pezzuline half carried, half dragged Peter from the cave. He stumbled dizzily, unaware. "We're taking him to the medical wagon," Pezzuline shouted.

"Wait!" Sytha's brow rippled with anger. "Give me the Long Dark Cloak."

They stopped while Davaan pulled the garment from Peter's bare chest and handed it to Sytha. He laid the cloak over Ivan and stepped back. There he waited for Sebastian's healing to begin.

"He's losing a lot of blood," Davaan said, staring at Ivan.

"Oh, God!" Ivan shrieked. "It burns deep inside. Help me—Sebastian."

"What's taking you so long?" Sytha grouched through gritted teeth.

There was a long pause, and Sebastian remained silent.

"Answer me," Sytha yelled. "Why aren't you healing him?"

Wayland squatted next to Ivan and wiped away the spittle from his mouth.

"I've repaired his vital organs and stopped the bleeding for now, but there's nothing more I can do." Sebastian's voice trembled from inside the cloak.

Sytha crouched next to Ivan. "Why? Why can't you help him?" He lifted Ivan's head and gently placed it on his lap. With delicate fingers, he smoothed his friend's sweaty forehead with soft strokes.

"I'm afraid," Sebastian said, "the sword was laced with the very same poison that nearly took Zephyrus's life. It's the same poison that killed Merridyn's husband and child."

Sytha gasped. His eyes went wide. "May the High Intervener bring comfort and mercy."

"P-poison?" Davaan stuttered. "What kind of poison, and where did it come from?"

"Long story," Wayland said and sighed with disgust. "It came from a Swamp Dragon's quills by the name of

Porcupine. It's wicked stuff." He bent next to Sytha and examined Ivan. "He's lookin' bad. Let's get him out of this hellhole. Maybe the doctor can do something and take the pain away."

Sytha and Wayland grasped Ivan by his arms and lifted him to his feet. Ivan's head fell forward, and he screamed. Pressing his free hand against his bloody stomach, he gasped for the needed oxygen in his lungs. He pleaded, "P-please—don't—don't move me. The fire—racing through my chest and neck."

And still, Ivan would not release the King's Scepter. His fingers stayed frozen around the golden handle.

"What's this?" Simon marched from the cave with a number of his soldiers. He gave sharp orders to his men and then stopped when he saw Ivan hunched over, holding his arms against his belly and the blood that had spread down his trousers.

"Stabbed by Hoxx with a poison-edged sword," Wayland explained, his breath coming in deep gulps. "Have to get him to a medical doctor at once." With grim faces, Sytha and Wayland continued to support Ivan on either side as they encouraged him to navigate the stone steps.

The soldier, who had picked up The Challenger, wiped the ghoul blood from its blade and followed them down the steep stairs and out the cave entrance.

"Soldier!" Simon yelled and gestured at one of his men who stood guarding the second cave entrance. "Go get the medical wagon and park it out front of the cave, now!" The soldier saluted and left his place in a hurry, his face distorted with fear.

Simon hurried to the stairs, where he caught up with Davaan and followed him to the bottom floor and out the main entrance.

Davaan's eyes grew large. "You-you have a medical wagon here—down the hill?"

"Of course," Simon said curtly. "You think we'd go ghoul hunting without medical supplies and food wagons? In fact, Dr. Sinclair is here."

"I don't believe the doctor can help him," Sebastian said from the cloak to Simon. "There was a powerful toxin on the edge of that sword. You will remember when Zephyrus was struck with the poisonous axe? This is that same poison circulating through Ivan's system."

Simon's face turned pale and froze with disbelief. "I'm so sorry," he mumbled. "It shouldn't have happened to our special Forest friend. H-he's so young."

The wagon approached at a rapid speed, and the driver pulled back on the reins. Shaking his long mane, the horse came to a jolting halt, whinnied, and pawed at the earth. "He smells blood—blood and violence," the driver explained.

"Be gentle with this boy." Simon motioned for more help, and several soldiers rushed to Wayland and Sytha's side, raising Ivan to the floor of the wagon. "He's been stabbed, Dr. Sinclair. See what you can do to close that wound until we can get him to the castle's infirmary."

As the men struggled to put Ivan into the wagon, Zello crept closer and stretched his long neck in their direction. "I can take him to the infirmary," he said.

Simon stared at the dragon with one eyebrow raised.

Turning his throbbing head, Ivan watched the soldiers through the thin slats of the wagon, where they panicked and scurried about. *Can no one help me?*

The ruby in the King's Scepter, lying at Ivan's side, glowed brightly once more. *Is it a signal that my life is ebbing away?*

"I recognize this lad," Dr. Sinclair said with surprise. "Didn't I take care of his eyes that were pressed into their sockets by a Vaguer? A head wound where he'd fallen on a rock? That was only about a month ago."

"Same one." Simon raked his fingers through his damp hair. "Name's Ivan Kimble—from the outside."

The doctor nodded, and his memory filled in the void.

"Should I take the scepter from him?" Sytha asked.

"Leave it for now." Simon waved the question away. "But stick around, Sytha, and see if you can help the doctor. And you, Wayland, check how many men need medical attention. Then, get them out of the cave as far away from the entrance as possible."

Wayland gave him a curious stare, but he didn't question the order. He returned to the cave opening and watched as men evacuated on their horses or limped out on foot. They dragged several dead soldiers out and helped the injured leave the dreadful hole. Many were wounded with gaping flesh on their bloody arms and legs. Serious infections couldn't be left to chance.

A group of soldiers stumbled from the cavern, agonizing over their feats against the ghouls and the multiple injuries. Angry scowls fixed on their faces.

"Move away at once," Wayland shouted to the evacuating men, waving his hands forcefully. "Commander Simon's orders."

"Get all the soldiers out of the cave," Simon yelled between cupped hands to his lieutenant. "Leave no one behind."

"Yes, sir." Pezzuline saluted and left the supply wagon, where Peter was in a deep sleep. Stomping back into the cave, the lieutenant shouted as he went, "Out, out, everyone out!"

Commander Simon leaned over the wagon's side where Ivan lay and reached for the relic. "Now, give me the scepter." Simon took hold of the handle and tugged. "It has one final act to perform."

Ivan resisted and groaned when Simon tried to pry his fingers away.

"Please, Ivan, let go. It's safe in my hands, and I promise I'll return it to you when this final task is done."

Tightening his jaw, Ivan jerked in a spasm of pain. "Help me," he cried. "It hurts terrible."

Dr. Sinclair filled a syringe, and a deep frown marked his forehead. He ordered Sytha, "Hold your hand on the thick bandage over his stomach while I inject this into his arm. Poor lad. Why was he fighting that horde of creatures, anyway? Didn't Commanders Greendyn and Commander Simon have enough soldiers to take care of this?"

"You'd think so, wouldn't you?" Sytha glanced at Simon, who looked shame-faced from the doctor's remark,

Sytha followed the instructions as the doctor injected the liquid.

Reaching out, Simon pried Ivan's fingers open and took the scepter. Stepping away from the wagon, the commander forced his way through the men and horses, who had made a hasty retreat to the outside. They must've known by the sharpness in Simon's voice that something serious was about to happen.

Wayland turned on his heel to check on Ivan. "Hang on, dear friend. We're getting help for you soon."

Ivan blinked. His lips turned blue. A rattling sound

released from his lungs as he tried to talk. "Help me, Wayland. I feel like I'm on fire—burning alive."

"Oh, Ivan. I'm so sorry. We should've stopped you and helped to kill Hoxx." Wayland shuddered, and his voice shook with tears.

"Are they all out?" Simon asked. "Are you sure the injured and dead soldiers were removed?" Simon questioned Commander Greendyn. He gave a swift nod and wiped his bloody hands on his uniform's trousers.

"All Clear," Greendyn shouted.

Simon ran toward the cave's mouth, gripping the scepter. "Move back—way back," he shouted and waved his hand frantically at them. "I sure hope this works the way Zephyrus said it would, or I'll look like a crazy fool."

"Do your duty, now," Simon said to the scepter. He made a swift shaking gesture into the cave as though dispersing the bright beam. The ruby gem shot a red glow inside the gloom causing a mighty explosion farther into the cave—and then another blast closer to the front. Simon spun around and ran fast. The flash shot fire and debris at top speed out the entrance. He'd just made it to safety, diving on his stomach, dropping the scepter to the ground with his arms crossed to protect his head.

In moments, after the interior imploded, all the ghoul bodies were incinerated.

Wayland dashed toward the commander, squatted, and brushed small stones and dirt off his back. "Are you okay?"

"I ate a little dust and skinned my hands, but I'm still alive. Thank you."

"I can fly him to the castle's infirmary," Zello said again and lumbered closer to the wagon where he stretched his neck and brushed his muzzle against Ivan's forehead. A tear slipped over the dragon's lower lid and down his rough scales. "He shouldn't suffer this way. He wears the Forest's Medallion for Bravery."

Simon got to his feet and eyed the dragon like he was thinking about Zello's suggestion again.

"W-where is Peter?" Ivan pressed his cold lips together, his face distorted with pain.

"We've already tucked him into a wagon." Simon cocked his head. "Over there—he's sleeping soundly."

"What do you think, Sebastian?" Sytha reached in and touched the fabric of the cloak. "Can Ivan endure the long ride to the castle?"

Sebastian released his spirit from the garment with a burst of colored smoke, swirled midair, and quickly solidified into a man. Ivan cried out, his hands pressed against his wound. "Sorry," the spirit said. "I didn't mean to pull so hard on the fabric."

"A trip in a wagon would be too rough and too far," Sebastian said, jerking on his whiskers and staring at the boy. "I believe Zello has a capital idea, but instead of flying him to the infirmary, take him to Fungoda, the healing tree, near the west border of the Forest."

The hard ridge over Zello's eyes lowered as he gave the suggestion deeper thought. "How will he survive a ride on my back if he can't ride in a wagon?"

Sebastian thought for a moment. "It's faster, and there won't be many ruts to jounce him about. It's the only option we have to save Ivan's life. His face is without color, and he's shivering."

The soldier, who held the Challenger, pulled a blanket from another wagon and draped it over the injured young man.

"Let's see what Dr. Sinclair can do for him right now." Sebastian leaned over the top, staring at Ivan with sadness. He took Ivan's hand and squeezed it.

"I've already given him all that I dare to numb the pain. However, it doesn't seem real effective. But fortunately, and thanks to Sebastian, his blood has coagulated and the bleeding has stopped."

"What's the Fungoda Tree?" Davaan asked when he drew closer to hear the conversation.

Sebastian answered, "When Zephyrus was struck with the poison-edged axe a couple of months ago, it was Ivan and me that traveled to Fungoda to get the healing sap that eventually saved Zephyrus's life. It took him a long time to heal and for Zephyrus to return to his healthy self."

"The Fungoda Tree you speak of releases a healing sap and can save Ivan's life?" Davaan had a befuddled look on his face.

"Yes." Sebastian tenderly laid his hands over Ivan's. "Once again, I'm inadequate to help him." His eyes glistened while his brows knitted with deep concern.

Sytha put his arm around Sebastian's shoulder to comfort him. "We all do the best we can with our gifts," he said.

Sniffing, Sebastian suddenly lifted his head and said in a panic, "I remember—it takes a long time for Fungoda to bring up the sap from his roots. We need to contact him at once—start the sapping process, and be on our way—like right now!"

Searching the area, Sytha said, "We need a dependable Root-Underground tree that can send a message." He called with cupped hands that encircled his mouth, "Is there a pine tree here that can send an urgent message? Speak up at once. We need communication."

A scraggly pine, not far from them, spoke, "I will do it for you." The tree's eyes poked out from its trunk where previous bark had been ripped away and it exposed a bare area. A thin piece of wood squeaked out and protruded, taking on the shape of a peaked nose. Below that, a thin bark mouth formed.

"Are you sure?" Sebastian lifted a bushy eyebrow.

"I believe I can still send electrical currents and connect with another pine lower on the mountain. He will, in turn, pass on the message."

"It's urgent." Wayland eyed the tree with skepticism. "You don't look so healthy."

"My health will improve, sir, as it will for all my tree brothers now that the ghouls have been destroyed. We are grateful to you and the soldiers for your bravery."

Simon cleared his throat. "Yes, well. It's him that's brave." He pointed at Ivan, who groaned and cried in the wagon. "He and Zello, the dragon over there, killed the Woman of Flame."

"All right then." Sebastian approached the pine. "Send a message to Fungoda, the healing tree, who lives near the border. He is certain to remember Ivan. Tell him to bring up his sap. We'll be there soon to catch it in a vial and administer it to the lad."

"Yes, sir. I'm forming the message now—preparing to send." After a long moment, the pine announced with a grin, "Message sent."

"Good. Thank you." Sebastian exhaled with relief.

"I'm not sure the boy can survive a rough flight from here to that Fungoda tree you speak of." Dr. Sinclair peeked under the layers of bandages on Ivan's stomach. "Not sure at all."

"You could be quite right, doctor." Sebastian took several steps away and motioned to the Elften. "For that reason, I'm going to call on you, Sytha."

"Me? What can I do?"

"I happen to know you possess more magic in that wand than you are allowed to use at this time in your life." Sebastian gave a knowing nod. "Maturity will gain you more access to it in the future, but for now, we need you to tightly seal Ivan's wound and put him into a suspended state."

Sytha covered his wand with his hand in a protective manner, and worry lines appeared on his brow. "Only our elders with decades of experience can understand the Elften rules. How—how do you know these things?"

"Your father, Anton, of course. We do talk, you know. I enjoy the times he comes to visit Zephyrus, which is not nearly often enough, I must say."

"But, Sebastian, you don't realize. My father, he…he monitors the wand's use, which is already over burdened by killing hundreds of ghouls. What will he say to me?"

"I know you are restricted on how much and how often you can use this kind of magic, but our loyal friend's life is hanging in the balance. You must do this and risk your father's wrath."

"You are a wise spirit." Sytha bowed his head.

"We must not let him die." Sebastian gazed at Ivan, who moaned in anguish.

"Take the pain away, p-please." His weak voice trailed. "Please…"

Chapter 23

Journey to Fungoda

"He *must* live," Zello wailed. "It says so in the Black Book of Pearls—the Forest Mantra."

Sytha studied the dragon, one eyebrow lifted. It was a time for surprises—there seemed to be no secrets. "How do you know about that?"

"I've lived for almost as long as Zephyrus. Remember, I was a gift to him when I was as small as the Great Crested Newt. We talk about things, and I know my history."

Twisting the wand in his delicate fingers, Sytha uttered the last sentence of the mantra, "Your duty is to keep him alive."

"Yeah. That's right." Zello snorted for emphasis.

Sebastian took Sytha by the elbow and led him to the side of the medical wagon where Ivan lay, clenching his teeth. Tears seeped from his lids. "Once you are under the suspended state," Sebastian said to Ivan, "your pain will ease and healing can begin. I fear it will be some time before you can ride a horse or a flying steed again. But I believe Zello may be your ticket to survival."

"J-just take the pain away," Ivan whimpered.

"Proceed," Sebastian said to the Elften. "Remove Ivan's hands from his stomach and touch his wound with your wand, and that should seal it for the long trip ahead."

"My father will be furious," Sytha muttered and looked in another direction, not meeting Sebastian's fretful eyes. "But our friend is worth any punishment I may endure."

"Saving this boy's life, after all he's done for us— the Forest—is what matters. Do you agree with me, Sytha, Son of Anton?"

The Elften conceded. "You are right, of course."

Dr. Sinclair gave an approving nod. Although it was unlikely he fully understood the power of the magic wand or the conversation.

Drawing Ivan's blood-soaked shirt aside, Sytha lifted the bandage. The wound was gruesome, seeping blood. He rested the tip of his wand against it, and with a sizzling sound, the trickle of blood stopped. In his Elften language, Sytha chanted in a soft, rhythmic voice. Then in English, he said, *"Take him to the place of full sleep and there, protect him until Fungoda's sap can help neutralize the dreadful poison within."* In a quieter tone, he added, "Forgive me, father. It's better he lives than to worry about my punishment for breaking Elften rules. He is a true friend of the Forest."

Ivan's face and body relaxed, and shortly, his breathing sounded natural.

Zello pushed the lingering soldiers and men aside and made a path for his bulk. There, he crouched down and lowered his head to the ground. The dragon said, "Wayland and Davaan pull Ivan up and have him straddle my neck. And then, Sytha, sit behind him and hold the boy against you with your arm across his lower waist. Don't touch his wound."

Tucking his wand into his quiver, Sytha agreed, as

though there was never a doubt who'd ride with Ivan. The maneuver was done slowly and carefully, with Wayland standing on one side and Davaan next to him. Sytha's arm went around Ivan's upper chest, hauling him along while trying to balance himself on Zello's muscled forearm. "Ivan, I didn't know you were so heavy," Sytha said and grunted.

Sebastian, Wayland, and Davaan tried to help, but there was only space for two people that could manipulate their way to the cradle of Zello's neck, and there was nothing substantial to grab hold of and pull their weight forward until they grabbed a spine.

Sytha positioned Ivan in front while he threw his long leg over and spanned the opening. With one arm wrapped around his passenger, Sytha's other hand clutched the dragon's front spine. He breathed in deeply. Only a jerk of Ivan's head and a small groan came from him, like he'd had a bad dream.

"Wait for me." Sebastian's spirit circled with ochre and gray smoke while he disappeared into the Long Dark Cloak that rested over Ivan's slumped shoulders. "Hold on, my dear lad. Soon we'll have Fungoda's sap to help your recovery."

"We're ready to go." Sytha gave the dragon a nudge with the heel of his boot. He yelled to his friends, "Don't forget to take the horses back to Zephyrus—oh, and our rucksacks, and the beagles, too."

"Not likely we'd forget," Davaan shouted. "Have a safe journey to Fungoda."

"I'm sure the beagles will follow us without being coaxed." Wayland waved with tears shining in his eyes.

Zello snorted a puff of smoke and took several running steps toward the ridge of the mountain. He pushed off, raising his membranous wings, flapping them with effort against the air. "I won't grieve for this mountain or the ghouls," he muttered. "This should've been done a long time ago. I've nagged Zephyrus for years, but he wouldn't listen."

"What did you say?" Sytha shouted.

"I said, it's about time he gave the order to rid our Forest of those nasty creatures. They are destructive and cruel."

"Everything in its own time," Sytha said, his concentration keen on keeping himself and Ivan seated on Zello's back.

With a glance at the ground, Sytha whispered, "Do you see the tiny figures below, Ivan, getting smaller and smaller? This must be what you saw when you rode on Fluorescent's back and retrieved the Golden Lantern from Zello. You were incredibly brave." He swallowed hard and tightened his hand onto the dragon's spine when Zello tipped a bit to his right.

Ivan's head rocked back and forth against the Elften's chest, and he made small grunting sounds as Zello pumped his wings harder to gain altitude.

"Be careful, don't climb too quickly," Sytha said to the dragon. "I'm trying to stay seated and hold fast to our precious passenger."

They flew down the mountain, leaving Commanders Simon and Greendyn behind, their soldiers, as well as the Elftens and Wolflords. They passed the rich farmland of the Gootsays' Village, past the awful Troll Transformation Prison. The Witches' Village swept by them, with their tall narrow homes perched on rolling hillsides and their revered Sacred Hill.

"It seems a shame that Lyla coveted that hill and

number 13 cottage," Sytha commented. "Such a waste."

Ivan let out a long groan.

"This is thrilling," Sytha said into Ivan's ear. "I'd like to go flying more often if only Bellion, the flying stallion, weren't so ill-tempered." He gave a little laugh. "Do you remember, Ivan, when that cantankerous horse snubbed you and refused you to mount him?"

The wind drew Sytha's silvery hair back from his forehead. He squinted. "We should've eaten before we left," he said a bit louder. "Wouldn't some vegetables and fruits be just the ticket right now? I did notice several wagons full of food and a large supply of water, but I didn't think to bring anything with us. Well, you probably aren't much interested in eating now, anyway."

Soon, Sytha lost his motivation to talk to the wind. It was obvious Ivan wasn't interested, either.

Zello was a dragon on a mission. His head projected forward, his attention riveted on the western border of the Forest and the location of Fungoda.

"I hope that ornery tree got our message about bringing up his sap," Sebastian raised his voice from the cloak. "We must wait for as long as it takes. Otherwise, it could mean death for the boy. I don't know how much time he has left."

"You are right." Sytha spit after an insect flew into his mouth.

Zello laughed at Sytha's insect misfortune. Then he glided gently and banked toward the western border of the Forest.

They flew on for some time when Zello exclaimed, "There! There's the clearing near Fungoda."

"Now remember," Sebastian warned, "the healing tree can be crotchety and insulting, so hold your sharp tongue and try not to upset him."

"I'll do my best." Sytha nodded. "We want the remedy, not a verbal jousting match."

"That's right!" Sebastian said.

"It's getting late, and the sky is darkening. Do you want light from my wand?" Though he asked the question, the Elften didn't know how he would fumble for the wand from its quiver and still hold tightly to Ivan, his first consideration.

"I'm going to need light to land." Zello snorted and coughed. "Dang! I just got a big bug up my nose."

Sytha couldn't hold back his own laughter. "Serves you right!"

Turning his head, Zello sneezed, and the flying insect with a yellow and black body propelled out, spinning as it fell to earth.

"Will we be too late?" Sytha asked Sebastian in the cloak, who had said very little since the beginning of the trip. "I mean, will the sap stop the deadly effects of the poison?"

"I'm trying to neutralize it now, but I don't seem to be very successful. Nor was I effective with Zephyrus. Our only hope is Fungoda's sap. And still, I remember Zephyrus's agonizing and slow recovery after the axe sent the same poison into his side. I cared for him and prayed and wept every day."

Zello stretched his wide wings and circled above the clearing. Each time he dropped lower and lower. His breathing labored, and his wings beat to control his descent. "Now I need your light, Sytha," he said.

With care and balance, Sytha removed his wand from its quiver and rolled it between his fingers. He gave it a gentle tap. Nothing happened. The Elften sucked in his breath, panicked that his power had been canceled. Again, he tapped the surface, and suddenly, light flashed, illuminating the clearing just before the tangle of oak limbs that led to Fungoda. "Only a few more moments, Ivan. Hold on, we're almost there."

At last, the dragon's sturdy feet hit the ground. He took several running steps to achieve balance and then came to a halt. "Aaargh," he groaned loudly. "That was one long flight." He flattened his bulk onto the ground and allowed his passengers to disembark.

"I can help." Sebastian appeared from the Long Dark Cloak in a swirl of gray and orange mist, looking lost at what he was supposed to do.

Sytha arched and massaged his back. Pushing himself up, he supported Ivan with his arm around him while Sebastian stood next to him and helped to heft the boy from the cradle of Zello's neck. They guided Ivan down the dragon's quivering forearm and onto the spongy ground of decaying leaves, fungi, and moss. "Did I tell you that you are heavy, Ivan?" Sytha's breathing intensified.

The thick stand of timeworn oaks with their interlocked branches seemed to support one another, holding each other upright.

Suddenly aware that strangers were trespassing, the tangled oaks griped. "Who are you, and what are you doing here?"

Zello turned his powerful head and said, "None of your leafless business. Go back to sleep."

The trees gasped. Obviously, they'd never been spoken to like that before.

"Shush," Sebastian warned. "They are the gatekeepers to Fungoda, and they protect him from marauders."

"Ah...then I shouldn't have said that." Zello blinked, but not looking regretful for his rude remark. "We're here to get Fungoda's sap stuff to heal this boy."

"We have received your message," one of the ancient oaks said. "The men may enter, but there's no space for a huge dragon. You'll have to stay here in the clearing."

"Sure," Zello said cheerfully. "I hear a flowing river nearby. I'm going for a long drink and rest my weary wings."

"That'd be the King William's River," the same oak said.

"As long as there's water there." Zello lifted an eyebrow. "I don't care what it's called." He turned his body around, dragging his long tail behind, and lumbered away.

Sebastian had left the cloak just in time to roll his eyes at the dragon.

"Some of these trees are over a thousand years old," Sebastian told Sytha as they moved in the direction of the healing tree. "And Fungoda is over five thousand. You'll see what I mean when you meet him. They were created by the High Intervener a long time ago to keep the Forest safe until Zephyrus became the new king."

Ducking under the black spidery branches, Sebastian said, "I'd forgotten how dark and dreary it is under all these oaks." He wheezed from the burden of supporting Ivan.

A curious, brownish-colored hare peeked from behind a rotted root of an ancient tree. He stared, sniffed, and dashed away. "It's good to see wildlife around this area," Sebastian said with a laugh. "That means Fungoda hasn't driven every living animal away with his disagreeable temperament."

"Thank goodness we're here," Sytha panted. "Dragging Ivan is a most difficult task."

In the darkening shadows stood a single, short twisted oak, missing limbs and leaves, its moss-covered trunk leaning to the left. They laid Ivan gently onto the leaf-strewn ground, where it provided a soft bed. He let out a long, painful moan.

Chapter 24

A Vial of Cure

Sytha withdrew his wand and lit the area.

"Mystical One. Wake up," Sebastian chanted, and then he whispered, "I have to call his attention in order to make him feel important." He winked at the curious Elften.

"Who turned on the lights?" Fungoda's sleepy eyes pushed out from his weatherworn gray trunk. A wide nose followed. "Who are you, and what are you doing here?"

"You know who I am. We've come for your healing sap."

Fungoda's crusty old face and thick bark brows relaxed. "And you, there." He glared at Sytha. "The skinny one with no color in his skin. Who are you?"

"I'm Sytha, Son of King Anton of the Elften Kingdom. I've come to help my friend. Do you have the healing sap for us, or not?" he said sharply.

"Cheeky young fellow, aren't you?" the gnarled tree scowled.

"You remember Ivan Kimble?" Sebastian put the flat of his hand on the large protruding growth on Fungoda's trunk that gave him a hunchback appearance. "A couple of months ago, we were here for your sap to heal Zephyrus."

"Ah!" The tree diverted his attention, and stared at the ground where the boy had his hands overlapped on his stomach. "He looks in a bad way."

"He was stabbed with a sword, covered with the same poison that nearly took Zephyrus's life."

"Where do we get this sap?" Sytha looked Fungoda up and down but could see no obvious place to pluck a vial from him. "This boy is near death—we must administer the sap at once."

Fungoda's eyes widened. "Quickly, then. Here, inside my burl is a spigot and a glass vial. You'll recall, Sebastian, you'll need to screw the spigot into the existing hole and hook the vial's handle there. Then the liquid will flow."

Sytha took on the job with shaky hands. He opened the small door on the distorted hump, feeling around for the items, while Sebastian held the light of the wand. When he found it, he pushed the spigot in and tightened it until it squeaked.

"Ouch. Be a little easy there, Skinny-one. Now place the vial's wire handle over it."

The Elften's quick and efficient fingers completed the job. When done, he stepped back to watch the sap drip to the bottom of the vial.

While they waited, Sebastian explained to Fungoda what happened in the Mountain of Smoke and Fire. "We fought those awful ghouls until every last one was destroyed. The tragedy is the condition of this brave boy before you. The price he paid is unaccountably high, and we are greatly saddened about it." After a moment passed, Sebastian slapped his hands together. "No more worries, though. With the power of the King's Scepter, the mountain, and all the ghouls were incinerated."

Whether Fungoda was paying attention or not couldn't be known. His eyes were pressed shut while he concentrated on his task. From time to time, he mumbled some words that neither Sytha nor Sebastian could decipher.

The vial filled to the top rather quickly, and Sytha gingerly removed it. "Do you know what is to be done now?" he asked Sebastian.

Squatting to his knees, a real effort for Sebastian's old bones, he handed Sytha the wand. "Hold the light close. We can't waste a drop."

"I have enough sap to fill another vial," Fungoda said with pride.

Pulling the front hem of the cloak away, Sebastian unbuttoned Ivan's jacket and shirt and exclaimed, "Oo-aah! It's infected—yellowish-green pus and already smells of rot. High Intervener, please cure the infection and stay the pain away. Neutralize the poison within."

Turning his head from the awful smell, Sytha dry heaved in the leaves.

"More light, Sytha."

The Elften pointed his wand at the boy with his free hand over his mouth.

"Hold very still now, Ivan, while I spread the skin. I have the healing sap from Fungoda. You remember him, don't you? We got this same antidote for Zephyrus, and it saved his life."

Sebastian dribbled sap into the wound.

Ivan screamed a blood-curdling sound, and his body arched. His arms swung out where he grabbed a fistful of moist leaves and bits of bark and squeezed it hard in his hands. "Sebastian, help me. It's burning me alive. I can't endure it—please." Tears collected and raced down the side of his face. Mucus ran from his nose.

"Can't you help him?" Sytha dropped to his knees beside Ivan. "Don't let him suffer this way."

"There's nothing I can do," Sebastian said while he wept along with Ivan.

He thrashed, turning this way and that, clutching his belly, wailing out for help, but nothing seemed to alleviate the agonizing pain.

Because of Ivan's bellowing, they didn't hear the swish of flapping wings overhead, or the sound of hooves that landed softly on the gatekeepers' ground. Small footsteps raced into Fungoda's domain.

"What can I do to help?" she cried.

"Anna-Iza!" Sebastian's head swung toward her, his eyes wide. "How-how did you know?"

With great effort, Ivan quieted his moans and listened to the goddess's words.

"The urgent message you sent to Fungoda through Root-Underground spun off in several directions, and we happened to catch it from one of our more dependable pine trees." Anna-Iza slipped gracefully from her silvery flying horse. The hem of her light-blue cloak brushed against the moist leaves as she approached.

"Can you help him?" Sytha's lips quivered. "He's in an awful way."

"What about your wand?" She stared at the Elften, her brow arched with dread.

"It seemed to work until we made that long flight here to Fungoda. I'd closed the wound and put him in a suspended state." Sytha studied the wand held with his fingers, hiding his shame. "Besides, my father has closed off its properties because of over misuse. The only thing it can do now is emit light."

"Ivan, I am here." The goddess went to her knees and knelt next to him.

He opened his eyes and blinked. "Anna...Anna-Iza. I didn't know y-you would come."

"Sssh. I will help you." She leaned over him and put her lips to his.

She raised her head with a blank look on her face.

Sebastian asked, "What have you found?"

****

Ivan knew Anna-Iza had the ability to learn what kind of person you were by a single kiss. It was called the Kiss of Discernment. Months ago, she had tested him as a newcomer and confessed she'd found his character exceptional. Now, Ivan guessed, she was searching for the extent of poison in him—and his chances for survival.

The goddess didn't answer but pulled on Ivan's chin to open his mouth and placed her tongue under his. After a moment, she straightened her back. Ripples of worry marked her smooth forehead. "The poison is strong in his system. He will need several dosages of Fungoda's sap and many weeks of rest." Taking a handkerchief from her cloak's pocket, she wiped the sweat from his brow and neck.

"I have more sap," Fungoda proudly said again. "You can use the extra vial in my trunk. But remember to bring them back someday."

She pressed her finger and thumb together on his wound where blood had seeped out, and she gently squeezed. The skin appeared to seal. Ivan shuddered and gave a sigh.

"What did you just do?" Sytha's light eyebrows rose.

"Don't look so surprised." Her serious frown gave way to a small smile. "My hands can seal and perform the same suspended state as your wand. But, I too, am restricted on how often I can do this. For now"—she nodded thoughtfully—"I'm in good standing."

"We make a fine team," Sytha said.

****

Anna-Iza came to see me and even kissed me. Ivan inwardly smiled. She cares for me. I think she even loves me, as I love her.

His pleasant thoughts faded, and he drifted into a deep sleep, far, far away. Nightmares invaded…taking his peace with them.

He was on his feet, staring at the vial as he waited for it to fill. '"You are the one,"' Fungoda had said to him. Ivan remembered those words from his first visit while he and Sebastian waited for the sap that would save Zephyrus's life. Even now, Ivan wondered what the words had meant. He was just about to ask the meaning when the wind swept in, lifted, and took him away. The Long Dark Cloak fluttered behind him and helped him to fly. "Where am I going?" he asked aloud in his dream.

Suddenly, he was returned to Zephyrus's Circle. With a shy grin on his face, Ivan approached the Great Tree. "I have the King's Scepter. Please open the sanctuary door, and I will replace it on its hook." But when he looked at his hands, he only held one of Zello's spines. The scepter had disappeared.

Once more, he was carried away and delighted to be sitting across the small table at Cookie's Crunching Crumb, where Coreena licked sugar from her fingers. "I could eat sugary things all day long." She giggled, taking a bite of her scone. Ivan smiled, reaching over to give her hand an affectionate squeeze.

Her anger was sudden and explosive. "I warned you not to go into the Forest—it's a very dangerous place. Now look what's happened to you!"

Ivan stammered, not knowing how to calm Coreena's wrath. "I-I must go—it's important that I find Peter."

****

Anna-Iza stood to her feet. Her delicate, curved eyebrows came in at the corners, and sadness passed through her. "Take the extra remedy that Fungoda offers. Ivan will need it."

Sytha rose to complete the task. He felt around the large hole in Fungoda's hump and lifted out the vial. He knew what to do and did it with haste.

"But, one vial cured Zephyrus." Sebastian's tone pleaded for a more favorable report, though he must've sensed the goddess was right.

"Zephyrus is a tree," Anna-Iza said. "And he went into dormancy, a natural suspended state until the poison could be neutralized. Ivan is not a tree. His system has limited abilities." She sighed, shaking her head. "You poor dear. You will need much care and tending in the weeks ahead. I wish…" She didn't complete her words but was certain that Sebastian and Sytha guessed her affection and devotion.

Staring at her, Sytha opened his mouth as if to speak, but Sebastian nudged him and pursed his lips. "Well, then," the Elften cleared his throat and said, "I hope he has as many friends on the outside as he does on the inside of the Forest." He moved closer and squatted and took Ivan's hand, rubbing warmth into them.

Sebastian reached for the second vial, now full, from

the healing tree and mumbled, "I'd better tell Zello we're staying here for the night."

"I have thought to bring you a basket of food," Anna-Iza said. "Though it's doubtful Ivan will want to eat. When I arrived, Zello begged for the apple, and of course, I gave it to him."

"Thank you. My stomach is grateful." Sytha bowed from the waist where he was kneeling.

"May you heal quickly, my dear friend." She touched Ivan's cheek, her eyes misted. "And may the gods of Olympia keep you safe.

Chapter 25

Return to Zephyrus

They curled up against Zello, where Sytha tried to sleep on the moist ground with his arms wrapped protectively around Ivan. The Long Dark Cloak lay over them, giving them some amount of warmth. Refusing to sleep on the cold ground, Sebastian returned to the cloak. During the late night and early morning, Zello snored and snorted. It was no good. There was no sleep for the Elften.

"We might as well get up and leave." Sytha sat upright using both hands, and rubbed his back.

When the chill of morning overcame Ivan, he groaned and reached for the covering that had kept him warm. "Time to face the day," Sytha said and jerked on the fabric. With some difficulty, the two pulled Ivan to his feet and wrapped the cloak around him.

Sytha and Sebastian once again struggled to drag Ivan onto the dragon's back, and when this was finally accomplished, the spirit swept back into the cloak. "I'll be here if you need me," he said to them.

Zello yawned and stretched before he took several running steps in the clearing and then rose to the sky, flapping his wide, dark wings. His flank muscles jerked, and his lungs breathed in and released air rapidly.

Ivan felt a cold rush of wind against his face. The

sun was rising but brought no warmth. "Hold still, Ivan. We're flying back to Zephyrus," the voice behind him said.

That same person held him tightly around his lower waist. *Who is it? Why is it so cold?* Dark clouds drifted over him, leaving the chill of moisture. Tightness pulled the folds of the skin on his belly. It threatened to release pain on him, but something unexplainable held it in check. It must be Anna-Iza's tender touch, he thought dimly.

Time froze. *Where am I, and where am I going? Is it time to milk my cows and go to school?*

"It's miserably cold," the shivering voice behind him said.

Ivan finally recognized it was Sytha speaking, and holding him. *What happened to Anna-Iza? Wasn't she with me, kissing me? I liked her kiss very much.*

After some time, the wind stopped whipping against his face, and the heavy bulk that carried him landed on the ground in an abrupt manner, stumbling numerous steps to catch his balance.

Several people rushed forward and gathered around. Ivan heard them moving and breathing deeply. He sensed their worry, asking questions with quiet voices.

"Is he going to be all right?" The fearful voice sounded like Wayland's.

Hands lifted and carried him somewhere and laid him flat. Blankets covered him to his chin, and his head rested on a pillow that smelled of warm wood.

Someone moved closer to the wagon and quietly nestled the King's Scepter by Ivan's side. "I told you I'd return the scepter to you, and then you can present it to Zephyrus with all its glory." Simon patted Ivan on his shoulder. "Be well, my friend."

"How are you feeling, Ivan?" Kindly green eyes looked down at him.

He blinked and rubbed his fingers over sleep-gummed eyes. "Where am I?"

"You are lying in a wagon in the clearing where I stand. We are happy to have you back." Zephyrus gave a great sigh. "You are safe with us, now."

Warmth returned to his body with blankets that covered and revived him. He grasped something by his side with a long, cold handle, heavy in his hand. The King's Scepter!

"I b-brought this—for the Sanctuary of Truth," Ivan said in a low, thick voice. He raised the object only a short distance above his head and examined its beauty. *Where has it been? I know it wasn't with me when I flew on Zello's back.*

"Thank you, Ivan. Even in your weakened state, you think of the relic's return." Zephyrus moaned. "All I ever wanted was for you—all of you, to come back safely."

Sytha folded his arms over the top of the wagon's side and leaned forward, looking at their patient. His dazzling blue eyes were sympathetic and caring. "We have another vial of potion from Fungoda. You'll need it for your recovery."

Sebastian's cheek muscle flexed as he came beside Sytha. "You gave us quite a scare. We weren't sure you'd make it. Thank the High Intervener you did," they said in unison.

"Where's Peter?" Ivan managed to ask. His eyes were dry, his stomach burned, and he felt the need to sleep.

"He was taken to your farm home by a couple of

Simon's soldiers." Wayland smiled at him and tucked the blanket over Ivan's shoulders. "Dr. Sinclair did what he could for Peter and said he needed to rest and recover from his terrible ordeal. Your brother didn't want to leave without you, but we told him you were badly injured and had flown on Zello to get the healing sap."

"Did we see Fungoda?" Ivan raised his eyebrows.

"Yes, don't you remember, and I was there with you?" Sytha made a sullen face. "Suffering the damp and the cold, I might say."

"Bounty? Alfred and Canute? Are they here?" Ivan coughed, trying to clear his scratchy throat. The gesture tore at his raw wound, and he cried out.

Davaan joined them and answered Ivan's question, "We gathered the horses and your beagles from the second cave. They followed the soldiers with Peter in the medical wagon. In a couple of days, Peter will return and take you home."

"Yes, I'll go home with Peter," Ivan mumbled. "It's time I returned to my farm."

"We hope you'll be in better shape by then," Sytha said. "But it's probably best that your brother takes care of you."

Staring off into the warm gray sky, Ivan asked, "Was it my dream, or did Anna-Iza come to see me?"

"She did and was very anxious about you." Sebastian also rested his arms on the top of the wagon and leaned forward. "The goddess stayed with us for some time when we were with Fungoda until at last, she had to leave because she was shivering with cold. She flew on her horse, Moonbeam, to her Crystal Palace."

Ivan's cracked lips turned into a small smile. Closing his eyes, he drifted off, remembering her gentle kiss.

"Speaking of Anna-Iza," Sebastian said and waved his hands above his head to get attention, a serious frown spread on his brow. "Our lovely goddess told me the men must all bathe with strong soap, washing every body part, including their clothing and their horses. The ghouls carry a deadly disease that can spread and take your lives as well as your loved ones'. The soldiers, Wolflords, and Elftens have been informed, and I've heard they've complied with the Forest's command."

"Does this include Zello?" Sytha wiggled his pale eyebrows at the dragon.

"I'll do it myself." Zello raised his head high and shook it. "It's undignified to have men wash a dragon."

"We'll bathe Ivan." Wayland turned to Davaan, looking for agreement. "Let's take him to the barracks." He grabbed the horse's bridle. "Come with me and move easy," he said. "We don't want to jostle our precious passenger." The animal whinnied softly like he understood.

"Davaan, go with your brother and help with Ivan's bath." Sebastian gave a quick nod and a worried frown. "We need to have a word with Zephyrus." He turned and motioned for Sytha to accompany him.

The three of them reached the barracks with Zello lumbering behind, cautioning them on every bump and move. "Stay on the path, you clumsy horse. Don't move too fast," he yelled.

When Davaan caught up with his brother, he stared at the ground in front of him, trailing silently.

"What's the matter?" Wayland asked as they trudged along the pathway. "Are you sad about Ivan being stabbed and in great pain?"

"Yes, that, too." The werewolf shook his head. "Well…I was thinking…"

"What about?"

"I—I think I want to…I'd like to change into a man, become a Wolflord like you, and leave my werewolf life behind."

Wayland gave a sudden burst of laughter and threw his arms into the air. "I've tried for years to convince you to make the *turn*, but you always refused me."

"Now, seeing how you all work together, how you care for each other, even willing to give your lives for your friends, it makes me want what you have."

Tears filled Wayland's eyes. "That would make me very happy." He embraced his brother and squeezed.

"Every day, I worry about how we will fill our stomachs." Davaan's bottom lip quivered. "Or who in our own pack will betray me and demand my place as leader. I worry about where our families of werewolves will sleep safely at night."

"I remember when I had those same worries. I want you with me and our Wolflord families more than anything in the world, just as Ivan wants Peter home with him. Ours is not a perfect life. We have our squabbles, but it's better than being a werewolf—by far!"

They were quiet for a time, each thinking their own thoughts as they led the horse and wagon to room number five in the barracks.

Ivan heard it all, and in spite of his painful condition, he grinned with joy.

Davaan glanced worriedly at his brother. "Tell me, is the transition painful, like I hear?"

"Very painful. Once in a lifetime is enough."

"I want Ivan at my ceremony." He glanced over at

Wayland.

"I'll personally invite him." Wayland looked over the top of the wagon. "Hear that, Ivan? My brother is finally willing to convert to a Wolflord. Glory be." His lips spread wide over white teeth.

"We're at the barracks," Wayland said for Ivan's sake. "We'll take you in and wash you, tuck you in for a long sleep. Hope it's warm in there."

They worked together to maneuver Ivan from the wagon and help him into the barracks. He cried out, making a rasping sound several times when the skin pulled on his wound and the poison burned in his system.

"We make a good team." Wayland chortled, and Davaan agreed. "Put him here on this bed. You lift his feet, and I'll take him under his arms."

Davaan pushed the covers away, and together they laid him down on the soft bed.

"I'll start a fire in the fireplace to take the chill off." Davaan patted Ivan's shoulder and ducked outside the door, where Ivan heard him select several chunks of wood from the wood box.

Davaan stood and admired the fire he'd made. "I'll unhook the wagon and take the horse to the stable—give him hay and oats. You go ahead and start scrubbing the disease from Ivan." He turned at the door and waved. He almost hid his grin.

Wayland knew his brother was smiling in triumph to get out of the unpleasant chore of washing another man. It's something a werewolf just wouldn't do.

Ivan whimpered and moaned as Wayland bathed him. He was especially gentle when he slipped the clean nightshirt over Ivan's head and pulled the hem down below his knees. He breathed a weary sigh, happy to have the chore complete. "All set for the night. Don't worry. We'll be in the beds next to you if you want anything. Sebastian should be here shortly and will enter the cloak to keep you safe and warm."

Ivan mumbled his gratitude, and he slept.

Chapter 26

Journey Home

Sytha pushed the barracks door open with his foot. His hands held a silver tray where he tried to balance a teapot and cup. "Good morning, Ivan. I brought you some porridge. You must be very hungry."

"I'm not." Ivan forced his eyes open and tried to move, but his body was stiff.

Wayland sat up, yawning and stretching. "Other than a lot of groaning and a few yelps, you seemed to sleep quite well."

Sytha went to the edge of Ivan's bed. "Can you sit up so I can spoon this into your mouth?"

"No. I'm not hungry. Is Peter here so I can go home?"

"I don't know. I hesitate to have you leave until you're feeling a little stronger."

Wayland leaped out from under the covers and helped Sytha pull Ivan into a slouched but sitting position. Ivan screamed, and his eyes squeezed shut.

"Oh, sorry," Wayland said. "I wasn't thinking…"

"Be quiet over there," Davaan grumbled. "I'm trying to get some sleep." He rolled over and chuckled.

"Commander Simon and some of his soldiers are eating their breakfast." Leaning over, Sytha felt Ivan's forehead. He grunted softly. "They're asking about you and would like to say their goodbyes before you leave, but I told them you were not in the best of shape." Sytha's smooth brow rippled along with a serious set to his mouth. "Zello is curled up in front of Zephyrus, telling the story of your brave ride to kill Manila. To hear his version, he did all the work, and you just rode along for the joy of it. I was going to correct his story, but I have a feeling Zephyrus figured it out."

"Where are Sebastian and the Long Dark Cloak?" Ivan glanced around.

"It needed washing," Wayland said. "Saturated with your blood and ghoul guts."

"And Sebastian left here early this morning to continue his conversation with Zephyrus, no doubt talking about our plight yesterday." Sytha stirred the porridge. "I overheard Zephyrus saying he never should've allowed us to go. He feels terrible about it."

"It was our decision to go to the mountain," Ivan said in a hoarse voice.

"You may not be visiting us for some time." Wayland placed a cloth napkin under Ivan's chin while Sytha offered their patient the first spoonful of porridge.

"Why?"

"Well, it'll be winter soon, and the Forest goes quiet," Wayland said. "Trees are dormant, the critters go underground, and birds go to warmer climates, or they find places to stay out of the cold. It's the same for you on the farm, isn't it?"

"Yes, it is." Closing his eyes, Ivan nearly drifted off to sleep.

Sytha managed to coax a couple more spoonfuls into Ivan's mouth that he swallowed with some difficulty.

"Were all the ghouls destroyed?" Ivan's eyebrows

tightened. "Even the queen and her children?"

"I believe so." Sytha looked away for a moment. "It was bound to happen sooner or later. We can't have those creatures killing our livestock and tearing flesh from humans. I appreciate your compassion, but in this case, it's misplaced."

"One last dreadful task." Wayland's dark brows squeezed together.

"What?"

"We have to spread your wound open again and dribble the last of this bottle of sap." He picked up the full vial from the window sill. "And this one, you take home with you. Have Peter apply it twice a day."

"No, no." Ivan ducked his head. "Please, no more of that stuff, no more pain."

Lifting Ivan's nightshirt, Sytha folded the bandage back. He looked disheartened and then straightened for a moment. "It looks kind of raw. Hold his shoulders, Wayland."

Now Davaan leaped out of bed and held Ivan's feet. "I would take this punishment instead of you, Ivan, if it were possible. I swear I would."

"Spoken like a true man." Wayland emphasized the word *man* and gave a positive nod at his werewolf brother.

Sytha's long fingers pressed the skin apart, and he poured the sap into the small gap.

Shrieking, Ivan shot up, arms flailing so fast that Sytha almost dropped the now empty vial. "Oh, High Intervener, it burns like a hot poker. Stop the pain, pleeease—Sytha—stop!" He laid his head back onto the pillow, his breathing deep and fast. "I'm dying. Tereus wants me dead."

He spun away in a cold, dark world, where the rock crevices, much like the ones in the mountain caves, threatened to pull him in and squeeze him to death.

The terrible voice of his enemy tormented him. "Now you will die, and all my powers will return. Peter will come willingly, and I'll make him my thrall once more."

"Go away! Go away, you dreadful monster," Ivan yelled.

The threesome looked at each other, guessing who had silently spoken to their injured friend.

Will Tereus never stop tormenting me?

****

Two days passed before Peter felt well enough to return to the Forest with Bounty pulling the wagon. King Canute and King Albert jumped out and raced around Zephyrus, yelping and barking. They must've known by the smells that their master had been there. Peter stepped from the wagon, watching his wobbly feet negotiate his first step to the ground.

"How are you feeling?" Zephyrus asked Peter. "You still look pale, although the terrible bruise near your eye and the cuts on your face seemed to have healed completely."

"Thanks to the Long Dark Cloak and its healing fingers. Still, I'm a bit groggy and weak, but each day I'm improving." Peter faced the Great Oak, and his chin quivered. "How is Ivan? Can I take him home?"

Zephyrus stared into the meadow before him. "His recovery is slow and painful, as it was with me." He looked at the boy, his twig and moss eyebrows pulled in.

Peter glanced away. "I…h-how can you ever forgive me for what I did to you?"

Zephyrus didn't answer.

"You do know what I did?" Peter slowly raised his head and met Zephyrus's eyes.

"Yes. The evidence was there. You struck me in my side several times with the poison-edged Silver Axe, one of our own Ancient Relics. You intended to kill me."

A look of self-disgust covered Peter's face. "How could I've done such a thing to a true friend?" His shoulders shook. Tears streamed down his cheeks.

"I refused to believe you would betray me, so I closed my mind to your cruel deeds. The master you serve rose as a menacing phantom, and he deceived you." Zephyrus's wooden lips pressed together as though it was difficult to continue. "Tereus snitched, admitting it was you who axed me and that he threatened your life to do his bidding."

Peter's sobs were so loud he couldn't speak or glance up. He dropped to his knees, his chin pressed against his chest.

"I love you, Peter, with all my heart."

"I know." He cleared his throat. "I feel the same about you. I can't explain the spiteful change in me, but Tereus had a stronghold."

"Tereus knew what you wanted more than anything, and he encouraged it, promising you wealth and kingship." When Peter didn't deny it, Zephyrus continued, "He is powerful and convincing. Centuries of evil, serving only his own needs have made him this way. That's why the High Intervener sentenced him to the underground to roam alone in his own wickedness. Then, having a void above ground, the High Intervener chose me to serve until another could take my place. You know these things. I didn't keep them secret from you."

He nodded and looked up reluctantly. "You confided in me long ago. That's true." Peter covered his face with his hands and wept bitterly. "I see it now. It's clear. The malicious thing I did to you and to my own dear brother."

"You can make amends."

"What must I do?" he asked between sobs, searching Zephyrus's face for the answers.

"You must ask Ivan for forgiveness. For the lies you've told, for money squandered, for abandoning him when your parents died. Ivan has an exceptional heart, never thinking ill toward anyone—not even you."

Peter wiped his nose on the sleeve of his jacket and watched Zephyrus. "W-will you forgive me for what I-I've done?"

Zephyrus considered this for a moment. "I do forgive you. And I encourage you to stay with Ivan on your farm and nurse him back to health."

"Yes, I will. I'll take very good care of him."

The Forest's wagon, with Wayland and Davaan in the driver's seat, slowly approached from the barracks, where they stopped in front of Zephyrus. Tied behind the wagon were three horses that followed along. Sytha and Sebastian sat in the back with Ivan, soothing and fussing over him. The Elften didn't speak to Peter, not even to greet him, but gave him a cold glare.

Peter wiped his eyes and avoided Sytha and Wayland's scrutiny. He rose from his knees, moved toward Ivan, and reached for his hand where he stroked it tenderly. "You don't look so healthy."

Blinking, Ivan smiled and gave a little laugh until it caused him to cross his arms over his stomach and whimper. "I'm not feeling well. Hoxx stabbed me with his poison-edged sword."

"I know, and I'm real sorry I couldn't be more helpful. I was chained to the wall and in a bad way until all of you rescued me." He gazed at Sytha. He gazed at Wayland. His last look was at Davaan and Sebastian.

"Your face is pale," Ivan said. "Have you recovered?"

"I'm getting better. These last couple of nights, I've had nightmares that have left me screaming and sweating."

"They tortured you in the cave. It's understandable."

"Yes, they were very cruel. Their orders came from Tereus, you can be sure."

"Let's transfer Ivan into your wagon," Wayland said to Peter. They jumped from the wagon's seat and moved toward their patient.

Sytha helped Ivan sit up while Wayland and Davaan inched him forward by pulling on his legs.

"Please be careful with him," Sebastian cautioned and wrung his hands together.

"Just relax." Wayland calmed Ivan and caught him in his arms, steadying him on his feet.

Alfred and Canute barked madly, scratching first at the wagon's wheels and then pawing at Ivan's bare legs. Even Bounty turned his head and softly whinnied.

Squatting, Davaan pulled the beagles away. "Your master is hurting. Give him time to heal, and then you can jump on him.

"You're wearing the Long Dark Cloak." Ivan pointed weakly at Sebastian.

"I know it looks better on you, but it did get a good washing." He pursed his lips before smiling.

"What's this around your neck?" Peter traced the

circle of the Forest's Golden Medallion.

"It was bestowed to him a few days ago," Zephyrus said with pride. "Awarded by the Forest with gratitude for his bravery."

"Ivan…brave?" Peter cocked his head and studied his brother. "That's a very high honor."

"He deserves it." Wayland gestured toward Ivan. "Let's move him now."

They maneuvered their patient into the back of the wagon that would take him home. Peter drew several blankets over him and adjusted a pillow under his head. "Is that comfortable for you, little brother of mine?"

Ivan moaned when they laid him flat in the wagon. He went very still, his body rigid with pain. "It…it's fine," he lied. "Thank you."

"Then I think we're ready to leave." Peter walked toward Bounty gliding his hand across his smooth flank. "Be careful how you move," he said to the horse. "My brother—and your master, is resting."

"May I ask where you think you're going?" Zephyrus addressed Sytha, Wayland, and Davaan. He must've wondered about the three horses tied to the back of the wagon.

"What?" Peter turned to ask, thinking the question was for him.

Wayland faced Zephyrus. "We talked about it last night and decided, with your permission, sir, that we will accompany Ivan to his home."

"You decided?" Zephyrus's eyebrows rose and twitched. "You know you are not allowed to leave the Forest. It's written in the Black Book of Pearls."

"Please, sir, this one time. Let us follow Peter, and when Ivan is safe, we'll return at once." Sytha drew a knit hat from his jacket pocket and pulled it over his ears. "Look! No one will see my Elften ears if I wear this at all times."

Davaan and Wayland did the same. "We promise we'll be careful not to be seen as a Wolflord—and a werewolf." Wayland stared at Zephyrus with pleading eyes. "Peter is sure to need our help getting Ivan from the wagon and into their farm home."

"Right now," Davaan said, tucking his ears under his hat, "nothing's more important than the safety and comfort of our patient. Don't you agree?"

Zephyrus stared into the distance, his wooden lips working up and down like he was chewing on a chunk of fungus. He closed his eyes, appearing to think this over for a long moment. "You are right. I grant you this privilege once and only once. Ivan must be safe."

"Thank you, sir," they chimed together and clutched each other's forearms, a gesture of friendship and agreement.

"Do be careful with our hero," Zephyrus said. "His wound is still very tender and it might start bleeding again. Remember to use the sap twice a day. Oh, and wash the wound with disinfectant several times to keep the infection away, and—"

"Yes, yes, Zephyrus. We all know what to do." Sytha gave a knowing smile.

"I won't be going with you, of course, but I certainly wish I could." Sebastian stepped close to the wagon, and after saying his goodbyes, he stroked Ivan's face. "May the High Intervener be with you on your journey to recovery."

Sytha put his hand on Sebastian's shoulder and reassured him. "We'll watch over him like a mother cat and her kittens."

"And we'll ride behind you," Sytha said blandly to Peter. "We want to be there in case Ivan needs help."

"I can take care of him." Peter frowned, curtness edged his voice.

Wayland scooped up Alfred while Davaan grabbed Canute. They placed them in the wagon next to their master.

"We're going home, boys," Ivan managed to murmur to his beloved beagles. They licked his face and nuzzled his neck, yipping with happiness.

Chapter 27

Home

Sytha and Wayland tightened their grip on Ivan and struggled to drag him up the porch steps and into his farmhouse. Gritting his teeth, Ivan groaned from a long spasm of pain.

"Be careful," Wayland cautioned, "we're pulling on his wound."

In front of them, Peter opened the door and directed them to Ivan's bedroom. "Lay him here." He motioned with a dip of his head. After they'd maneuvered him into bed, Peter drew the blankets over his brother and bent to kiss both cheeks. "At last, my dear brother is home."

"Are the beagles allowed in the house?" Davaan entered with the extra blankets, a pillow, and Ivan's clothing in a bag that he'd retrieved from the wagon.

"Better not." Peter stared at his brother, lying so helpless and in pain. "They might jump on him and cause more damage."

"May the High Intervener heal you quickly, my dear friend." Sytha bent over Ivan and kissed his forehead.

When no one spoke, Peter said, "I—I'm sorry I got you into a terrible fix."

Davaan blinked, and his jaw tightened. "The rescue wasn't as smooth as we'd hoped."

"It nearly cost your brother's life," Sytha growled.

"Maybe now you'll put your selfish ambitions aside and think of someone else."

Wayland laid his hand on the Elften's forearm. "Let it go. The important thing is for Ivan to recover and be on his feet." He reached into his shirt pocket under his jacket. "This is the healing sap from Fungoda. You'll need to apply it to the wound twice a day until it's gone."

Peter took the precious vial. He studied it and rolled it between his fingers. "I'll do exactly as you say."

Glancing around the bedroom, Wayland said, "For a bachelor, Ivan keeps a tidy house."

"He's always been that way." Peter glimpsed proudly at his brother. "A habit from our mother."

"Listen…I hear a horse approaching." Davaan dashed to the kitchen window and searched the yard. "It's a boy. Who is he?"

Wayland and Davaan pulled their knit hats lower onto their heads, covering their wolf-like ears. Though more delicately shaped, Sytha jerked his hat from his pocket again and did the same. "We can't take any chances."

The door swung open. The boy's eyes grew large. "Where is Ivan Kimble? Who…who are all of you?" He knew Peter, of course, since he'd continued to care for the farm while Peter mended from his trauma in the forest.

The threesome greeted the boy. "We're friends of Ivan's and decided to drop by to see him."

"And you are…?" Sytha asked and put his hand forward, which the boy shook.

"I'm Dan Jacobs. I come every morning and evening to milk the cows and feed the chickens when Ivan's away in the forest on business. I don't know what kind of business he does there, but I wouldn't dare go into that forest for anything. It's too scary." He finally stopped talking.

"Have you been doing chores all morning?" Peter stood back and eyed Dan like he wondered why he was still at the farm. "It's nearly ten o'clock. Shouldn't you be in school?"

"Yeah. I'm a bit late finishing up. I mean, I've been cleaning the barn and a few extra chores that needed to be done because I figured Ivan would come home today. And I was right, huh?" Dan brushed his long bangs from his forehead, but they slipped back over his eyes. "Where is he? I saw the wagon and Bounty out front with three other horses tied to the hitching post. They must belong to all of you."

Sytha was grateful he'd left his light blue horse at the barracks' stable and rode one of the soldier's stallions. A light blue horse with a darker mane and tail would certainly stand out, and the villagers would ask questions.

"Ivan is quite sick," Peter said. "I'm taking care of him."

"What's his ailment?" Dan looked at them with eyebrows lifted. He didn't give Peter a chance to answer. "Can I see him? Let him know I'm here, and I've done the chores. He isn't contagious, is he?"

"No," Sytha said, scratching under his knit hat until Wayland grabbed his hand to remind him not to expose his ears. "He'll feel better in a few days, and then I'm sure he'd enjoy your company."

"I'll help out until he mends." Dan glanced curiously at Peter. "Maybe my sister can come when she's finished with school in the afternoons."

Peter frowned at the boy when he mentioned his sister, but he didn't disagree.

"We'd better leave." Wayland cleared his throat and made a move toward the front door. He faced Peter. "But if you need us for any reason, let us know, and we'll be here as soon as we can."

"Please take care of him." Davaan put his hand on Peter's shoulder and squeezed.

"Look, I…" Peter began, stumbling. Redness returned to his cheeks. "I'm so sorry for the trouble I've caused." Sytha and Wayland stopped and turned to listen. "Remember the good times we've had, and," Peter's voice was contrite, "maybe you'll forgive me for the dark path I've taken. I-I couldn't help…Tereus wouldn't let me go."

Seemingly unconvinced, Sytha's light eyebrows drew together.

"We hope you've learned a hard lesson." Wayland paused, his hand on the doorknob, and said just above a whisper, "We tried to tell you he was evil through and through."

"Who's Tereus?" Dan looked from Sytha to Peter to Wayland and Davaan. When no one answered, he said, "Well, nice to meet you all. I'm already late for school, so I'd better leave." With that, Dan gave a quick bow as he'd seen Ivan do. He skirted past Wayland at the door and left.

"Be careful what you say in front of the boy." Sytha frowned, pressing his lips. "That information belongs strictly to the forest. There's no sharing."

"I know that," Wayland answered in a defensive manner.

The three left the house and stood on the porch with

their hands resting on the rail as they watched Dan gallop away. Canute barked and growled at Davaan while Alfred whimpered and scratched at the closed front door.

"He can smell my werewolf intentions." Davaan gave a friendly laugh. "Well, it won't be for long, you furry mutts. Soon, I'll be changed into a man, just like Wayland, here."

Sytha shifted on his feet and said quietly, "Do you think Ivan will be okay if we leave him?"

"We have no choice." Wayland shrugged his shoulders. "And, yes, I think Peter regrets his misguided life, his poor choices, and he'll be devoted to his brother."

"Something. Just something doesn't place right." Sytha tapped his finger against his forehead and frowned. "I can't figure it out now. But Peter's motivations are more complicated than one would first think."

Davaan bit on his lower lip. "He seemed sincere to me. But then, I'm a simple werewolf, and we haven't been trained in the social skills that you have."

"Let's put the wagon over by the barn and find a stall for Ivan's wretched horse." Wayland stepped off the porch and took hold of Bounty's bridle, leading him away.

After a short time, they completed their tasks, mounted their own stallions, and rode toward the West Forest.

****

"Ivan, are you awake?"

"P-Peter. It's you. H-how did I get here?"

"We brought you from the forest this morning. Don't you remember riding in a bumpy wagon and being dragged up the porch steps to your bed?"

"Who…?"

"Your devoted friends, Sytha, Wayland, and Davaan." Peter sat on the edge of the bed and reached for his brother's hand where he stroked it with tenderness.

"How can that be? They aren't allowed to leave the…"

"They got special permission from Zephyrus and left the forest to follow me here."

"I'm grateful they cared enough." Ivan gave a low moan.

"You're looking a little better."

"I'm so glad you're with me." Ivan scanned his brother's face like he'd seen it for the first time. "I've dreamed of this for so long."

Peter gave a quick nod. "I've missed you, too, little brother of mine."

Ivan remembered the endearing phrase from when he was just a youngster. It made him feel loved and protected.

"Where do I start?" Peter paused, looking overwhelmed, embarrassed, and regretful, all at the same time. "I'm sorry for my selfishness and greed. That's what Sytha said, and he's right."

Ivan gave Peter's hand a squeeze. "I don't always agree with Sytha's opinion. He can sometimes be a bit terse with others. It's his privileged position as royalty, I think. You are a good and true brother, and I love you."

Peter smiled. The first time since he'd left the forest. "W-will you forgive me for the things I've done—and not done for you?"

Blinking, Ivan said, "Yes, of course. The thing is, I've missed you and wanted you home with me. Here, where we could look after one another."

Peter sniffed and gazed at his brother with hopefulness.

"Sometimes it's awfully lonely by myself, what with mother and father gone, too. I try to cover my loneliness by reading a lot, even doing my homework far ahead of our assignments, but it's not as good as being with you."

That brought a grin to Peter's lips.

"You'll remember I went into the forest where I'd heard you were seen throwing wood into a wagon. I made many new friends, had adventures, and—nearly lost my life more than once. I don't think—" He paused for a moment to take a deep breath. "—I don't think I'm cut out for the adventurous life."

"You'll have to tell me about it when you are feeling stronger. But for now, I must use Fungoda's sap on your wound. Sytha gave me orders to apply it twice a day, and I know it's for your own good." He rolled the covers down and unbuttoned Ivan's shirt, noting the streaks of dried blood. "I'd better change your clothes and put on a clean nightshirt." He found Ivan's nightclothes neatly folded in a dresser.

"Where are my shoes, socks, and trousers?"

"There, in that bag. Davaan brought them in with the blankets."

When Peter dragged Ivan to a sitting position, he let out a painful cry and squeezed his eyes shut. The nightshirt was harder to remove, causing the wound to stretch and double on itself.

"I—I'm so sorry, Ivan." Carefully, he maneuvered a clean shirt over Ivan's head and tucked his arms into the sleeves.

Groaning with pain, Ivan allowed his brother to peel back the bandages. "H-how does it look?" His chin quivered, and his head flopped to the side, not wanting to see it.

"It's getting better." Peter stared, his face stricken. "You have a distance to go before it's healed. But don't worry. I'm here to help, and maybe later this evening, you'll feel well enough to have dinner with me."

"I'd like that." He licked his dry lips. "Peter, you must do something for me."

"Sure, anything."

"I promised to take a job at Turlow's Gristmill on the weekends. Would you ride to the mill tomorrow and tell Mr. Turlow that I'm ill and can't work for a while?"

Peter hesitated. "Well…you see, I owe him money." He ran his fingers through his light-colored hair, his forehead wrinkled. "I went several times to purchase grain and flour—Tereus said his army needed to be fed. Mr. Turlow trusted me, believing I'd come back and make good on the charges. The Kimbles have a solid reputation with them. Did you know that?" He shifted his gaze away in a moment of shame. "But I didn't have any money to pay him, and I still don't."

Ivan waved a feeble hand into the air. "I paid your invoices in full, not knowing when you'd return." He waited for Peter to admit he also owed money to Jay Whittaker, but his brother said nothing.

"Thank you." Peter rubbed his sleeve across his nose and sniffed. "When I feel it's safe to leave you for a while, I'll go see Mr. Turlow and tell him you are ill. Make an apology for my negligence."

"Okay." Ivan reached up and touched Peter's chin. "Your scar is quite visible from this angle." He scowled.

"I wonder why Cecil bit you so many years ago. He acted like a mad dog for no reason that I can tell."

"I guess I'll never know, but he's a mean one—ever since he was punished and sent to Troll Transformation Prison. Are you stalling, Ivan Kimble? You know I have to perform my nursey-duties. Now hold still."

Peter lifted the nightshirt and pressed his fingers into Ivan's stomach, separating the wound just a little. He dribbled several drops of the liquid into the small opening.

Ivan clenched his teeth, trying to be brave and hold back a scream. Tears welled in his eyes, and he closed them tightly. "No, no…please…it burns terrible."

"I'm sorry—so sorry little brother. I didn't mean to hurt you, but this must be done." Peter's voice faded. Ivan shuddered, closed his eyes, and fell into a deep sleep.

Chapter 28

Coreena's Visit

Ivan heard a female's voice. Sweet and laced with worry.

"I want to see Ivan. Maybe I can help."

"Thank you for coming, Coreena." Peter closed the front door behind her. "It's nice to see you again. Been a long time."

She gave a quick lift to her brow. "What happened? You look pale."

"Nothing to worry about. I'm feeling better now. Tragic about Phillip dying in that tractor accident." It seemed that Peter intentionally changed the subject. "I know how fond you were of him."

"That's all in the past now, though I still grieve for him," she said with abruptness.

"Ivan's been asleep all day, and I haven't wakened him. He needs to heal."

"Heal? Danny didn't tell me what was wrong, but he assured me Ivan's not contagious. Is he?"

"No. A deep and painful stomach wound."

"Oh, no. How did it happen?" She covered her mouth with her hands, and her eyes widened.

"He can tell you." Peter looked away. "When he awakes—and he should soon. Will you spoon-feed him? There's soup on the counter, over there."

"I'd be happy to. Where is he?"

"That way." Peter pointed to a hallway off the kitchen. "Just follow the sound of heavy snoring."

Dan walked through the front door like he was part owner of the farm. "Hi, Peter. How's Ivan? I've come to do the evening milking, and Coreena insisted she wanted to come. She thinks she's Florence Nightingale. You know, the nurse. And sometimes she does seem to have a gift for healing."

"She wants to be a nurse, then?"

"I don't know." Danny threw his arms into the air. "You'll have to ask her."

"With Coreena to coax him to eat, I believe he'll soon recover." Peter moved to the front door. "I'll put on my boots and help you in the barn."

"You still remember how to milk a cow?" Dan made a comical face as if in doubt.

Glancing at his smooth hands, Peter shook his head. "I'll need a bit of practice."

Before Peter and Dan could leave, they heard Coreena call, "Hey! Come here and do your job."

They hurried to the bedroom.

"What happened?" Peter's breathing was rapid.

Dan stretched his neck around Peter and gaped at the sick patient. "You don't look so good, Ivan."

Coreena removed her coat and wool scarf and draped them over a chair. "You must sponge bathe him and change him into a clean gown. He smells awful."

"That would probably be the infection, but I did change the nightshirt he's wearing," Peter muttered in his own defense. "He's been in so much pain, I..."

"Well," she said huffily, "now is the time. I'll put on a pot of tea and warm the soup."

Dan stared down at Ivan. "I've never bathed anyone before. Where do we start?"

"First, we remove the nightshirt."

Together they struggled to pull off Ivan's clothes. Peter lifted the bandages and shook his head. "Coreena's right. The bandage has to be changed."

Groaning, Ivan pushed his brother's hands away. "No. No," he cried. "No more."

"I'm sorry," Peter said. "But this must be done. I promised your friends."

Turning his head away, Dan squeezed his eyes closed. "It looks awful. How did he get this terrible wound?"

Ivan pretended to drift off to sleep, not wanting to explain. He hoped to observe how his brother answered Dan's question.

Peter gave a lift of his left shoulder, sensing Dan's gaze on him. "I can't say. If Ivan wants to tell his story, he will."

"I don't mean to be nosy, but if Ivan's in some kind of trouble, I want to help."

"I know, and I feel the same way. That's why I'm here taking care of him. But it's not for me to say."

"Coreena's been nagging me to find out how Ivan got hurt. She's really very fond of him, you know?"

"Yes, I can see that." Peter frowned, almost undetected. He gathered the used dressing and tossed them in the dustbin next to the bed.

"Where does he keep the bandages?" Dan moved toward the bedroom door.

"Don't know. I haven't explored the house much since I've been home. I've felt so awful." He scratched the side of his head. "Well—" He rethought the question.

"—try the hall closet. That seems like the best place for such a thing."

Dan returned in a moment and tossed a range of bandages on the bed. "You haven't even told me why you were in a bad way. Did you both tangle with some wicked creature in that terrible forest? No wonder Coreena hates that place."

"Never mind that now," Peter said and soothed Ivan's forehead. "Let's get this job done so your sis can spoil him."

When they finished bathing him and changed his dressing, they left the bedroom. In a rush, they grabbed their jackets from the wooden coat rack by the kitchen door. "We're leaving," Peter called over his shoulder to Coreena. "Don't let Ivan get away with anything." He laughed.

She turned from the stove and scowled.

"Ivan," she softly called as she entered the bedroom. "It's Coreena Filmore. I've come to feed you. Are you up to it?"

"After the clumsy scrubbing I've just had, I'm very awake and in a lot of agony." He couldn't hold back a moan. When he spoke, he could smell his own sour breath and hoped she wouldn't get too close to him.

"Dan told me you were sick. How did you get a stomach wound?"

He looked up into her bright turquoise-blue eyes and tried to force a smile. "It's a long story. I'd rather not speak of it right now."

Her smooth brow rippled. The same look she'd worn when he'd told her at the Crunching Crumb that he was going into the forest. She must've forgotten how angry she was toward him after he'd treated her so rudely that day.

"Cozy," she said after looking around Ivan's bedroom, sounding like she approved. "What's this?" she suddenly asked and moved toward the dresser.

Ivan tried to sit up to see what she'd asked about, but he whimpered and eased back onto his pillow. "It's a medallion," he simply said.

"Where did it…? Look at that! It says on the front, beneath the jewel, it's the Forest's Medallion for Bravery." Flipping it over, she said, "And there's your name, Ivan Kimble, at the bottom, with a dragon and a big tree at the top. Remarkable." She swiftly turned with surprise and curiosity. "What did you do to deserve such a high honor?"

"I-I…" He stilled, closing his eyes, holding his stomach with both hands.

Coreena went to him. "I'm so sorry. I didn't mean to cause you pain." She took a face flannel, rinsed it in a dish pan nearby, and wiped his sweaty face. "You can tell me the story when you feel better."

After a moment or two, he said, "I'm hungry."

"The soup should be hot, and I have tea for you—for us."

"Where's Peter?" He made a small noise in his throat, forcing back a cry. He didn't want her to think he was weak and out of control, especially after she'd seen the medal.

"He and Danny went to milk the cows." She explained, going into a sing-song voice, "Then they'll release them from their stanchions so they can drink from the barnyard trough, then they'll water and feed the chickens, then put the cows back into the barn and give them hay." Coreena wrinkled her nose and grinned. "I hear the same routine from Danny when he comes home." She sighed and rose from the chair. "I'll be right back."

Ivan lay there after the spasm of pain had passed, feeling happy because he was in Coreena's care. She's beautiful, he thought. Her long blonde hair and lavender fragrance lifted his spirits.

What about Anna-Iza? I deeply care for her, though our friendship is not allowed. What must I do?

He thought back on his terrible encounter with Hoxx. *Why did I act so foolishly? Reaching for the King's Scepter when I knew the ghoul had a sword by his side. That was reckless enough, but what I didn't know was the weapon had a poisonous blade. Oh, God. It hurts.* The heat of the poison scraped along his veins like a rake, boiling its way through his chest. *Will I ever feel well again?* What about Zephyrus and how he, too, must have suffered because of the Swamp Dragon's poison that covered the blade of the Silver Axe? He still wondered about the mysterious man in the gray-hooded cloak that struck Zephyrus in his side, nearly causing his death.

He listened for her footsteps, hoping she would hurry. He licked his lips.

Ivan must have dozed off for only a short time when Coreena returned, holding a tray with a bowl of something that looked like broth with small chunks of potato, along with slice of buttered bread. He breathed in the hot aroma, eyeing the meal with eagerness.

"I'll pour us some tea." Her arched brows lifted as she concentrated on filling first one cup and then another. "I remember you don't take sugar or milk. Can you sit up?"

He tried, but his muscles wouldn't cooperate, and the throbbing was great across his middle.

"Maybe I can help you." Coreena rolled the covers away, grasped him under his arms, and tugged. "One more time, and I think we have it." When she lifted again, he was sitting upright, leaning against the headboard.

"You're amazingly strong for a girl," he said, grinding his teeth to mask the pain. He didn't cry out, even though he wanted to.

They laughed about his remark that she was strong. It hurt his stomach, but their laughter was just what Ivan needed. *How long has it been since I've experienced such a delightful thing?*

Instead of questioning him about his dilemma, which he was grateful for, Coreena told him about her day at school. "You see," she said, lifting the spoon to his mouth, "my teacher, Mr. Bankus, asked me to take over his class again. He does this a lot. I don't know where he goes, but he disappears for several hours," she whispered, believing she'd betrayed a secret. "When he returns, I smell alcohol on his breath. I enjoy teaching the students, so I haven't complained, even though I'm still a student myself. Here, open your mouth and swallow." Ivan did as she asked, enjoying the flavors and warmth going down his raw throat.

She broke off pieces of bread and handed them to him. With her urging, he ate every spoonful. Dabbing his lips with a napkin, she smiled and seemed proud of her accomplishment.

She continued, "I read *Gulliver's Travels* by Jonathan Swift to the students. Do you know the book?"

He shook his head.

"Then I'll bring it tomorrow and read to you. Now, how about a nice spot of tea?"

He took the hot cup from her hands and raised it to his lips. "Good," he mumbled. After a couple of sips, his eyes drooped. He wanted to talk, to ask her questions, but the need to sleep overtook him.

"I...I'm sorry, but..." He yawned behind his palm.

"You're getting sleepy. It's naptime for you." She removed the teacup. "I don't know how you can drink this without lots of sugar and milk. It's simply unthinkable."

Ivan grinned and murmured something about brushing his teeth.

"Let's see if I can return you to your back." Coreena cradled him in her arms, holding him close to her, and manipulated his body into a flat position. When he seemed comfortable enough, she leaned over and brought her lips to his. She kissed him, a long, soft kiss. "That should help make you feel better." She giggled, trying to cover a bit of embarrassment. "I hope you don't mind."

"I...liked it...very much." He gave a big smile, and his eyes closed.

She sat in the chair next to him with her hand covering his. "Oh, Ivan. I hate to see you in such pain. If I had the skill to heal you, I would." He heard her deep sigh.

A lovely dream came and took him away. He drifted into the forest, passing over Zephyrus's wide crown of golden and crimson leaves, past a flying carpet where Rounds, the bald-headed druid, sat waving, and past a beautiful lake that Ivan knew to be Lake Emerald. The vision sparkled like it was touched by Sytha's magic wand. There was an ache in his heart to return to the forest…to return to his friends.

He thought he was still dreaming when he heard Coreena's quiet voice. "You don't need Anna-Iza's Kiss of Discernment to learn what kind of man you are. I know you are quite remarkable, Ivan Kimble."

Chapter 29

Road to Recovery

The next morning, Dan showed up early to help Peter milk the cows.

"You're slower than a magpie flying upside down." Dan roared with laughter. "You might as well be pullin' on sticks instead of a cow's teats—cuz' nothing comes out."

After they'd completed the milking, Peter chased Dan up the porch steps and into the house. "I told you I would need some practice." Their footsteps moved quickly, scraping across the kitchen floor.

Ivan heard their laughter, and it soothed his befuddled dream. He thought about what Coreena had said? *How does she know anything about Anna-Iza's Kiss of Discernment? Surely my worlds are mixed up and make no sense. Of course, that's it. Or is it guilt visiting me? Didn't I kiss Anna-Iza and confess my love for her? How can I be so fickle? I should only care for one girl at a time.*

After three days of confinement, he was anxious to do something fun with Peter and Dan.

His back had bed sores. Shifting, Ivan tried to get comfortable. This morning, he felt a bit better and even considered helping to prepare breakfast.

"Are you staying to eat with us, Dan?" A pan

clunked when Peter set it on the wood stove.

"No, thanks. I've been late to school for the last week, and my teacher at Graydon Hill School threatened to make me sit outside the classroom. I don't think that's a bad punishment, do you?"

Peter chuckled at the statement and pulled off his jacket.

"Then I'll see you this afternoon with Coreena," Dan said. "She thinks she can help Ivan get well."

"It could be true. Go say goodbye, and tell Ivan breakfast will be served shortly."

Dan entered the bedroom. "How are you feeling today? Coreena plans to come with me this afternoon and read to you. She'll bring some scones she's making. Here's my advice, Ivan, don't eat them. She's not a good cook, and her baking is even worse. I try to help her, but it seems hopeless."

Ivan wondered how bad it could be. "Could you stop by the Graydon Village School and tell Mrs. Hambuckle not to worry about me. I'll be back just as soon as I've recovered?"

"Yeah. I'll tell her this afternoon. I already told her you had some unusual tropical disease and must be confined at home for a long while." He wore a serious expression.

"You told her *what*?"

"Well, see you later." He laughed as he turned and left the room.

Peter walked in when Dan walked out, and he asked his brother, "Would you like to join me for breakfast this morning?" He pushed the chamber pot under the bed with his foot so Ivan wouldn't trip on it.

"That would be nice. I'm weary of being in bed and

sleeping all day."

"Great." Peter clapped his hands. "I'll go fry some eggs, potatoes, bangers, and make some toast. Okay?"

"Sounds delicious."

"Then, I'll bathe you and apply what is probably the last of Fungoda's sap. I hope it means you'll be completely healed. Unless…"

"Unless, what?"

"You're trying to get out of farm chores." Peter threw a dishtowel at him, catching Ivan by surprise. "I want to see you there sitting on a milk stool across from me, and I'll challenge you to a milk fight."

"Like we used to do?" Ivan grinned broadly. He knew it would be a happy reunion once Peter left the forest, and Tereus no longer held him in his grip.

After his brother left the room, Ivan heard him shoving wood into the stove and the sharp strike of a match. The sound of pots and pans shifted and clunked on the burners, and soon the aroma of fried bangers wafted into his bedroom. He licked his lips.

Peter maneuvered Ivan out of bed, lifting with his arms around him. "Put your feet into these slippers." Together they shuffled to the warm kitchen, where Ivan eased himself onto a cushioned chair.

The table was covered with their mother's favorite lace tablecloth. Fancy plates and cups were waiting there, with gleaming cutlery resting beside them. It was an impressive effort on Peter's part, and Ivan smiled with appreciation. The setting invited the brothers to enjoy their first meal together since Peter had left for the war. Ivan couldn't be happier, and he was sure his face showed it.

"You need to put on weight that you've lost since

the accident." Peter turned to glance at him from the stove. "You're getting rather gaunt." He divided the eggs and bangers and brought buttered toast to the table. "Eat up."

When Peter was seated, they made small talk for a while. Ivan asked after the cows and how much they were producing. "Did Dan tell you about filling out the milk charts?"

"He did. We're up to date on that—no worry."

Ivan cut the banger into bite-size rounds and chewed before asking his first question. "Why did the ghouls turn on you when they were under Tereus's control?"

Peter's jaw muscle jerked, and his eyes opened wide.

Did I insult him? Is it too early to ask?

"You want to talk about that now, just when you're recovering from the vicious battle with the ghouls?"

He nodded, staying his eyes on his brother.

"From what I've figured, and I've thought about it ever since I was chained and tortured in that miserable cave. Somehow, Tereus learned that I'd contacted Davaan and asked him to help me escape the mountain without being seen—no trace of me." Peter rubbed the back of his neck, where he still had scars from the torture during his capture. "Since Davaan's a werewolf and has the skills, stealth, and intelligence, I knew he would be best to help carry out the plan. More importantly, he was willing because of you."

"Why include me in the rescue?" Ivan raised his teacup to his lips and sipped. His hand shook a bit, afraid of how Peter would answer.

He faced him. "No one cares for me like you, little brother. I trust you more than anyone. You are loyal and have the devotion of the Forest behind you…Sytha, Commander Simon, and the Wolflords. I could tell they all have a high opinion of you."

"But they weren't invited. Only Davaan, Wayland, and me. The armies weren't included."

"That's right. I thought it best not to alert the ghouls. They are not very smart, but they are savage, and there are—were—so many of them." Peter rolled his eyes.

"The Elftens helped, too," Ivan added, realizing how lucky he was to have so many dependable friends.

"Yes, the Elftens. Their magic is priceless, and Sytha is quick and accurate when it comes to the bow and arrow. We used to practice archery together, but I could scarcely beat him. My consolation prize was a couple of his golden-tipped arrows."

"I know he gave you them as a gift." Ivan dabbed his mouth with a napkin. "I've watched Sytha in action, and his accuracy is amazing."

"I think Sytha is angry with me and holds a grudge for the bad decisions I've made." He bit into his toast and chewed. "We were famously close, you know? Wayland, Sytha, and me—the fun-loving terrors of the forest." Peter laughed. He must've flashed back in the past and to the mischief they'd caused.

"So I've heard." Ivan glanced shyly at his brother. "I'm wondering, did Maloof and Cecil visit our farm a second time and I wasn't aware of it?"

Again, Peter appeared surprised, if not embarrassed to answer the question. "Yes, they did. They tried to convince me to seek Tereus and join him in his mission and to sit upon the throne as a king. The offer appealed to me and so, this time I agreed to a meeting." He lowered his forehead into his open palm. "It was foolish of me. So shortsighted."

Ivan nodded a time or two. Yes, he thought, it was very foolish, but he couldn't say it aloud. There would be no purpose to it.

"Ivan." Peter put down his fork and leaned forward. "I must warn you. Now that Tereus knows you helped free me from the mountain and you've killed Hoxx, his wrath will be even more powerful against both of us. You cannot return, no matter what. I tried to tell you this on your first visit to the Forest, but you insisted your friends would protect you." He reached across the table and took Ivan's hand. "Please promise me you won't go there."

After a moment, Ivan pulled back his hand and went very still. "I-I don't know. But…now that you're home with me, there's no reason to return and search for you."

"That's good. We'll both live longer that way." He gave a cautious smile.

"Did Coreena ask you to tell me this?"

Peter pulled up his shoulders. "She did mention it, and I said I felt the same way, that the forest is a dangerous place. I think the pretty lass has a crush on you." He wiggled his eyebrows up and down in a comical way.

"I'm fond of her, too." His cheeks turned warm. Although he'd already admitted it to Peter, it felt good to voice his fondness for Coreena.

"Well, I can't blame you. I liked Coreena for years, but she wasn't interested in me." Peter gave a little laugh like his admission embarrassed him. I think she saw me as Phillip's friend, and I was too old for her." He shrugged.

Avoiding Peter's eyes, hoping, indeed, there was

nothing between them, Ivan encouraged some eggs onto the back of his fork with his table knife and ate them. *Yes, it's true. The forest is a dangerous place. Haven't my two previous visits proven this? My fight with the Black Knights, the Forest war, nearly losing my Essence to a Vaguer. Now, Peter and I can work the farm together and be happy, just like we were before he was enlisted into the British Army.* Although his brother confirmed he'd never gone to fight the war. Instead, he entered the West Forest and stayed safely at the South Castle, enjoying himself and his new friends until peace had been declared.

"You still look thin and pale." Peter shifted in his chair and seemed uncomfortable with Ivan's silence. "There are dark circles under your eyes. Are you sleeping well enough?"

"That's all I've been doing, and I'm anxious to do something more." He didn't tell Peter about his nightmares. "Winter will be here soon, and there's much to be done on the farm."

"Don't worry. I'll help you, and Dan said he'd come by whenever you needed him."

"The breakfast you made is delicious." Ivan thanked him.

Peter blinked with pleasure and pressed his lips together. "I thought I'd go into the village today and buy some groceries, if you feel well enough for me to leave." His eyebrows lifted. "I don't think I can eat eggs at every meal. I'll go see Mr. Turlow and tell him you're ill…and make my apologies for not paying the invoices in a timely manner. If Jay Whittaker is still working there, I'll pay him, too."

Pleased that Peter remembered his promise to speak

with Mr. Turlow and Jay at the mill, Ivan nodded. "Oh, and would you buy some cracked corn for the chickens? I'll give you money."

Ivan suddenly pushed upright from the table and froze. The quick motion caused him to shiver as pain shot through him.

"W-what's wrong?" Peter dropped his fork onto his plate.

"Thunder. I hear—something that sounds like—"

Peter jumped from his chair and went to the kitchen window. "Oh, my God! It's…"

"Who? Who is it?"

"It's Zello! That crazy dragon is circling and about to land on our lawn. He's going to get hung for this, breaking Forest Law by leaving its borders."

Returning to the table, Peter held Ivan under his arms and guided him. "Hold on to me, and I'll open the door. Easy now. You haven't been on your feet much these last few days, and your legs are sure to be weak."

They went onto the porch to see the great beast as he glided and lowered his wide, dark wings. His large feet came to an abrupt halt not far from where Peter and Ivan stood. The dragon folded his powerful wings next to his body and stretched his long neck, eyeing everything around him. His nostrils flexed when he smelled the smoke from the Kimbles' chimney. Ivan knew that dragons didn't like smoke or fire unless it was their own.

"What are you doing here, Zello?" Ivan's mouth hung open.

The dragon lowered his head. "I've been looking for you," he said with ease. "I didn't properly say goodbye when they put you into a wagon and took you away." He squinted. "Who's that beside you?"

"I-I'm Peter, Ivan's brother, of course. You must remember me."

The dragon seemed to analyze the comment and jerked his head forward. "Yes, now I remember. There was a time, after you betrayed us and disappeared, that I promised myself I'd eat you if I ever found you again."

Peter leaped back, muscles tightened in his cheeks.

"Why would you even think such a thing?" Ivan glowered, more than a little confused. *What did his brother do to cause Zello's wrath?* He glanced at Peter, whose head hung low. Alfred and Canute were muddled to see the huge dragon on their property, and they woofed several times.

The dragon didn't answer but drew in closer to examine Ivan. He tipped his head and snorted. His breath was truly rotten, and Ivan would've pulled away, except he needed the porch railing to lean upon.

"How are you feeling?" the dragon asked with a sympathetic voice.

"I'm getting better every day. Peter is taking good care of me."

With a robust huff, Zello asked, "Do you need more sap from Fungoda? If so, I'll go now to get it for you. I'm sure one of your friends from the forest would ride with me."

Ivan shook his head. "We'll use the last of it today, and I'm hoping it will do the trick."

Peter interjected, raising his skeptical brow, "Did Zephyrus give you permission to leave the forest?"

"He doesn't know. I left from the South Road Entrance, near the Azurite Mountains. No one thought to name it the South Road Exit." He raised his head high, where his throaty snorting sounded like laughter. "That was a good joke. But I don't think anyone saw me leave."

"What if they did? Will you be punished?" Ivan clenched his teeth to stop the nagging pain. He wasn't accustomed to standing for long periods, and besides, the cold morning air chilled his bare legs. He wished he would've grabbed a jacket or even a blanket to cover his shoulders.

The dragon's eyes narrowed like he considered this for the first time. "I don't know. I'll probably be put on trial and found guilty." He exhaled hot air and changed the subject entirely. "The good news is the dragon's stable is nearly finished. I've been helping almost every day since I burned it down. It's looking quite splendid."

"Hooray!" Ivan said and turned to Peter. "Do you know about the dragons' stable that burned to the ground?"

"I was someplace else when that happened, though I did hear a brief rumor about it."

"It was me." Zello lowered his lids, his tone remorseful. "I was trying to relight the wick of the Golden Lantern in the old stable with my fiery breath, and the straw made me sneeze. Well, it was a disaster, and the building went up in flames. Fortunately, the other dragons, including two young males and an infant, got out safely."

"Thank goodness." Peter breathed a sigh.

"When are you coming back, Ivan? You can ride with me anytime you wish. Zephyrus may approve of my leaving the forest to come get you."

Ivan pursed his lips and said, "I don't think he would be in favor of that."

Alfred and Canute ran up the porch, barking at

Zello. "Shush," Ivan said. They whimpered before finally settling down near Ivan's slippered feet.

"I'd better go feed the horses and then hook Darkly to the carriage." Easing down the steps, Peter hugged the railing to avoid getting close to Zello.

"Don't forget, I'll give you money for the supplies in the village." Peter gave a brief nod indicating he'd understood.

After he'd left, Ivan asked, "What did Peter do that's so terrible?"

Zello paused and watched as the blond-haired brother ran toward the barn. "I thought Zephyrus would've told you."

Shaking his head, Ivan answered, "I've had little conversation with him about Peter. He doesn't bring up the subject, so I don't ask."

"Why the heck not? Aren't you curious?"

"Yes, I am. But it's not good manners to pry." Ivan glanced away, making sure Peter had moved out of earshot. "I'm not sure I want to hear the truth."

"It was some time ago." Zello looked off into the distance, wrinkling his brow. "He went to the dark side and joined that vile creature beneath the earth—Tereus."

"I've heard something of that nature, but what did he do?" Ivan was careful with the little information Peter had entrusted to him.

"Well." Zello licked his lips with his long tongue. "He fed the Dark Army with grain that he got from somewhere. He told our secrets. And he fought in the Forest War against us."

"No, that's not true." Ivan made a halting gesture with his right hand. "Peter wouldn't have betrayed us. He told me he wasn't part of their hideous war but that he stayed hidden until the fighting was over."

Zello eyed him, snorting in disbelief. "You know that Tereus is Zephyrus's brother, don't you?"

Ivan nodded, wondering how two brothers could be so different. "Peter told me he'd joined with Tereus to help out the Forest Army, and the strong hold Tereus had on him. Since then, Peter has asked for my forgiveness, and said he was sorry for drawing me and Davaan into his dangerous plan to travel to the Mountain of Smoke and Fire. He had no other way to escape the ghouls. Now," Ivan said with relief, "my brother is staying here on the farm with me. Already I see the pain and worry leave his face."

"So, you'll come back with me…sometime—to see all your friends?"

"It'll be winter soon." Ivan grabbed the porch post, his body slumped from fatigue. "I understand the Forest closes down until spring arrives. Maybe then, I'll visit." In his heart, he'd promised never to return, but he wanted to give Zello hope. Though Ivan would miss his friends and their adventures terribly, he also needed to be with Peter and live a normal life.

The announcement seemed to crush Zello's feelings. His dragon eyes watered, and his voice was heavy and forlorn. "I'd better get back to the castle. Lord Graydon will be missing me soon."

Seeing the sadness in Zello's eyes, Ivan wanted to assure him that he'd find a way to return to the Forest—eventually. *Though I've promised Peter not to go there.*

Zello blew a sigh in Ivan's face. "Where's your Golden Medallion for Bravery?" His own medal hung around his neck, looking tiny against his tough, brown scales.

Amused the dragon would think of the special award that bonded them, Ivan pointed toward the house. "In my bedroom, where it's safe from plundering hands." A quick grin showed he was teasing.

With that, the great beast said, "Take care of yourself until we meet again."

"Wait! I-I wanted to ask you, well, on that day I flew on Fluorescent's back to catch the Golden Lantern…"

Zello pushed his maw closer. "What about it?"

"Did you mean to see me fall to my death and keep the lantern for yourself?"

"I have no use for it. I was mad for being accused of things I didn't do, and the people of the Forest didn't believe me. So, I wanted to draw attention and make them sorry for their short-sightedness."

"But—but I could've fallen to my death."

"I would never let that happen." Zello winked. "The Black Book of Pearls wouldn't allow it."

"What? I don't understand…y-you, but you…" Ivan sputtered, trying to get a clear answer.

"Someday, you will understand. It will all be known to you." The dragon turned around, took several measured steps, and said, "May the High Intervener be with you." Then faster and faster, he moved until his wings lifted and pumped hard to get airborne. His effort to take off swirled dust and leaves in his wake. Ivan watched in awe as his dragon friend rose from the ground, dropping and rising until he caught an updraft. There, he blew a long stream of fire into the blue-gray sky. This foolish lark could get him into a great deal of trouble if anyone in the village spotted such a thing. Ivan hoped they hadn't.

Scratching his head, he watched the huge beast as he

flew west, wondering what he would *someday* understand.

Chapter 30

Time with Coreena

Shivering from the cold, Ivan walked toward the door just as he heard Peter pull the carriage from the barn.

Sad to be left alone on the porch, the beagles whimpered. Ivan wished he could take them into his arms and stroke their backs and tell them how much he loved them.

Wheels crunched on hard ground as Peter rode the buggy from the stable, bringing Darkly to a halt. He hopped off, took Ivan by his arm, and led him to his bedroom. "It's time for your final dosage of sap," he said, throwing his arms wide, "before I leave you."

They both grimaced.

Peter cradled his brother onto the bed and eased his head against the pillow. "Are you comfortable?"

"I'm very tired." He wondered if there was more to Zello's story, and only Peter could tell it. Finally, he found the courage to ask. "Why is Zello mad at you?"

"Didn't he tell you?"

"Not much, just that you gave your loyalty to Tereus."

"Well, that's plenty of betrayal. Tereus makes you do wicked things while promising you glory and fame. I was taken in, Ivan. Too naïve to know the difference."

He turned red and averted his eyes.

Peter brought a dishpan with warm water, along with a face flannel, and placed it on a nightstand. Ivan's nightshirt showed blood stains, and they concluded the wound had been pulled open and drained during Zello's visit. "Too much excitement for you." Peter pursed his lips. He washed his brother's chest and legs, along with a gentle pass across his middle, finishing by scrubbing Ivan's arms and face.

"You already smell better." Peter laughed and gave him a poke in his bicep.

Shaking, Ivan clenched his teeth for what he knew was sure to come.

"I wish I could ease your pain." Peter lightly shook the liquid in the vial. Examining it against the light of the window, he affirmed that this would be the last application of Fungoda's sap. He pulled away the bandage. "It's better, but still red and raw. Maybe this last dosage will take care of that." He blew out a puff of breath.

Ivan's body stiffened, his fists curled against his side, waiting for the inevitable. Moments passed. He felt a stinging sensation and the liquid that dribbled down his side. "Did you use it all?"

"Yes, that's it."

"It must be healing. There was little pain." He took Peter's hand in his. "Thank you, dear brother. I don't know how I would bear this without you."

Peter's face lit up. His grin was genuine. "That's what brothers are for." He covered the wound with clean bandages and pulled Ivan's nightshirt down past his knees. "Now, if you tell me where the money is, I'll take what I need and be on my way to the village."

"There," he said, pointing his finger toward the dresser. "Top drawer."

He opened it and exclaimed, "Goodness! Where'd you get all this?"

"I've saved and stashed it there for my use." Ivan didn't tell Peter that Zephyrus had paid him generously each time he visited the forest. "That reminds me, would you pay Dan when he comes this afternoon?"

"Sure. I think there's plenty here for that." He stuffed the cash into his pocket and returned to fold the covers to Ivan's chin. "Sleep well. I'll be back as soon as I can."

"I hate to see you go. It will be lonely without you."

"You've had enough excitement for the morning, what with Zello's unexpected visit."

"It was great to see him, but I fear he may be in trouble for coming here." Ivan said goodbye and had planned to question more, but knew Peter needed to be on his way.

He was fed. He was warm. He was happy.

****

"Wake up, sleepy head." Coreena peered into Ivan's bedroom. "Where's Peter? I thought he'd be looking after you."

Ivan groaned and tried to turn to his side. His back was sore from lying in one position for what seemed like hours. "Why are you here so early?" he said and yawned.

"It's not early. Danny went straight to the barn to start the milking. It's cold out there, and it may freeze tonight, so he hoped to finish quickly."

"Peter left late morning to go into the village and buy groceries." He struggled to raise himself by his elbows, but it was too painful. "I thought he'd be back by now." Glancing shyly at her lovey rose-colored cheeks, he watched while Coreena removed her coat and plaid scarf, and draped them over a chair. *Does she know I stare at her?* "Could you help pull me into a sitting position?"

She did as she'd done the day before, lifting and dragging until he leaned against the headboard. "There, how's that?" she said with a lilt in her voice.

"Much better." He had hoped she'd kiss him again, but she didn't. Was she embarrassed? Stretching against the stiffness in his neck and shoulders, he was again surprised at how strong she was in her upper torso. "Are you going to read to me?"

"Yes, as I promised. I think you'll find this book quite delightful." Coreena showed him the cover of *Gulliver's Travels,* and Ivan hummed his approval.

He stayed silent when she began to read about the Lilliputians from the land of Lilliput. Just how the tiny inhabitants had captured a full-sized man named Lemuel Gulliver, and held him prisoner, Ivan couldn't figure.

"Strength in numbers," Coreena explained, and Ivan thought of the ghouls.

Near the middle of the third chapter, she scowled and said, "It reminds me of you, Ivan, always looking for an adventure. Taking chances, risking your life in the forest—and for what reason?"

Ivan argued. "I...I didn't go there to find adventure. I went into the forest to find Peter—and I found him."

Coreena pressed her lips together, like she was trying to decide if she should believe him. "So...you won't be going back?"

"No reason. Peter and I are together and safe on our farm."

Reaching for his hand, she gave it a squeeze and grinned widely.

He closed his eyes and said, "Besides, the adventures of Gulliver's travels were mostly out of his control, as they were for me. Now, continue on about the Lilliputians. I want to learn if he escapes and returns to his wife and family."

After reading for several chapters, Coreena stood and handed him the book. You can read until I find something for you to eat. I brought some scones that I made for you, too." Her smile was warm and genuine.

Since he'd missed lunch, even Coreena's scones sounded good, in spite of what Dan had told him. He hoped she hadn't sprinkled sugar on top. His empty stomach rumbled dreadfully, and Ivan laughed to hide his embarrassment.

Coreena's hand went to her mouth to stifle a giggle. "I'll see what I can find for you."

She went into the kitchen, where clanking sounded. "Oh," she said, "there's no fire in the stove. I thought it was chilly in here when I came. Well, I know how to do this." Ivan listened to logs being stuffed into the stove, and a match was lit. Ivan recognized the familiar sounds, having done it plenty of times.

When he heard a horse neighing and a carriage outside the house, he knew Peter must've returned. He considered getting up to help Coreena with the fire and to find out what had taken Peter so long in the village, but when he threw off the covers and tried to sit up, nausea hit him. Feeling wheezy and without energy, he lay back down. *Is it hunger or the poison that still circulates in my bloodstream?*

"Hello, Coreena. How's our patient?" Peter called in

his easy, unbothered manner.

"He's very hungry. You neglected his lunch." Her voice was tight, and Ivan detected a strong reprimanding tone.

"You're right. I was held up in the village." Peter set a bag of groceries on the table, where it made a dull thud.

"There are several more bags in the carriage. It's been so long since I've shopped that it took quite some time to finish the task. Then, of course, to further excuse my tardiness, I talked with several people who still remembered me. They wanted to know all about my war experience."

Ivan strained to hear past their moving feet and the rustle of items being pulled from the grocery bag.

"You know, Coreena, we could take up where we left off before I went to war." Peter teased in his cocky manner.

She couldn't know that Peter never went to war unless he'd told her, which Ivan doubted.

Quiet followed.

"There never was a beginning," she said in a stiff voice.

Peter mumbled something. It sounded like he said, "I liked you."

I liked you? Left off? He swallowed hard. *Does that mean Peter still had eyes for Coreena all this time, and I was too blind to see? And why not? Peter is tall and handsome with a chiseled jaw and straight nose. His quick wit and engaging tongue would charm anyone. Haven't people always been drawn to him—especially the girls?*

Tears formed in Ivan's eyes. *I've had a crush on Peter's girl, and I never realized it. Why hadn't Peter told me? Because...because Peter is too kind and must've decided to step aside and see where the romance took them.* Ivan's face and neck burned with shame. *How did I not see it?*

No. I'd never intrude on Peter's girl. But how can I erase my own feelings for her? She's been so attentive and caring toward me. Is it to impress Peter, or does she truly feel affection for me? And yet, she kissed me.

Peter poked his head into Ivan's bedroom door and said, "I'm going to help Dan with the milking. When we're done, we'll make a splendid dinner for us."

Ivan turned to look at him and forced a grin. "I'd like that."

Humming a lovely little tune, Coreena entered the bedroom after Peter had left and helped Ivan struggle from the bed. Holding his forearm with her hands, she guided him to the kitchen table. She gave him a lovely smile when she brought a small bowl of hot lentil soup, along with buttered bread, and carefully set it in front of him. Ivan thanked her but could find nothing to say. His feelings of humiliation overwhelmed him as he spooned the soup into his mouth. *She feels sorry for me. That's what it is.*

"Are you okay?" She looked up under her light lashes.

Ivan lifted an eyebrow as his answer, but he couldn't speak. His raw throat might release his sadness to tears.

"Don't worry about this meager amount. When Danny and Peter finish the chores, they'll prepare a dinner of chicken and boiled potatoes. Doesn't that sound delicious?"

He sensed her attempt to bring joy to his late lunch, but it failed to lighten Ivan's mood.

"I know what will cheer you." Her face brightened with enthusiasm. She jumped up and brought the basket of scones to the table. Lifting the dishtowel, she handed one to Ivan on the empty saucer meant for his teacup.

After a couple of bites, he gave a weak smile, forcing politeness. It was as Dan had said. Dry and flavorless, it crumbled into pieces. He suspected she'd forgotten the salt and maybe a second egg. But Ivan was grateful she cared enough to make them for him. "Thank you," he mumbled.

"You're very quiet this afternoon. Are you sure you feel all right?"

Ivan stared at his empty bowl, avoiding her bewildered gaze. His chest felt hot with disappointment, not knowing how to hide his hurt feelings. He thought Coreena was fond of him, enjoying his company, but Peter's words suggested otherwise.

Their silence lingered as Ivan sipped his tea, unable to speak.

Finally, he said, "I'm sorry, but I'm tired." Ivan stood from his chair and held out a halting hand. "No need to help me. I can manage." After hesitating, he said, "T-thank you for the soup and the…the scones." He stared at the floor, watching his short steps, wondering for a moment if he'd been wrong. But I heard what Peter said, though Coreena had rejected his statement. *Does she mean it? Or did she try to cover her feelings for Peter in case I overheard? I don't know. It's all too complicated to make sense.*

"I-Ivan. What? I don't understand." Her voice trembled. A small animal-like cry escaped.

Closing the bedroom door, Ivan removed his bathrobe and draped it over the chair. The effort to crawl into bed was painful and he was glad. Nothing could hurt like the tear in his heart. He hadn't realized until now how much happiness she'd brought into his life these past few days.

He tried to doze off, but sadness pushed sleep away. *What am I to do?*

Later, the door to his bedroom opened slowly. Ivan hoped it would be Coreena, and he'd apologize and ask her how she felt about him.

"Ivan, will you join us?" It was Peter's voice. "Dinner is ready and if I must say, we did a splendid job. Ivan?"

"I…I'm too tired to eat. I'm sorry." He yawned to make it seem real.

"Okay." Peter paused for a moment, like he was about to say more, but then didn't. "I'll check on you later."

Time passed. They must've finished their chicken dinner. Ivan heard her delicate footsteps come into his dark room. She sat in the same chair near his bed where she'd read Gulliver's Travels to him.

Coreena took his hand that rested on his stomach and held it to her wet cheek. "Please, don't be angry with me. Tell me what I've done wrong." She sniffed. "I'll try to make it better."

Ivan did not stir, but pretended to sleep. If he spoke, he'd surely weaken and take her in his arms. He might even cry out loud. *She's Peter's girl, and I have no right to interfere. Hasn't Peter admitted he'd liked Coreena for years?*

She blew her nose into a handkerchief and stood, reaching for her coat and scarf. "I won't be back, Ivan," she said quietly. "I don't think you care for my company

any longer."

The bedroom was very dark after she closed the door behind her. Tears formed in his eyes.

His whole body trembled. A bit of vomit came up and dribbled over his chin and met the neckline of his nightshirt. He couldn't forget her final, unhappy words.

How can I let her go so easily without asking for an explanation? A harsh voice inside tormented him. *Maybe you're a bigger fool than you care to admit, Ivan Kimble.*

Chapter 31

The Truth

December swept in with freezing temperatures, along with a light dusting of snow. Though Ivan had days of pain and nausea, he had more good days than bad, and he continued to heal. He and Peter did the chores in the morning, with Peter doing most of the work, which he insisted was fine with him. Often, Ivan would collapse on a pile of straw and take a nap listening to the cows shifting on their heavy feet and the rhythmic splash of milk hitting the metal pail. "It's better you get enough rest and heal completely." Peter would grin and kiss Ivan on both his cheeks.

There were times like these and many more that Ivan truly appreciated his brother and loved him even more.

Some days, Peter would harness Darkly and ride into the village. Just what he did there, Ivan wasn't sure, and Peter didn't explain much—only about seeing old friends he'd met. He told Ivan that he visited the Rouster, Mule's favorite pub, and played cards along with a few games of checkers. Ivan suspected that Peter was bored with the farmer's life and went there to mingle with more people. And the girls.

When Ivan was feeling especially gloomy and vulnerable, he'd imagine Peter meeting secretly with Coreena in the Crunching Crumb Tea Parlor, and there, they'd hold hands and gaze into each other's eyes. The thought nearly doubled him over with sadness. He would fabricate conversations between them, where his brother would say something amusing, and Coreena would giggle. Many nights he wept while trying to stifle the noise so Peter wouldn't hear. Ivan would press his fingers against his eyes to hold back tears, but it rarely helped. He missed her sharing with him, missed her reading to him, and he especially missed her kisses and laughter.

He thought on his foolish decision to let her go without explanation. Now, he felt shame and uncertainty, but he couldn't see a graceful way to make amends.

Dan asked and asked, looking hurt. "Why were you so mean to my sister? What did you say to break her heart?"

Ivan would shake his head and look away, giving no answer. Finally, Dan stopped asking, but Ivan could tell he was deeply troubled over the matter. After the cold set in and night came quickly, Dan no longer showed up to help with the milking. Most mornings and evenings, Ivan and Peter managed the farm chores well enough, but their friends were greatly missed.

Sometimes, his brother gave him a curious glance, like he was waiting for an explanation, but Ivan wasn't ready to divulge his confused feelings.

Almost a month had passed since Ivan returned to the farm with a life-threatening wound. One morning after Peter had gone into the village, a buggy pulled up the driveway, crunching frosty gravel as it approached. A horse neighed. Alfred and Canute barked to warn their master they had visitors.

"Aye, Ivan!"

Ivan knew the voice, and he was at once overjoyed. Moving carefully, he grabbed a jacket and went out onto the porch. There, he met his neighbor Mueller McKay and Emma, his wife, and he gave her a welcoming embrace. Their son, Max, held a box full of what must've been food, for Ivan could smell yeast from freshly baked bread protected under a white dishtowel.

"Come in," Ivan said, grinning joyfully. He stepped aside, making way for them to enter.

"I brought you Steak and Kidney Pie. I hope you like it." Emma moved her hefty figure into the house, indicating to her son with a waggle of her finger to place the box on the table. "Some Christmas pudding. There's a pheasant there, too. Plucked and ready for the oven."

"Shot it myself." Max lifted his chin, wearing a proud grin.

Ivan chuckled and ruffled Max's hair. "In that case, it will surely taste ever so good. Thank you, Max."

"Sure." The boy flushed with pride, shoving his hands into his overall pockets.

"Goodness Sakes," Emma's voice rose. "We heard you had something contagious, and so we stayed away. Then—" She looked back at Mule. "—he got pneumonia. And Elmer, you remember little Elmer—the bawl-baby of the family? He got the measles, and then Max caught a mild case of them. It's been one long nursing bout with this brood." She wiped her forehead and whistled out a puff of breath.

"What was the tropical disease you had, and how in the world would you get such a thing?" Mule's voice was packed with concern.

"It wasn't a tropical disease," Ivan said, trying to

laugh off the foolish rumor. "I believe it was…ah, influenza, of sorts, that I just couldn't seem to recover from." He hated to lie to his good neighbors, but he couldn't tell them the truth, or the village constable might come and ask him questions, bringing a net and shackles with him.

Noticing Emma's enlarged belly, pregnant with a child, Mule had told Ivan, he asked, "How are you feeling?"

"Oh." She sighed. "Some days are pretty good, and some days I'm weary. But with our brood of boys, I scarcely have time to pamper myself." She gave a weak smile.

"When you coming back to school?" Max met Ivan's eyes. "We all miss you. Even little Mercy cries for you."

"Soon," Ivan said, remembering Mercy with her bouncing blonde curls. "I'm anxious to get back to my studies and see Mrs. Hambuckle."

Max nodded and grinned. "I'll tell her you are better and not contagious anymore."

"Give Ivan his homework," Emma said, nudging her son.

He handed Ivan a cloth bag that hung over his shoulder. Glancing inside, Ivan spotted a couple books and a stack of papers.

You didn't miss much," Max insisted. "Mrs. Hambuckle spends a lot of time daydreaming and talking about her husband, who came back from the forest. She's so grateful to you for making it happen, and she mentions it almost every day."

"That's nice of her." Ivan grinned and glanced at the stove. "Can I make you some tea? I'd be happy for your company."

"Sorry, Ivan. Goin' into the village to do some Christmas shopping. Max and the boys need clothes and stuff like that." Mule unpacked the box while Emma gave instructions on the time and temperature to cook the fowl. "There are some apples from our cellar, too. Thought you'd enjoy them." Mule looked mighty proud of himself.

Ivan thanked them again and returned their box. He knew boxes were hard to come by since the war. "Too bad Peter's not here to see you. He's in the village today, but I'll tell him you stopped by with this wonderful gift."

"Yup." Mule pursed his lips and scowled. "Be good to see the rascal and find out what kind of trouble he's got himself into after living in that wicked forest."

"Oh, you be quiet. It's none of your business." Emma gave him a push with her hip and Mule, being thinner and somewhat shorter than his wife, nearly fell over from the impact.

Months ago, Mule had told Ivan that a friend of theirs saw Peter in the forest, loading a wagon with free firewood. That explained Ivan's first venture into the formidable West Forest. He could hardly believe the rumor, but he did, indeed, find Peter. And he was grateful for it.

"Best we leave now before the weather gets worse." Mule and his family said their goodbyes and left the house.

Ivan waved from the porch as they turned the buggy around and headed for the village. After they were gone, Ivan felt lonely—even emptier. Leaning on the cold porch rail, he stared to the west. Something warm and inviting stirred, nudging him to return to the forest. He wanted to see Zephyrus and Sebastian, to have adventures with Sytha and Wayland—maybe Davaan would even join them. For a long time, Ivan stood there, remembering. He kneeled with some effort and roughed Alfred and Canute's ears, stroking their backs. They loved his attention, woofed, and licked his fingers. Finally, he exhaled and went into the house.

****

That evening, while Peter washed dishes at the kitchen sink and Ivan dried, Peter turned a worried face to his brother, his voice forceful. "Why doesn't Coreena come by to see you anymore?"

Ivan's brow shot up. "I…well—it's too cold for her—them to come." He figured Peter already knew the reason and wondered how much he should share. *Did he ask the same question of Dan?*

"That's not the answer I'm looking for, little brother. I saw clearly that you and Coreena were fond of each other. You even admitted it. Did you have a disagreement or something?"

Reaching for a plate, Ivan wiped it and placed it in the cupboard. His chest grew hot, and his hand trembled a bit. Now was the time for them to talk. The loneliness he felt from Coreena's absence caused him to curl up in bed at night and groan with misery. He wanted to hear her cheery voice, watch her pretty, animated face, and gaze into her attentive turquoise-blue eyes.

"I…I…"

"Okay. Tell me." Peter turned his head and looked, truly looked at him. His light eyebrows pulled together. "Maybe I can help you with your love life. I've had a few disappointments myself, you know?"

Ivan couldn't imagine. He swallowed past the

burning in his throat. "Almost a week ago…" He stalled for a moment and took a deep breath. "I heard you talking…here in the kitchen. I thought Coreena was your girl, and so I withdrew my affection for her. I w-would never interfere with someone you cared for."

Peter froze like he couldn't believe what he'd just heard. "What—?"

Now, Ivan was even more humiliated. *Did I hurt Coreena's feelings by jumping to a conclusion and not understanding?*

"Tell me. What did I say to give you such a crazy idea?" Peter's eyes grew large, and his mouth stayed open.

"You…you said, 'We could take up where we left off before I went to war.' " Ivan lowered his head and stared at the counter, feeling heat circle his neck and creep to his cheeks.

"Oh, goodness, Ivan. I don't believe—how could you take such an idle remark seriously? She was just a kid then. I teased her sometimes when I went to visit Phillip. She would blush and giggle—like she giggles now."

Holding the dishtowel in a twist, Ivan didn't move. "You admitted you liked her, but she wasn't interested in you."

"Well, that's just it. She wasn't and still isn't interested in me. It's you she likes—in fact, a great deal."

Ivan raised his eyes and studied his brother's face. *Is he telling me the truth?*

"She lived next door to Phillip and Dan at the time. Remember?"

"No," Ivan said softly and frowned. He didn't remember and hadn't known them. "Was she with her

329

family?"

"I don't believe she had a family, never said. She did have a guardianship or something like that."

"Oh. Yes, I'd heard that." Ivan felt the blood drain from his face. Peter looked stricken.

"I'm so sorry you misunderstood my…well. I guess it was a stupid thing to say. I tend to be flirtatious when I clearly shouldn't. It makes me feel like I'm important to the females." Peter put his arms around his brother and held him. "Please forgive me—again."

When he released him, Ivan pulled a hanky from his back pocket, blew his nose, and wiped his eyes. "I'm glad we straightened this out. I've been very sad."

"Please, never feel timid about asking me anything. We are brothers, and we have no one but each other." Peter paused for a long moment, nodding his head, and thinking about the things he'd said. "Now that you know it was a careless remark, why don't you go see her and apologize for your rudeness and my thoughtlessness?" A muscle twitched in his jaw, proving to Ivan that his brother was truly ashamed.

Grabbing several pieces of cutlery, Ivan wiped them so hard he thought he'd rub the silver right off. "I don't think she cares to see me after the way I've treated her."

****

The next morning, after the chores were done, Peter helped Ivan harness Bounty to the buggy.

The animal whinnied and stomped his front hooves and then turned to nuzzle Ivan's neck.

"Stop that, Bounty. You're rubbing snot all over me." Just the same, Ivan was as delighted to see his horse as he was to see him. "I've missed you, too."

"I think you going into the village will be just the

ticket for you." Peter stroked Bounty on his shoulder. "I'd love to ride with you, but this influenza—" He sneezed. "—has gotten me down."

"Are you sure I should leave you?" Ivan paused before he buttoned his jacket and pulled on his hat.

"I'll be fine. Just need some hot tea and a bit more sleep."

Ivan was glad Peter gave his okay to go into the village. The money he'd kept in the top drawer of his dresser was nearly gone, and he needed to visit the Graydon Village Bank and withdraw from his account. *It's surprising how much more expensive it is for the two of us to live.* But Ivan didn't mind. Having his brother with him brought him comfort and a great deal of happiness. Besides, Peter deserved to be paid for his labor on the farm.

"You're sure you're up to riding the distance to the village?" Peter asked a second time. "We could wait until tomorrow. I'm sure I'll feel better by then." He sneezed into the palm of his hand.

Chuckling, Ivan said, "You're fussing, and you'll surely spoil me. Go to bed. I'll be back in a couple of hours."

He climbed up onto the buggy seat, pulled a blanket over his knees, and gave the reins a gentle shake. Bounty moved forward into the cold gray morning. Though he was headed toward the village, Ivan wished he could turn around in the opposite direction and ride into the West Forest. His friends were there. Zephyrus must be in full dormancy by now, his sap returning to his roots that would allow his system to shut down during the long winter. *Sytha? What would he be doing? Surely he was home with his father, the king, who may have taken his wand privileges away and lectured him severely.* Ivan had no way of knowing. *Will Davaan change his mind about turning into a man and leaving his werewolf life behind?* Ivan recalled Peter's words about never returning to the forest. *We promised each other. Should we ignore Tereus's threats and attend Davaan's ceremony next year?* Ivan hoped so, and he would look forward to it.

Overhead he watched as blackcaps and redstarts flew away to warmer climates. They were later than usual to migrate to their annual destinations. Probably because of the long warm autumn, he figured. A startled hare ran in front of Bounty and hid under a roadside bush. These common sights of home made him smile, and he was glad for them.

Peter was right. It felt good to breathe the crisp air and travel the familiar road into the village.

By the time he'd reached his first stop, his stomach had taken quite a jostling, feeling hot and sore. He sat straight and inhaled a deep breath, determined to ignore the pain. During the ride, he considered how he could see Coreena again and apologize for his stupidity. Should he stop at her house before he left for home this afternoon? *What will she think of me, jumping to conclusions about Peter's remark?* He eased down from the buggy and stepped carefully onto the frosty ground. Examining his list, he checked to be sure he wouldn't forget any of his errands.

Just as he left the Graydon Village Bank, with his wallet thick in his back pocket, he spotted her coming his way. He couldn't believe his good luck. Then, realizing what he needed to do, his mouth went dry, and his throat closed up.

Coreena wore a long coat the color of a young fawn. The royal blue scarf wrapped around her neck was knotted in front with short fringe hanging down. His legs froze where he stood, unable to move. *Will she talk to me or walk on by?*

When her eyes met his, she zigzagged and picked up a brisk pace.

"Coreena, wait. I—I want to talk to you."

Though he'd been awarded the Forest Medallion for Bravery, this encounter set his heart to pounding. *What will I say and not sound like a babbling fool?*

Without slowing, she stepped to her right to avoid a collision with him.

"Please. I need to explain." He held out his hand to grasp her sleeve, hoping she would stop.

"Too late for weak apologies." She gave him a surly glance and jerked her arm away.

Now he moved in front of her, and she did stop but looked determined to move aside at any moment and hurry on.

"It—it was a huge mistake. I-I misunderstood Peter's words—his intentions."

Her eyes opened wide. "What does Peter have to do with your rudeness toward me?" She pressed her lips together and crossed her arms. Her purse swung in the bend of her elbow.

Ivan didn't care to make a confession here on the street with curious villagers passing by. He pointed behind her. "Can I buy you a cup of tea at the Crunching Crumb Tea Parlor—and a-an ickleberry scone?" he added as an enticement. "It will be easier if we are warm and sharing a pot of tea, don't you think?" *Does she see my lips quivering?*

Coreena lifted her head.

Is she thinking about the invitation while silently arguing with herself?

"Besides, my knees are shaking so hard I may collapse right here."

"Are you nervous with me?"

"Yes, a bit."

She seemed to appreciate his honesty and humility. Her stern face softened, and she gave a single nod of her head. Turning, they walked together toward the tea parlor.

He held the door for her, careful not to get too close and ruin his chances. The strained feeling between them was awkward and alien to him. His emotions kept back-peddling, trying to find solid ground. Overhead, the little bell tinkled, just as it had when they'd first met here which seemed like ages ago. Coreena led the way until Ivan maneuvered forward and pulled out a chair for her to sit at a small but cozy table in the corner by the window. She didn't remove her coat. That was a bad sign, possibly meaning she didn't plan to stay long. Sitting slowly, he lifted his hat and stuffed it in his jacket pocket. He inwardly grimaced, remembering the uncomfortable wrought iron chairs. Well, he would have to suffer through it.

Cookie, the owner, quickly moved her bulk toward them, jerking the sales pad from her pocket. "I see your beau is back. Kissed and made up, did ya?" She gave a snort of laughter. It appeared that Coreena didn't appreciate the remark. Her cheeks reddened to match the color of her cold, red nose.

"A pot of tea, please, Cookie," Ivan said politely. "And perhaps an ickleberry scone with clotted cream for

Coreena." She looked up under her eyebrows at him, but he couldn't tell if she was pleased or annoyed.

"Do you mean blueberry?" Cookie scowled at him. "Don't know what ickleberry is, so I'm sure we don't have 'em."

"Oh, sorry." Ivan quickly covered his blunder. "I do mean blueberry, of course." He swept his fingers through his hair. *Great beginning, Ivan,* he reprimanded himself.

To his surprise, Coreena released a small smile.

He drew in his breath and decided to plunge in before he lost his nerve and before Coreena lost her patience and left in a huff. This might be his only chance to set things right. He studied his fingers, waiting for the courage to flood over him.

"This shouldn't be so difficult for you," she said with a dry tone. "After all, you were awarded the Forest Medallion for Bravery."

"You'd think so, wouldn't you?"

She waited.

"I...I'm so sorry. A couple days ago, I spoke with Peter and asked him about a remark I'd

overheard him say in the kitchen. He suggested you were his girl and...well, I felt I was interfering."

There was a small flare to her nostrils. "What are you saying?"

He repeated Peter's statement about *taking up* where they'd left off and how badly Ivan felt that he'd drawn on her sympathies because of his injuries. "I thought you were being kind to me but truly liked Peter."

"I don't know how you got such an idea from a meaningless remark like that." Her eyebrows jerked together, and her mouth parted, like she would say more, yet nothing followed. He sensed her frustration.

"It does seem rather weak now that I put words aloud to it." Ivan unbuttoned his jacket and at once felt relief from the heat. "It was very real at the time and…and it broke my heart." He stopped and stared at his nervous fingers once more. "B-because, I, well…Coreena, I'm terribly fond of you."

Now I've said it. Does she feel the same? A glance at her showed only frozen astonishment.

What do I say now after my confession?

Cookie set the two cups of tea on saucers. "Thought I should pour your tea. Looks like you're in a serious trance. One scone with clotted cream for the young lady." She walked away, muttering, "Young love. How tender, how sweet."

"What did Peter say when you asked him about this?" She spooned in sugar and added cream, stirring slowly.

"H-he was as surprised as you are and denied there was ever anything between you." Ivan bit his bottom lip, wondering if she would laugh or throw her scone at him.

"You're very sensitive and loyal to your brother, aren't you?" Her voice had softened.

"He's the only family I have. Now that he's home and we're together again, he's like the Peter I always knew. I don't want any problems between us."

She stopped stirring. Her slender hand reached across the table to his and squeezed. "I should've guessed it," she said, lifting her head in a knowing way.

"Guessed what?" His dark eyes opened wider.

"It was a big misunderstanding. Your behavior didn't fit what I'd come to admire about you."

Her opinion pleased him, though he tried to keep a straight face. "What…what is your opinion of me? I mean, is it still good, even though I caused you sadness?"

"It's *very* good, Ivan."

His grin said it all. "Let's put it aside and think only on the joy of being together." Watching her expression, he was afraid his statement sounded immature.

He took a sip of tea, hoping the pause would soothe his anxious thoughts.

"Yes. And, by the way, I'm very fond of you, too. Ever since we attended the fundraiser for the Graydon Hill School. We danced, we laughed, and we talked. It was a wonderful evening."

"It was." Ivan smiled and squeezed her hand that now rested in his. He was happier than he'd been in many days. He felt the heavy gloom lift from his heart. "Come, I'll walk you to your buggy." Glancing out the window, he said, "I've noticed the weather has turned quite threatening."

Ivan laid the money on the table and put his hat over his head. Cookie moved quickly and handed Coreena a sheet of brown wrapping paper. "For your scone," she said. "It's too hard to eat when you're having a lover's spat, and your mouth is dry as powder." Her thick eyebrows lifted with a show of empathy. Nodding, she picked up the money and returned to her tea parlor duties.

On the way out, Ivan said under his breath, "How would Cookie know that? Do you think she's ever had a boyfriend?"

Coreena glanced at Ivan and gave him a wink. "Women have an intuition for these things."

The day had turned colder, and Ivan suspected more than a dusting of snow would soon follow. He hoped he would make it home before the snow fell heavily.

Coreena swung the blue scarf around her neck and held the wrapping with the scone in a tight grip. "How would it be if I walked you to your carriage since I have one more errand to do before leaving the village?"

"Fine." He tucked his arm through hers and smiled. "I'm glad we're good friends again. I've missed your company terribly."

"Me, too." She looked up at him and gave a cheerful smile. "You know, I do believe the sky is more menacing. I'm fortunate that I live close by, but you best be on your way."

They strode to Ivan's buggy, where Bounty lifted his head and whinnied.

I'm going to kiss her. That will help make up for the way I've treated her, and it will remove any doubt she may have. With a quick breath of courage, he turned and pulled her to him. He lowered his head and brought his lips to hers, where he kissed her several times. The sweet taste of her mouth was better with each kiss.

She gasped, blinking. "Did you like that?"

"I liked it very much." His grin told the whole story.

Chapter 32

Hunger for the West Forest

Ivan pulled himself onto the buggy seat, immediately feeling the chill on his rear end. "Brrr," he said and laughed with happiness. "There, I've done it. I kissed her—and kissed her several times, too." He could tell by the way her soft lips moved under his that she also liked it very much. *Should I tell Peter or keep it my secret?*

He watched the road carefully once he left the village and felt the threat of the oncoming storm. Beyond the ditch and the roadside bushes to his right, he saw a herd of cattle huddled under the trees and wondered why they weren't in their warm barn.

Bounty hurried his pace, showing no interest in the cows. He must've known a snowstorm was moving in quickly, threatening their safety. Ivan drew his shoulders together hoping to hold in his body heat, and to warm the frozen mask on his face. In spite of his leather gloves, his hands were soon stiff with cold.

Shortly, wet snow blew with the gusts of wind. Ivan blinked the frozen flakes from his eyelashes, wondering if he'd make it home before freezing to death. He suddenly saw something moving at the wood's edge, again to his right. It looked like a young girl wearing a crimson-colored cloak with white fur trim around the hood. *What was she doing walking in a risky storm like this?* He couldn't see her face, but the diminutive figure reminded him of Anna-Iza. *Of course, that couldn't be. She and her sister goddesses are forbidden to leave the West Forest.* There were no other horses or carriages on the road.

Ivan jerked back the reins and called, "Hello, can I help you? Are you lost in the blizzard?" She turned her head slightly like she'd heard his call and then continued floating through the dense trees. He suddenly remembered a scene from a dream when he was in the West Forest that both surprised and disturbed him.

In his daydream, Coreena and Anna-Iza were walking slowly from opposite directions in a forested area until they met each other. Coreena had said to Anna-Iza, "He is meant for me,"

With her head bowed low, sorrow in her voice, Anna-Iza answered, "I know. I know."

Had his dream visited reality?

He swallowed hard, staring at the girl, whose ghostly image broke, and vanished before his eyes. *Was she an illusion, or did she get lost in the trees?* He clutched Bounty's reins with stiff fingers and gave them a quick shake. *Is there a message in the girl's appearance and disappearance? Did Anna-Iza need me?*

A shameful reminder of his promise to the High Goddess rushed over him. As soon as Ivan had left the West Forest, she faded from his memory, and he couldn't understand why. He confessed that he loved her and agreed to wait for her—forever. Already he'd broken his word. Now, he must face his promise of betrayal. *What am I to do? How did my simple life become so complicated?*

His horse shook his head and swished his impatient tail, not much caring what was on the side of the road, cattle or a young girl. "She wasn't real, Bounty," he said. "The storm is getting the best of me. Let's go." Ivan clicked his tongue, thinking about the illusion all the way home. But no answer came to him.

The buggy made long tracks in the two inches of snow as Ivan entered the road to his farm. Sighing with relief and deep gratitude, he exhaled. "We made it, Bounty." He unharnessed the horse and encouraged him into the stable. "Extra oats for you as a reward."

"The girl wasn't real," he said, trying to convince himself. Filled with doubt, he laid his head against his horse's neck, stroking its quivering shoulder. "Should I have gone to her—tried to help? I just don't know."

Entering the house, he pulled off his gloves and jacket, hanging them on the wooden peg rack near the door.

Peter coughed.

"How are you feeling?" Ivan quietly entered Peter's bedroom. It still needed organizing and cleaning out, something Ivan had promised he'd do if Peter would come home. There were boxes and furniture stacked neatly against the walls and in the corners. Ivan made a mental note that he'd take care of it as soon as he felt completely well and his strength returned.

"Not much better." Peter rolled over and looked at Ivan. "You know, I never once got sick or caught influenza when I lived in the forest. Not once."

"There's a terrible snowstorm out there. I barely made it home before freezing to death." Ivan shivered and leaned against the doorframe. "I'll put more wood on the fire, so it's nice and cozy in here. Then, I'll make you some potato soup for your dinner."

"That would be nice." Peter blew his nose and cleared his throat. "How was your trip to the village?"

Ivan stalled for a few moments, then took a chair from the corner and sat next to Peter's bed, trying to decide if he should tell him about the cloaked illusion in the woods. *Or should I tell him about Coreena?* His joy spilled over. "I ran into Coreena today just as I left the bank."

"Oh?" Peter was at once interested.

"At first, she snubbed me, and she had every right to. I treated her shabbily." Ivan related the conversation to Peter, reliving the experience he'd had with her.

"Sounds promising." Peter sniffed, and his eyebrows rose.

"I kissed her, Peter, and it was…wonderful. Right there on the main street of Graydon Village."

"Just wait until that scandal circulates." His laugh was nasal. "She must've forgiven you for your foolish behavior."

"She did." Ivan's thoughts went back to the girl who appeared from nowhere on the side of the road. He couldn't be sure if it was Anna-Iza in a long sweeping cloak, but it *seemed* like her. *Who could explain the illusion? Was it all in my head or the poison that still lingered in my system?*

"You know," Peter said hesitantly, "someday you're going to have to tell Coreena about your time in the forest—the danger. Your stomach wound, your close relationship with a tree, and a spirit that lives inside a cloak. Who'd believe such nonsense?"

"Have you told her anything about my adventures there?" Ivan leaned forward, his elbows resting on his knees.

"When she questioned me, I told her she needed to talk to you, and I believe it was the right answer. Maybe she'll think we're both daft."

"She'd probably be right." Ivan grinned.

"You like her a lot?"

"I do. I'm terribly fond of her. Thinking about her almost makes me giddy."

"Ha! I'd never think of you as giddy. Serious, sober, and sensible, yes—but not giddy."

They were silent while Ivan considered his brother's assessment of him. He guessed it was quite accurate, but he didn't know how to change his behavior.

"Don't look so glum." Peter gave a throaty laugh. "You have to appreciate where our parents came from and the strictness of our upbringing. It stands to reason that we'd be influenced by their rules."

"Not you," Ivan said, hoping he hadn't offended his brother. "You live and enjoy life and don't seem to worry about much. During the war, you were at the South Castle, making friends and having a good time. The forest was lenient and generous to you."

"Yes, it certainly was, and I'm grateful for it. I hope someday to return and make amends, especially to Lord Graydon."

Ivan looked down at his hands and wove his fingers together. *Did Peter mean what he'd just said? That he considered returning to the forest in spite of their promise to each other and Tereus's death threat against them?*

Peter took a deep breath and placed his hand on Ivan's knee. "You are a wonderful brother, and I love you very much. I would probably be dead by now if it weren't for you and your thoughtfulness. I wish I could be like you, but I know I'm too self-centered."

"People change. I remember not long ago when you saved me from the Vaguer. If you hadn't been there, I'd be like a sleepwalker—no memories, no spirit—maybe no life."

Tears misted Peter's eyes. "I thank God I was there in time to kill that terrible creature."

Ivan nodded and lowered his head. "I'll put more logs on the fire and start the soup." He rose from the chair. "Don't worry about the barn chores. I've done them by myself in the past, and I can do them now. You just get well."

As he left the room, he rubbed the tender stomach wound that pained him during the tense ride home. It had been a sweet day…astonishing and disturbing, all mixed together.

****

Mid-December ushered in a heavy snowstorm that kept most people close to home, including Ivan and Peter. During this time, the brothers cut a pine tree from their own forest and erected it in the living room. With a couple of Christmas decorations, constructed when they were young, and adding a few strands of holly berries, the house looked and smelled festive.

They invited Coreena and Dan to join them for a delicious roasted pheasant with potatoes, yams, cranberries, boiled cabbage, and Christmas pudding. Ivan attempted a mince pie until he realized he didn't have enough dough to lattice the top. He scratched his head and reread the recipe. Though he was sure he'd made the correct amount, where had it disappeared? When Peter came in from outside after shoveling snow from the porch steps, Ivan shared his blunder. "I don't know what happened. How did I come up short?"

Peter looked sheepish. "I—well. Before I went outside, I was having a little fun and made a ball of the dough and threw it into the air, intending to catch it behind my back. But I missed when it came down and smacked on the floor." His face twisted.

"You th-threw it away?"

"Sorry." He shrugged his shoulders. "I forgot to tell you. Let's make it again—together."

Ivan got the flour and sifter from the flour bin, and they started over.

Peter wrapped a towel around his head and tied an apron up to his chest, pretending to be a famous chef. Speaking a few words of Russian, he measured and dumped in the lard. Ivan took a pinch of salt and tossed it into the flour mixture.

They laughed as they worked on their project. When Ivan rolled out the pie dough with a wooden rolling pin, Peter walked his two fingers down the middle of it, insisting the marks meant they'd always be together. Happiness swelled Ivan's heart. He loved being with his brother and his natural quirkiness.

Ivan decided to keep Peter's finger tracks in the pie dough as he fluted the edges. He would share the story with Dan and Coreena, and they would certainly be tickled.

"How well did you know Anna-Iza, the High Goddess of the forest?" He lifted his gaze to meet Peter's.

"Well enough for her to kiss me." Peter gave a sly smile.

"A Kiss of Discernment?"

"Oh, you know about the test, then?" Peter cocked his head, realizing his bluff had been called. "Every serious visitor gets a Kiss of Discernment," he admitted, his face turned pink.

"Did you pass?"

"I believe so. She was complimentary about my character."

"Of course."

"Did you spend any time with her or her sister goddesses?" Ivan hoped he didn't sound overly anxious for his brother's answer.

"No. I didn't see her often since I spent my time at the South Castle with Lord Graydon, Commander Simon, and his troops. I'd always hoped for an invitation to visit her at their Crystal Palace, but the invitation never came."

Ivan couldn't hide the slight turn of his lips.

"You had a crush on Anna-Iza, too?" Peter gave him a quick glance.

"I was—I was very taken by her. She's special and has a kind of magic and a lovely disposition that I like very much." *Should I share my sighting of the lone girl I saw in the snow-covered meadow?*

"Leave it alone." Peter wiped his hands on a dishtowel. "She can't be touched, and neither should her sister goddesses. For what reason, I can't figure. Some silly rule about their Olympian gods in the faraway east, I think, wherever that is. I've never seen her gods, and no one else has either. So I don't know if they're real or invented."

Ivan shrugged. "I'm not sure about them either." He decided at that moment to share his strange sighting—or vision of the goddess during the snowstorm. "It seemed like her in her crimson-colored cloak walking toward a forested area just off the road. I called, but she just kept walking and soon disappeared. I can't figure it out."

"And I can't imagine a sensible girl like Anna-Iza leaving the forest and traipsing through a freezing storm. Besides, the outside world is forbidden to her and her sister goddesses, too."

Ivan's forehead wrinkled a bit, and he turned his head away. Of course, he knew this. *Does he sense my guilt for loving both girls?* "Seems we have the same good taste in women."

"Yeah. Too bad." Peter gave a snort. "She's one unique girl. I would've liked to know her better, but she wasn't interested in any mortal—especially one from the outside."

Holding up the pie, Ivan asked, "There, what do you think?"

"Beautiful job, little brother. You paid close attention when Mother made pies. Do you plan to eat a small piece and betray your sensitive teeth?"

Ivan laughed, and his smile lingered. "I don't know. I'll have to think about it."

Changing the subject, Ivan asked, "Why did you get involved with Tereus?"

Peter exhaled deeply, seemingly weary of the subject. "I thought I already covered that question. We are royalty, Ivan. I know you haven't forgotten, and I know you don't care—but I do. If our parents had stayed, we would be sitting on the throne of Russia right now,"

"Not likely," Ivan said. "Nicolai abdicated the throne—though it was under pressure. Remember? The Romanovs were officially removed from their royal position when the brutal Bolsheviks took over."

"Well…Tereus asked me to share the kingdom with him." Peter lifted his chin. "We'd rule the forest together and make it strong and worthy, rich and powerful. It was all planned, and Tereus asked me to be part of it. How could I turn it down?"

Ivan shook his head. "You got out alive. Don't regret what could never be yours. He's evil, and you would come to no good end with him." Ivan took the used cutlery to the sink to wash them, hoping to break their tension with their serious discussion. Peter seemed to still yearn for a partnership with the demon, and talking about it made Ivan nervous.

"You're right…no good end. But I can't help but feel I've been cheated."

"Not so. Life is good here. We're together, happy, and healthy."

"Sure." Peter seemed to consider this for a moment. "When did you become so wise and good with words?"

Turning to look at him, Ivan felt a rush of pride. He'd always hungered for his brother's approval, and now he'd gotten his wish.

"We should get the chores done before Coreena and Dan arrive for our splendid Christmas dinner." Peter poked his brother in his arm.

"I'll be along shortly." Ivan thought about Peter's compliment and grinned into the open oven, where he basted the pheasant. His mouth watered, thinking on the delicious feast.

Dressing quickly into his barn clothes, a milk pail swinging in his hand, Ivan left the house. He stopped and stared when he saw Peter standing near the road, facing west. His shoulders slumped. *Was he nostalgic for the forest, his friends, and the excitement?* Ivan didn't know, but it suddenly concerned him. Coming beside Peter, they walked together, arm in arm to the barn.

After their talk earlier at the kitchen table, Ivan too, longed to return and see his friends in the West Forest. But hadn't they promised each other never to go there again? It was too dangerous—life threatening. Now, Tereus, the creature of the deep caverns, was hell bent on revenge for the both of them. Shuddering, Ivan thought back on the things Tereus had done to try to destroy him, and the beating he'd forced on Peter. *How can I risk endangering our lives?*

In the barn, they had their first milk fight. Chuckling, Ivan turned the Holstein's teat to the side, giving it a long, hard squeeze toward Peter. He didn't see it coming, but he reacted quickly and did the same with the cow he was milking. Surprised, Peter's aim was off by nearly a foot. Ivan shot him again. Hot milk arched across the walkway, striking Peter's head, and wetting his hair.

"Hey! That's my ear," he yelled.

It was all in fun. They laughed and hugged, wishing each other a Merry Christmas.

They anxiously left the barn and closed the door behind them.

"Look. There are strange buggy and horse tracks in the snow, but there is no sign of anyone visiting us." Ivan pointed. "Someone was here while we were milking the cows."

"Yes, and human footprints, too. It's a bit too early for Dan and Coreena." With his head bent, Peter followed the tracks toward the house.

Alfred and Canute raced them to the porch, barking and spinning in circles. They could smell the pheasant and potatoes roasting, anticipating their share of the meal. Coreena and Dan would be along shortly, so Ivan and Peter must hurry to get dressed for the festivities.

"What's this?" Ivan spotted an envelope lying on the porch bench with two acorns resting on top. "Who could've delivered this?" He opened it right there.

Peter stopped to scrape his boot on the bottom step. "Drat! I stepped in some cow poop." He glanced up at his brother and said, "What does it say?"

Our Dear Friends, Ivan and Peter,

Ivan, we hope you've healed from your dreadful sword wound. We think of you every day.

Please come to Davaan's Transition Ceremony. Yes, he still agrees to become a man.

He wants you both to be here. It's a huge event in a werewolf's life to transition. Davaan is hopeful his family and pack will someday decide to join him.

We are planning it next year in May when it is warmer. Will you and Peter be our guests? We love you, Wayland & Davaan

Post Script: Sytha had to write this for us. Maynard agreed to deliver it.

Ivan faced Peter with a long and surprised stare. A small smile lifted the corners of their lips.

A dark-haired lad will come seeking and find maturity, wisdom, and friendship.

He will risk his life for the Forest's survival. He will find himself in his search.

Your duty is to keep him alive.

A word about the author…

In an earlier career, Vicki Price was a freelance fashion illustrator in Los Angeles, working for both wholesale and retail fashion houses. After she retired from her business, she taught watercolor classes to young people for over a decade. Now, she's an active fine art watercolor and acrylic artist and a passionate writer of young adult fantasy.

Vicki and her husband live on a lovely mountain in the Sierra Nevada Mountains, not far from Yosemite National Park, where the deer and the quail come to eat the cracked corn they've provided, next to the ravens that squawk for their treat of peanuts.

https://www.vickithomasauthor.com/
https://www.vickithomasartist.net